WHEN TOMORROW COMES

Part one of the
Behind Blue Eyes Trilogy

By

Joanna Lambert

*auth*ors
On Line

Visit us online at www.authorsonline.co.uk

An Authors OnLine Book

ISBN 978-07552-0484-7

Authors OnLine Ltd
19 The Cinques
Gamlingay, Sandy
Bedfordshire SG19 3NU
England

This book is also available in e-book format, details of which are available at
www.authorsonline.co.uk

To my Grandparents with Love and for Dad, a special star who touched so many lives in the short time he was here

ACKNOWLEGEMENTS

MANY THANKS TO GAYNOR AND ALL AT AUTHORS ONLINE FOR THEIR HELP AND ENCOURAGEMENT IN GETTING THIS PROJECT OFF THE GROUND. ALSO THANKS TO BARBARA AND JUDY FOR READING THE ORIGINAL DRAFT AND CONVINCING ME I HAD SOMETHING WORTH PUBLISHING. LOVE YOU BOTH.

To Jan

With Best Wishes

Audrey (aka Joanna).

v

ABOUT THE AUTHOR

Joanna Lambert lives in a village on the outskirts of Bath with her husband, Ruby the Mini and Ziggy her much-loved ginger cat.

1965

ONE

Friday 20th August

'It's beautiful. When did you say it was built?'

'Mid seventeen hundreds I think.' Robin Goddard replied staring up at the ivy-clad walls of his father's farmhouse. His companion, an auburn haired woman in her early forties nodded and fell in behind him as he made his way up the path to the front door. 'My great grandfather won it on a wager at Exeter Races in eighteen forty three.' He added as his hand went into his pocket, searching for the key.

'All this on a lucky horse? The gods must have smiled on him that day!'

'Indeed and he treasured the place until the day he died.' Robin smiled. Mary O'Farrell wasn't just an attractive woman with a soft Irish accent; from their conversation, he discovered farming was in her blood. In her hands, this would remain a working farm, and with this knowledge he realised that letting go of Paddocks might not be as difficult as he first thought, although first he had to persuade her to buy it.

He unlocked the door and let her in, the place empty, the familiar furniture of his childhood long gone. Bare rooms resonated to the sound of their voices. No time to get nostalgic, he thought as he looked around and memories came flooding back. I live overseas; taking over this old place was never an option.

He took her from room to room, watching her face, trying to gauge whether she liked what she was seeing, hoping she did. Then they were climbing the stairs and he stood back as hands in the pockets of her jacket she wandered in and out of each room with leisurely ease. Her expression was giving no secrets away until she walked into the last room. The bedroom where he had been born.

'What a wonderful view!' Her face lit up as she reached window. 'I can see the village from here. Is it a large place?'

'Meridan Cross? No,' He paused for a second. 'Quite small really. There's a pub and a village shop though.'

'I can see a large house with lots of chimneys. Elizabethan?'

'Little Court? Yes it is. Laura Kendrick lives there. The family have been in the manor since the fifteenth century. Laura is very traditional,' he laughed. 'takes her responsibilities to the village very seriously. The villagers adore her.'

'And we have company.' She turned to look at him with a smile.

Curiosity drew him to the window. In the field, which fronted the house a Land Rover had pulled up and two men were getting out.

'That's Richard Evas.' He nodded towards the taller of them. 'and his foreman Jake Carr. They're doing their regular check of the boundary fence between Paddocks and Willowbrook.'

'The next door neighbour.'

Robin nodded. 'He's a good man. I grew up with his son; we were great friends as children. Joined the army together.' He smiled. 'Thought we could make a difference, you know what young men are like, full of passion and ideology.'

'And now you're both older and wiser of course.'

'Me maybe. Sadly, Mike didn't make it back. He was killed in action in Burma.'

Mary watched the tall fair-haired figure of Richard Evas as he walked the boundary stopping at each post to check its soundness. 'Poor man,' she said gently. 'So many didn't come home.'

'No,' Robin replied, 'and you cannot imagine what he and his wife Peggy have gone through since. Peggy was very ill after Mike died and then just as she was getting over it, her son in law was killed in a plane crash and then to crown it all, months later their daughter disappeared from the village leaving them to bring up the two grandchildren. Dreadful, simply dreadful. Sorry,' he raised an apologetic hand. 'I must sound like some gossiping old woman.'

'No, please, do continue.' The corners of her mouth lifted in a soft smile. 'After all, if the Evas's are going to be my next door neighbours I'll.....'

'You're going to buy Paddocks?' He interrupted her, unable to conceal his delight.

'Yes, it's wonderful! I love everything about it!' She moved away from the window. 'Now, perhaps we could discuss the finer points of the sale over some lunch? You can tell me all about the village and perhaps a little more about my new neighbours.'

'Of course.' Robin indicated the door with a smile. 'I know just the place.'

Monday 23rd August

Fifteen-year-old Ella Kendrick rode into the farmyard and slowing her grey hunter Merlin to a walk steered him towards the stables. Once inside she dismounted carefully before lifting off the twin bags containing the remnants of the harvesters' lunch. Each day for the last week, she had ridden out daily to the fields with tea, lemon barley, sandwiches and cake for the men who were busy bringing in the harvest. In the front parlour at Willowbrook Farm previous generations of Evas's had used the walls to record a pictorial history of past harvests and her grandfather was no exception. The photographs of his Massey Ferguson combines now stood proudly beside those muted sepia shots of men in smocks, shouldering scythes and posing proudly in front of heavily loaded wagons. Modern combines were not only time saving, they were also labour-saving, which was just as well, Ella thought, because village lads no longer wanted to work the land. Most of them left school and found jobs in nearby Abbotsbridge or Kingsford in factories or offices with more money and better hours than those offered to farmhands. However, as far as the harvest was concerned, traditions were still very much alive and there was no shortage of helpers.

Storing the saddle and bridle in the tack room Ella released Merlin into the back paddock, retrieved the bags and crossed the yard towards the farmhouse. The clock on All Hallows church tower struck three as she pushed through the small side gate and reached the back door. Pulling off her riding boots in the utility, she unpacked the contents of the bags, rinsed out the flasks and bottles and wiped out the sandwich boxes and cake tins. Her chores over, she went to find her grandmother.

As she entered the kitchen, the aroma of Peggy Evas's weekly baking session still lingered. An assortment of fruit and savoury pies cooling on top of the Aga - crusty loaves nudging each other on cooling trays and her grandmother's speciality, a deep Victoria sandwich cooling in solitary splendour on a small wire rack, awaiting its filling of vanilla butter icing. Spying the pottery bowl containing the icing, Ella could not resist running a sneaky finger around the rim.

'Hello!' She called out, stopping to suck the residue of sweetness from the tip of her finger before moving into the hall. 'Grandma I'm home!'

She stood on the bottom stair, looking up to the landing, wondering if her grandmother was having her usual afternoon lie down. '*So I can have a proper rest without any disturbance.*' She had insisted. She looked at her watch. The refreshment run to the harvesters had taken less time than usual today. Perhaps she could find something else to do until she woke up. She stepped off the bottom stair, and then hesitated. Tilting her head, she listened. Yes, there it was, the faint strains of music. Old music. Curious, she began to climb the stairs.

It was coming from the attic room right at the top of the house. The stairs to it were narrow and twisting; dark wood treads which had long lost their colour through the countless numbers of feet that had climbed this way. The door at the top, which opened inwards, was partially open. She could hear it clearly now, the strains of an old gramophone playing a scratchy 78. *I'm in the mood*

3

for love, simply because you're near me floated through the door. Cautiously she pushed it open.

A single light bulb lit a windowless room full of boxes and trunks. On a small table stood an old wind up gramophone, a black disc revolving unevenly under the heavy arm of the stylus. Over in the far corner her grandmother sat on a chair in front of a large brown-lidded trunk, a book on her lap, hair in her eyes, staring down and muttering.

'Grandma?' Ella said softly. 'Whatever are you doing up here?'

Peggy pulled off her glasses and sat bolt upright. She pushed her hair from her face and stared at Ella, mouth open, eyes wide with fright, a choking sound coming from her throat.

'What's the matter?' Ella stared at her. 'Are you ill? Shall I get granddad?'

'No! Please! No!'

Ella's gaze fell on her grandmother's lap. What she'd thought was a book was, in fact, an album, full of old photographs. Peggy snapped it shut and clutched it protectively to her chest. 'I need to have her near me like this,' she gasped. 'I need to be able to remember how she was.'

'It's all right.' Ella approached her slowly. 'I'm sorry I didn't mean to frighten you.'

Peggy lowered the album to her lap once more.

'He doesn't understand you see.' She said, fumbling in the pocket of her apron for a handkerchief. 'He thinks he's doing the right thing, he really does. He thinks if we don't mention your mother's name we'll all forget her eventually.' she dabbed at her eyes. 'She ran away so many years ago but I can't forget her. I loved my Michael but he was his dad's boy. Went everywhere with him. It was terrible when he died. I was ill.' she shook her head. 'Very ill, but I still had my girl.' She turned to look at Ella, her face wet with tears. 'Maybe he resented that. Not having anyone. He never really had much time for her, you know. Not like he did for Michael.'

A continuous blip announced the record had ended. Ella walked over to the gramophone, lifted the arm and turned it off.

'She loved that song.' She heard Peggy say, her voice much calmer now. 'One of her favourites when she was courting your father. Poor Christopher,' there was a heavy sigh. 'Just like Michael, taken from us too soon.'

Ella turned. Her grandmother was holding the album open, showing a tantalising glimpse of photographs.

'Would you like to see?' Peggy patted the lid of the chest. 'Come, sit here, let me show you.'

Ella crossed the room and settled herself down, watching curiously as Peggy flipped the pages back to the beginning.

'Now this is your mother at her christening.' She gently caressed the sepia surface of the photo. 'She was *such* a beautiful baby.'

Half an hour later Peggy closed the album; getting to her feet she fixed solemn blue eyes on Ella.

4

'You do understand don't you?' She reached down and stroked Ella's dark curly hair. 'Why I have to come here?'

Ella nodded.

'The pictures and the music,' Peggy continued. 'They're all that's left of my Mel. Your grandfather brought every photograph of her up here while I was in hospital,' she said, lifting the lid and placing the album carefully back in the chest. 'Of course he didn't think I would find them. And if he ever finds out, I don't know what he'll do.' She shivered nervously.

Ella placed a reassuring hand on her grandmother's arm, now realising why she had been running errands every afternoon. She stared at the chest. This was the very thing her grandfather felt her grandmother needed protecting from but strangely it appeared to be the one thing that she needed. Of course, she knew this was not the behaviour of a rational person. Grandma had a sickness, brought about by the death of her uncle and the disappearance of her mother. She knew she should tell her grandfather what was going on. However, if she did it might make matters worse. He might take the photos and the records away and destroy them. And goodness knows what might happen then. Peggy might end up in hospital again and she couldn't - wouldn't be responsible for that.

She felt the older woman's hand on her shoulder and looked into her sad, worn face.

'Promise me you won't say anything,' she pleaded. 'He mustn't know. He mustn't.'

Ella gave her grandmother's hand a gentle squeeze. 'Don't worry,' she said. 'I promise I won't say a thing. It can be our special secret.'

Sunday 5th September

Ella skirted the northern edge of Hundred Acre. Tomorrow she would be back in uniform, starting a new term at school, but for now, she was enjoying a last ride out on Merlin. Ahead in the distance, she heard barking and could see up ahead where the wood met the field, someone walking towards her with two border collies.

Catching sight of her, they left their owner and bounded towards her. The figure started to run, whistling after the dogs, calling them back, but they had already reached her and were circling Merlin, barking noisily. Merlin's ears went back and he began to snort, his feet dancing on the spot. Ella reined him in, patting his neck and talking reassuringly to him as the young man reached her and grabbed the dogs, clipping them both onto leads. He stood there for a moment looking at her, trying to get his breath back

'I'm so sorry,' He said apologetically. 'Can't think what got into them. Are you O.K?'

All Ella could do was stare at the stranger. Broad shouldered and deeply tanned he was beautiful, there was no other word for it. His teeth were white and even, his eyes the most vivid blue and his short, thick hair was golden blond.

'I'm fine thank you.' She finally found her voice, leaning forward to place a steadying hand on Merlin's neck. 'You shouldn't really be here you know. This is private property. There are signs.'

'I'm just walking dogs.' He shrugged. 'I'm not doing any harm.'

'Dogs which should have been on a lead.' Ella bristled, irritated by his arrogant attitude. 'I could quite easily have been thrown, the way they were jumping all around me.'

'And if you had, my little princess,' He grinned. 'I would have taken you in my arms and revived you with the kiss of life.'

Ella kneed Merlin towards the stranger, staring down at him for a moment, feeling hot anger colour her face. 'I'm nobody's princess.' She said coldly. 'Least of all yours.' And yanking Merlin's head towards the direction of Willowbrook she rode away, unable to cope with the mocking amusement in his blue eyes and the fluttering butterflies in her stomach.

Reaching the top of the hill, she turned to look back towards the wood. He was still watching, the dogs at his feet.

'Good looking wasn't he Merlin?' She said, leaning over the horse's neck and whispering into his ear. 'Full of himself though. Kiss of life indeed!'

The horse nickered softly in response and chewed his bit. Looking towards the wood again, she saw the stranger had gone. Her pulse steadied, the flush in her cheeks cooled. The butterflies settled. She took a deep breath and glanced at her watch, realising she should be home. Her brother Nick was catching the six forty train to Bristol tonight. Beginning his first term at university. She had promised to be at the station with the rest of the family to see him off and she did not want to be late. Pulling Merlin round she headed him in the direction of Willowbrook, thoughts of the handsome stranger fading as she rode.

Monday 6th September

Ella sat watching trees and fields pass the window by as the train clattered its way through the Somerset countryside towards Kingsford. It seemed impossible that the eight weeks of the summer holiday had gone and now here she was, about to begin another year at High School. She always enjoyed the start of a new term. New classroom. New syllabus. And this year was even more important than all the others had been, because she would be studying for her 'O' levels. The beginning of a three-year journey towards university and her chosen career as a vet. The thought of university made her wonder how Nick's first day was going.

The family had gathered at Meridan Cross station yesterday evening to wave him off. Ella had hugged him tightly, called him a lucky dog and told him how she envied the freedom he was about to experience. Grandmothers Laura and Peggy stood side by side; women of similar ages but physically the exact opposites of each other. Plump Laura, clear skinned and bright eyed in her tweed skirt and twin set, pearls at her throat and Peggy small, sad and colourless in her beige dress and brown cardigan. When everyone else had finished their goodbyes Peggy shuffled forward, reaching up to touch his face gently with the palm of her hand, tears in her eyes. 'I'm going to miss you Michael.' She said softly, reaching for the handkerchief tucked into her sleeve. 'You mind and take care of yourself now son and come back safely.'

'It's Nick, Peggy,' Richard corrected gently. 'He's off to university in Bristol, remember?'

Peggy turned to look at all of them, confusion in her face. 'Not Michael?'

'No Peggy.' Laura Kendrick had stepped forward and affectionately looped arms with Peggy. 'Nick your grandson.'

'Ah yes.' Peggy's expression changed. She gave a tired sigh and smiled. 'Of course.'

The diesel's claxon sounded loudly, distracting Ella from her thoughts. She felt the train slowing and caught a patchy glimpse of Kingsford through the trees ahead. The small town was a mixture of stone and red-bricked houses clinging to both sides of a winding river valley. With its origins as a Saxon settlement, it had a wealth of historic buildings and was a favourite stop off for tourists.

From the train window, Ella could now clearly see the school, a magnificent seventeenth century manor house, leaded windows catching the morning sunlight. Originally the home of Sir Edward Conran-Hill, who made his fortune in wool and cloth, it was now Kingsford High, a co-educational grammar school with an excellent academic reputation. Thoughts of school now reminded Ella that her friends Issy and Jenny would be waiting at the station to meet her.

Familiar buildings slipped past her carriage as the train slid into the station. Doors banged and people poured out onto the platform. Ella joined the queue filtering out into Station Road. Passing the porter collecting tickets at the barrier, she finally emerged into the pale morning sunshine.

They were waiting for her by the taxi rank as they always did on the first morning of a new term. A small brown-eyed brunette and a blue-eyed blonde. After hugs of reunion, Ella stood back smiling at them both.

'Thank you both for my birthday cards and presents. I just love your hair.' She said, admiring Jenny's geometric chin length bob.

'Mum took me up to London. Vidal Sassoon!' Jenny said, pirouetting to give Ella the full benefit of her new look. 'I'd better not tell you what it cost! Iz has had hers cut like Cathy McGowan, not at Vidal Sassoon's though.'

Issy poked her tongue out at Jenny. Her thick blonde hair fell smoothly onto her shoulders, her fringe falling in a neat line into her blue eyes just like the presenter of *Ready Steady Go*.

'Wherever it was cut, you both look great.' Ella said with a smile, and then added. 'What's this about a new club you've found?'

'The Mill you mean? It's fantastic. Dad's company did the renovations!' Jenny said proudly. 'He said it cost a fortune!'

'It has live bands and all the latest sounds.' Issy joined in enthusiastically. 'Jen knows the bouncer, don't you?' then to Jenny's nod. 'That's how we manage to get in.'

'There was this boy. Duncan. He was a Mod.' Jenny's eyes widened excitedly. 'You should have seen him! He had all the gear on! Mohair suit! Lambretta covered in lights. And the way he danced!' Her eyes widened. 'He was fantastic!'

'He wasn't *that* fantastic!' Issy was eager to get her own back after the comment about her hair.

'Well I thought he was!' Jenny protested, annoyed at the way Issy had trampled all over her daydream.

'Don't talk to me about boys.' Ella said, remembering her encounter. 'I met one too. Blond, good looking. Just like Steve McQueen, but *so* conceited.'

'Really?' Issy and Jenny chorused, their verbal tussle suddenly forgotten.

'Yes. He called me princess!' She put her hand to her face. 'Yuk!'

'Oh Ella!' Jenny clapped her hands. 'This is really exciting. You are always telling us how dull the village boys are. We want to know more, don't we Iz!'

'Yes.' Issy nodded eagerly. 'Where did you meet him? What's his name?'

'Like how old is he?' Added Jenny just as the church clock struck in the distance. 'Has he got a scooter or maybe even a car?'

'So many questions!' Ella said, checking her watch. 'Do you realise what the time is? We are going to be late for assembly. Let's talk about it at lunch time.'

'Oh Ella, come on that's mean!'

Laughing at Issy's protest, she laced her arms in theirs and steered them out of the station car park. 'All right, all right! I'll tell you everything you could *possibly* want to know. But please, let's hurry!'

Friday 17th September

Mending fence posts with his foreman Jake Carr on the edge of the south pasture, Richard Evas noticed a woman rider approaching out of Hundred Acre. He guessed immediately it must be their new neighbour Mary O'Farrell as he had seen the coal black mare she rode grazing in the pasture just below Paddocks Farm only days ago.

She approached the two men slowly, reined in and dismounted, pulling off her riding gloves as she walked over to them. She wore a green jacket and jodhpurs tucked into brown shiny riding boots, a slim elegant figure with thick, wavy auburn hair curling around the edge of her riding hat.

'Hello there!' She called out.

'Good morning.' Richard returned her smile and extended a hand in greeting. 'I believe we're neighbours. I'm Richard Evas and this is my foreman Jake Carr. I own Willowbrook Farm.'

'Mary O'Farrell. Pleased to meet you.' She shook his hand. 'I saw you both on the day I looked over Paddocks. You were checking fence posts then.'

'A never ending task.' Richard smiled. 'How are you settling in?'

'Very well.' She nodded.

'Bit of a change isn't it? Moving from Ireland to the wilds of Somerset?'

'Oh I haven't lived in Ireland for years.' She laughed. 'My husband Sam died eighteen months ago and my eldest son Martyn has taken over the running of the family farm in Sussex. I have been thinking about a move for some time now. Striking out on my own. I have friends who farm just outside Dunster. They told me about Paddocks. It's a beautiful old place.'

'It certainly is.' Richard agreed. 'What's your specialty?'

'Horses, although my husband was a cattle man. Paddocks has come with cattle, mostly beef, which I'm keeping for the time being. The vet's calling round this morning to check them over for me.'

'Mr Evas has a fine herd.' Jake chipped in. 'Channel Island. Bath and West champions too. Got the trophies to prove it!'

'Jake, you are embarrassing Mrs O'Farrell, I'm sure she is not at all interested in my herd.'

'Ah sure, but I'd love to see them. If you can spare the time, of course.' She nodded towards the fence. 'I can see you're busy.'

'No, you're welcome to drop in any time. I'm sure my wife Peggy would love to meet you.' Richard gave her a broad smile. 'And there's another member of my family who will be very interested in seeing you. My granddaughter Ella - she is hoping to become a vet. I'm sure she'll want to quiz you about horses.'

'And I know Niall my youngest will be very interested in your herd. He hopes to keep to family tradition and farm eventually…..'

Across the valley, the sound of the church clock caused her to pause.

'Was that eleven?' She looked at them both, puzzled.

'No, twelve,' Jake replied

'Sorry, I'll have to be going. The vet's due at 12.30, mustn't keep him waiting.' She said, as she gathered up her reins and swung herself back into the saddle. 'Thank you for your invitation, I will ride out and see you all soon, that is a promise.' And with a final wave, she swung her horse's head around and cantered off into the distance.

9

TWO

Saturday 25th September

'Here we are, all peeled and chopped.' Ella said, placing a basin of Bramley apple pieces on the table where her grandmother was rolling out pastry.

Dusting her hands down the front of her apron, Peggy took the basin from her. 'Thank you,' she said, touching Ella gently on the shoulder. 'You're a good girl.'

'I'm only too pleased to help.' Ella replied, seeing her grandmother's expression suddenly sag, aware that the door to painful memories was creaking open in her mind once again.

'Your mother was good too.' Peggy's mouth wobbled and she chewed her bottom lip. 'Do anything for me, she would.' she said, walking over to the sink. 'Absolutely anything.' A solitary tear trickled down her cheek and she brushed it away with the back of a floury hand. She stared out of the kitchen window, the bowl still clasped in her arms. 'I miss her so much.' she sighed, 'so very, very much.'

'Is there anything else you'd like me to do?' Ella asked, trying to distract her grandmother and pull her out of her melancholy. As she spoke, she noticed the wrapped cake and flask of tea still standing on the dresser.

'Look what Grandfather's forgotten.' She said, picking up the greaseproof bag and thermos. 'I suppose that's because he was in such a rush this morning.'

'Yes. Jake was late. Overslept. Put him all out.' Peggy viewed the kitchen clock with a worried look. Her preoccupation with the past dissolved as she realised the time was just after ten. 'He'll be so upset when he realises he's left it behind.'

'Don't worry, I can take it to him now if you like.' Ella volunteered.

'Would you?' Peggy looked relieved. 'Thank you Pet. I'd hate to think of him out there without a drink and something to keep him going till lunch.'

Grabbing the navy duffel bag from the back of the kitchen door, Ella packed the thermos and cake into it and pulled the drawstring handle tight.

'Did Granddad say where they'd be working?'

10

'Out by Fox Cottage.'

'What time shall I tell him you'll have lunch ready?'

'Better make it one.' Peggy turned to gaze at the table. 'Oh dear, now where was I?' She put the bowl of apple pieces down and shuffled over to pick up her rolling pin once more. 'I must get on.' she shook her head at Ella. 'Otherwise I'll be all behind.'

'Poor Grandma Peg.' Ella said to Merlin as she put his saddle on. 'What are we going to do? She's getting worse.' Tightening the girth she lowered the stirrups and swung herself onto his back. 'If only Mother would come back.' She sighed, turning him towards the stable door and out into the daylight. 'It might make all the difference. But we know that's not going to happen, don't we?'

She took Merlin at a steady walk down the farm track to the road and then on into the village, eventually reaching the High Street and beyond that the village shop. From out of nowhere, its owner Margaret Sylvester suddenly appeared. Her pink overall wrapped tightly around her thin body, she looked up and down the road, arms clasped tightly against her chest. Catching sight of Ella, she watched her pass, a pinched expression on her miserable face. Ella ignored her. She had not forgotten what Margaret had done. Rachel, Margaret's daughter had been her best friend since they were small. They were inseparable. Until the day the eleven plus results arrived.

'I don't want you seeing my Rachel any more.' Margaret had told her abruptly when she came to call for Rachel one afternoon. 'Time you went your separate ways; found other friends at your fancy new school.' And following this outburst she simply shut the door in her face.

'It's nothing but sour grapes.' Granddad said. 'Because Rachel is going to secondary school. Silly, pathetic woman.'

However, Ella was sure Margaret had been waiting for an opportunity to part them for a long time. There was something in her attitude, something beyond the normal miserable face she presented to the world. At times Ella was sure she hated her, but she had no idea why. Rachel, Ella had learned through Peggy's chats to Margaret, was now best friends with Trish, eldest daughter of the unruly Robinson clan from Field Way cottages. They had started secondary school together and were in the same class. Trish, a girl with rather too much to say for herself was only going to do one thing Ella decided, and that was get Rachel into a whole lot of trouble!

The sound of Merlin's hooves echoed off the rose coloured cottages as she continued her journey. Just outside the village, the Miller boys passed her in their father's battered old American army jeep. Rowan, the eldest, staring in fixed concentration as he drove while Ash leaned out and blew her a kiss. Laughing, she blew one back, stopping and turning in her saddle to watch them go. The two small grubby gypsy boys she remembered from childhood had now grown into dark, handsome, wild young men who worked for their father Nelson in his scrap business run from the family smallholding, Saddlers End, just outside the village. There the outbuildings were bursting with an untidy jumble of second hand farm machinery and tractor parts. Although the place was a complete tip, the business was a little goldmine and Nelson, despite his scruffy appearance was reputed to be one of the wealthiest men in the area.

The last cottage left behind, she was now in open countryside. High banks on either side of the road obscured the view for a while and then the landscape opened out again into wire fences and neatly clipped hedges.

The blare of a car horn made her pull Merlin to a halt; through the gaps in the hedge she glimpsed a vehicle approaching at speed in the twist of the lane ahead. A red, open top Austin Healey Sprite suddenly loomed large in the road in front of her and continued to approach at speed. Instantly she turned Merlin into a convenient gateway, waiting until the car passed.

'Idiot!' She shouted after him as he disappeared into the distance, wondering what kind of madness possessed anyone to drive like that on narrow country lanes. Once it was quiet, she continued her journey, upping Merlin's pace to a slow trot. She rounded the bend. The road ran on straight ahead into the distance and she could just make out the slight flick to the right where the lane led up to Fox Cottage, the place where they had lived before her mother's departure. She pulled Merlin up with a frown. Something was in the road up ahead. It looked like a large piece of bent metal. Digging her heels into Merlin's flanks, she rode forward to investigate.

Rachel Sylvester lay very still. She gradually increased the depth of her breathing, pushing her lungs out to their full capacity. Tentatively she felt down her ribs, first the left then the right. No pain, but she could see she had left fine pink imprints on the front of her white cotton blouse. She turned her hands over to look at them; both palms were scraped quite badly, blood spotting through her skin in several places and as the numbness subsided, they were beginning to sting. Instinctively she put her fingers into her mouth one by one and sucked them, leaving the taste of blood on her tongue.

Propping herself up on her elbows she looked down the length of her body. The knee on the left leg of her trousers was badly torn. Her best trousers. Her only pair of trousers. She felt like crying. This was all her own fault. She had gone off without saying a word to her mother. There would be big trouble when she got home, even bigger when her mother saw the state she was in. But she needed to get out; she had to find the car. It was white, expensive - a sports car. Not many people would own a car like that round here. Once she discovered where it came from she figured out she could ask around, find out who the owner was. She felt like Sherlock Holmes, hot on the trail, full of optimism. Unfortunately, all her detective work had come to an abrupt end only moments ago when someone driving a red blur had run her off the road.

Of course, the easiest way would have been to ask her mother who her mystery man was. She knew everything about the village, who came and went; but to do that would be to draw attention to herself, and she desperately needed to keep this a secret. Being found out would only get her into trouble. For what chance did a plain fifteen-year-old stand in the boyfriend stakes with this gorgeous god like figure she had seen behind the wheel. He was way out of her league and she knew it, but that did not stifle her hopes. If anything it made her more determined.

The sound of hooves told her a rider was approaching. What if it was him? She had seen him once or twice on horseback when she was out running errands for her mother. She lay back in the grass and closed her eyes, fantasising about what would happen when he saw her bruised and bleeding in the ditch. She imagined him dismounting, rushing to her side and lifting her into his arms. The thought made her quite dizzy. The horse had come to a halt now. There were footfalls on the road, coming nearer. She closed her eyes, waiting, willing her dream to become reality.

'Rachel?'

She opened them again. 'Ella?'

Ella knelt beside Rachel. 'Are you all right?'

'Well,' Rachel pushed herself up onto one elbow again. 'I don't think anything's broken, but look at my trousers! My mother will go mad!'

'I'm afraid your bike's had it too.'

'Oh no!' She sat bolt upright.

'Was it a madman in a red sports car?'

'I think so.' Rachel brushed her blonde hair back from her face. 'It all happened so quickly. One moment I was riding along, next the bike and me had parted company and I was lying here.'

'Come on.' Ella hauled her to her feet.

She has changed, Ella thought to herself as she pulled grass from Rachel's hair and clothes and helped her tidy herself up. That bright face, the happy smile, all gone. That awful aggressive mother of hers has turned her into this thin, pale frightened creature. Eventually she stood back and gave Rachel a smile of encouragement as she made her final assessment.

'A torn trouser leg, scraped hands, a wrecked bike. No broken bones though,' she said cheerfully. 'What were you doing out here anyway?'

Rachel coloured. 'Oh, I was just out for a cycle ride. I enjoy the countryside and as I can't afford a horse - well, I can't even ride actually - it's the next best thing.' She blurted out.

'Are you still interested in riding then?'

'Oh yes, I loved it when we, you know, used to go out on your other pony - what was he called - Butterscotch wasn't it? But lessons are so expensive; my mum could never afford them.'

Ella thought for a moment then an idea came to her.

'I could teach you to ride on Saturday mornings after I've finished my chores. There is a spare horse at Willowbrook, so once you are proficient enough there's no reason why you couldn't come up and take him out when you felt like it. His name is Buster and he is very gentle. I know Granddad would be pleased to have someone do that for him.'

13

'I can't Ella.' A sudden horrific realisation crossed Rachel's mind. 'My mother said I wasn't ever to see you again!'

'Rachel, that was five years ago.'

'I know.'

'Why did she do that anyway? What had I done?'

'I don't know.' Rachel shook her head. The only thing still imprinted on her mind was the depth of her mother's anger and her own fear of the consequences of disobeying her.

'Well, it doesn't matter anyway.' Ella shrugged, determined Margaret was not going to get in the way this time. 'Riding lessons will be good for you. She'll soon come round.'

'Oh Ella!' Rachel threw her arms around her and gave her an enthusiastic hug as Ella's matter-of-fact attitude to her mother caused her own fear to evaporate. 'Thank you!' she relaxed her grip slightly and looked at her. 'I've missed you, you know. Really, really missed you.'

'I've missed you too Rachel. What are you doing now? Are you still at school?'

'No, I left last year. I help in the shop now full time. What about you?'

'I'm doing my O levels this year.'

'I wish I could have done something but I'm not clever like you.' Rachel looked at her enviously.

'You could learn to type. Work in an office.'

'Mum might allow me to later on.' Rachel gave a half-hearted shrug. 'But at the moment she thinks I should be with her in the shop.'

Ella nodded. So Margaret thought Rachel should be in the shop did she? The thought of Rachel's days being spent serving behind the counter or filling shelves angered her. She deserved more from life than being stuck within the four walls of her mother's narrow world or hanging around the bus shelter talking to the village lads with Trish Robinson. It made her even more determined to do something about it. Teaching her to ride, she decided, would be just the start.

'I've always dreamed of learning to ride.' Rachel was saying. 'And now....' the enthusiasm suddenly drained from her face. 'Oh, but I haven't any suitable clothes to wear!' She wailed, looking down at the rip in her one and only pair of trousers.

'Don't worry.' Ella laughed. 'I can find you something. Let's have a look at you.' She pulled Rachel against her. 'As I thought, we're about the same height. It shouldn't be a problem.'

She walked back to Merlin and grabbed his reins. 'Now then,' she said. 'Can you just stay there for a few minutes? I have to deliver this food up to my grandfather.' she indicated the duffel bag over the saddle. 'I'll ask him if he'll drop your bike back home for you later. Then I'll come back and give you a lift home on Merlin. O.K?'

Rachel nodded as she watched Ella mount effortlessly and move off. A

14

great joy washed over her. Ella was back in her life again; an Ella obviously not scared of her mother! And she was going to learn to ride! There was a horse she could use too. Pursuit of her mystery man was very much on again!

'Oh dear oh dear.' Richard Evas came into the kitchen, peeled off his jacket and hung it on the door. 'That wretched woman. No wonder her husband ran off!'

Facing each other across the heavy white Formica topped kitchen table, Peggy and Ella looked up from their pre lunch cups of tea.

'No need to guess who you're talking about.' Ella smiled.

Silently Peggy got up and retrieved a cup and saucer from the dresser. 'Tea Richard?' she brandished the pot at him.

'Please.' He sat down at the far end of the table and sighed. 'Yes,' he turned to Ella. 'Mrs Sylvester no less! I do her a favour by taking what is left of her daughter's bike home and you would think it was my fault! She really let rip!'

'Well, that's Margaret for you.' Peggy said placing the tea in front of him and pushing the blue and white sugar bowl towards him. 'Never happy unless she's having an argument with someone.'

'I understand you've offered to give young Rachel riding lessons.' Richard raised an eyebrow at Ella as he picked up his cup.

Ella nodded. 'Is that a problem?'

'There was a bit of resistance at first, but she soon saw the advantages.' He smiled. 'I think she sees it as an opportunity to get Rachel away from Trish Robinson. Bit of a bad 'un that girl. When's the first lesson?'

'Next Saturday, she's coming round at eleven.'

Saturday 2nd October

Ella walked back to the stable with Rachel, trailing Merlin and Buster behind them.

'I was scared about coming here today, you know,' Rachel confessed as they unsaddled the horses and stored the tack away. 'thought I'd make an absolute idiot of myself. I thought if I couldn't ride a bike, what chance would I have on a horse. But,' her face lit up. 'I enjoyed it! It was really great!'

'You did well.' Ella agreed. 'Of course riding's the fun part. Looking after a horse is generally quite hard work. So for part of next week's lesson we'll do some grooming and I'll show you how to look after tack, it needs regular cleaning and checking.'

'Great. I love it all!' Rachel nodded enthusiastically.

'Hello Rachel!' Peggy, crossing the yard with a basket of eggs, joined the girls on their way back to the house. 'Enjoying yourself are you?'

'Oh yes Mrs Evas! Very much!' Rachel smiled back, happiness radiating from her pale little face.

15

'You need fattening up Rachel, you're far too thin.' Peggy said, looking at the two of them standing side by side. 'There's cake and a glass of milk in the kitchen if you're interested. Better still, I can get the frying pan out. Bacon, eggs, fried bread - the works. That'll put some colour in those cheeks!'

'Cake will be fine Mrs Evas.' Rachel gave Ella an amused grin.

As they entered, the kitchen there was the sound of front doorbell in the hallway.

'Now I wonder who that can be?' Peggy frowned. 'Here, take these will you?' she handed the egg basket to Ella. 'I'll go and see.'

Ella took the eggs to the far corner of the kitchen and helped by Rachel, began stacking them in a cardboard tray on the worktop. She heard voices in the hallway, one of them her grandfather's, then collective laughter and footsteps coming nearer.

'She's here at last!' Richard said as he entered the kitchen. 'Met her in the High Street and twisted her arm. Said you were all dying to meet her.'

A slim, attractive middle-aged woman with auburn hair appeared behind him, Peggy following. The new arrival was wearing jodhpurs, a white blouse and a green jacket trimmed with black velvet. Ella thought she looked positively stunning. The smile when it came was warm and friendly and as she was introduced, she extended a hand in greeting to Peggy.

'Pleased to meet you Peggy.'

Watching, Ella noticed the immediate change in her grandmother's face. The sudden arrival of high colour in her cheeks. Eyes moistening, tears threatening. Then a smile appeared on Peggy's face. 'Welcome.' She said breathlessly, taking Mary's hand and squeezing it tightly. 'Welcome.'

Quickly Ella stepped forward to stand beside her grandmother.

'This,' Peggy turned to look at Ella. 'Is my granddaughter Ella.' She transferred Mary's hand across to her. 'She's going to be a vet one day.'

Ella looked at Peggy for a moment, before turning her attention back to Mary, smiling politely as they shook hands. As she looked into her face, she realised what her grandmother had seen. The similarity to her mother was striking.

As Rachel was being introduced, the doorbell rang again and Richard left the room, muttering something Ella could not quite hear. Again voices in the hall. 'Come on through, we are all in the kitchen.' she heard him say.

'Sorry,' he apologised to Mary as he joined them again. 'I completely forgot your boy was parking the Land Rover.' He gave a short laugh. 'Right everyone; this is Niall, Mary's younger son. Niall, this is Peggy my wife and Ella my granddaughter. And last but not least, her friend Rachel.'

'Pleased to meet you.' Niall shook Peggy's hand, then Rachel's and lastly Ella's, holding onto it just a little longer than necessary. 'So! We meet again Princess.' he said with amusement in his vivid blue eyes.

For Rachel the meeting was bitter sweet. Her greatest wish had come true because at last she knew the identity of the young man she had been mooning over for weeks. However, this was overshadowed by the fact that not only had he already met Ella; from the way he was looking at her he was obviously totally smitten.

Friday 15th October

'Peggy?'

Laura Kendrick pushed open the door and walked into a warm kitchen smelling of freshly baked bread and cake. The radio was on, Max Bygraves floating through its speaker.

'Peggy!' Laura called again, crossing the kitchen, amazed at the marathon cooking session that had been taking place. Four halves of Victoria sponges rested on wire cooling racks. Next to them, a clutch of large loaves dusty with flour sat side by side, their tins on the draining board, ready for washing. She counted three pies and from the smell coming from the Aga knew there was more cooking.

'Laura! What brings you here?' Peggy appeared in the doorway, wiping her hands on her apron, all smiles.

Laura stared at her in surprise. She was wearing a blue and green patterned dress, her hair freshly cut, falling in soft waves around her face. Her eyes were bright and the lines, which had previously cut deep furrows in her face, appeared to have gone into mass retreat. Even the round-shouldered stoop had disappeared. She stood there upright; full of life and energy, almost her old self.

'I came to see you about the church cleaning rota.' Laura gazed at the cooking then back at Peggy. 'Goodness, there's enough to feed an army here!'

'Oh!' Peggy bustled around the table to join her. 'This isn't all for us!'

'I should think not.' Laura laughed. 'I know Richard has a healthy appetite, but...'

'It's for Mary.' Peggy interrupted. 'And the boy of course. Well, she's busy with the farm. Doesn't have a lot of time for cooking. So I thought...'

'That's very kind of you Peggy. Very generous.'

'Oh it's nothing.' Peggy shrugged off the compliment. 'No more than I should do really.' Then moving closer to Laura she lowered her voice. 'You know who she is don't you?'

'No.' Laura frowned, wondering what piece of village gossip Peggy had discovered.

'My Mel!'

'Mel?'

'Yes!' There was an excited glint in Peggy's blue eyes. 'God's brought her back to me!'

'Oh Peggy!' Laura looked at her sadly. 'I don't think so, my dear.'

'And two more grandsons.' Peggy continued, ignoring Laura's concern. 'Wonderful isn't it?'

'What?' Laura stared at her in amazement.

'I'm so excited!' Peggy beamed, moving across to the Aga and lifting the kettle. 'Although it's a secret at the moment of course. I can't tell Richard. Not yet.' She said, moving over to the sink. 'But I know I can talk to you about it Laura. You understand dear. I'll make us some tea.' She turned to look at Laura, her face aglow with happiness. 'Then we can have a proper chat about it.'

Escape, Laura realised, was out of the question. Pulling out a chair, she sat down with a feeling of deep unease.

Saturday 30th October

'I look terrible.'

'No you don't, red suits you, and it goes with your colouring exactly.'

'It's not the colour, it's me. I'm shapeless. I look like a ruler.'

'Don't be so silly Rachel; we're all different shapes and sizes. Look, why don't you stuff hankies in your bra if you're that worried?'

'Because they'll know.'

'Who, for heaven's sake?'

'Boys.'

'If anyone touched me there I'd slap them,' Ella said indignantly.

'It's all right for you.'

'Don't be silly. Come here, before your hair dries completely. After I've put this setting gel on it I'm going to wind it on big rollers to give it more body. And please do stop moaning, I'm going to make you look really glamorous.' Rachel sat at the dressing table obediently, thinking that it would take nothing short of a miracle to do that.

Ella sighed as she wound the long blonde hair around the big plastic rollers and secured each one with a pin. Rachel had permission to stay over at the farm for the Young Farmers Halloween Dance in the Village Hall. There was going to be a live local band, a disco and Peggy and some of the other local wives had been at the hall all afternoon preparing the food. The scouts had been busy decorating the hall and she knew they were all going to have a great evening. Rachel, however, had been driving her mad with her worries and insecurities ever since she arrived.

Fixing the last roller, Ella stood back with satisfaction. 'Right,' she said, 'I'll give it a once over with the hair dryer then we'll leave it and concentrate on doing your nails. I have some wonderful new polish that will just go with your dress.'

'You're so lucky.' Rachel said casting an appreciative eye around Ella's room with its comfortable furniture, pretty curtains and wall of pop posters. Her record collection, sitting in a small cupboard next to her record player was full of the latest sounds, her wardrobe full of fashionable clothes. She had everything she wanted and Rachel felt quite envious when she thought of the small square bedroom she occupied which doubled up as an overspill for the shop's stockroom.

'I know,' Ella replied. 'But tonight I promise you, you'll be the one with all the boys will want to dance with.'

'I know someone who won't want to dance with me.' Rachel said miserably as she watched Ella plug the hairdryer into the socket next to the dressing table.

'Who?'

'Niall.'

'I shouldn't let that worry you.' Ella said, shouting over the noise of the hair dryer. 'He's no loss.'

'Why don't you like him Ella?'

'Because I met him before he came to Willowbrook.' Ella said, the memory making her feel hot and angry. 'He's arrogant. And he's patronising. Thinks he's God's gift to women!'

'But Ella, can't you see? He's mad about you. At the Harvest Supper, I noticed he was watching you all evening and in church on Sundays, he always turns to look at you when you arrive. Then at Young Farmers, each time he asks you to dance you go off with someone else, but no matter what you do, he still seems to adore you. I think he might be in love with you.'

'Of course he isn't!' Ella laughed. 'You've been reading too many of those romantic paperbacks your mother sells, that's your trouble! Now do be quiet and let me dry your hair.'

'To be sure, Ella has worked wonders with Rachel.' Mary O'Farrell remarked to Peggy as they sat drinking their port and lemon and watching the dancers later that evening.

Peggy nodded in agreement. Rachel, wearing a red mini dress, lipstick and eye shadow, looked much older than her sixteen years. 'I'm not sure her mother would approve though.' She said, 'it's just as well she's staying at the farm tonight. Wouldn't do for her to go home looking like that.'

'No.' Mary agreed, catching sight of her son watching Ella intently as she danced with one of the Miller boys. 'Margaret must be the most miserable woman I've ever met. Something terrible must have happened to her. I can't believe she was born that way.'

'It was losing Christopher,' Peggy said simply.

'Who?'

'Laura's son.' Peggy gave Mary a sweet smile. *I know my darling you can't reveal yourself yet. Not even to me. Don't worry, I understand. I'm happy to play this little game with you for now.* 'She never spoke to Mel again after they got engaged you know. Said she had stolen him. Of course it was complete nonsense.' She looked across at Mary and seeing no reaction, continued. 'Mel would never do such a thing. She was a sweet, caring girl. In the end Margaret ended up marrying this other fellow, one of the salesmen who called regularly at her mother's shop. Sold haberdashery or something. Didn't last of course. He did a moonlight flit with her mother's savings and the barmaid from the Blue Boar at Higher Padbury just after Rachel was born. The shock of it put Margaret's mother in her grave less than six months afterwards.'

'Oh!' Mary's face was full of sympathy. 'What a sad business! All the more reason to do our best for Rachel then, don't you agree?'

'Yes.' Peggy looked across to where Rachel sat and smiled, thinking how kind and generous it was of Mel to put the past behind her and want to help the daughter of her old rival Margaret. 'Of course we must.'

Ella had finished dancing and was talking to Rowan Miller as they left the floor. As she passed Niall, he reached out and touched her arm.

'Dance Ella?' He smiled pleasantly. Dark eyed Rowan gave her an amused grin before wandering off to join his younger brother.

Abandoned by Rowan, Ella stood there wondering how to get rid of Niall. 'I'm sorry.' She shook her head politely. 'But I really would like to sit this one out. Maybe later?'

'Maybe never eh?' He mimicked. 'What's the matter Ella, frightened of me?'

'Frightened? Of you? Don't be so childish.'

'Well dance with me then!'

'I don't want to. Just leave me alone please.'

'Find me someone on their own as beautiful as you and I will.' He threw out the challenge with the normal confident grin she had come to detest. She turned around; everyone around her, attractive or not was with someone and then she caught sight of Rachel sitting on her own in the corner watching them both with her sad little face.

'Wait there.' She crossed over to where Rachel sat and grabbing her by the wrist, hauled her out of her seat.

'What are you doing Ella?' Rachel resisted, a confused look on her face.

'Making your dream come true. Come on, Niall wants a dance.'

'Not with me he doesn't.'

Ella tightened her grip. 'Rachel just stop arguing please and come with me.'

'Well would you look at that,' Peggy said with a laugh as she watched what was taking place across the room. 'Ella's doing a spot of match making.'

'Rachel and Niall?' Mary studied her son and the thin girl he was now holding in his arms. 'Never in a million years Peggy. My money's on Ella.'

'Ella? With Niall?' Peggy's hand went to her throat, shocked at the thought of what was being suggested. 'No,' she said breathlessly. 'Impossible.'

'Impossible?' Mary looked puzzled.

'Yes.' Peggy was adamant. 'Surely you of all people must realise that!'

'Must I?' Mary frowned, wondering why the older woman was so upset.

'Yes.' Peggy patted Mary's hand gently reassuringly. 'Take it from me he's far better off with Rachel.'

1966

THREE

Sunday 2nd January

A group of around twenty red and black jacketed riders sat in the car park of the Somerset Arms on a cold frosty morning for the first hunt of the New Year. Both riders' and horses' breath hung in the air and there was the stamp of impatient hooves and the accompanying whine of hounds as they circled round, eager to be off in pursuit of the as yet unseen quarry.

Ella, on Merlin, sat between Mary O'Farrell and her grandfather. They were finishing off the mulled wine stirrup cup, served by publican Tom Bennett and his wife Lily.

Checking his watch, Master of hounds Rex Gallagher, a tall thin man in a tight fitting breeches and red jacket, put his brass horn to his lips and blew, signalling the time for drinking was over and the hunt was about to move off.

Ella reached down and returned her glass to Lily's tray with a smile. Sitting back, she surveyed the group with its customary cluster of local farmers and landowners, noticing at once the golden head of Niall O'Farrell, surrounded by a group of girls from the local Pony Club. He had certainly made an impact since his arrival in the village. Everybody adored him. All the girls, including Rachel dreamed he would ask them out. However, they were all disappointed. Niall, it appeared, did not date although he liked to flirt and tease and make them laugh. At the local barn dances or Young Farmers Disco evenings, he would make sure he danced with every girl in the room, but he always left alone and Mary would always smile and say his studies at Cirencester Agricultural College came first and there would be plenty of time for romance once he had passed his exams.

Since their first encounter on the edge of Hundred Acre, the previous September Ella was of the opinion that he was a good-looking know-all who thought women were putty in his hands. Everyone except her of course. Purposely ignoring him had now become a regular hobby of hers. The problem

21

was that her attitude, which sometimes bordered on rudeness, seemed to encourage him even more. What did not help was that Mary had become a frequent visitor to Willowbrook and quite often, when home from college, Niall accompanied her. There were occasions, therefore, when she could not avoid him, unlike Rachel, who would spend every spare minute of her time at Willowbrook hoping to see him. Her trips out on Buster were also, Ella suspected, carried out in order to waylay him if she could. Today, as a group of four girls on horseback sat laughing and chatting with Niall, Rachel hung around in the immediate vicinity, gazing adoringly at him, caught in her usual daydream as Buster stamped impatiently. Ella shook her head, caught by the irony of the situation. Rachel she knew, would love to be in her shoes.

The hunt began to move off through the village, the gentle clip clop of hooves resonating off the walls of the cottages. The grass was white with frost and although it was a clear day with vivid blue skies and unrestricted sunshine, the ice was slow to melt.

Ella found herself alone as Mary and Richard rode ahead together. It was such a beautiful day and she realised just how much she loved Meridan Cross and the way it looked, settled and peaceful on the edge of the valley, smoke from its chimneys drifting upwards towards the dark expanse of the wood above. As she rode her thoughts were of the rest of the day, returning home after the hunt to a relaxing bath and Sunday lunch. Afterwards her grandfather would settle in front of a roaring fire for his customary nap before making his way in the fading light with Jake and the dogs to the south pasture to get the herd in for afternoon milking. It was a warm, comforting pattern of life, which she knew would one day have to be temporarily broken when she left for veterinary college.

She had approached local vet John Bembridge back in the summer to tell him of her career plans and he had offered her weekend work to give her a taste of what the job was all about. For the last few months, she had been assisting at the practice at weekends, working on reception and helping with the animals. She was enjoying every minute of it and John had now promised to take her on a couple of farm visits in the new year. Ella was now more than sure she had made the right decision about her future and hopefully once she had qualified, she would return to the village and its peaceful way of life to work with him in his practice.

After a ten-minute ride into open countryside, they reached the uneven track leading to Fox Cottage. From there the stream of horses swung right, through a small gap in the wall and cantered along the edge of the barley field, now a wide expanse of black, which ran down through the valley between the edge of Hundred Acre wood and the main road through the village.

Ella slowed slightly and waited for the main body of the hunt to string itself along the perimeter of the boundary wall between the wood and the field before she followed. One rider drew up just slightly behind her and kept pace. She turned and found Niall watching her, a smile on his face. She kicked at Merlin, moving his pace up a notch.

'Why are you always avoiding me Ella?' He asked, upping his pace to join her.

'I'm not.' She kicked her heels into Merlin again and he responded, drawing level with her.

'At the Halloween Dance, you refused to dance with me, you gave me Rachel instead. At the Christmas Dance too, you turned me down again. Why?'

'Does there have to be a reason?' She snapped, irritated by this unwarranted intrusion into her quiet privacy.

'Of course there does!'

'Well I haven't got one!'

'You must have!'

Ella let the last few riders pass her, intending to spur Merlin into a gallop to follow them, but a gloved hand reached out and grabbed her reins.

'Will you let go please?'

'Not before you give me an answer. Why don't you like me? Everyone else does.'

'I don't think you'd be very happy if I told you.' She said, resting her hands on her saddle.

'Try me.' His blue eyes challenged hers.

'Well, you're arrogant, self centred, vain, rude, oh and patronising!'

'I'm impressed,' His eyes were full of amusement again. 'You've recognised all my star qualities.'

'Oh, do me a favour, get lost.' Angered, Ella snatched the reins free, kicked Merlin's flanks and set off at a gallop, annoyed that despite her anger her heart was pounding madly and her face felt unnaturally hot.

Determined to lose him, she turned Merlin into the thickness of Hundred Acre, where out of the sun a thin, smoky mist swirled around the trees. She could hear the hunt up ahead, the sound of the hounds and call of the huntsmen as they negotiated their way through the wood. A low dry stone wall loomed ahead of her, with an open clearing and wide path through the trees beyond. Catching a flash of red jacket, she kneed Merlin towards the wall. This would be a piece of cake in comparison to the jumps she regularly used at Willowbrook. However, as he took off, quite unexpectedly a pheasant flew out of nearby undergrowth with a raucous screech. Merlin, in mid flight, shied and landed awkwardly, tipping Ella straight over his head. With a shriek, she landed on a soft bed of wet brown leaves. Flat on her back she opened her eyes, trying to focus as winded, she fought to get her breath back.

'Ella, Ella, are you all right.' Niall was suddenly there at her side, releasing the chinstrap of her riding hat, lifting her head gently. 'Say something, please, oh God, this is all my fault! Have you broken anything?'

Ella shook her head as she found herself staring up into eyes of incredible blue. He studied her for a moment, gently brushed the mud from her face with his gloved hand then bent his head and kissed her very softly on the mouth. She offered him no resistance, a combination of the fall; his closeness and the kiss itself making her feel weak and helpless.

'I've wanted to do that since the first day I met you.' He said as he held her there, looking down at her with a rapt expression. 'Do you know how wonderful you looked?' Then he bent his head and kissed her again.

Twenty yards away a rider reined in. Rachel had heard the scream and seen a riderless Merlin weaving through the trees. Retrieving him, she had made her way back through the wood. All she could feel was bitter disappointment as she watched the scene in front of her. The day had started so well, so full of opportunity, it might just have been the day when Niall O'Farrell actually noticed she was something other than just another young girl rider in the hunt. Now as she watched she knew that it was even more hopeless, for she, like all the others had simply been a mere distraction.

When Ella pulled them together on the night of the Village Halloween Dance, he had taken her in his arms and as they had slowly circled the room together, all her dreams had come true. For days afterwards, she could close her eyes and still feel the pressure of his hands on her back, breathe in the scent of his aftershave and imagine it was happening all over again. But she had only been fooling herself. For although he had paid her compliments and chatted with her as they danced, all the time Ella was the one he had really wanted. Until this moment, she believed Ella when she said she couldn't stand him because he was pompous and conceited. But then how could anyone possibly resist someone like Niall O'Farrell? Especially when he caught hold of you and kissed you like that?

Rachel knew she ought to hate them both, but she couldn't. Ella was her best friend. She deserved the love of someone like Niall, for just seeing them together made her realise what a perfect couple they made. One blond and one dark; his handsome to her pretty. Yet she knew that even the enormity of her emotional generosity was not quite large enough to anaesthetise the hurt of unrequited love that filled her heart and threatened to choke her at that moment. As Niall helped Ella to her feet, Rachel urged Buster forward, trailing Merlin behind her.

'Are you OK?' She called out. 'I found Merlin wandering, I was worried.'

'I'm fine.' Ella said rubbing mud from her jodhpurs. 'It was a pheasant, gave Merlin a bit of a fright. One moment I was in the saddle, the next on the floor!' she laughed as she took the reins from Rachel's outstretched hand.

'Thank you. God I feel such an idiot.' She said hauling herself into the saddle.

'It's a good job Niall was close by.' Rachel gave him a haunting smile.

Niall and Ella's eyes met for a second in conspiratorial silence.

'Yes,' Ella said slowly, her gaze never leaving his face. 'It was.'

Rachel suddenly felt she had to leave them, she had put on a brave face but she could feel the pain returning. 'I'll be off then.' She said quickly turning Buster's head back towards the wood.

'No, wait, I'll ride with you.' Ella nudged Merlin forward to join her. She turned back to look at Niall, standing by his horse's head. 'Thanks Niall,' she said and then she was gone, riding away with Rachel into the mist.

Niall smiled to himself as he watched them go, pleased with the way things had gone. So unexpectedly too. 'Now. 'He smiled to himself. 'Let's lower the heat and allow to simmer gently.'

Sunday 27th February

'Rachel whatever is taking you so long?' Margaret Sylvester stood at the bottom of the stairs, pulling on her brown overcoat, aware that they were with every minute, getting nearer to a situation that would make them late for church. Since very early that morning, Rachel had been in her room, even choosing to miss breakfast. She had then transferred herself into the bathroom where she had been ever since.

'Ready.' A voice replied as the door opened suddenly and she stood there in a red tartan mini skirt and black polo neck jumper, her fair hair tumbling in curls around her shoulders, make up on her face.

'Good heavens!' Margaret's mouth fell open. 'Your face! And where did you get those clothes?'

'Ella gave them to me.'

'Did she now?' She waved an outraged hand at her daughter. 'Well you can take it all off! It's totally inappropriate!'

'It's not!' Rachel's eyes widened indignantly. 'It's fashionable!'

Margaret started up the stairs towards her daughter. 'Yes and fashion does not belong in the House of God!' She peered at her. 'You'll give Reverend Farr a heart attack!'

Grabbing Rachel by the arm, she whisked her back towards the bathroom, shoving her through the door. 'Just go in there and clean that face off while I find you something more appropriate to wear! And tie that hair back!'

As the door closed behind her, Rachel stood looking at her reflection in the mirror. She filled the basin with water and soaped the flannel, feeling disappointed that her attempt to look more adult had now been completely wrecked by her mother. No doubt, she was rummaging through her wardrobe looking for the drabbest thing she could find. The bottle green dress with the white lace Peter Pan collar, that's what she'll choose she decided. It was a horrible thing, more appropriate for a twelve year old.

As the flannel returned her face to its fresh innocence, she resolved not to feel too downhearted. The most important thing was that Niall was free! The kiss in the woods six weeks ago had not seen the beginning of the great romance with Ella after all. Of course there had been changes; Ella's frostiness had disappeared and she now treated him like all the other boys. He was charming too, taking her out to dance and flirting with her just like he did with all the other girls. But they weren't dating; there was definitely nothing going on between them, she was sure of that. She smiled at her reflection. It meant there was still a chance for her. And knowing that she could cope with having to go to church looking like a twelve year old because in the huge scope of things it didn't matter, it was merely a small setback a........

A sharp tap at the bathroom door brought her back to reality.

'Rachel!' She heard her mother's familiar bark. 'Have you finished?'

'Yes! Coming!' She replied breezily, throwing open the door and finding herself face to face with her mother and the dreaded dress.

Saturday 19th March

Ella, on Merlin, followed a well-worn path through Hundred Acre. A warm spell had breathed Spring into Hundred Acre and celandines were everywhere in large yellow sprawls covering the floor of the wood. Soon she heard the familiar sound of water over rocks and decided to rest Merlin and give him a drink.

Rachel was supposed to have been riding with her today, but Margaret had insisted she spend her morning tidying the stock room instead. Ella thought that was mean, but knew it was pointless arguing. The way to handle Margaret was to simply ignore her. It was far more important to concentrate on making the most of the time she did have with Rachel. She had made good progress with her riding and Ella had now turned her attention to clothes. Over the last few weeks, with unwanted items from her own wardrobe, she had been teaching Rachel about mixing and matching colours and showing her what suited her. The results were very positive and now she was having her hair cut and styled regularly at the village hairdressers instead of letting her mother hack it, she was attracting interest from some of the boys at Young Farmers. It was only a matter of time now before someone asked her out. Who knew, once Rachel had landed her first proper boyfriend perhaps the crush she had on Niall would die a natural death.

Leaving Merlin at the stream, Ella sat down on a tree stump and turned her face up to the sun. Niall. Now there was an enigma. Since their encounter in the wood back in January, she had been in his company at dances and other Young Farmers gatherings, but while he was always friendly, he had not attempted to ask her out. Why had he kissed her? He told her he had wanted to do it ever since he met her. Was that true? Or was that just something he said to all the girls? Maybe she had been a disappointment. She had never really kissed a boy properly before. However, as he had done it twice, she decided she couldn't have been that bad.

Issy and Jenny had not been very helpful either. Jenny said that if he had not asked her out yet he probably wasn't worth bothering with, whereas Issy, as outrageous as ever, suggested that perhaps she ought to ask him out. Ella was horrified; there was no way she could ever do something like that! It would be far too embarrassing. She sighed. Jenny was right of course, if he couldn't make the effort, he really wasn't worth bothering about. Anyway, currently there were far more important things to occupy her thoughts, like exams. The results of her mock 'O' levels in January had been encouraging, the real thing now only weeks away. She needed to work hard if she was to be certain of a place in the sixth form and that took priority over any thoughts of romance. The sound of approaching hooves drew her back to the present. She looked up and saw Mary O'Farrell approaching on Cassie.

'Mary!' She got slowly to her feet. 'What brings you this far into the wood?'

'Rex Gallagher's lost a calf.' Mary reined in, immaculate as ever, in pale cream jodhpurs and a tan jacket. 'Little black and white thing. Looks as though it managed to get through a break in the hedge. Rex is looking farther down the valley and as I was out riding, I said I would help. I came this way as I thought it might have strayed up into Hundred Acre.'

'I'll help too if you like.' Ella said unhitching Merlin.

'Thanks. You take the east side of the wood and I will go west.

Ella and Mary rode off in opposite directions. The thickness of Hundred Acre soon enveloped Ella, branches brushed her face and pulled at her clothes and the ground beneath Merlin's hooves became boggy and sticky.

Suddenly she pulled him to a halt and listened, she was sure she could hear something. Urging Merlin towards the sound, she saw the calf up ahead, standing in a small clearing crying pathetically.

Dismounting she tied Merlin to a nearby tree, then cautiously approached the animal, calming it with soft words. It stood there looking at her meekly, brown eyes under long lashes, it's nose wet, a sad, mournful sound coming from its mouth. She edged forward and made a grab at it, her fingers closing around its thick coat, but as she did, the calf moved, dragging her with him and she fell forward, straight into the soft black earth. Ella sat up; the calf stood there looking at her silently, appraising her and the mud, which now clung to her clothes.

'You little beast.' She said, getting to her feet. Her second attempt was more successful; she held on tightly, pulling against him, but he was strong and she went down again. She got to her feet, dirty but unwilling to give up. Reaching the calf again she put her arm around his neck, just like she'd seen on rodeo films, twisting his head, she levered her body against him and he fell on his side.

Somebody was clapping. She looked up smiling, expecting to see Mary, but instead found Niall. He slipped from his horse, rope in hand and secured it around the calf's neck tying him to the branch of a heavy trunk that straddled the edge of the clearing. When he got back to Ella, she was leaning against a tree, brushing the dirt from her jodhpurs.

'Well done,' He said. 'We've been looking for him all morning. Sparky little thing isn't he?'

'He certainly is. 'She laughed. 'I wouldn't want to tackle him again in a hurry.'

She was aware of a sudden silence between them and looked up to see she was the subject of his blue-eyed scrutiny.

'What?' She stared back at him, realising the way he was looking at her was making her heart thud.

'Ella, is everything all right?' He looked at her seriously, secretly delighted his mother, worried in case Ella got into trouble in this notoriously boggy part of the wood, had sent him after her. It was just the opportunity he had been waiting for.

'Yes. Why?'

'You seem to have been avoiding me since January. Have I done something wrong?' He sounded hurt.

'No.' she shook her head, the way he was looking at her making her feel quite weak. 'I just thought you weren't interested.'

'Not interested? You must be joking!' He gave her a smile which set her heart pounding even faster. He was perfection. He looked just like a male model in his denim jeans and shirt. He was irresistible and he knew it. He came nearer to her, leaning against the tree, resting one arm just above her head as he looked down into her face.

'How old are you Ella Kendrick?' He asked.

'Seventeen in September.'

'Old enough then.' He laughed, his eyes never leaving hers.

'Old enough for what?'

'For this.' He pulled her mouth to his and kissed her hard. This kiss felt nothing like the one he had given her in January, she thought as she found herself responding. This was a man's kiss, it spoke of many things, including sex. She felt his hand wander down the front of her shirt, cupping her left breast, feeling for the nipple through the fabric, before it travelled further down and began gently easing the material out of her jodhpurs. Realising where this was going Ella removed his hand, pushing it away.

'And how old are you, Niall O'Farrell?' She cocked her head cheekily at him.

'Nineteen next month.' Amusement danced in his blue eyes.

'Old enough then.' She mimicked.

'For what?' He frowned.

'To know the difference between girls who do and girls who don't.'

'Oh yes.' A slow smile spread across his face and he bent his head to kiss her again.

'Well I don't.' She said, ducking under his arm and walking out into the clearing towards Merlin.

'Ella, wait.' He called after her. 'I'm sorry, I shouldn't have behaved like that.'

'No you shouldn't.' She replied, pushing her shirt back into her jodhpurs. 'I don't know what kind of girls you've been with in the past, Niall but I'm not like that and you'll just have to accept that. *If* you still want to go out with me.'

'Oh I do. I really do.' God she was irresistible when she was angry he thought as he looked at her standing in front of him, grey eyes like a storm at sea.

28

'Right then.' The storm in her eyes calmed and her smile returned as she walked over to where he stood. 'Now we've got that sorted, can you do something for me?'

'Anything. Your wish is my command.'

She rested her palms on his chest and looked into his face. 'Kiss me again, will you?'

FOUR

Tuesday 19th April

'God he's gorgeous!' Issy said, looking at the photo of Niall Ella had just handed her.

It was their second day back at school after the Easter Holidays. Wandering into the town during their lunch break they were now sitting on a bench facing the river only yards from the front of The Bridge Hotel where Issy lived.

'How can you have ever thought about avoiding someone like this?' Issy was amazed.

'Well, when I first met him he was rude, I didn't like him very much. Of course I didn't know him very well then.'

'Well, a man like this could give me all the hassle he liked and I'd put up with it. What do you think Jen?' Issy gazed appreciatively at Niall for a moment longer then handed the photo to Jenny.

'He's very nice Ella.' Jenny agreed.

'Nice!' Issy exclaimed. 'He's the most perfect human specimen I've ever seen!'

'And this is Nick isn't it?' Jenny pointed to the figure beside him.

'The one and only.'

'He's changed.'

'Yes.' Ella nodded. 'I think he's filled out a bit.'

'He's very handsome.' Jenny smiled thoughtfully, her eyes fixed on the tall fair haired young man leaning on the gate. She remembered he had been Head Boy during the last school year. 'I bet he's breaking hearts in Bristol. Has he got a regular girlfriend?'

'You can ask him yourself when you come to stay.'

'Will he be there then, I thought you said he'd be in Cornwall?'

'He leaves the week after your visit. He's looking forward to seeing you again.'

'You're just saying that.' Jenny laughed.

'No I'm not. He does remember you.'

'Maths Wiz you mean?'

'That was just a silly name he called you. He's a bit more adult now.'

'Mmm.' Jenny handed the snapshot back to Ella.

'Right,' Issy stood up and checked her watch. 'There's time for a free Coke at our Coffee Bar and even better, new Tamla Motown on the juke box.'

The Bridge Coffee Bar was busy but a bent sixpence jammed in the juke box meant music was coming from a tinny transistor on the shelf above the bar. Opting to take their drinks outside, Issy, Ella and Jenny found an empty table. It was a pleasant day with no breeze and sun rays spilled lazily through the shade of the mature chestnut trees above their heads, dappling the tables with moving patterns of light and shade.

'Only two more months and it will all be over.' Issy said stretching back in her chair and turning her face towards the sun.

'I'm going to flunk Geography.' Jenny sighed. 'The rivers; I can never remember the names of the rivers. Mrs McCabe nearly had a fit the other day when I said Germany's largest river was the Rhone. I meant the Rhine but got my O's and I's mixed up.'

'You'll be fine.' Ella drew a mouthful of Coca Cola through the straw and watched as a coach pulled up in the car park, its passengers spilling out in an enthusiastic jumble ready to explore the sights of Kingsford. 'We'll revise together, I'll test you and you can test me, that way we'll both learn.'

'Of course you'll walk sciences.' Issy looked enviously at Ella. Here was someone who seemed to soak up knowledge like blotting paper. She was so quick at everything and appeared to have no trouble in understanding anything they were taught.

'Nothing's certain.' Ella replied modestly.

'Oh go on.' Jenny argued. 'You'll breeze into Langford. And at least you know what you want to do. Iz and I haven't got a clue.'

'There's plenty of time to make your mind up during the summer break.' Ella said. 'The results aren't in till August.' She took a deep breath, closed her eyes and like Issy and Jenny, turned her face to the sun. Her mind drifted to the coming summer. Eight whole weeks at Willowbrook, riding, swimming, barbecues and dances with Niall home from Cirencester. It was her idea of bliss. Of course two of those weeks would be spent entertaining Jenny. Jenny. She smiled to herself. The spellbound expression on her face when she'd been looking at Nick's photo. Now what was that all about?

'Nice to see some people have time to enjoy the sunshine.'

A male voice suddenly interrupted Ella's thoughts and she opened her eyes to see a stocky, sandy haired young man standing there looking at all of them. Broad shoulders and strong arms filled his red checked shirt and his faded blue jeans were coated in cement dust.

'Mick!' Jenny who had also closed her eyes now opened them wide with surprise at the sight of her brother. 'What are you doing here?'

'I've been to Sutton's builders merchants up the road to get some odds and ends for the site. I passed you on the way out, thought you'd be coming here, so I decided to drop in and say hello.' His gaze drifted slowly over Issy for a moment before turning to look at Ella.

'I've seen you before. On many occasions.'

'Yes you have.' She nodded.

'You waved at me once.'

'I did. It's good to meet you at last.'

'Jen tells me you're the clever one.' He grinned. 'Going to be a vet.'

'I hope to.' Ella returned his friendly smile.

'And where's Bodgit the Builder working today?' The mockery in Issy's voice was clear as she put her bottle on the table.

'Well Ermintrude my darling,' Mick retaliated. 'we're in Hanover Street, refurbishing a row of weaver's cottages.' He pulled up a chair and joined them. 'They're lovely. Better than all those modern boxes Dad and old man Macayne usually have us working on. Although I have to say, the new stuff is what brings the money in these days.'

'Could we see them?' Jenny asked. 'We've got a home revision afternoon tomorrow. We could come then.'

'Yes, I'd like have a look around.' Ella agreed. 'What about you Is?'

'S'pose so' Issy looked at her and gave a bored yawn before turning her attention to the river.

'I don't think so Sis.' Mick shook his head doubtfully. 'It's Bob Macayne you see, he's got strict rules about women on building sites. Suppose it's understandable. After the accident.'

'What accident? Who's Bob Macayne?' Ella frowned, reaching forward to leave her empty bottle on the table.

'Dad's partner.' Jenny answered. 'It happened years ago. In one of those big places overlooking the park. He'd just bought it. It was almost derelict and he had plans to renovate it. His dream home so Dad said. Bob was supposed to meet his wife there one afternoon to show her around, but he got delayed - some meeting or other. When he finally got there she was lying in the hallway, dead.'

'The handrail on the landing was rotten,' Mick added. 'She must have leaned against it. It gave way and she fell straight into the hall below. Broke her neck. So it would be more than my life's worth to let you girls anywhere near Hanover Street until everything is finished.'

The blare of a horn intruded into the conversation. A figure in a flatbed truck parked at the edge of the bus stop lay-by was gesturing at them.

'Sorry, that's for me. Gotta go.' He gave an acknowledging wave to the van. 'Andy,' he said to Jenny. 'Just started with us. I'm looking after him.'

'But I thought he was destined for university in the autumn.' Jenny frowned, her gaze still on the van. 'Didn't Bob have great plans for him to become an architect?'

'Yes, but he was expelled from St Mark's last week.'

'Ooh.' Jenny's eyes lit up with interest. 'Why?

32

'Don't ask.' Mick looked uncomfortable. 'I've said too much already.'

'Oh come on,' Jenny prodded, 'you can tell us.'

Mick shook his head.

Issy stood up and collected up the Coke bottles from the table. 'I heard Andy was kicked out of school.' she said, 'because he was caught in the showers in the sports pavilion with a girl!'

Mick glared at her.

'And from the colour of your face,' Issy said with undisguised smugness, 'and your none-too-pleased expression I would say I'm right.'

Mick didn't answer. He sat watching Issy with a murderous glare as she walked back into the coffee bar . The horn sounded again, pulling him to his feet. 'I'd better go.' He said irritably.

'Time we made a move too.' With a scrape of chairs Ella and Jenny were on their feet. Jenny patted Mick's shoulder. 'Don't take it personally,' she said. 'If Issy knows then so do heaps of other people.'

'It's not that. It's the way she is always so pleased with herself when she thinks she's got one over me. Bloody Ermintrude,' he said as he backed away from them, 'why can't she just grow up!'

'Why does he call Issy Ermintrude?' Ella frowned as they watched Mick head off towards the van.

'It started as a joke. She wore a blue felt hat to The Mill one night. He told her she looked like Ermintrude from the Magic Roundabout.'

'And all this confrontation is because of that?'

'No, there's the other thing.'

'What *other thing*?'

Jenny sighed. 'The incident in the restaurant with Mr Davies, remember? It was all round school, Issy nearly died of embarrassment. She blames Mick for the whole thing and has never forgiven him.'

'Won't ever forgive him!' Issy added as she joined them. 'What's the matter, have I upset him again?'

'Yes you have!' Jenny said angrily. 'And I wish you would stop it.'

'Well, it's about time he grew up!'

'Strangely enough, Is.' Ella laughed. 'He said just the same thing about you!'

Back behind the wheel, Mick gave a final wave as the three girls passed him by, his eyes lingering on Issy for a moment before he turned to his passenger.

'Sorry. Got held up.'

Andy Macayne cast dark, humourless eyes in the direction of the three departing girls, the hard set of his mouth indicating he was not happy to have been kept waiting.

'Who's the girl with the dark curly hair?'

'That's Ella.' Mick replied, noticing the glitter of interest in his dark eyes.

'Ella who?'

'I didn't ask.'

'You're pretty useless Mick do you know that? I saw you chatting her up and what have you found out? Sod all.'

'So?' Mick gave a couldn't-care-less shrug.

Andy took a deep breath and gave his colleague a look that conveyed total exasperation. 'Well if you don't take advantage of a situation, you'll always be left behind where women are concerned.'

'If I don't take advantage as you put it,' Mick replied, annoyed. 'It's because firstly she's my kid sister's friend and secondly a girl like that wouldn't fancy me anyway. I'm a realist Andy, unlike you.'

Andy laughed. 'What I felt when I saw her was very real, believe me.'

'Oh yeah, until the next pretty face passes by.' Mick laughed, sliding the van into first gear and waiting for a gap in the traffic.

Ignoring him, Andy rested his arm on the open window of the cab, waiting until it caught up and eventually drew level with the three girls. As the van passed them, Mick gave a blast on the horn and Andy leaned out, giving Ella the benefit of one of his most seductive smiles.

'Make the most of it.' Mick shouted above the noise of the engine. 'That's the last you'll see of her.'

'Maybe,' Andy wound up the window and turned to Mick. He was smiling. 'then again, maybe not.'

Friday 22nd April

Rachel was standing at the top of the small ladder, arranging boxes of cereal when the shop door bell jangled.

'Shan't be a minute.' She called out, pushing the very last box of Rice Crispies into place.

'Don't worry I'm not in a hurry.' A voice replied and she nearly fell off the ladder as she turned to find Niall O'Farrell looking up at her.

'Rachel.' He stared at her open mouthed for a moment. 'I didn't recognise you. Your hair; you look...' he searched for the word. 'Gorgeous!'

'Do I? Thank you.' She smiled back, holding onto the ladder tightly as she climbed down, aware that her legs felt like jelly. 'Thought it was time for a change. Miriam Hollis did it for me at The Salon,' she said as she faced him. 'She said I looked like Julie Christie.'

He stood back for a moment, frowning at her. 'Mmm I can see what she means.' He agreed. 'She's my favourite actress you know.'

'You're teasing me Niall O'Farrell.'

'No, it's the truth, she is.' He grinned. 'Um, Mum's weekly order. Is it ready?'

'Yes, of course.' She pushed through the beaded curtain at the rear of the shop and reappeared with a large cardboard box full of groceries.

'Here we are.' She smiled again at him as she lifted it onto the counter. 'The bill's tucked into the side.

'I'll settle up now.' He said, pulling his wallet from the back pocket of his jeans and extracting a sheaf of notes.

'Going to the dance tonight?' She asked as she took the money and opened the till, encouraged by his friendliness.

'Yes. You?'

'Of course,' She handed him his change, staring into his eyes for as long as she dared, 'I'm really looking forward to it. I'm hoping the new glamorous me,' she lifted the ends of her hair, 'will make all the difference.'

'No doubt about that.' He said, his eyes fixed on her as he tucked the wallet back into his jeans and lifted the box off the counter. 'They'll be queuing up to dance with you. Right behind me.'

'You're teasing again.' Rachel replied breathlessly as she lifted the counter flap and crossed to open the door for him.

'No I'm not.' He stared at her again, and then smiled. 'And if I'm not at the front of the queue I'll push everyone out of the way to get there.'

'Niall!' She laughed, feeling colour flood into her cheeks.

'Rachel.' He looked at her seriously for a moment then leaned forward and kissed her gently on the cheek. 'I mean it. Honestly.'

'But I thought you were going out with Ella.'

'Me with Ella?' He looked puzzled. 'Whatever gave you that idea?'

She stood transfixed in the doorway as he left, making his way down the steps, into the road and out to the Land Rover.

Stashing the box in the rear he closed the tail gate and gave her a cheeky wink. 'See you later then Julie.' he said.

She returned his wave, watching him from the top of the steps as he drove off. Her heart soared. It had finally happened, the moment she'd dreamed about. Not only had he noticed her, he'd kissed her too; only on the cheek, but a kiss nevertheless. And she'd been right all along! He wasn't with Ella. He was free. She couldn't believe her luck! She ran back into the shop her heart thumping, her mind already full of what she would say and do, but most importantly what she would wear.

Ella's thoughts were on Niall as she made her way across the gravelled car park of the Village Hall. Since their meeting in the wood five weeks ago she had been seeing him regularly. He had taken her up to Weston Super Mare to see The Who in concert at the Winter Gardens, arranged various trips to the cinema, wined and dined her and spent hours riding around the quieter parts of Meridan Cross. If anyone had seen them, nothing had so far been said, but tonight, the first Young Farmer's dance since they got together, would certainly give the village something to talk about.

The more she saw him, the more addictive he became and she felt amused that after months of purposely being rude to him she had now discovered how

much she liked him.   They had so much in common too; the love of the
countryside, horses, music, even the same sense of humour.   And of course that
kiss.   She felt weak at the thought of it.

The hall was buzzing with people when she walked in. Simon Maddox, the
Young Farmer's regular DJ was on stage setting up his equipment with assistance
from the Miller boys, while people were standing round in little groups chatting.
Waving to Ash and Rowan she bought herself a Coke at the bar and turned to see
whether Niall was around.   Suddenly her gaze fell on a familiar figure in a blue
mini dress and patterned tights sitting at a corner table alone.

'Hello.'   Rachel looked up and smiled as Ella arrived at her table and sat
down beside her.

'Well what a difference.'

'Do you like it?' Rachel's face lit up.

'I do. It suits you.' Ella smiled. 'Who did it? Miriam?'

'Yes. She said it made me look like Julie Christie. Imagine.' She gave a
sigh. 'Me looking like a film star. Well it's a start Ella.' her face became
serious. 'I'm fed up with how I look, how I am. I want to change. I want.....'
she broke off as her attention was drawn to something beyond Ella.   A joyful
smile lifted the corners of her mouth.

Ella turned and saw Niall who waved out before joining the Miller boys at
the bar.   At that moment Simon Maddox announced his intention to kick off the
evening, launching straight in with the Four Seasons *Let's Hang On.'*

'I have to go, Niall's arrived. I saw him earlier today.' She looked at Ella,
her eyes shining.   'He liked my hair.   He said I looked like Julie Christie too.
She's his favourite actress you know! Ella, he's noticed me at last! I think he
likes me!'

'Rachel, there's something you ought to know.'   Ella's hand shot out to
intercept Rachel but she was on her feet and gone. Niall saw her approach and
moved away from the bar, drink in hand. He smiled as he reached her and
stopped, the flat of his hand hovering around her shoulders as he leaned forward
to listen to what she was saying. Rachel took Niall's glass from him and placed
it on a nearby table.   Looking across at Ella, Niall gave a shrug and smiled
before being led out onto the floor.

Ella closed her eyes, wondering what kind of madness had taken hold of
Rachel and how she was going to react when she found out Niall was with her.
Four dances later, Niall managed to extract himself from Rachel, pairing her off
with Rowan Miller before retrieving his drink and coming to sit with Ella.

'God I thought I'd never get away. Can't think what's got into her tonight.'

'Maybe it had something to do with what you said to her today.' Ella eyed
him suspiciously.

'Me?' He looked at her, all wide eyed innocence.

'Yes, she said you came into the shop.'

'That's right. We chatted and she asked me if I was coming here tonight.'

'And what did you say?'

'I said I was. Said I liked her hair. Teased her a bit. Told her all the boys would be queuing up to dance with her.' He shrugged. 'And that I'd save a dance for her. That was all. I'd say that was pretty harmless wouldn't you?'

'Not when she's obviously still got a huge crush on you.' Ella shook her head wearily.

'Has she? I can't say I've ever noticed.'

'You must be blind then. She's been like it ever since you arrived in the village. All she's ever wanted is for you to notice her and today for the first time you have.'

'Do I detect a little jealousy?'

'Don't be silly. I don't want her hurt, that's all.'

'So what do you suggest?'

Ella thought for a moment. 'I suppose I could take her out riding tomorrow and tell her then. There's no best time for this but it's got to be sooner rather than later before she builds her dreams any higher.'

Rachel, on the dance floor, was having the time of her life. The perm seemed to have opened the door into a new world Not only had her mother approved, but Niall had shown her the kind of interest she'd dreamed of for months and now Rowan Miller was whispering compliments in her ear and brother Ash was lined up for the next dance. She smiled, her thoughts returning to Niall again, her attention drawn to the edge of the dance floor as she looked for him. Eventually she saw him sitting with Ella, their heads together in close conversation. Why, she wondered, was Ella looking so serious? Was something wrong? She closed her eyes and concentrated on the beat of the music. Suddenly she didn't care what Ella thought or felt; for the first time in her life everything was going her way and that was all that mattered.

'Have you seen Niall anywhere?'

An anxious Rachel met the Miller Boys as they stepped from the hall into the darkness of the car park. The evening was over, the music had faded. Back inside tables were being cleared, glasses collected and washed. Outside in the sharp coldness of an early spring night one by one cars were vacating the car park.

'I think he went some time ago.' Rowan gave her an easy smile.

'He can't have.' Rachel shook her head. 'His car is still here.' She pointed to where the white E-type was parked. 'I have to stay.' She sounded panicky. 'I have to find him.'

'Hey, calm down, I'm sure he's around somewhere.' Rowan patted her shoulder and he and Ash left her, heading across the car park towards their Land Rover. Rachel watched them leave her anxiety returning. Where could Niall be? He had been on the dance floor for most of the evening, partnering nearly every girl there, but she knew deep down that she was his special one and she merely sat sipping her Coke, watching and waiting for the end of the evening when he would almost certainly cross the room and have the last dance with her.

Only he hadn't. He seemed to have disappeared into thin air. She pulled her coat around her. She couldn't go back in without looking clingy and that was the last thing she wanted him to think she was. So she decided to wait by his car instead, surely he couldn't be much longer?

Ten minutes later, despite stamping her feet and pacing back and forth, cold began to seep through her. With a shiver she tried the car door and surprisingly found it unlocked. Within minutes of slipping into the passenger seat, she saw him appear in the doorway of the hall, helping Simon carry his equipment out to the van. She smiled to herself. So that's where he'd got to. She settled down in the seat. It wouldn't be much longer then they would be alone together. The thought of kissing him goodnight made her shiver with excitement.

She closed her eyes for a moment, snuggling into her coat, pushing her hands deep into her pockets to keep herself warm. The sound of approaching voices made her open them again. She sat up straight, wiping the condensation from the window with her sleeve. She could see someone locking the main door of the village hall while a small group of shadowy figures drifted in twos and threes across the dimly lit car park. One couple waved, broke away from the rest and headed in her direction. She peered into the darkness; they were walking very closely together and as they drew nearer she could see the man had his arm around the girl's shoulder. It was too dark, however, for her to recognise either of them. As they reached the car she realised the man was Niall. Smiling he reached up and placing his hands either side of the girl's face, drew her gently to him and kissed her. Rachel felt hot and angry. After all he said to her he was with someone else!

As she continued to watch, the headlights of a departing car caught the couple in its beam and a cold sick feeling seeped into her stomach as she realised the girl was Ella. She panicked, knowing she couldn't let them find her here; it would be too humiliating. Hot anger exploded in her head as she shoved at the door, pushing her way out into the blackness of the night.

Ella let out a scream of fright as the car door flew open and a dark figure fled past her into the night.

'What the hell's going on! I was sure I locked that door!' Niall dived into the car, checking that everything was still there. 'Thank goodness.' He emerged looking relieved. 'Nothing's been taken. Who was it anyway, did you recognise them?'

'No.' Ella paused, looking out into the darkness in the direction the figure had gone. 'But I have a funny feeling it might have been Rachel!'

'Rachel? I thought she'd gone.'

'She did. To sit in your car and wait for you. Niall what *is* going on?'

'Nothing!' He shook his head. 'Nothing at all. Oh God!' he put his hands to his face for a moment then took them away. 'What are you going to do?'

'I don't know.' Ella shook her head. 'Try and see her tomorrow and explain. That's if she'll believe me.''

Margaret Sylvester sat up in bed with a jolt, head on one side, listening. There it was again. Carefully she pushed back the blankets and dropped her feet to the floor, pushing them into slippers before padding silently across to the door. She opened it just a fraction, pausing to listen again as she pulled on her dressing gown. In the hall a light came on. Margaret crept onto the landing, peering over the stairwell as she picked up the wooden copper stick resting in the corner, kept there specifically for occasions like this.

'Who's there?' She yelled out holding the stick tightly in her hand as she strode forcefully down the stairs. As she got to the bottom she could hear a small whimpering noise coming from the sitting room. Reaching the door she prodded it slowly open with the stick, her fingers stretching for the light switch. 'Rachel!' Her eyes widened at the sight of her daughter hunched forward in the chair by the fireplace, clutching a handkerchief, her tearstained face streaked with black mascara.

Rachel looked up and seeing her mother burst into fresh floods of tears. Instantly Margaret dropped the copper stick and crossed the room, easing herself onto the arm of the chair, her sharp features softening into genuine concern as she placed a gentle arm around Rachel's shoulder.

'Whatever's happened?'

'He lied to me Mum! He told me he wanted me and all the time he didn't. He wanted her instead!'

'Is this Niall we're talking about?' Margaret frowned.

'Yes,' Rachel sniffed loudly. 'He danced with me, he was really enjoying himself. Then I didn't see him again all evening, so I waited for him after the dance, and he came out with her and they were kissing!' her face began to crumple. 'I felt so stupid. She didn't want him until she saw him with me. I thought she was my friend, how could I have been so stupid!?'

The tears began to trickle down her face as she bent her head and sobbed into her soggy handkerchief.

'I knew this would happen!' Margaret reacted angrily. 'That bloody girl, she's just like her mother!'

'What are you talking about?' Rachel pulled the handkerchief away from her tearstained face.

'The reason I always tried to keep you apart.' Margaret said abruptly. 'Because of what happened to me.'

'Because of Ella's mother?'

Margaret nodded. 'And Christopher Kendrick.'

She looked at her daughter's astonished face.

'Oh I know what you're thinking. But I didn't always look like this, you know.'

She pushed herself off the arm of the chair and walked over to the old oak bureau. Pulling open one of the drawers she took something out and brought it back to where Rachel sat. 'Here.' she said, handing her an old photograph with curled edges. 'This was taken when I was eighteen.'

Rachel stared down at the picture. Two pretty girls standing together at the bottom of the shop steps in front of the lilac tree. Both were wearing summer dresses, their arms interlocked. The smaller one had shoulder length hair, her head thrown back in a wide, confident smile. The other, a lighter haired girl, with similar features to her own, had a quieter, shyer expression.

'We were friends, you see. Me and Mel Evas. Shared everything. Just like you and Ella. We had no secrets. When Christopher Kendrick returned from the war, he set the village alight. He was dark, handsome; a hero. In our young eyes he was just like a Hollywood star. They had a dance up at the manor to celebrate his return. Mrs Kendrick invited the entire village. It was a wonderful evening. We were sitting in one corner, us village girls. All dressed up, watching him. He came across that room and he took every one of us out for a dance, but at the end of the evening it was me he asked to see again. I thought he was wonderful. I also thought Mel was my friend. I was too trusting.' Her face softened as she reached out smoothing a stray strand of hair back off Rachel's face. 'She wasn't interested in him at all you know, not at first. But she couldn't bear someone having something she didn't. She went behind my back! She stole him from me! I hated her, but I hated him too. I thought he loved me. But he didn't really care about me at all. If I'd meant anything to him she would never have been able to come between us. He was as shallow as she was. They deserved each other!'

'Oh Mum!' Rachel threw her arms around her mother and sobbed.

'Come along.' Margaret said, reaching up to prise her daughter's hands away. 'No more tears.' She looked into Rachel's red rimmed eyes. 'You have to pick yourself up. Dust yourself off.'

Finding a dry corner of the damp handkerchief she began to gently wipe her daughter's face. 'Plenty more fish in the sea Rachel. That's what you've got to tell yourself. You're worthy of far better!'

Saturday 23rd April

Ella rode Merlin slowly up the High Street, past the sprawl of whitewashed and pink stone cottages, towards the village shop. Behind her trotted Buster on a long lead, saddled and ready for Rachel. As she rode, Ella was aware of what the task might be ahead of her. If, indeed, it had been Rachel in the car last night then she could still be very upset. She cursed Niall's stupidity. How could he have been so naive as to have encouraged her like that? She closed her eyes and prayed that her friendship with Rachel was strong enough to convince her that there had been no conspiracy, although exactly how she was going to explain things in a plausible way at this very moment escaped her.

Reaching the shop she dismounted and tied both horses to the lilac tree. At the front door she knocked twice and waited. She saw the reflection of Margaret through the semi-opaque glass, then the door was flung open.

'Well!' Margaret's eyes narrowed as she looked at her. 'You have some nerve turning up here! What do you want?'

'I brought Buster, I thought Rachel might like to come out riding this morning.' Ella replied calmly, aware of the hostility she was now facing.

'Did you now?' The smile which appeared on Margaret's face was quite malicious. 'And what brought this about?' she moved so close that Ella could feel the warmth of her breath against her cheeks. 'A fit of conscience was it?'

'I don't know what you mean.' Ella was taken aback at the ferocity of the accusation.

'Don't give me that! You're a deceitful girl Ella Kendrick, going behind my daughter's back! Stealing Niall from her!'

'I didn't steal Niall from Rachel!' Ella replied, annoyed at the accusations Margaret was making. 'I came to explain. There been a terrible misunderstanding!'

'A misunderstanding eh?' Margaret gave an indignant snort.

'Yes, and if I can just see Rachel I can explain....'

'I don't think there's anything she'd want to listen to from you.' Margaret shook her head. 'The damage is done. But let me tell you something, young lady,' she stabbed a threatening finger at Ella. 'You'll pay for this. Maybe not this week, or next month but some time in the future, when you're least expecting it, I'll make sure you suffer for what you've done to my daughter. Now get out of my sight!'

Friday 24th June

Mary O'Farrell turned Cassie back towards home, following the edge of Hundred Acre towards the village. The afternoon was warm, a heat haze rippling over the ripening barley field, skylarks in full song above it. She felt relaxed, her mind turning to thoughts of the forthcoming weekend when Richard and Peggy would be her guests for Sunday lunch and decisions on what she should cook for them.

As she reached the edge of the barley field and turned into the road she noticed a blonde figure in jeans and a short sleeved blouse sitting on the five bar gate of the field opposite.

'Rachel! What are you doing here?'

'Not a lot Mrs O'Farrell, just sitting.' Rachel said with a weak smile.

She studied the girl's face; the usual bright, happy smile was missing. In fact, she looked quite miserable. She knew from Peggy that there was some sort of rift between her and Ella; that she no longer came up to the farm to take Buster out. The cause of this was a mystery. Peggy knew nothing and Ella it seemed was reluctant to discuss it. Knowing that Ella was not the kind of girl to let things like a silly spat drag on she realised that Rachel's continued absence from Willowbrook must be down to one person; her mother. Seeing Rachel sitting there she decided perhaps it was time to get to the bottom of it all.

'I've not seen you at the farm recently.' She said quietly. 'Buster misses you taking him out you know.'

'Does he?' There was a glimmer of interest in Rachel's face.

Mary dismounted and tied Cassie to the gate, hauling herself up beside Rachel.

'Rachel what is it? Why have you fallen out with Ella? You were such good friends.'

'I know we were and I miss her, even though.......' Rachel looked at Mary with an unhappy shake of her head. 'Oh Mrs O'Farrell, it's such a mess. I just don't know what to do!'

'You could try talking to me. I'm a good listener and impartial!'

Rachel looked uncomfortable. 'Sorry, I can't...'

'Has Niall something to do with all this?'

'Someone's told you haven't they?' She bit her lip nervously.

'Actually they haven't, but I do know my son. He breaks hearts wherever he goes, never very faithful for very long. Although I did think at the beginning of April things were going to change. He seemed very keen on Ella and....'

'The beginning of April?' Rachel interrupted. 'Was he seeing her then?'

'Yes. Why?'

'Oh no!' She jumped down from the gate. 'I got it all wrong!' She looked up at Mary for a moment then was gone, running down the road towards the village. Staring after her, Mary felt even more confused than ever.

'That's it!' Issy walked through the wrought iron entrance gates to Kingsford High and threw her school hat in the air. Twirling around, she caught it, laughing at Jenny and Ella who were following quietly behind her. Together the three of them walked down the tree lined avenue towards the river and the Bridge Hotel's Coffee Bar. The last 'O' level examination had been taken, it was time to celebrate and think of summer holidays.

Sitting at a table in the sun they discussed their grand plans for the future. They had all met the Careers Officer just before the start of their exams. Jenny, with her aptitude for figures, had decided to look for a job with one of the local banks and Ella to return for her A levels to get into Langford. Issy, who found learning tedious and sometimes quite pointless, was ever hopeful of her favourite Beatle turning up at the hotel and getting down on one knee to propose. But as that was never likely to happen, she'd decided on Plan B. Her father had made her an offer to come and work for him. He had expansion plans. He was going to build a banqueting suite at the rear of the hotel for wedding receptions and functions. And he wanted Issy to help set it up and run it.

Saturday 25th June

Ella had decided to set the day aside for a good clear out in the stables. She had got up early, taken Merlin out for an hour and was now sitting on a wooden crate sorting through a pile of tack. All of a sudden she was aware of movement in the open doorway where sunlight streamed through onto the concrete floor, catching the edge of the stall with its brightness.

'Hello?' She called out. There was no reply. She bent her head again, her concentration taken on checking the leather as she ran it through her fingers.

'Hello Ella.'

She looked up to see a figure hovering uncertainly.

'Rachel!' Surprised, Ella got to her feet, dropping the tack onto a nearby bale. She gave her an encouraging smile.

'Oh Ella!' Rachel took a few hesitant steps forward. 'I just had to see you. I want to apologise for making an idiot of myself with Niall and blaming you because it all went wrong.'

'I came to the shop.' Ella said with a shake of her head. 'But your mother wouldn't let me see you.'

'I know. She was very angry. That was my fault too. I really thought, well, that you'd stolen him you see. He came to the shop to collect the groceries earlier that day. He kissed me on the cheek. Called me Gorgeous.' She hung her head. 'I honestly believed he was interested in me. When I asked him about you and him said there was nothing going on.'

'Well he lied.' Ella said, reaching out and squeezing her hand. 'But it's my fault too. I should have told you earlier that we were seeing each other.'

'I was so angry and humiliated that night Ella.' Rachel continued, her blue eyes misty. 'When my mother found out what had happened, she said you were cruel and selfish just like your mother and that I was to stay away from you. But when I really thought about it I realised you were the best friend I'd ever had.' She hung her head briefly before looking up with a small smile. 'And then I saw Mrs O'Farrell yesterday and she told me about how you and Niall had been seeing each other since early April. I had to come then, to apologise and ask if we could be friends again.'

'Of course we can.'

'Oh Ella!'

'Buster has missed you.'

'Yes, Mrs O'Farrell said. Is he around?'

'Granddad's put him in the field behind the farm, said he needed to stretch his legs. Did you want to take him out?'

'Could I?'

'Of course, just give me a hand with clearing up here, then we'll go catch him.'

Relieved and happy Rachel picked up a nearby brush. Everything was back to normal. She'd got her best friend back, she was free to come to the farm again and take Buster out when she wanted to. But more than that, she'd learned a valuable lesson; that looks were only skin deep. Niall might be the best looking man on the planet but he was vain and silly. In fact Ella was welcome to him.

Thursday 28th July

Ella stood on the platform at Meridan Cross looking up the line. The station clock showed 11.32. She checked it against her watch. Spot on. The train, she calculated, was only minutes away from the station now. As if in answer, the twin tone of the diesel was heard far the distance followed by a sudden flurry of activity in the nearby signal box. Levers were pulled and signals just outside the station responded. Alerted by this, Mr Mortimer the Station Master emerged from within the station buildings, checking his fob watch against the station clock, smiling up at it with satisfaction, then at Ella. He touched his cap to her as he passed, she returned his greeting with a smile.

She could see the yellow front of the train in the distance as it rounded the bend out of the deep cut which took the line south west towards Taunton. The scattering of passengers who stood around her on the platform began to gather up their belongings, readying themselves to get on board as soon as it stopped.

Within seconds the square of yellow had taken a defined shape, she could see the cab with its windows and the driver in his blue short sleeved shirt. A rumble accompanied by a shriek of brakes followed the train into the station where it came to a halt with a slow shudder, filling the station with a strong aroma of diesel.

Doors opened and banged against the side of the train, followed by a voice calling 'Meridan Cross, this is Meridan Cross, next stop Morden Junction.' A cluster of people emerged from the train, most of them villagers returning from an early morning's shop out of Abbotsbridge. Mr and Mrs Lawrence, a retired couple who lived in the High Street, Mrs Baxter and Mrs Hinden, both widows from Tucker's Lane and Mrs Robinson and three of her boisterous children from Field Way. Then she saw Jenny.

Dressed in pink jeans and a matching short sleeved gingham shirt she was standing at the end of the platform, suitcase in hand. Ella rushed to greet her, throwing her arms around her with such a force that she dropped her case.

'I can't believe I'm here, it's been a wonderful journey! I've never travelled so far on a train before.' Jenny's eyes were sparkling. 'There was such a lot to see. You miss so much in a car.'

'Come on.' Ella grabbed the suitcase and guided her towards the gate where porter Stan Jefferies was taking tickets. 'Granddad's waiting outside in the car park. Welcome to Meridan Cross.'

Nick Kendrick sat astride Merlin watching the peaceful valley below him. This was his third holiday return since starting in Bristol last September and as usual he had quickly slotted himself back into farm life, finding plenty of jobs to do under the guidance of his grandfather and Jake.

Nick took a deep breath; Bristol was a great place, full of bustle and life and he had settled down well into student life in his first year. But looking at the countryside around him now, he realised how much he had missed the village and that despite enjoying the variety of pubs and music clubs the city had to offer, he was still a country boy at heart. He shaded his eyes against the late morning sun, and gazed out to the east, over the barley field. The light breeze stirred the yellowing heads of the grain causing a silky liquid ripple across the breadth of the field. He smiled as he noticed movement to his far right, and turned to watch the progress of the Land Rover as it journeyed steadily through the village. From his vantage point on the edge of Hundred Acre where lush green pastureland sloped gently away down to the road he had a clear view and recognised his grandfather at the wheel. He urged Merlin forward across the field, calculating that he would reach the turning up to the farm at the same moment as the vehicle and be able to race it to the house.

Jenny saw the horse and rider just ahead of them and nudged Ella.

'Isn't that Nick?' She shouted over the noise of the engine.

Ella nodded. 'Yes, it looks as though he's going to race us to the farm.'

Richard smiled and pushed his foot down hard on the accelerator. The Land Rover shot forward as it turned into the track up to Willowbrook, Nick urging Merlin forward to keep pace in the field beside it. Ella was laughing as she saw her brother kick Merlin to move him slightly ahead. Neck and neck horse and vehicle closed in on the farmhouse, Nick finally putting Merlin over the fence to land just yards ahead of his grandfather. By the time they had pulled up outside the front of the house, Nick had already ridden out of sight into the yard. As Ella climbed out and helped Jenny with her suitcase he reappeared, leading Merlin, smiling broadly.

'The winner!' He said triumphantly

'You always are.' Richard grinned amicably at him. 'You have a distinct advantage, young man. You can cut corners, I can't'

'Nothing like real horsepower.' He eyed the Land Rover with a grin. 'beats the socks off the man-made variety.'

'Don't you be rude about this old girl,' Richard patted the bonnet affectionately. 'She's been worth her weight in gold over the years!'

Jenny stood there silently, listening to their banter, her mind going back to the first time she'd met Nick. It was love at first sight and had lasted four whole years, while he was still at Kingsford. Of course, once he had left for university she'd convinced herself she had merely been the victim of a schoolgirl crush. However, when she saw the photograph she realised maybe it hadn't been a crush after all, and now she was standing here next to him she realised from the way her heart was thudding, that she was right.

He saw her then, small and shy, standing slightly behind his sister.

'Ah the Maths Wiz.' He smiled down at her, then seeing she was embarrassed, said. 'Sorry, didn't mean to be rude, I was only teasing. Girls and maths don't usually go together, you know. Here, Sis.' he handed Merlin's reins to Ella, his gaze still fixed on. Jenny. 'Tie him up will you while I see to our guest? 'He bent down to retrieve her suitcase. 'Let me give you a hand with this.'

She watched as his fingers closed around the handle. Warm, strong hands she thought. He's wonderful; just wonderful.

With a smile he lifted the case and opened the gate for her. 'This way.' He said and ushered her through it and up the garden path towards the front door and the smiling figure of Peggy Evas.

FIVE

Saturday 30th July

Collin's Barn, a modern, concrete floored building which normally stored tractors and combines, had been completely transformed for the Young Farmer's Midsummer Barn Dance. Vehicles had been moved out and two Portaloos offloaded at the rear of the building. Inside a bar had been set up at one end and a stage erected at the other for the group and disco. For most of the morning a band of volunteers, including Ella and Jenny had been busy with preparations for the evening.

Jenny was currently helping Ella assemble trestle tables for the buffet. It was the second full day of her stay and she was really enjoying what she realised was a way of life totally different to her own in Abbotsbridge. She loved the old farmhouse with its warm stone walls, cosy bedrooms and profusion of flowers in the garden. And Little Court, Laura Kendrick's Elizabethan manor house was just amazing.

Niall, she had to agree with Issy, was one of the most handsome boys she had ever seen with his blond hair and striking blue eyes. He and Ella made a perfect couple and looked so happy together. She had also met Ella's friend Rachel who lived in the village shop with a real sourpuss of a mother. She, like Ella, felt sorry for Rachel, a girl even shyer than herself. And then, of course, there was Nick. At school he had merely been Ella's older brother - quiet, studious, an enigma. Now, here she was, spending time, getting to know him and enjoying every precious minute. He had made up a foursome with Niall, Ella and herself when they'd visited the pub on Friday night and had played darts and kept them amused with his stories of student life in Bristol.

This evening she was really looking forward to the dance; Nick would be there and she hoped she would have the opportunity to dance with him. She loved everything about him, his broad shoulders, the sparkle in his deep blue eyes and the way he continually ran his fingers through his fair hair to push it back off his face. She knew he was quite studious, keen to get his degree and become a teacher. She dreamed of the possibilities the evening might bring, but realistically knew that he probably had a girlfriend at University and his friendliness was only good manners while entertaining his sister's friend.

Returning to the barn later that evening Jenny saw how the morning's work had paid off. The whole place looked colourful and inviting. Straw bales had been arranged in a large square around the barn and someone at the bar was ladling out glasses of punch for new arrivals. She sat with Ella, Rachel and Niall, chatting and laughing; Ella introduced her to the Miller Boys, two years apart but almost duplicates of each other with their curly black hair and dark eyes. Rowan the eldest promised her a dance later on.

Nick arrived at 9.00 with pretty brown haired girl who he introduced as Helen Beckwith, the local doctor's daughter. Jenny's heart dipped disappointedly as she watched him get her a drink.

Moments later the band started up and the caller stood up and announced the first dance. Leaving their drinks on a nearby table, Nick took Helen's hand and led her out onto the floor, Ella and Niall joining them and a dozen other couples. Trying to put her disappointment behind her, Jenny watched, amazed at the way everyone seemed to know all the right steps in what seemed to be quite a complex set of manoeuvres.

'It's not as difficult as it looks,' Rachel said, leaning towards her. 'Everyone here's been doing it for years that is why they make it look so easy. Still, you wait till they've all had a bit to drink; it gets really silly then, especially if the Miller Boys are on the floor!'

By the time the band had finished that evening everyone was having a thoroughly good time, and Jenny found herself in the thick of it, partnering Rowan Miller. All her past disappointment at finding Nick with another girl was swept away as he swung her around whooping joyfully and deliberately bumping into his brother. When the music stopped he had given her a soft hug and thanked her for the dance before kissing her hand and walking her back to her seat.

She sat down, breathless and laughing, only to be back on her feet almost immediately as the band finished and the buffet was announced. As she returned to her seat with a plateful of food and sat down beside Rachel she noticed a young bearded man had joined Nick and Helen.

'That's Tom Andrews, Helen's fiancé.' Rachel said, chicken drumstick in hand, nodding in their direction. 'Nick's been holding the fort. Tom was in London today, couldn't get back on time. Nick's a nice bloke, isn't he? Bit of a swot though, doesn't seem to have much time for girls.'

Jenny looked at him a preoccupied smile on her face. 'That's a shame,' she said.

Rachel picked up her serviette and slowly wiped her hands. 'Actually Jenny.' she looked at her seriously. 'I think he quite likes you.'

'Me? You're imagining things.' Jenny shook her head.

'Yes, he's been watching you all evening, you know.'

After the food it was the turn of the disco to get everyone up dancing, kicking off with Manfred Mann's *'Pretty Flamingo'*. Apart from the surroundings they could have been at The Mill Jenny thought as she joined the others on the floor. She did not see Nick amongst the dancers during an evening that remained full of partners - Ash, Rowan again, Niall and several other boys from Young Farmers. Eventually, the evening drew to a close, Simon the DJ announced the last dance and people paired off and wandered out onto the floor. Jenny, alone on her bench, was aware of a touch on her shoulder and looked up to see Nick standing behind her.

'I'm sorry, I haven't been very good company tonight have I?' he said. 'So I'm going to make it up to you now by asking for the last dance.'

Remembering Rachel's words, all Jenny could manage was an embarrassed nod as she got to her feet. Gently she slipped into his arms and out onto the floor to join the others.

'So?' He said with a smile. 'Enjoying your stay so far?'

'Yes, it's so different from home, but I like it. I can understand how Ella loves this place so much.'

'Do you ride?'

'I used to.' Jenny nodded. 'I had lessons as a child but I've sort of lapsed.' Realisation of her lack of competence caused her confidence to come to an abrupt halt and she made a face. 'If I tell the truth, I'm probably a bit rusty. In fact I'm probably quite useless.'

'Well, we can't have that can we?' Amusement lit his face. 'Did Ella tell you Niall's mother used to be a riding instructor?'

'Yes.'

'Well Jenny Taylor, here's a challenge for you.' He looked at her with a warm, disarming smile. 'You go and see Mary, brush up on your riding and if I think you're competent enough, I'll take you out for the whole day on Wednesday.'

'You will?' She couldn't believe what he was saying, she felt like pinching herself to make sure it was really happening.

'Yes, just you, me and a picnic lunch if the weather's good enough. Would you like that?'

'Oh yes, yes I would.' Jenny gave him a radiant smile as the conversation with Rachel earlier on that evening echoed in her ears. This was a bet she wasn't going to lose.

Wednesday 3rd August

The late afternoon sun was settling in the west as two riders skirted the eastern edge of Hundred Acre and out towards the lane and the track to the farm. Jenny, astride Buster, followed at a gentle pace behind Nick who had borrowed Merlin for the day.

It had been wonderful. They had ridden the boundaries of the farm, meandered through Hundred Acre and had lunched leisurely by the river. They had talked and exchanged views on music, books, films, fashion and his great love history. She knew by the afternoon that he liked her company because he'd asked her if she'd like to go to Kingsford with him the next evening to see *A Man for All Seasons* at the Gaumont.

Just before six they rode slowly back to the farm and into the stables where Nick dismounted and helped Jenny as she slid from Buster's back, reaching out to support her. As her feet made contact with the stable floor, Buster moved against her, knocking her sideways. It was only Nick's well timed grab which prevented her from falling.

Jenny felt herself colouring as he released her. He was so close, his expression gentle and she knew beyond any doubt what was about to happen. She closed her eyes and waited. The kiss when it came was however, not quite what she had expected. She felt the first firm pressure of his lips against her skin, but it was her forehead he kissed, not her mouth.

'Thank you for a lovely day Jenny Taylor, I haven't enjoyed myself so much for a long time.'

She opened her eyes to find him standing in front of her, a soft smile playing on his lips.

'Me too.' She nodded, embarrassed, trying to hide the way her heart had begun to pound against her ribs, hoping the way he was looking at her that he might be about to kiss her properly now.

'Good, I'm glad,' He said, then quite unexpectedly turned his attentions to Buster, pulling at his girth, the moment suddenly lost as she heard him say. 'Right then, let's get these horses unsaddled and settled for the evening shall we?'

Jenny felt disappointed as she followed him into the tack room carrying Buster's saddle. She was sure that for a split second they were on the verge of their first real kiss, but something had stopped him. She watched him lift the saddle onto a nearby rack wondering whether the problem was maybe just a simple one. That he was as shy as she was.

'I think little Jenny has a bit of a crush on Nick.' Peggy said to Mary over coffee in the big kitchen at Paddocks. 'I've caught her once or twice staring at him all dewy eyed.'

Mary laughed as she poured out two cups of coffee and pushed a plate of chocolate biscuits in Peggy's direction. 'I knew something was up. She put so much energy into getting her riding skills up to scratch. Said Nick had promised to take her out for the whole day. You should have seen the determination in her face.'

They both laughed.

'I wonder if Nick's noticed.' Peggy stared thoughtfully as she brought the cup to her lips.

'Oh I would imagine so, he doesn't miss much. Not that he's much of a ladies man.' Mary shook her head. 'He's far too studious. I think his romantic inclinations are collecting dust on a shelf somewhere until he finishes university.'

'You're probably right there.' Peggy agreed. 'Pity really, she's a nice girl.'

'Yes she is. And you know something? This riding business, well it got me thinking. The village could do with a riding school, there isn't a decent one for miles.'

'But where would you locate it?'

'Charlie Cooper's small holding.'

'Ah, I heard he was selling up.'

'It's ideal, stabling for six and four acres of land.'

'There'll be a lot of interest in that, my dear. You'd better get your skates on.'

'I already have.' Mary said with a broad smile. 'I signed the contract yesterday. I move in next week.'

Thursday 11th August

Jenny stifled a yawn as she came down the stairs to breakfast on what was to be her last morning at Willowbrook. The spell of fine weather had deserted them, leaving a grey, overcast sky which looked as though it could turn to rain. A fitting end to her holiday, she decided, to be leaving on the day the weather had turned. A smell of toasting bread greeted her as she walked into the dining room, where Ella was helping Peggy lay the breakfast table.

'Where is everybody?' She asked, looking around a room where Richard and Nick were usually sitting in the corner busy discussing farm topics in the run up to breakfast.

'Down the south pasture.' Peggy replied as she set out the cereal bowls. 'One of the cows has fallen into a ditch, stupid thing. They're trying to haul her out.'

'Are you planning to go down there after breakfast?' Jenny asked innocently, thinking it would be an opportunity to be near Nick. 'I'll come with you if you like.'

'I don't think that would be a good idea.' Ella replied as she brought in a selection of cereal packets and left them in the middle of the table. 'It's in a cramped corner of the field near the wood. The vet's there and Granddad's been back once for more rope. They're going to try to pull her out with a tractor, but if that doesn't work they'll have to get the fire brigade. She's big, heavily pregnant and quite distressed so they are having to be very careful.'

Jenny walked over to the window and looked out towards Hundred Acre. Low cloud threaded itself through the trees as light slashes of rain appeared on the glass. This had been a magical fortnight; there had been so many new experiences. She had made new friends, including Nick, but friendship wasn't what she wanted from him was it? She knew she was only sixteen, probably just a kid to him, but she also knew that what she felt for him was special and she had not experienced anything like it in her life before.

'Breakfast Jen!' Ella called to her as she brought in a large jug of cold milk and sat down at the table.

Jenny turned away from the window, deciding that despite her feelings she had to be realistic. Next week she would be starting her new job at Midland Bank and time, distance and other young men she would meet there would probably make her see this whole thing with Nick in a completely different light. It was time to go back to Abbotsbridge, her family and the real world. Joining Ella she sat down and began helping herself to cornflakes.

The hands of the station clock swung to 11.00. Jenny sat with Ella on a brown and cream bench, her suitcase between them. The grey skies had parted slightly to reveal patches of blue sky and the sun was trying to break through. The air felt slightly muggy. Somewhere in the station a bell rang.

'That means the train's just left Morden,' Ella said. 'It should only take a few minutes to get here.'

'It's been a lovely holiday.' Jenny looked pensive. 'Do you think I could I come back again some time?'

At that moment signals just outside the station clanked into position, causing them both to look up the line, which stretched emptily into the distance.

Ella put her arm around Jenny's shoulder and gave her an affectionate hug. 'Grandma and Granddad would be pleased to see you any time. They've enjoyed having you.'

'Will you say goodbye to your grandfather and Nick for me? I'm sorry they weren't back in time.'

'Of course I will.'

Jenny felt sad that the incident with the cow had prevented her saying goodbye to Nick properly. She had hoped to have seen him before they left for the station but neither he nor Ella's grandfather had returned. He was leaving for Cornwall tomorrow to stay with friends in Falmouth for the rest of the summer. She would probably never see him again.

The blare of the diesel's klaxon sounded in the distance, followed almost immediately by its appearance way down the track. It rumbled nearer and nearer, until with a protest of brakes it slowed and stretched itself along the length of the platform.

Ella helped Jenny onto the train with her case and then stood on the platform near the open window of the carriage. Within minutes the train was preparing to leave. Doors slammed and Ella reached out and patted Jenny's shoulder.

'Good luck with the new job! Give me a call; let me know how you're getting on.

Jenny smiled. 'Thanks, I will.'

'Maybe we can all get together for lunch sometime.' Ella shouted over the drum of the engine, but Jenny wasn't listening, she was looking beyond Ella and smiling. As she felt the first jolt of the train's movement out of the station, he came running down the platform towards them, his fair hair bouncing against his forehead, his smile just for her.

'Jenny!' He called out to her as he reached the window and briefly touched her hand. 'I couldn't get away, I'm sorry.'

'I know, it's all right, I understand.' She said, looking down at him as he kept pace with the train.

'Jenny, will you write to me? I'll leave my address with Ella.'

She saw Ella look at both of them and smile.

'Please, don't lose touch.' His blue eyes held hers. 'I've enjoyed the holiday so much, it's been special, really special. And so have you.'

'Yes, yes, I'll write, I will.' Jenny agreed eagerly, as the platform ended suddenly and the train slipped away, leaving him standing there. She stood at the window until both Nick and the station disappeared from sight. Sitting down, she pressed the back of her head against the seat, closing her eyes and then opening them again, hardly daring to believe what had just happened. He wanted to keep in touch, he wanted her to write. It wasn't over at all. It was just beginning.

Sunday 14th August

Ella and Nick stepped down from Richard's Land Rover and stood together looking at the dilapidated stable block in front of them.

'Mary must have been mad buying this.' Nick said, gazing at the peeling paintwork, rotting wood and the untidy jumble of rusting farm machinery which had been abandoned around the site.

'Don't you worry,' Richard replied as he joined them. 'There's an army of workmen coming in here next week to put things to rights. Come back next Sunday and you won't recognise the place. She'll soon be up and running.'

'What about stock?' Ella looked out on the empty field. 'If she's planning to open the second week in September she'll need to get that organised fairly quickly.'

'Ah that's sorted. I said I'd go to Taunton with her. There's a horse sale on in the livestock market on the 25th.'

'Oh dear!' Ella laughed. 'You've forgotten something haven't you?'

'What?'

'That's a Thursday. You take Grandma to Abbotsbridge every Thursday.'

'Oh drat, so I do.' Richard cursed, and then he smiled. 'Never mind, I expect she'll enjoy Taunton just as much.'

'Honestly Richard it doesn't matter, it really doesn't. I'm sure you're right, I'd have a lovely day out in Taunton, but on this occasion I'd really prefer to go to Abbotsbridge.'

'Oh now you've made me feel awful, leaving you to fend for yourself like this.'

'Look, the train's no bother, honestly. I haven't got much to get anyway, just some material for a dress for the Harvest Festival Supper next month.'

'Are you sure now Peggy? I really do feel bad about it.'

'Tsh, get away with you Richard Evas. I know you're dying to pick out some good horses for the girl, and I can't wait to see the place when it's finished. You know she's spoken of nothing else but her stables lately, she's really wrapped up in this project, bless her!'

'Yes I know she is. But I still feel a bit bad about deserting you like this.'

'Well please don't. I'll enjoy the train; it'll be a nice change.' She cupped his face in her hands and kissed him. 'Richard, forget about me, you must do this for Mary. After all she is our.....' she hesitated, then realised perhaps this wasn't the moment. 'very good friend!'

Thursday 25th August

It was 3.45. The Town Hall clock chimed and Peggy, emerging from Langleys' Department Store, checked her watch, noted it was five minutes fast and stopped to adjust it. Her shopping was now finished, material and pattern purchased and it was time to return to the station to catch the 4.15 back to Meridan Cross.

On her way there she interrupted her journey for a short browse around the market, where she met up with Sybil Masterson, the village schoolmaster's wife and the two walked back to the station chatting. As they arrived on the platform, the train pulled in, the hum of the diesel clear on the afternoon air. Sybil and Peggy settled down together in a second class carriage facing each other next to the window. Sybil immediately opened her vast handbag, pulling a half finished green knitted sleeve from its depths.

'For Henry's birthday.' She said by way of explanation and putting on her glasses began to knit furiously.

Peggy gazed out of the window, admiring the hanging baskets and floral tubs on the opposite platform. She smiled across at Sybil then checked her watch.

'We're late.' She said. Sybil nodded in agreement and continued knitting.

A guard passed the open doorway. Peggy called out to him and he returned, leaning into the compartment.

'Excuse me, when are we leaving?'

'When the London express gets in,' He said with a smile. 'We have to cross the incoming line to get onto the Taunton track. Can't do that until it arrives. Don't worry.' he reassured them both. 'It won't be long.'

He disappeared, his footfalls trailing off down the corridor, leaving Peggy to gaze out of the window again. She looked at the people on the opposite platform - a large matron in a tweed suit and flat sensible shoes. Next to her, a smartly dressed woman in blue, holding tightly onto two small boys. Several business men with their brief cases wandering slowly up and down and...

The woman was pacing impatiently, glancing at her watch then up at the station clock. She was dressed in red with matching high heels, an elegant hat perched on her blonde head. She looked out of place; overdressed for a town like Abbotsbridge. She belonged to the big city Peggy decided and immediately wondered who she was and what she was doing there. The way she held her head, the elegant way she walked. It was just like Mel. But Mel was in Taunton, choosing horses with Richard. She stared at the woman again.

'It can't be.' She shook her head, looking first at Sybil then back at the stranger, who had now turned her back to her and was reading an advertising poster.

'What is it Peggy?' Sybil halted her knitting, looking over the top of her glasses at her companion.

Peggy ignored her, continuing to watch the woman, willing her to turn around again. She needed to see her properly. She needed to make sure.

A train whistle shrieked in the distance and the woman turned to look down the track.

'I have to do something.' Peggy announced abruptly, getting to her feet. 'I won't be a moment!'

'Peggy what *is* the matter?' Sybil Masterson stared at her.

Peggy stood up and began gathering up her shopping, talking to herself in silly breathless bursts which Sybil couldn't understand.

'Peggy, what are you doing?' She watched the older woman's frantic scrabble to collect all her shopping together. 'You can't go, the train will be leaving soon. If you miss it, there won't be another one until seven thirty.'

'I need to check something!' Peggy said firmly as she left the compartment. 'I won't be long! I just need to make sure!'

Spearing the ball of wool with her needles and dropping her knitting onto the seat, Sybil pulled off her glasses, got up and followed Peggy into the corridor.

'Peggy.' She called after her. 'Make sure about what?'

But Peggy had now stepped off the train and slamming the carriage door shut was beginning to make her way down the platform to the crossing board at the end of the station.

'Peggy!' Sybil summoned all her strength and shouted. 'Where are you going?'

Peggy turned for a moment, smiled and replied, but her words were lost in the shriek of the incoming train and the throb of the stationary diesel.

'The express is coming.' The guard said, passing her on his return from the front of the train. 'I should take your seat if I were you Madam, we'll be leaving shortly.'

Sybil returned to the carriage, wondering what could possibly have triggered Peggy's bizarre behaviour. She heard the roar of the approaching train on the other line and gazed across at the opposite platform, frowning as she wondered what it was Peggy had spotted that was important enough to miss a train for.

As she picked up her knitting and settled herself down again, she felt the vibration and heard the approaching express as it slowed for the station. The noise seemed to continue for an eternity, then all at once it was in the station, passing her compartment with a great rush of noise through the small aperture in the window, its closeness causing the carriage to rock slightly.

Sybil dropped a stitch and frowned. The express was no longer moving but strangely she could still hear the high pitched squeal of brakes. She tilted her head, listening carefully and realised it wasn't brakes at all. It was the sound of people screaming. She stood up, heard the sound of running feet along the platform, followed by shouting. Abandoning her knitting she left the compartment. Outside people were pouring off the train, all heading towards the end of the platform. Curious, Sybil left the train and joined them.

'Well, I would say all in all we've had a very successful day,' Richard said with a satisfied smile as they drove into Meridan Cross village.

'Yes, what a surprise! Five horses, all good quality. I had no idea we would achieve so much.' Mary clapped her hands together girlishly and laughed. 'I'd say we were spoilt for choice wouldn't you?'

'We certainly were.'

Richard could not believe their day had gone so well. They had arrived mid morning and spent the first hour looking over the auction stock, picking out animals they were going to bid for. Over lunch they short-listed and set themselves a ceiling for each bid when they attended the auction proper. At the end of the afternoon they had come away with two Exmoor, a New Forest and a couple of older hunters. Their return journey had been filled with excited discussion over the plans for the riding stable and its eventual opening.

'Richard,' Mary said quietly. 'I still feel bad about dragging you off to Taunton today. Poor Peggy, having to get the train to Abbotsbridge, it was most unfair.'

'Not at all, I did give her the option of coming along today, I even tried to persuade her the market in Taunton would have far more to offer than anything in Abbotsbridge, but she would have none of it. She didn't mind, really. She's gone on the train before, said she'd enjoy the change.'

'Nevertheless, I feel I must make amends. As soon as I get home I shall be booking a table at the Charlton Cat for Saturday night. My treat, I insist.'

'That's very kind of you Mary but not at all necessary.'

'Please, Richard I really want to do this.'

'Well, if you insist,' He nodded in agreement as he slowed the vehicle to turn into the high banked lane which led to Paddocks Farm. 'But the wine's on me.'

'Sure, I'm in agreement with that.' Mary smiled; everything was coming together so well. She was almost there, hopefully opening for business in mid-September.

The Land Rover followed the twists and turns of the narrow lane, brushing the rich overhang of ferns, foxgloves and grasses which narrowed it in parts and obscured vision. As they rounded the last bend before the farmhouse where the road widened out slightly, Richard found himself face to face with an on-coming vehicle and swung the wheel to the left, hitting the bank and bouncing off it back into the lane. The Land Rover shuddered heavily and stopped.

'Are you OK?' He looked at Mary. She nodded, white faced.

'What the hell does he think he's playing at!' She said angrily as she pushed open the door and jumped out, running to where the other vehicle had come to rest on the edge of the ditch.

Niall pulled himself from the Jaguar, looking pale and shaken.

'How many more times do I have to remind you about driving like a madman in that thing?'

'I'm sorry, I'm sorry!' He raised his hands in a placatory gesture, his face ashen, his voice breathless. 'I was on my way to Willowbrook. Oh God, I'm so glad you're back. Laura has just phoned. She's there with Ella.' He looked at them both. 'It's Peggy. There's been a terrible accident!'

Friday 26th August

'Sybil.' Henry Masterson leaned over and touched his wife's cheek. She opened her eyes at once.

Seeing her confused expression he gave her a reassuring kiss on the cheek. 'You're at home dear, in the sun lounge.'

She looked around. 'Yes, so I am.' She closed her eyes again.

'Sybil,' Henry whispered gently. 'Richard's here. He would like to talk to you.'

'Talk to me?' She frowned.

'About the accident.' He squeezed her hand. 'Do you feel up to it?'

'Yes, yes of course. Where is he?'

Henry looked up and motioned to Richard, standing in the doorway, to come forward and seat himself in one of the cane chairs.

He settled himself quietly opposite her.

'I've already given the police a statement Richard.' She said quietly, resting against her pillows, her face pale against the darkness of her hair.

'I know, I've talked to them. I just wanted you to tell me, it's not really the same hearing it from strangers.' He lowered his head, rubbing tired hands over his face.

Sybil pushed herself upright. 'There's not much to tell really,' she said gently. 'I met her on the way to the station. We chatted. Sat in the same carriage by the window, facing each other. There was a delay. The express. We had to wait for the express.' She stared out of the window, concentrating, trying to remember every detail. 'I was knitting and she was watching people on the platform opposite. Then suddenly she became really agitated. Started talking to herself. Said she had to go. That it wouldn't take long. Said she had to make sure about something. I couldn't make head nor tail of what she meant. Then she just got to her feet, grabbed all her shopping and got off the train.' She pushed her lips tightly together as the rawness of the memory returned and she sat there, trying to compose herself.

Richard watched her with concern. 'I'm sorry; this is so selfish of me. I shouldn't have come.' He got to his feet to leave

'No, no, I'm fine.' She waved a hand at him to sit down again.

'Did you notice who was on the opposite platform?'

'People,' She said looking at him helplessly. 'Just people. Men with brief cases, a woman with small children and there were a couple of women on their own. Both impatient, both checking watches. Pacing up and down. Waiting for someone I suppose. One was in her fifties, a large matronly type, the other was younger, wore a suit. I remember thinking how smart she looked.'

'When Peggy got up to leave, how did she look to you?'

'Odd.' She shook her head. 'Confused.'

Richard nodded.

'I did try to call her back, I really did.' Sybil shook her head, her voice trailing away to a tired whisper. 'She just didn't seem to hear me.'

'It seems to me,' Henry Masterson said, his face sad and serious. 'That something caused Peggy to have some sort of relapse. I'm so very sorry Richard. This past year, well she's been so different. So happy. I really thought she'd finally got over all that business with Mel.'

'So did I Henry,' Richard said sadly. 'So did I.'

1967

SIX

Sunday 25th June

The sun had just slipped behind the trees to the west and dusk was approaching as Laura Kendrick emerged from the kitchen with Ettie. They were carrying large plates of sandwiches which they had both been busy preparing to feed the handful of villagers who had stayed behind to clear up after the Annual Fête, held as usual in the field fronting Little Court. It had been a splendid day, with only one or two odd showers which had sent the crowds rushing for cover into the beer tent, much to publican Tom Bennett's delight.

Laura felt pleased with the days events; there had been an abundance of well thought out stalls, donkey rides, bowling for a pig (which Richard and Mary had overseen), tombola and a coconut shy. Even Doggy Barker, the village's odd job man, had joined in this year, dressing as a clown with painted face and garish clothes to entertain the village children.

The WI cake stall had surpassed itself, Winnie Jenkins, Laura's friend from Higher Padbury producing the most mouth-watering Victoria sponges. She had also pledged a trio of luxury fruit cakes in the raffle. Mary's riding school protégés had given an entertaining display prior to the gymkhana, which to everyone's surprise Rachel won on Buster. Ella and Niall had been in charge of the Young Farmers events and were now dismantling the jumps and stacking the poles in one corner of the field. Laura smiled. Only the young could be guaranteed to have so much energy after the lively way they had whirled around to the music Nelson Miller and his boys had provided at the impromptu barn dance which wound up the afternoon's proceedings.

Setting the sandwiches down on an empty trestle table, she called out to everyone to come and get something to eat. As if by magic, Tom Bennett appeared from his tent, carrying a huge jug of cider, his wife Lily following behind with a tray of glasses.

'Here we are Mrs Kendrick,' Tom said, handing Laura a half pint glass filled with golden brown liquid. 'I guess this isn't your normal tipple, but I can thoroughly recommend it for thirsty workers.'

'Thank you Tom.' Laura smiled. She took the glass and perching herself on one of the remaining straw bales sat quietly for a moment. She had been so busy all day; this was the very first time she had been able to relax. She made the most of it, taking note of who was still here and what they were doing. In one corner of the field, Rachel was helping her mother box up what was left over from the white elephant stall. Margaret, sour as ever, was berating her daughter, instructing her to take more care with the china she was busily wrapping in newspaper. The Miller boys and their father had finished packing away their assorted menagerie of musical instruments and were now enjoying pints of Tom's free brew. Another guaranteed boisterous night down at Saddler's End, Laura thought with a smile.

On the edge of the field she saw Richard and Mary making their way towards Richard's Land Rover. Last year she remembered it had been Peggy keeping pace with Richard's long stride, a brace of pheasants in her hand. It seemed impossible that she was no longer living among them all. The village would remember her as a good, honest, hard working woman who had sacrificed her later years to bring up her grandchildren. Now, slowly Meridan Cross, like her family, was learning to live without her.

Laura remembered the day of the funeral. The brilliance of the floral tributes around the grave dramatically contrasting with the solemn black of the mourners. And afterwards the tears and self-reproach. Firstly, Ella admitting that for years she knew her grandmother was regularly spending time in the attic with music and old photos of Mel. Followed by Mary saying she should have cancelled the visit to the livestock market when she realised it clashed with Peggy's shopping trip. And finally Richard regretting the fact that he allowed Peggy to go alone to Abbotsbridge when she obviously was in no fit mental state. Even Laura had added her own revelation; her secret knowledge of Peggy's fixation that Mary was Mel. Everyone, it appeared, could have saved Peggy if only they had taken a different path. But what was done was done and in truth maybe Peggy was also partly to blame. Her life long obsession with her daughter had made her ill, driven her to the borders of insanity and almost certainly played its part in the accident. Aware of the troubled family around her, Mary cancelled the opening of her riding school for six months in order to take hold of the situation, supporting and guiding them through their grief and confusion.

A year on Mary's hard work with the family was beginning to pay off. Ella's school work was picking up again after a dramatic downturn. Nick, who had taken permanent refuge in Bristol, was returning regularly to spend weekends at the farm. From Richard there was praise and admiration from someone he told Laura he thought of as not only a most remarkable woman but also one of his closest and best friends.

At the far end of the field the plump form of Winnie Jenkins emerged from the main marquee, carrying a stack of empty boxes, heading towards her car which was parked in the cobbled yard by the stable block. Watching her progress, Laura could see she was struggling and abandoning her drink, went to intercept her.

'Winnie!' She scolded as she reached her. 'You really shouldn't be carrying great heavy things like that.'

'Oh don't fuss so Laura!' The older woman replied as she came to a halt, face pink with exertion under her halo of white hair. 'I'm quite able, really I am.'

'Nonsense, look at you now, fighting for your breath.'

'You do exaggerate so, I'm not an invalid.' Winnie protested as she peered at her friend over the top of her burden.

'Come along, let me help you.' Laura was insistent. With a small sigh of defeat, Winnie obliged, dumping the boxes onto the grass in front of her. Laura smiled; she was a battler was Winnie. Seventy four, widowed for more than a decade, totally independent and quite cantankerous.

'Right, now divide the boxes into two piles and I'll take half. I don't want a heart attack to mar what has been a wonderful afternoon.'

'Heart attack indeed,' Winnie made an exasperated face and bent down, separating the cardboard containers into two lots, and giving Laura half.

'I think you've gained a hefty reputation here today.' Laura laughed, as they made their way across the field and out of the gate into the lane which ran down towards the stable block. 'Your cakes have been the talk of the fête. By the way who won the raffle?'

'Oh a lovely lady,' Winnie's eyes crinkled with amusement. 'In fact it was quite strange really. She was with this man. I naturally thought they were just friends. He was a good bit older than her you see. But when he picked up the cakes for her he said that they would be just right for a wedding and he supposed he'd have to marry her now so as not to waste them. She laughed and asked him if he that constituted a proposal, and he said yes it did.' As she opened the boot of the car she gave Laura a happy little shrug.

'And?' Laura asked, her curiosity mounting as she handed her the boxes.

'Well, then she looked at him a bit straight and said *You're serious about this aren't you?* and he said, *Of course I am* and then she kissed him. Quite lady-like it was, under the circumstances, and said *In that case I accept.*

'I wonder who that could have been?'

'Just a minute, I think I've still got the ticket here.' Winnie pushed her hand deep into the pocket of her dress and pulled out a folded raffle ticket. 'Here we are, 327.' she turned it over, peering at the writing on the rear. 'Her name was O'Farrell, Mary O'Farrell. Do you know her?'

'Yes I do,' Laura replied, realising that two of her best friends had suddenly turned their relationship into something quite different and wondering what the reaction from the rest of the family would be when they found out.

Thursday 29th June

Edie Moffatt pedalled her old black bicycle up the vicarage driveway and out into Down Lane, then turned left towards the High Street. Her morning had been busy; there had been furniture to polish, carpets to vacuum and the last and most tedious job of the day - the Reverend Farr's weekly wash to iron. Still, working for the vicar had its bonuses. Not only did the monotony of housework pay fairly well, but also the place was a real fly trap for snippets of juicy information; and what better place to exchange her weekly store of knowledge than at the village stores with her great friend and gossip Margaret Sylvester.

Edie was a large round woman with a florid complexion and greying hair, nearly twenty years older than Margaret. She had known Margaret's parents Frank and Elsie Duncan well, Elsie being as avid a gossip as her daughter was now, but not as generous. For Margaret was not averse to parting with a pound of Typhoo tea or half a pound of bacon for the juicer pieces of information Edie brought her. Today, Edie reflected as she freewheeled past the Somerset Arms, what she had to tell Margaret would be worth half the shop.

Saturday 1st July

Ella stood flowers in hand, looking down at the simple pale marble grave with its black lettering. Rachel standing silently beside her, allowed her friend this private moment, her only gesture to hand over a bottle of water. Ella knelt down and took out the wilting blooms from the previous week, refilling the metal receptacle with water before carefully arranging the fresh chrysanthemums. Picking up the dead heads she stood up and took a step back.

'There,' she said quietly. 'I hope she likes them. They came from her garden.'

'I'm sure she does,' Rachel said looking at Ella, wanting to say more, but knowing it would almost certainly be something totally inappropriate.

Ella walked away from the grave, brushing away the wetness from her eyes with the tips of her fingers. She discarded the dead flowers on a nearby heap of grass cuttings as she walked towards the lych-gate where Merlin was tethered. Rachel heaved herself into Buster's saddle and rode silently after her. They were in the High Street before she spoke again.

'You know it's nearly a year since she died,' she said quietly. 'Willowbrook is so empty without her. I should have let Grandfather know about the attic. She was ill Rachel and I didn't let them know. I feel I'm partly to blame and it hurts so much. Do you think I'll ever get over this?'

Rachel shook her head. 'I don't know Ella; I guess you will in time. What's happening about university? Will you still go next year?'

'That's the plan.' Ella made a face. 'Although I must admit I've found it hard going this year. I just don't seem to be able to concentrate the way I used to. It's not only losing Grandma, I miss having Jenny and Issy around.' She looked bleakly at Rachel. 'Nothing seems to be the same any more.'

They had reached the shop now and Rachel dismounted, handing Buster's reins over to Ella.

'Sorry I can't come back to the farm with you but Mum wants me to help clean out the freezer.'

'No problem,' Ella replied. 'Are you OK for tomorrow?'

'I think so. Shall we say ten thirty?' Rachel gave Buster a farewell pat.

'Ah there you are.' Margaret Sylvester in familiar pink nylon overall appeared at the top of the steps, arms folded, her mouth in its usual disapproving set as she fixed Ella with a frosty stare. Despite all her warnings, Rachel was still keeping her company. She grudgingly acknowledged that Rachel had made a mistake about Ella and Niall, but she still sensed danger and felt annoyed that from being in control she had gone back to being a helpless spectator in all this. One thing, sure as God made little apples, she decided, nothing but trouble and pain would come for Rachel if she continued with this so-called friendship.

'Not late am I?' Rachel asked, looking at her watch.

'No love.'

Ella suddenly found herself the subject of pale eyed scrutiny. She tugged on Buster's rein, drawing him in closer to Merlin, trying to ignore the woman's blatant stare.

'Going to be bridesmaid are you?' Margaret called out with an unusual hint of amusement on her thin lips.

'I'm sorry?' Ella frowned at her wondering what sort of trouble she was in the throes of making now.

'At your grandfather's wedding.'

'Wedding? He's not getting married.'

'Oh yes he is. The banns are being called at All Hallows tomorrow.'

'Mrs Sylvester,' Ella smiled uncomfortably. 'If that was about to happen, don't you think I would know? I've no idea where you've got this from but it simply isn't true. Who is my grandfather meant to be marrying anyway?'

'Mary O'Farrell, of course.' She gave a harsh laugh. 'That'll make Niall your uncle won't it?'

'I don't believe you.' Ella shook her head uneasily. 'You must be wrong. She's......'

'Nearly young enough to be his daughter, yes, we all know that.' Margaret smirked. 'Right old cradle snatcher your grandfather!'

'Mum, that's a horrible thing to say!' Rachel looked at her mother in dismay.

'Yes it is,' Ella replied, steadying Merlin. 'I don't know where this came from, but it's totally untrue.'

'Is it now?' Margaret rose to the challenge. 'Then I suggest you get yourself home and ask him yourself!'

'That's just what I intend to do.' Ella replied angrily, turning Merlin back towards the farm. Thirty minutes later, after settling Buster and Merlin down for the night, Ella walked back to the farmhouse. She noticed that during her time in the stables Mary had arrived, leaving her Land Rover on the rough gravel at the front of the house. She felt pleased, she would be able to ask both of them now and dispel once and for all this awful gossip Margaret and her evil tongue were putting about the village. As she came in through the kitchen door she heard voices.

'Well, I think you've really hit on a good choice there, this hall is in definite need of something to lift it out of the doldrums. And I do like the rust tones; they go well with the carpet.'

Opening the door which led into the hall she came face to face with her grandfather and Mary O'Farrell. Mary was holding an open wallpaper sample book against the wall.

'What are you doing?' Ella looked at them both, feeling a sudden rush of unease.

Richard smiled uncomfortably. 'Oh, Mary thought the hall could do with a bit of brightening up. She's chosen some wallpaper.'

'It's kind of you to take an interest.' Ella fixed her eyes on Mary. 'But surely things like that should be our decision, after all we're the ones who live here.'

The look which passed between Richard and Mary made Ella feel distinctly uncomfortable.

'Ella, I've been meaning to talk to you.'

'What, about wallpaper?' She said sharply, knowing now almost certainly that Margaret had been telling the truth.

'No, about Mary and me.' He walked over to Ella, looking down at her with a smile. 'We're going to get married.'

'Yes I know.' Ella felt a tightness in her throat and a sensation that she was about to suffocate.

'You do? Who told you?' Richard said his eyes wide with surprise.

'Margaret Sylvester. About ten minutes ago.'

Richard closed his eyes and sucked his breath in hard. 'Oh Ella, honestly love it wasn't meant to happen this way. We were going to tell you, but I was very aware what a tough year you've had. It was all a matter of choosing the right moment. Believe me, the last thing I ever wanted was to hurt you.' He reached out and laid his hand softly on her shoulder.

'Please! Don't touch me!' She brushed him away, tears in her eyes. 'How could you both humiliate me like this? How could you!' She shouted and turned and ran from the room.

Niall hung his jacket in the hall and walked slowly into the kitchen at Paddocks Farm, border collies Tinker and Zeb following at his heels. He expected, as usual, to find his mother there. Today, however, she was not. Instead, propped against the teapot on the kitchen table was a note telling him she was at

Willowbrook and he would find his tea in the fridge. While he waited for the kettle to boil he buttered himself a hunk of bread and picked at the neatly arranged salad with its cold new potatoes and generous portion of chicken breast. He wondered why his mother had needed to go to Willowbrook at this time of day. Wedding matters no doubt. He smiled to himself. Not long now and they would all be living at Willowbrook. He was surprised no one had yet told Ella; the wedding was less than a month away and they were still hesitating, wanting the timing to be right, wanting to break it as gently as they could, knowing she was still emotionally fragile, afraid of the repercussions which might arise if they got it wrong. Well, they'd better get on with it, he thought, because if they didn't tell her soon, someone else surely would. Didn't they know there was no such thing as a safe secret in Meridan Cross?

Tea made, he sat down to eat, only to be interrupted moments later by the shrill of the phone in the hall. Leaving his half eaten meal he went to answer it. When he returned he picked up his salad and returned the fridge. Cursing under his breath he grabbed his car keys and headed for the door.

Ella sat quietly, her back pressed up against the trunk of the huge willow which hugged the bank where Little Court's garden met the river. She had been here for three hours now, waiting patiently for her grandmother to come home from her bridge afternoon in Higher Padbury. She felt alienated and humiliated, the memory of Margaret Sylvester's smug expression still imprinted on her mind. The whole world seemed upside down, the upheaval which followed her grandmother's death, the emotional hole in her life and her inability to concentrate on her studies had been bad enough, but now the unthinkable had happened. How could she possibly go back to Willowbrook after this? Mary was already making changes, preparing to transform the farmhouse into something unrecognisable. She felt excluded. Shut out; unimportant in the grand scheme of things. She simply didn't belong there any more. And so, she reflected, she would have to leave, find somewhere else to settle, somewhere away from all the turmoil so she could concentrate on preparing herself for A levels next year.

As she turned to look at the house again she saw a figure emerge from under the sprawl of the rose arch at the back of the house. As he passed the ornamental fountain he saw her and began crossing the lawn in her direction.

'I thought I'd find you here. Are you OK?' Niall said quietly as he reached her.

She shook her head, turning away to watch the early evening sparkle of sun on the water, her throat tight with tears.

He sat down next to her, quiet for a moment, as if afraid to break the silence, then gently taking her hand he said. 'Do you want to talk about it?'

She turned to look at him, her expression desolate. 'Oh Niall,' she sobbed as his arms closed around her. 'How could they?'

Tuesday 4th July

'I don't believe this!' Richard Evas said as he poured the last of the Piesporter into his wine glass. 'I thought that Niall more than anyone would be able to bring her to her senses.'

'I'm sorry.' Mary looked sympathetic. 'Believe me, he has tried everything. She is convinced that she's in the way here, that she doesn't matter. He has managed to persuade her to come to the wedding but she's asked for her things to be packed and sent to Little Court.'

Richard looked aghast. 'Just like that, without even talking to us first?'

'Richard!'

'What!?'

'You've no right to be angry with her, you know,' Mary said with a sad shake of her head, pushing her plate to one side and retrieving her wine glass. 'I can imagine how she must feel about our wedding. Just as she said, it seems that she doesn't matter.'

'I suppose you're right.' He gave a tired sigh as he played with the stem of his glass. 'We've made a right pig's breakfast of it, haven't we? I just feel so frustrated that there's no way of righting the wrong. The last thing I wanted was to get married under a cloud. But I know Ella, she's stubborn like Laura. It's going to be a long, hard job winning back her trust, believe me.'

'All the more reason to stand back from it, give her some space,' Mary said wisely. 'Sure, Ella's a sensible girl, Richard, she'll come round, you'll see. Believe me, this is just a silly storm in a teacup.'

Friday 7th July

Two women stood together talking in the Dress Fabric Department of Langley's, Abbotsbridge's largest Department Store. One of them, a smart, grey haired, woman in her early fifties seemed distracted, running her fingers over the racks of dress material, while the other, a plump brunette in a navy suit, a tape measure looped around her neck, had pulled out a bale and was holding it up against her.

'I don't think you'd do a lot better than this Sheila,' she said with a professional bunching of the material to show its potential. 'This is just your colour, put navy shoes and bag with it and it will be look wonderful. We have the perfect Butterick pattern and Trica Neal our resident seamstress would do splendid job, as good anything you could buy upstairs. Trust me; I know what I'm talking about.'

'Ooh, I'm not sure Joyce.' Sheila Fitzallyn's face set itself in a frown, reflecting the confusion of one who is suddenly faced with an impossible decision. It had been her husband Charles' idea to have something specially made. He wanted her to have something unique for this important family wedding and now she wished she had brought him with her to help make the choice.

'What about the green?' She reached for a nearby bale and pulled it out. 'I quite like this.'

'Hello Sheila and what are we up to now?'

Sheila froze material in hand. She looked at Joyce and seeing her friend's tight smile knew exactly who was standing behind her.

A small immaculately dressed blonde eased herself between them, splaying her fingers across the bale of material. However, it was quite obvious that she had merely done this to admire the shade of her nail varnish rather than the colour or quality of the fabric.

'Actually green does you no favours darling.' She said, staring at the bale and then at Sheila. 'Makes you look a teensy bit sallow actually.'

The friendly smile on the woman's lips was not reflected in the iced blue brilliance of her eyes. Sheila knew as always that Mel Carpenter was the queen of the put down and prepared for humiliation once again.

'Oh I totally disagree Mrs Carpenter, I think the green's quite fresh.' Joyce argued. 'But it's not as good as the pale blue, now that really suits her, don't you agree?'

'What's it for?' Again pink tipped nails gave the material a disinterested feel.

'A dress and coat for a wedding.' Sheila replied. 'My niece Susan is getting married in August to one of Charles' junior partners.

'Well, if you're going to have something *run up*,' Mel said disdainfully. 'You might be safer with the *plain* navy.'

Sheila, good mannered as always, bit back the temptation to say what she really felt. Why couldn't Mel Carpenter leave people in peace, why did she always enjoy intruding into their lives and trying to make them feel insignificant? 'I'll take the light blue.' She said defiantly.

'I think you have made an excellent choice.' Joyce beamed. 'Talking of weddings Sheila,' she said lightly as she wrapped the material carefully back around the bale ready to carry it to the counter for cutting. 'I see that farmer from Meridan Cross is getting married.'

'Which farmer's that dear?' Sheila turned her back on Mel as she replaced the bale of green back in the rack and moved closer to Joyce.

'You know the one who lost his wife in that dreadful accident at the station last year.' Joyce said as she patted the flat of her hand down the rack to even up the bales. 'Oh what was the name now? Evas, that's right Evas. The announcement's in the paper today.' She smiled. 'Nice to see a happy ending isn't it? Don't you agree Mrs Carpenter?'

Turning from the counter to find no one there she looked at Sheila and smiled. 'Well, I wonder where she went?'

'Haven't a clue.' Sheila shook her head. 'Maybe it was something you said.'

Monday 10th July

Mary was brewing tea in the kitchen when there was a knock at the front door. She walked into the hall, smoothing her hands down her skirt and checking her hair in the heavy gilt framed mirror before pulling back the brass catch which held the heavy oak door in place. With a creak it swung open to reveal a small blonde woman about her own age, immaculately dressed in a pink shirt and cream slacks. Pearls circled her throat, matching studs in her ears and Mary was struck not only by the perfection of the woman's overall appearance, but also the brilliant ice blueness of her eyes.

'Yes?' Mary smiled politely. 'Can I help you?'

The stranger did not smile back, she merely stood there appraising every inch of Mary carefully, her eyes like sapphire frost, her mouth set in a straight, tight line.

'Is Richard Evas at home?' She spoke at last, her voice soft and well educated.

'Yes, he's here,' Mary replied, noticing the fine gold band and three diamond cluster on the woman's left hand. 'Mrs....?'

'Carpenter.' The woman replied coolly catching Mary unaware as she eased past her into the house. She turned in the hall eyes taking in the walls first then the furniture. 'Not much change here I see.' she said with a sorry shake of her head. 'New paper but still a drab old place.'

'Exactly what do you want Mrs Carpenter?'

'I've come to see Richard Evas.' She said, looking thoughtfully at Mary as she studied her reflection in the mirror. 'And your mother if she's here.'

'My mother?' Mary frowned, confused.

'Yes, Mary O'Farrell, the woman my father going to marry.'

'You're Mel?'

'That's right.'

'I'm Mary.'

'There must be some mistake.'

'No mistake.' Mary smiled and extended her hand hospitably.

Mel ignored the gesture. 'My father, please.' Her hand was already on the front parlour door knob. 'I'll wait in here.'

Mel Carpenter locked the door of her red Sunbeam and walked towards the front door of her house. She felt irritable and depressed. The visit to Meridan Cross had been a nightmare. She knew her first face-to-face encounter with her father was going to be difficult, but what was far worse was finding out her new stepmother was only five years older than herself. How could he contemplate such a marriage? It was unthinkable.

She climbed the stairs feeling quite shaken. Of course it had been a gamble just turning up out of the blue like that. But at the time she'd been feeling strong, in control, prepared for anything. That was until she actually came face to face with him. The contempt he'd held for her hadn't diminished, but then had she honestly expected that it would have? He was a hard man who lived to a strict moral code and she was, as she always had been, the wastrel child, adored by her mother, but never quite reaching his impossibly high standards, always a huge disappointment.

'So the bad penny's returned at last. Still the same, apart from a change of hair colour.' He stood facing her, his back to the window, hands clasped behind him, eyebrows drawn together like gathering thunder clouds. 'Thought you were never to be seen again. Australia wasn't it?'

She sat quietly, her hands folded in her lap determined to ride out his anger.

'Yes it was', She replied calmly. 'But we're back for good now Dad.'

'*We* now is it?' He studied her left hand, noticing the wedding band and engagement ring. 'A new husband too. How long since?'

She thought for a moment then shrugged. 'Eight, nine years.'

'Can't you remember?'

'Does it matter? I'm back, that's the most important thing.   Liam, my husband, is an architect. He's bought a practice in Abbotsbridge.'

'Has he now? Is that the reason you've come scuttling to my door today? Do you think after the way you behaved I'm even the slightest bit interested!?'

She ignored his anger, feeling a desperate need to placate him. In order to be in a position to protect her inheritance from her new stepmother, the sole reason for her visit, she knew she would have to swallow her pride, turn the other cheek, even grovel to be accepted back into the family once more.

'I guess not.' She gave a weak smile. 'But I've come with an olive branch. I wanted to see if we could repair the damage I caused. Make a fresh start. With the wedding imminent I thought it might be an appropriate time. I was so sorry to hear about poor Mum.'

'Were you now?' He looked at her sceptically. 'You know, I'm not sure I could trust anything you said any more Mel. Not after all the lies.'

'If I ever lied, there was always a good reason for it Dad,' she said defensively.

Richard left the window and sat himself down opposite her, a tired expression on his face.

'Like the way you lied about Laura I suppose?

'What do you mean?'

'You said she threw you out.'

'Well she did in a manner of speaking.'

'I think I would have too, after what you did.'

Mel looked at him blankly.

'Bankrolling Wing Commander Snowdon and his chinchilla farm with investment money which you stole from the children's bank accounts.   That money wasn't yours to take!'

'I didn't steal it.' She protested. 'I invested for them.'

'You handed it over to a con man! I warned you when he arrived in the village, didn't I? I said he was a bad lot. And, of course, you going back to work afterwards had nothing to do with having freedom and meeting people. You had to because you'd lost all the money!'

'You should be proud of me!' She glared at him. 'Yes, I made a mistake! Yes, I went out to work because I had to! I had my children to think of didn't I?'

'Your children, would they be the same ones you abandoned?'

'That's not fair! It was impossible to take them with me.'

'Oh and why was that?' He got to his feet and stood over her.

'Because....' She put her hands to her face, feeling the heat flooding into her cheeks.

Richard left her and moved towards the door. 'You dumped them here to run away with this Liam fellow didn't you?' He rested his hand on the brass handle watching her closely. When there was no response he said. 'I think I've heard enough. You'd better go!'

'Please, at least let me see the children.' She was desperate now, clinging to anything that would delay her departure. Make him change his mind.

'I don't think that would be appropriate. Besides, they are not children any more. They are young adults.'

'Then if they are adults, they should be allowed to make their own minds up about me.'

'They already have. You leave them be!' He opened the door. 'Now, please go.'

Seated at her dressing table Mel stared at her reflection in the mirror. Leave them be indeed! That was the last thing she was going to do.

SEVEN

Wednesday 12th July

Nick and Jenny emerged from the Peking House Chinese restaurant just off the Horsefair. They had spent the morning browsing in Bristol's Broadmead shopping centre, Jenny making one or two purchases for her forthcoming holiday with the family in the South of France. The special businessman's lunch, filling and cheap, had made a pleasant change from the usual beans or spaghetti on toast Nick was used to preparing in the shared kitchen in his student digs. And the icing on the cake was that he had Jenny for company. It was great to spend time with someone he was hopelessly in love with.

Reaching the edge of the pavement he automatically took her hand in his as they prepared to cross the road.

'Nick! Nick!'

Out of nowhere came the voice. Feminine, unfamiliar. He hesitated, looking around to see where it had come from. Then he saw her; a small, blonde woman dressed in a pink and navy sundress and high sandals with dark American style sun glasses running up the street towards them, waving.

She reached them, slightly breathless. 'Sorry! Your flatmate said you were down here shopping. I thought it would be like looking for a needle in a haystack, but, well, you look so like your father!'

Nick stared at her blankly. 'I'm sorry, do I know you?'

'It's the hair isn't it? No more red.' The woman laughed. 'Blondes are supposed to have more fun, you know.'

Nick frowned at Jenny then looked back at the woman. 'You'll have to forgive me I still have no idea who you are.'

'I'm Mel.' She beamed at him. 'Your mother.'

'What?'

'Yes, I've come back.' The smile was there again. 'Actually *we've* come back. I'm married. My husband Liam is an architect. He's recently opened a practice in Abbotsbridge.'

'Is that Liam Carpenter?' Jenny joined the conversation.

'That's right.' Mel frowned. 'How do you know him?'

71

'He's doing some work for my father's company.'

'And you are?'

'Jenny Taylor. My father is joint owner of Taylor Macayne Construction.'

Mel's smile faded. 'You're Jack Taylor's daughter?'

'That's right.'

Ice blue eyes fanned slowly over Jenny.

'Jenny's my girlfriend.' Nick tightened his grip on Jenny's hand. Disapproval was written all over his mother's face.

'Really!' Mel stared at both of them. 'Nick, I think you and I need to talk. We've got a lot of catching up to do and,' she eyed Jenny, 'things that need discussing. I'm sure Jenny won't mind if we slip away for an hour,' she waved a hand at the shops. 'There's plenty here to distract her.'

'Jenny's not going anywhere.' Nick's expression hardened. 'How dare you be so rude! So presumptuous! How long is it now? Eleven years? You walk out of our lives. We don't hear a thing from you and then suddenly here you are, behaving as if nothing's happened.'

'But that's why I want to talk to you. I need to explain about...'

'I don't want to hear.' Nick interrupted. 'Nothing you have to say to me is relevant.'

'But I'm your mother.' Mel said indignantly.

'You lost the right to be that when you left us.'

'My God!' Mel's eyes narrowed. 'You sound just like the old man!'

'You've seen grandfather then have you?'

'Oh yes, him and his child bride! I thought at least I could count on you having an open mind even if his was closed. Let's hope Ella....'

'You keep away from Ella.' He raised a warning finger at her.

'Or what Nick?' She backed away, an unpleasant smile slowly forming on her face, then she was gone, heading in the direction of the Fairfax House car park.

Later that evening Nick rang the farm.

'I thought Mel would ignore my warning about seeing you,' Richard said. 'I'm afraid there's not much I can do about Ella. I'm already in hot water with her about the wedding. If I go round to Little Court to talk to her about her mother, the mood she's in she'll probably welcome her with open arms.'

'But someone needs to say something.' Nick argued. 'Don't worry, I'll phone her myself.'

'I wish you the best of luck.'

Ettie answered the phone at Little Court. Nick heard her footsteps trailing away to the bottom of the stairs. Moments later Ella picked up the receiver.

'Nick, how are you?'

'Fine, just fine. Ella I thought I ought to ring you to let you know mother's back.'

'Mother, where?'

72

'She was here in Bristol yesterday. She's married again, just settled back in Abbotsbridge. She told me she wants to see you.'

'Does she? Well fancy that, after all this time! Is there a problem?'

'She's the problem Ella.'

'What do you mean?'

'Rude, arrogant, she's just walked back in as if nothing's happened. No apology. No explanation. Wanted to discuss things with me and one of those things was Jenny.'

'Jenny?'

'She was with me when we bumped into her. Mother made it very clear she doesn't like her. It's got something to do with the Taylor family.'

'That's crazy. I'm sure there's a perfectly simple explanation to all this.'

'Ella, promise me if you see her you will be careful.'

'Nick, I'll be fine, just fine.'

Thursday 13th July

As Ella left school to catch her train home that afternoon she noticed a red sports car parked a short distance up the road from the main gates. As she reached it a small blonde woman emerged from the driver's seat. Everything about her was immaculate, from her green and beige dress and jacket to the single strand of pearls at her throat.

'Hello Mother.' Ella greeted her calmly. 'Nick said you'd be coming to see me.'

'Did he?'

'It's been a long time.'

'Yes darling, it has.' The woman replied with an embarrassed shake of her head. 'I know have a lot of apologising and explaining to do. Please say you'll listen. Don't turn me away like Nick, I couldn't bear it.'

Ella watched her mother's hand go to her face to brush away tears. She reminded her of a small, fragile bird. She at least deserved a hearing and unlike her brother she was prepared to listen. She wanted to fill in the gaps, to hear her mother's side of things and then once she had all the information make her own mind up. 'Don't worry, I won't.' she said quietly.

'Darling, thank you so much!' With a sob Mel stepped forward and folded her tightly into her arms.

Friday 14th July

'Please, choose anything you like. I can thoroughly recommend the carbonara.'

'Yes, I think I'd like that.' Ella looked up from her menu with a smile. 'I'd love an Italian coffee too, one of those frothy ones.'

73

'Of course,' Mel smiled indulgently, 'I'm just so pleased that you've given me the chance to meet with you like this. There's so much I have to tell you.' Her face was suddenly serious, 'and so much lost time to make up.'

They were sitting in a quiet corner of Ronaldo's, Abbotsbridge's most expensive Italian Restaurant in the High Street, with it's whitewashed walls, green checked table cloths and raffia covered Chianti bottles, a froth of red geraniums on each window ledge.

Despite Nick's warning, Ella's curiosity was aroused. She thought of all the times she had sat with her grandmother listening to her stories. Stories she knew were viewed from her grandmother's sad little world - but what else had there been to listen to when any mention of her mother had been banned under her grandfather's roof? Now she was sitting opposite her and she wanted to know everything. Outside the school, on the day they first met, she had broken away from her mother's tight embrace, her questions endless. Where had she been? Why had she gone? And now she was here, had she come back to Abbotsbridge for good? Her mother had silenced her with another hug and a kiss on the cheek.

'So many questions my darling.' Brilliant blue eyes filled with tears scanned Ella's face. 'Which you probably realise will take an eternity to answer. And right now I know you have a train to catch.'

Ella looked at her watch and realised she was indeed in danger of missing her only means of getting home.

'Oh no, I'll have to run!'

'No you won't.' Mel was insistent. 'Hop in; I'll take you to the station. And maybe on the way we can talk about where we can go for lunch.'

Now here they were at last. Friday afternoons were a free period for Ella, time usually spent in the library studying. But with exams finished and the summer term almost over, things were winding down and she knew her absence from school wouldn't be noticed. As arranged, Mel had picked her up outside the school gates and driven out of Kingsford towards Abbotsbridge. On the way Ella had chatted about life in Meridan Cross and her studies at Kingsford High, but now it was time to get down to the more serious business of listening to what her mother had to say.

Ronaldo hovered, dark and swarthy, pad in hand, gold filling glinting as he smiled, ready to take their order. Her mother decided on penne with a mushroom sauce and Ella said she would have the carbonara. The coffee arrived almost immediately, two white cups topped with froth and a sprinkling of chocolate. Ella added sugar to hers and stirred it gently, watching her mother's elegant fingers as she picked up her cup and brought it to her lips.

'Well,' Mel said, returning the cup to its saucer, the froth having made no impact on her perfect pink lip line. 'Here we are then, you and me together at last.' She took a deep breath. 'Ella, there is so much to say; but more than that, an apology to make.'

Ella watched her mother silently. She was warm and friendly not at all like the woman Nick had warned her about. There must be some mistake, maybe they had just had an unfortunate start.

'I must have appeared very selfish,' Mel continued, 'running out on you and Nick. Leaving you the way I did. But I was very unhappy in Meridan Cross. I felt my life was in a rut. When your father was killed so tragically I couldn't stay at Little Court any longer; Laura and I didn't get on, we never had. So I moved with you both out to Fox Cottage and my mother, Grandma Peggy encouraged me to return to work. That's where I met my current husband Liam.'

The conversation halted briefly as Ronaldo appeared placing the carbonara in front of Ella and a dish of penne in front of Mel, both of which he served with the flair of an artist, sprinkling Parmesan liberally over both dishes before retiring with a smile.

Ella watched the retreating Ronaldo before turning back to her mother. 'So when you went to Australia it was with Liam?'

'Yes.'

'But why didn't you tell them that?'

'Your grandfather was so strict, so critical about everything I did. He didn't approve of me working. Didn't approve of the friends I had made. If I'd come home and said I'd fallen in love and wanted to get married and take you two around the world for the next eleven years, can you imagine his reaction?'

'Yes.' Ella nodded, picking up her fork and pushing it into the pasta. 'I can.'

'Because of that,' Mel continued. 'I had to choose between the man I loved and my children. Make no mistake, it was a painful decision and I hated myself for what I had to do.'

'But couldn't you have talked to Grandma Peg about your dilemma. She would have understood. I know she would.'

'I don't think so Ella,' Mel shook her head, 'because ultimately your grandfather would have become involved. I knew how disapproving he was, so Liam had to be a secret right from the start. I lived a double life. Your grandparents knew nothing of Liam and he knew nothing of them. Then when he told me he was going abroad and said wanted to marry me and take me with him, you can see the impossible position I was put in. So I decided that the simplest solution was to write a letter telling mum and dad I wanted to start a new life away from England and leave, knowing you'd be taken care of by the best people in the world.' she sighed as she put her fork down and stared at her daughter.

'And how long did you stay in Australia?'

'Two years, then we moved to New Zealand and finally Canada. We came back to Abbotsbridge six months ago. Once we were settled, I thought about getting in touch, and then I heard about the accident.......'

'You knew about Grandma?' Ella frowned. 'But why didn't you come home then?'

'Because,' Mel said quietly. 'I guessed you'd all still be in a terrible state and I thought if I turned up, it might have been too much for you all to cope with. It would have been especially bad for your grandfather.'

'And Liam, does he know about us yet?'

'Yes, and he's very keen to meet you both. As you can imagine, he was very upset that I'd kept you secret all these years, but in the end I think he understood my reasons for doing what I did.'

'You didn't have any children with him?'

Mel shook her head.

'Has Liam any family?'

'Just his father, Philip. He's an architect too; he has lived and worked in California most of his life. Unfortunately he was badly injured in a hit and run accident a couple of years ago. He's in a private clinic now, undergoing long term treatment for his injuries. It was pretty bad, he'll never walk again. Liam says he's in the best place; that American doctors can give him the finest treatment there is. We pay all his medical bills. It costs a small fortune.'

Ella gave a sympathetic nod and continued with her meal quietly as she tried to cope with the enormity of all she had been told.

'What's Nick studying at university?' Mel asked as she finished her meal.

'He's taking Bachelor of Education Degree; hopes eventually to teach history.'

'A teacher?' She gave an approving smile then winced. 'I rather think we got off on the wrong foot the other day.'

'I think you did.' Ella agreed as she placed her spoon and fork neatly across her empty plate. 'Why don't you like Jenny?'

'There's nothing wrong with Jenny.' Mel smiled, pulling cigarettes and a lighter from her handbag. 'It's just that she's very young and Nick should be thinking about his career first. I can see I have a lot of bridge building to do, both with him and Dad.'

'You've seen Granddad?' Ella looked surprised.

'Yes, last week. I heard about the wedding from some friends here in Abbotsbridge. Naturally I was surprised, but then I thought it might be just the opportunity I was looking for to come home.' She shook her head. 'Of course as usual we ended up arguing.'

'What about?'

'Oh all sorts of things,' She said thoughtfully, cigarette poised on her finger. 'Mostly where I'd been during the last eleven years. Don't get me wrong, I didn't expect to have a smooth ride when I came back, but I thought your grandfather might have mellowed over the years. Needless to say that was wishful thinking!' she gave a sigh and blew smoke into the air. 'I have to say, Mary was a bit of a shock, I expected someone more his age. Do you get on with her?'

'She's O.K. I guess.' Ella shrugged.

'You don't seem very enthusiastic.'

'It doesn't bother me one way or the other,' Ella said calmly. 'I don't live at Willowbrook anymore.'

'Don't you?'

'No, I moved to Little Court two weeks ago.'

'May I ask why?'

'Because I was upset; do you know how I learned about the wedding? Through that dreadful Margaret Sylvester! Even Grandma didn't know, well not properly. I couldn't accept that the village gossip knew before I did. How could he? I just felt I didn't matter any more.' She bit her lip, the memory of it all still fresh and raw. 'Afterwards, Granddad said he was trying to pick a good moment to tell me, but by that time I really didn't want to listen. The damage was done.'

'Darling that's simply dreadful, see, doesn't that confirm everything I've been telling you about him? He really is terrible.' Mel sympathised. 'Still at least now you have Laura.'

'Well, yes, I do, but I can't stay there indefinitely. I don't want to put Grandma in a difficult position, you know, with Granddad. I did think,' She reflected with a sigh. 'that maybe I could find a flat after the summer holidays; somewhere nearer Abbotsbridge.'

Mel looked at her thoughtfully. 'You could always stay with us.' She reached across the table to grab Ella's hand enthusiastically. 'Yes, please come! We have heaps of room darling and we really would love to have you! You could continue your studies, and of course, you'd still be able to return to Meridan Cross to see your friends whenever you wanted!'

'It's very kind of you to offer.' Ella was hesitant. 'But think of all the extra work it would make for you. '

'Rubbish! Anyway I'm sure your grandfather wouldn't mind.'

'I don't care if he does!' Ella snatched her hand away. 'He certainly didn't consider me when he decided to marry Mary!'

She took her gaze out into the street, watching people hurry by. Why was she being so stupid? Wasn't this the answer to all her problems? She had always seen refuge at Little Court as short term, intending to eventually move into Abbotsbridge, and here was her mother offering her all she had planned for the future right now. She wouldn't have to wait, she could escape from Willowbrook and the village with all their sad memories and start a new life now; all she had to do was say yes.

'I'm sorry.' She said, turning back towards her mother. 'I didn't mean to be rude. Actually, I think it's a kind and wonderful offer and yes I'd love to come.'

'I don't believe I'm hearing this!' Richard Evas turned to face his granddaughter, his expression a mixture of anger and despair. 'You've been duped, you realise that do you?'

Mary and Ella sat facing each other in the front parlour while he paced between them, hands pushed deep into the pockets of his green corduroy trousers. When Ella had turned up at the farm this evening he thought she had come to make peace; instead she had dropped this bombshell.

'I haven't been duped as you put it.' Ella responded angrily. 'I've simply made an independent decision about my life, just like you have about yours!'

'Ella, oh Ella.' He moved to stand over her, a sadness enveloping him as he saw her usual warm expression now replaced by a steely hardness. 'What is all this? Tit for tat?'

'I'm not *quite* that childish.' She replied, her grey eyes cool as they met his. 'I've never known my mother properly. Now she's back I do want to get to know her. Besides, I can't come back here, you don't want me.'

'That's not true Ella....' Mary began, but Richard silenced her with a raised hand. 'Leave this to me please, Mary. Ella, your mother is dangerous.' He said as turned away to the window again. 'Very dangerous.' he swung around suddenly. 'You may think I'm a hard man, but let me tell you I've had good cause to be. She has done incredible damage to this family. Her only thought is for herself. She never does anything unless there's benefit in it for her. Beware Ella, if you agree to live with her, because believe me you will end up regretting it.'

He saw the stubborn tilt to Ella's chin, the defiance in her eyes and realised he was making no impact. 'All right, I can see from your face that you don't care about any of this, but just remember one important thing, when it suited her, she didn't think twice about abandoning you and Nick.'

'Just like you've abandoned me now!' Ella retaliated.

'Is that how you honestly see it?' He closed his eyes then opened them again, looking down at her with a sigh. 'Look, I'm sorry. I handled things very badly; believe me if I could turn back the clock I would. Are you telling me that I'm to be punished now for just one mistake in all the years I've loved and looked after you?'

Ella could not answer him truthfully, to do so would weaken her argument for going, and go she must. For the changes had started already; the wallpapering in the hall had been completed, there was a new dresser in the parlour, pictures had been removed and ornaments replaced. The house she called home was gradually disappearing.

Richard moved away from the window and walked over to sit beside Mary. He leaned forward, clasping his hands in front of him, then raised his eyes to meet Ella's.

'I think I should tell you,' He said slowly. 'She's already been here.'

'Yes I know.'

'Did she tell you what happened?'

'You argued.'

He nodded. 'Did she tell you what about?'

'No...Well, yes...about where she'd been all this time. But she told me everything. I know now about the terrible choice she had to make, to sacrifice her children for the man she loved because you wouldn't have approved of her getting married again.'

78

'Ella that is not true. My concern was always for you two. She was never here. I had no idea where she was or who with half the time. She never said. Just came and went as she pleased. During the last weeks before she left us, you almost lived here permanently. If I was ever angry with her it was because she showed very little commitment to either of you.'

'But she was in love! Torn between us and him! Surely you can understand her dilemma?'

'No Ella, I can't and I think you've been badly misled. She should have been honest with us, told us she was involved with someone.'

'But how could she? She was scared you would make her finish with him.'

'Ella, nobody ever made your mother do anything she didn't want to. She is the most stubborn creature God ever made.'

'There you are. See! How could she possibly deal with you when that's what you thought of her? Grandma Peg was right.'

'What's she got to do with all this?'

'When she was alive she told me all about Mother. Everything she said is just what Mother is telling me now. About her choices and the sacrifices she made. She may have been ill, but she knew all about mother, she really did.'

'You're grandmother *was* ill Ella. I know now that she never fully recovered from the second breakdown she had when your mother left. She lived in her own little world. And as far as I am concerned, anything she said or thought about your mother would therefore have been seriously flawed.'

'No, it was the truth, I know it!'

Richard looked at the uncompromising expression on his granddaughter's face and realised that arguing with her was a waste of time. She had been skilfully brainwashed by Peggy and Mel into seeing events as some sort of romantic tragedy. Right now, anything he said would go totally unheeded and if he pushed his point home it would send her running in the completely opposite direction, determined to prove him wrong. Reluctantly he knew he would have to let her go, but it hurt him deeply.

'If all this goes wrong, if it all lands back in your lap young lady,' He waved a warning finger at her. 'I will not pick up the pieces.'

'It won't.' Ella said confidently, getting up from her chair. 'I know what I'm doing. Now if you'll excuse me, I promised to meet Niall at 8.30.'

As she left the room, Mary turned to her husband to be, her voice gentle. 'Richard, can I say something?'

Richard looked hopefully towards his wife-to-be.

'I think painful as it is we're just going to have to accept Ella's decision.' She began softly. 'And if we're going to win her back, the first thing you have to do is to set your differences aside with Mel and invite her and her husband to the wedding. No, please don't make that face. Liam is your son in law and good manners dictate that we must welcome him into the family. After all it must have been quite a shock, discovering he has a whole new bunch of relations out here in Meridan Cross, don't you think?'

'Yes you're right.' He conceded with a resigned nod. 'But do be very careful won't you? We've lived very peacefully for the last eleven years without Mel. Don't let her get too close to us. She's capable of inflicting great damage. Believe me, this thing with Ella is only the beginning.'

Twelve miles away in Abbotsbridge, Mel was sitting facing Liam across the dining room table. She had thought it a fairly simple task to sit him down and reveal a past she had spent eleven years concealing, one which he knew nothing about. Liam was easy going, he adored her, he never objected to anything she did or said, why should now be different? With the confidence borne of one who is used to always getting their way without question, she had brought the subject up over dinner that evening. With most of the peeling, scraping and chopping done by Mrs Harris her daily, she had served him chicken in white wine with new potatoes, peas and carrots and a bottle of Muscadet thrown in for good measure. She believed a good meal and wine would go a long way to ease the passage of controversial news.

As she uttered the first sentence there was the unexpected clatter of cutlery against china as his knife and fork were placed heavily against his plate.

'What did you say?'

'I said my father's getting married again.'

'I see.' He hesitated for a moment before picking up his knife and fork resuming his meal. 'But you don't have a father; you told me all your family were killed in the war.'

Mel bit her lip. 'I lied.'

'Why? Were you ashamed of something?'

'No. My father is a tyrant, he'd have parted us. I had no choice.'

'And besides this ogre of a father of yours, are there any more relatives I don't know about?'

She nodded dumbly.

He watched her, waiting for her next words, when they did not come he coaxed.

'Come on then, tell me.'

'I have a son and a daughter. I....I was widowed quite young.'

'And exactly why did you wish to conveniently forget about them for all these years?'

'Well...' She hesitated, her confidence deserting her. 'Liam, I don't know where to start really.'

He watched her for a moment, stroking his beard, his green eyes thoughtful. Then refilling his wine glass he sat back in his chair. 'I think,' he said calmly. 'perhaps the beginning might be as good as anywhere.'

Sitting in the E-type on top of Lancombe Firs, Niall and Ella were in the middle of an argument.

'Ella, you can't just leave! We need to talk about this.'

'Niall there's nothing to discuss. I can't stay at Little Court indefinitely.'

'Why not?'

'Because it would put Grandma in a very difficult position.'

'Then come home. Please!'

'Home!' She rounded on him. 'And where's that? Your mother's already in the throes of turning Willowbrook into some place I don't recognise anymore. I can't go back there and you know it!'

'But Abbotsbridge for goodness sake, it's twelve miles away!'

'What's the problem with that?'

'I'll never see you.'

'Of course you will! I'll be back at weekends to stay with Grandma. It won't be any different than what happens now, with me here and you in Cirencester all week.'

'What if you don't come back at weekends?'

'Of course I will. What reason would I have to stay there?'

'You might meet someone else.'

'Oh Niall,' Her face softened and she touched his cheek, 'that will never happen. I love *you*, remember?'

'Honestly?'

'Cross my heart and hope to die.' She made a sign across her front. 'Now, give me a kiss. I hate fighting.'

'Me too.' He leaned across, his smile re-appearing as he brought his mouth to hers.

Sunday 16th July

Mel replaced the telephone receiver with a smile. Ella had just phoned. It appeared Richard had been extremely angry and upset at the news she was to move to Abbotsbridge. Well it served him right she decided, if he had only been a little more charitable about things all this could have been avoided. It could have been one big happy family, instead of which he had now managed to alienate both his daughter and his granddaughter.

Of course, Liam had initially been shocked by her revelations, but with expert manipulation on her part he now he appeared to have come to terms with the news and was actually looking forward to meeting Ella. She had booked a table at the Castle Hotel in mid-August specifically for this purpose. She smiled. Although originally wanting Ella back had been motivated by the need to get back at her father, on reflection she decided that having her back might be a bit of a social coup. What potential there was, having an attractive young daughter to show off around town. Who knew where that would eventually lead to? If Ella married into one of the town's wealthy and influential families, well, think of the benefits that would bring them!

And talking of weddings! Mel gave an amused laugh as she picked the invitation up from the hall table.   Now who had sent this?   No prizes for guessing it must be Richard's wife-to-be.   She looked like a peace maker, wanting to pour oil on troubled waters, to start her new life on the right footing with her new in-laws. Ah well, she would accept graciously, it would be a day out, it even might be a bit of a laugh, all those pathetic faces from the past queuing up to see her. Of course if she was going to give them value for money she would need a new outfit. Tossing the invitation back onto the table she picked up her handbag and car keys.   Time for her favourite occupation - shopping.

Saturday 19th August

Liam Carpenter was relaxing after an enjoyable meal at The Castle Hotel in Abbotsbridge. The Duck a l'Orange had been wonderful, the Claret superb. In fact the whole evening had all gone very well. And to think that he had been worried about this initial meeting with the first of the children he now found himself stepfather of. Ella. He looked at her across the table.   A pretty seventeen year old quite unlike her mother, with long black hair and intelligent grey eyes. She had a pleasant smile, good manners and seemed to have warmed to him right from the moment they met.

'Mel tells me you plan to return to school in September.' He said as he refilled his glass.

'Yes.' Ella smiled brightly. 'Upper Sixth next term.'

'And University to follow?'

'Hopefully.' Ella nodded. 'I didn't do as well as I could have this year. Grandma's death really affected me. But I'm over that now and I know I can get the grades I want.'

'Where do you hope to go?'

'Langford.'

'Langford? Where's that?'

'Somerset. It's Bristol University's Veterinary College.'

'You want to train to be a vet?' Liam seemed impressed. 'And how long will that take you?'

'Five years.'

'Five years?' Mel looked taken aback.

'Why so long?' Liam asked as the waitress appeared and began clearing away the sweet dishes.

'Because there are such wide variety of subjects to cover. Biology, Physics, Chemistry, Anatomy, Physiology, Biochemistry, Bacteriology, Pathology.' She reeled them off expertly. 'Oh and animal management and then there's surgery in the final year.' She finished with a confident smile. 'I'm quite looking forward to it actually. It will be a challenge and it's all I ever wanted to do. Eventually, when I qualify, I hope to work with our local vet.'

'John Bembridge!' Mel laughed. 'Will he still be alive by then?'

'He's not that old Mother! And he's a good vet, granddad swears by him.'

'Yes I'm sure he does darling, but do you honestly think that being a vet is the right sort of job for a woman?'

'Of course I do!' Ella seemed surprised. 'I think it's an excellent job for a woman. What do you think Liam?'

'Let's just say it's unusual.' Liam conceded with a smile, raising amused eyebrows at his wife. 'That's probably why your mother's a bit taken aback by the idea. Isn't that so darling?

Mel was hesitant, looking first at Liam then at her daughter. 'Yes, I suppose you could say that.'

Friday 1st September

'That's one more item to cross off the list.' Laura smiled cheerfully as she closed the front door of All Hallows behind her.

'The flowers look absolutely beautiful Laura, thank you.' Mary O'Farrell said, as they walked slowly down the path together towards her Land Rover which was parked in the shade of nearby chestnut trees. 'I had no idea Ted was so green fingered, or that you had such a flair for flower arranging.'

'It's nothing really.' Laura shrugged off the compliment. 'Just an extra little something from me. You've been a good friend since you arrived, to me and to many others in the village. I guarantee you'll have a splendid turn out tomorrow.'

'More from curiosity than anything else, I expect.'

'Nonsense, the people of the village are very fond of you.'

'Ah but it's not me I'm talking about. It's Mel and that husband of hers who'll be the main attraction.'

'Ah yes, Mel.' Reaching the Land Rover Laura paused for a moment. 'Can I ask exactly what made you invite her?'

'Because,' Mary said, with a sigh. 'I want tomorrow to be a new start for not just Richard and myself, but for the whole of the Evas family. And the Kendricks of course. Life's too short to fuss and fight. I was thinking of Liam too, he's an outsider like me, I wanted him to have a proper welcome into the family.'

'Has Ella met him yet?'

Mary nodded. 'Niall told me they had dinner in Abbotsbridge a couple of Saturdays ago. Ella likes him, says he's a very kind man. Apparently he adores Mel.'

'Oh dear,' Laura made a face. 'That sounds rather worrying.'

'I know Richard has very strong feelings about her but maybe we've got it all wrong you know.' Mary opened the driver's door of the Land Rover and got in. 'Maybe we should be a little more gracious, give her the benefit of the doubt.

Eleven years is a long time, she might well have mellowed. It's just unfortunate she got off on the wrong foot with Richard, if circumstances were different we'd probably have been saying how nice she was.'

'My dear,' Laura said seriously, climbing in beside Mary. 'Take it from me, nice is not the sort of adjective that has ever attached itself to Mel, nor ever will do. I am extremely worried about Ella. Is there's nothing we can do to deter her from this folly?'

'No.' Mary shook her head sadly, as she turned the key in the ignition and the engine coughed into life. 'We made a dreadful mistake not telling her about the wedding. Ella says she wants to get to know her mother, which I suppose is understandable, but at the back of it I'm sure she's really only punishing Richard. I was there, he tried very hard to stop her going, but she simply dug her heels in and refused to budge.'

'Perhaps if I had a word......'

Mary shook her head with a sympathetic smile as they reached the junction with the main road and turned left. 'You're wasting your time Laura.'

'What makes you so sure?'

'Because Ella is just like you; strong, determined and very single minded. And at the moment she's not listening to anyone, however persuasive their argument. I think we just have to let things run their course; I'm sure everything will work out. Now then, where's that list?'

'I have it here.' Laura pulled Mary's small black pad from her jacket pocket.

'What else is down there?'

'Check catering.'

'Right, that means Tom at the Somerset Arms; we're nearly there.' She shot a quick look at the older woman as she slowed up, ready to make a right turn into the pub car park. 'Come on, cheer up. Ella's a smart girl, she'll be fine.'

'I hope so Mary.' Laura said with a troubled smile. 'I really do hope so.'

EIGHT

Saturday 2nd September

Niall sat watching Ella out on the dance floor as he reflected on the events of the past twelve hours. For the villagers the centrepiece of the day appeared, as his mother predicted, not to have been the bride and groom, but the returning prodigal daughter and her husband.

Arriving for the wedding dressed in a jade green dress and coat with navy hat, matching accessories and Hollywood style sunglasses, she was the type of woman whose glamour automatically attracted attention. But she had a cool, aloof air about her, unwilling to mingle, her expression for the most part, one of total boredom. Her husband, although polite and smiling, looked uncomfortable. Shocked, Niall expected, at discovering what was here in Meridan Cross. On the whole he liked the look of Liam Carpenter, a tall, lean bearded man with the long, tapering fingers of a musician. He made an attractive match with Mel, dark brown hair going a distinguished grey at the temples and warm green eyes which looked directly into yours when he spoke. Niall had immediately taken to him, unlike Mel, whose arrogant stance told him she thought everyone in Meridan Cross was far too common to bother with.

The wedding had gone well, the day bright and warm, summer having not quite yet lost its hold. Mary, radiant in cream and carrying a bouquet of apricot roses, arrived on his brother Martyn's arm. Martyn's daughters, five year old Susanna and three year old Rebecca, wearing deep apricot shepherdess dresses with straw bonnets, had been her bridesmaids. The picture as they posed for photographs after the ceremony had, Niall thought, looked delightful; it had also drawn an adoring smile from his sister-in-law Hilary as she watched.

The church had been packed; not surprisingly the whole village had turned out to see the event, and an invitation had been extended to most of them to come to the evening. Niall felt it had been a perfect day for his mother, but Richard he knew was far from happy. He was frustrated and angry at his inability to make peace with Ella. He had apologised for all the upset he had caused and wanted her to come back to Willowbrook. But Ella had other ideas; the arrival of her mother couldn't have come at a better time as far as she was concerned. She was looking forward to living in Abbotsbridge and getting to know both her and Liam better. Niall, however, thought she was making a huge mistake.

He had been introduced to Mel and Liam after the service as photographs were being taken outside the church. Shaking her hand politely he was aware of a speculative interest in her eyes and initially a smile which spoke of approval. But when Liam asked him exactly where he fitted in to the Meridan Cross village family tree and he had revealed his identity, the warmth in Mel's expression had vanished immediately. She withdrew her hand quickly. Being Mary's son, he realised, meant he had now automatically become the enemy. But if he had problems, then so did she, judging what had happened shortly afterwards.

Still smarting from his encounter, he watched as the photographer organised Mary and the bridesmaids for a shot. He saw Mel usher Liam towards her father, who was standing talking to Nick.

'Dad, Nick, this is Liam my husband.' She announced proudly.

They all shook hands then after a few brief words Richard left the group, his presence required for the next shot. Nick also turned to go but Mel reached out, catching him by the arm.

'Nick, I am so sorry about the other day in Bristol. I was rude.' Niall heard her say. 'But we do need to talk.'

Nick looked at her for a moment. 'You're eleven years too late Mother.' He said and turned his back on her and walked away. Although she shrugged the whole thing off, she sat poker faced through the whole reception. They left around seven. Mel, complaining of an impending migraine, said the day had drained her and she needed her bed.

Richard and Mary left an hour later, planning an early start the next day for their journey north to their honeymoon destination. A small exodus followed; Nick with Laura and Niall's brother Martyn and wife Hilary carrying two tiny tired bridesmaids.

The barn dance finished, a disco took over and things livened up. Ella seemed to have been glued to the dance floor for most of the evening. In a pale green dress and jacket, her long dark hair falling loosely down her back, she was currently in the centre of the floor laughing happily and dancing outrageously between Ash and Rowan Miller.

From the start she had been different from the rest he thought as he watched her. She was not only pretty, she was smart as well. She'd turned the tables on him and frustrated his plans. He found himself accepting her rules, doing anything she asked in his attempt to snare her. There had been a silly flirtation with Rachel, but all that had done was to make him realise Ella really was the first girl he'd ever wanted long term. They had been together for just over a year now and he wasn't looking anywhere else. Meridan Cross was anticipating an engagement. And then the unthinkable. He couldn't believe what he was hearing the night she announced she was going to live in Abbotsbridge with her mother and stepfather. How could she make such a decision without talking it through with him? Didn't he matter? It appeared not. Because despite all his attempts to make her change her mind, nothing, it seemed, would move her from her determination to go.

Earlier today he had given her a very special present, for her birthday on Monday, a tiny gold heart on a chain. He recalled when she opened the box. The delight on her face; the way she had thrown her arms around his neck and kissed him, telling him it was the best present she'd ever had and how much she loved him. True she had worn it all day, proudly showing it off to everyone, but he still felt uneasy. He checked his watch. Eleven fifteen. He would be walking her home soon. Just the opportunity to find out exactly how genuine that love was.

The hall was a mass of movement. Currently Jeff Beck's *'Hi Ho Silver Lining'* was playing and people had abandoned their seats, flocking onto the floor with their partners. He saw Rachel in the crowd; someone had draped a bright blue feather boa around her neck and she was on the floor in the middle of a group from the Young Farmers Club who were jumping about and joyously waving their arms in the air to the chorus. He caught her looking at him, saw her smile and wave out. Rachel, of course, was the exact opposite of Ella; blonde to her brunette; steady to her impulsive; quiet to her gregarious. Watching her moving to the music, her blue mini dress riding up her thighs, he realised how much she had grown up in the last year.

Hi Ho Silver Lining came suddenly to an end. The Four Tops *'Reach Out and I'll Be There'* following and Ella, despite Rowan Miller's attempts to keep her there, came off the dance floor. Pushing her hair out of her eyes, she crossed the room back to the bar where Niall was staring out into the crowd.

'Penny for them.' She said as she reached him.

'What?' He frowned as if he didn't understand her.

'You were miles away!' She laughed, her grey eyes meeting his.

'Oh I was just watching everybody enjoying the fun. Going really well isn't it?'

'Yes, it's a shame Jenny's away in the South of France with her family, she'd have really enjoyed this. I think Nick's been a bit adrift today without her, I did try to pair him up with Rachel, but I don't think he was in the mood.'

She searched through the collection of glasses on the bar, retrieving a half empty glass of wine. Raising it to her lips, she stood silently beside him for a moment, watching the dancers. The Four Tops ended and Simon announced he was going to slow things down.

As the first strains of The Platters *'Smoke Gets In Your Eyes'* filtered from the speakers Niall took the glass from her hand and put it back on the bar.

'I thought you'd never ask.' She gave him a lazy smile as she gently folded herself into his arms.

They circled the floor, holding each other tightly and when it was over he took her lightly by the shoulders and pressed his lips softly against her forehead.

'Happy birthday for Monday.' He said gently.

'Thank you. And thank you for this.' She fingered the little gold heart that hung around her neck.

'I thought it was appropriate as you'll be taking my heart with you. Do you realise how much I'm going to miss you?' He hugged her tightly against his chest. 'I still wish we'd talked this through, found some other way.'

'Niall, I can't stay here,' she said sadly as the record came to an end and they walked hand in hand back to the bar. 'And this offer from my mother has come at the right time. I know she seems hostile towards you at the moment, but give her time, she'll change her mind, I know she will. Once I settle into Abbotsbridge I'll persuade her to let you come down and spend some time with us. Liam seems to like you, so you're half way there.' she ran her hand comfortingly down his cheek. 'I'm sure she'll think you're as wonderful as I do once she gets to know you.'

He forced a smile, upset that she still didn't appear to think there was a problem.

'Are you ready to go home?'

'Yes, just let me find Rachel I won't be long.' She disappeared, pushing into the jostle of bodies on the dance floor to find her friend.

Rachel was in the ladies re-applying her lipstick, the blue feather boa still draped around her shoulders.

'Hi!' Ella put her head around the door. 'Thought I ought to let you know we're just leaving. I've got an early start tomorrow and I need my beauty sleep.'

Dropping her lipstick back into her handbag, Rachel turned to look at Ella, her eyes filling with tears.

'Oh Rachel, please don't cry, you'll start me off!' Ella went over and gave her friend a hug, fighting back her own tears. 'Look, everything is going to be fine. As soon as I've settled in I'll be back every weekend, I promise. The train only takes half an hour.'

'Not for much longer.' Rachel said, sniffing as she broke away. 'Mum heard this morning. The station is being closed at the end of October.'

'You're joking!'

'I'm not. Mr Mortimer's taking retirement and Stan's got a job at the mushroom factory. They're going to increase the number of buses through the village instead.'

'But the bus takes ages to get to Abbotsbridge.'

'I know.'

'Then the sooner I start driving lessons the better.' Ella said, concerned that her regular return to the village for weekends was under threat.

'Actually,' Rachel sniffed again. 'I'm already having lessons.'

'You kept that a secret!'

'Sorry!' Rachel looked embarrassed. 'I've been out with Mum a few times, but for the last month I've been having lessons with Mr Davis over in Morden. I didn't want anyone knowing until I was quite proficient. Anyway, he's very pleased with me and last week he put me in for my test.'

'That's brilliant Rachel!' Ella gave her an enthusiastic hug.

'And there's something else. Tom has offered me some part time work at the pub. He managed to sweet talk Mum round. Told her it would be good for me to have a bit of variety in my working life. I'm starting next month after my eighteenth birthday.'

'Well done Tom! Hey, there's going to be so much to talk about when I come back!' Ella glanced at her watch. 'Sorry, I'd better go, Niall's waiting. Rach,' she hesitated as she reached the door. 'Can I ask a favour?'

'Sure.'

'Keep an eye on Niall for me will you? He's very upset about me going.'

'I know. Your mum doesn't like him either does she? He's having a bit of a tough time at the moment.'

'Oh I'm sure she'll come round, but for now I just need to know there's someone here to watch over him.'

'Well you can count on me; I'll be his guardian angel.' Rachel said slipping her bag over her shoulder and following Ella out of the cloakroom.

She said her last goodbyes, Niall finally prising her out of the clutches of the protesting Miller brothers. Her coat was slipped over her shoulders, the door opened and she was out into the coolness of the early September evening, a full moon bathing the countryside in its pale grey light.

Ella looked at her watch. 11.35. Her last night here in Meridan Cross. Tomorrow she would begin a new life miles away, a life totally removed from the one she lived now. She felt both sad and excited. They strolled hand in hand through the village until its lights gave way to a narrow unlit country road, the beam of Niall's torch throwing a warm, moving pool of light to guide their way. Somewhere to their left a cow coughed and Ella saw the indistinct grey shapes of her grandfather's herd dotted eerily around the moonlit field. Niall had hogged conversation since leaving the village hall, talking mostly about his next term at Cirencester. Then just where the road forked to the left and skirted part of Hundred Acre wood and the barley field he stopped.

'What's the matter?' Ella looked uncertainly into the darkness.

'Come with me.' He took her hand.

Slowly, they walked along the lane to where it followed the edge of the wood, emerging several hundred yards later to form part of the perimeter of the barley field. Harvesting had finished during the previous week; the field was now a carpet of uneven blonde stubble, rendered colourless by the light of the moon. Stopping at the new wooden five bar gate which Richard and Jake Carr had fitted earlier that spring, he pushed her gently against it and cradled her in his arms.

'I love you Ella Kendrick.' He said, pushing her hair back from her face. 'In fact I've adored you from the moment you rode into my life not more than two hundred yards away from this very spot. You're the only one who matters. Without you I'm nothing, you do realise that don't you?'

'Yes.' She said in almost a whisper, and reached up and softly brought her lips to his.

'Ella, I want our last night together to be special.' He said, pulling away from her. 'I want to make love to you here, tonight.'

She shook her head. 'Niall, we can't'

'Of course we can.'

'What if I get pregnant?'

'You won't, I'll be very careful.'

'What if *very careful* is not enough?'

'We'll just have to get married.' He said cheerfully. 'It wouldn't be the end of the world, would it?'

'Is that what you said to all the others?'

'What others?'

'Niall,' She looked up at him. 'I may be only seventeen but I'm not stupid. 'I wouldn't be the first would I?'

'No.'

'How many others have there been?'

He shrugged. 'I can't say I really remember.'

'And would you have married any of them if they'd got pregnant?'

'I don't think so. They weren't special.'

'So I'm special?'

'Yes, very.' He touched her face gently.

'And you are special too and that's the reason I want us to wait.' She reached for his hand. 'Can you understand that?'

'No! You don't really love me do you?' His voice was flat and full of disappointment.

'But I do, honestly.'

'What if something happens while you're away? What if you meet someone else?'

'I won't.'

'You might.'

'O.K. we'll make a pact.' She said, taking the little gold heart between her finger and thumb and holding it up to him. 'I swear to you Niall O'Farrell that this heart is a symbol of our love. As long as I wear it, it will show the world that we belong together.'

'You really mean that?'

'I do!' She said in a breathless voice, letting her arms snake slowly around his neck. 'I really, really do!'

Sunday 3rd September

Niall watched the road below. From where he stood he had a clear view of the last few cottages in the High Street and open countryside beyond. He leaned almost casually against the fence waiting for Liam's car to appear. One thing filled his mind; Ella's kiss and the warmth of her body against his as she had

90

made her promise to him. His decision not to go to Little Court to say a final goodbye to her this morning because of her mother, made the memory even more poignant. He caught sight of the Rover making its way slowly through the village, picking up speed as it passed the last of the cottages. He watched it, waiting for it to pass the entrance to Willowbrook, raising his hand in farewell. It was too far away to see any of the occupants but he hoped Ella had seen him. He gave a sigh, his elbows on the fence, his hands cupping his face.

'Morning, Niall.'

The voice took him by surprise. He turned to see Rachel sat astride Buster, frowning down at him.

'Are you all right?'

'I'll live.'

'I hate it too.' She said, dismounting. 'I've just come from Little Court. I wanted to give Ella a final hug and her birthday present.'

'I wasn't as brave as you, couldn't face her mother, I'm afraid.'

'You should have come. You shouldn't have let Cruella win.'

He looked at her again, his face softening into a grin. 'Cruella?'

'Yes, Cruella de Vil from 101 Dalmations. Don't you see the similarity? The snooty nose in the air manner, the evil look in those cold blue eyes?'

'Yes, you're right.' He laughed.

'I'm about to take Buster round Hundred Acre. Join me if you like. It might do you good. Take your mind off things.'

Niall looked at her for a moment, remembering the night before and the blue dress riding up over her thighs as she danced.   The vision of smooth flesh caused the beginnings of movement in his groin but he shook off the feeling, turning instead to watch the Rover finally disappear behind the hedge lined banks of the road to Abbotsbridge.

'Thanks, but maybe some other time eh?' He said and gave Buster's rump a friendly pat before turning to begin his walk back to the farmhouse.

'Did you both enjoy the wedding?' Ella asked once they were on the open road away from the village.

'Yes,' Liam answered, briefly looking at her in the car's rear view mirror. 'It was very educational. Village life certainly is different.'

'What about you, Mother?   How did you feel, coming back after all these years?'

'Absolutely nothing's changed Ella.' Mel replied, checking her make up in the car's vanity mirror. 'Sadly, darling they're still the same scruffy, small minded people they were when I left!'

'Mel, that's a bit harsh!'   Liam slowed the car as they approached the junction with the main road which ran west towards Abbotsbridge. 'I thought they were quite a friendly crowd.'

'That's because villagers are naturally curious about strangers.' Ella said as she fingered the heart, determined to defend the friends she had left behind.

'Is that what they think I am, a stranger?' Filled with indignation Mel twisted in her seat to look at her daughter. 'What's that?' She asked, seeing Ella's fingers clutching at something around her neck.

'It's a gold heart.'

'So it is. Where did it come from?'

'Niall gave it to me for my birthday.'

'Did he now?' She frowned. 'Ella I think we ought to get one thing straight, as far as I'm concerned you are far too young for any serious romantic attachment, and when the time does come,' she turned a reproachful eye towards the heart, 'there will be plenty of eligible young men in Abbotsbridge.'

'But Mother I love Niall.'

'Love indeed!' Mel snorted indignantly, 'What can you possibly know of love at your age? He's turned your head with his good looks and his fancy words. He's thoroughly unsuitable and I forbid you to have any more contact with him.'

'But you don't know him! Once you do things will be different.'

'Ella please do not argue. I don't want you seeing him and that's that.'

'I hardly think you can stop me.' Ella said defiantly. 'I'll be in Meridan Cross with Grandma at weekends. I'm bound to see him.'

'Not if I stop you coming back you won't!'

'But we agreed!'

'Ella just stop arguing will you?'

'Mother!'

'That's enough Ella!' Mel raised an authoritative hand. 'Please,' she softened her tone. 'I don't want to argue and fight, not with your birthday imminent. Darling,' she was all smiles now. 'I have the most wonderful surprise waiting for you back home. Wait till you see it, I know you'll just love it!'

Monday 4th September

Ella got out of bed and crossed to the window, drawing back the curtains. It was not only her eighteenth birthday but also the first day of her new life in Abbotsbridge and a lead grey sky welcomed her. Staring down into the back garden, a huge expanse of neatly mown lawn surrounded by colourful flower borders and mature trees, she thought about the conversation in the car yesterday. Of course her mother didn't mean what she'd said. She disapproved of Mary and Niall had somehow got mixed up with all of that. The answer was to get him invited down here so he could spend some time with them all. Liam liked him and with his irresistible charm she knew her mother would soon be won over.

She turned from the window to look at the room, remembering how excited her mother had been when she had whisked her from the car into the house and up the stairs. The objections to Niall had been quite lost as Mel clasped hands, an enthusiastic smile on her face and announced that the redecoration and refurnishing of her room was her birthday present from both of them. Ella had just stood and stared in disbelief.

Rosebuds; everything was rosebuds. Cream, red and pink rosebuds with deep green leaves. A theme which transferred itself to the bedspread, curtains and skirt which hung from the glass topped dressing table in the corner. The only items she did like were the new pale ash storage units along one wall (which her mother proudly told her were G Plan) giving her ample room to store all her clothes and personal things, and the rich green carpet, so thick her feet sank into it. Of course she couldn't say anything without hurting her mother's feelings and right at this moment she knew she needed to keep on her good side if she was to change her mind about Niall. So she had hugged her, enthused about everything in the room and pretended it was all absolutely wonderful.

As she was shown over the rest of the house Ella began to understand what had drawn her mother to the choices for her room; the whole house echoed this fussy theme. The lounge had an enormous television in a mahogany case, a huge glass cabinet full of china figurines and a very elaborate green three piece suite whose dramatic pattern was reflected in the wallpaper. Sanderson, her mother had informed her, just like her bedroom. 'It's the thing to have.' she told Ella. Ella nodded silently, seeing more of it repeated in the dining room. She had trailed from room to room behind her mother, amazed at the money which must have been lavished on the house, aware that such extravagance would not have been heard of at Willowbrook.

The only oasis in this desert of ostentatiousness was Liam's den and here he made sure he was the one who gave her a guided tour. She found herself stepping into a long, light airy room whose plain walls were painted white. In one corner stood a pale grey desk and matching storage cabinets lined the opposite wall. Above these was a large green felt notice board where various plans were pinned; his current projects he said. The opposite wall was covered with framed shots of previous achievements. Among these there was a marina and a large shopping complex. Liam told her it was a place called Kookaburra Falls in Australia where he and Mel had lived when they were first married. It was the first of the contracts which had kept them away from the UK for many years.

Ella walked around his drawing board and draughtsman's chair, placed next to the French doors he told her, so he could watch the peace and tranquillity of the garden as he worked. She ran her fingers over the trays of fine tipped pens and pencils, special templates for drawing, miniature pots of paint and multicolour inks.

'What's this?' She asked, looking at a detailed drawing of a circular building lying on his drawing board.

'I'm redeveloping a garage site for a local client.'

'Unusual shape.' She traced her finger around the outline of the building.

'Yes, they wanted something different. Building has started already. I've just got a few minor internal modifications to do.'

'Looks fascinating. Could I come and watch you sometime?' She asked, gazing around. 'I promise I'll be really quiet and won't get in the way.'

'Yes, I think I'd like that.' He said after a moment's thought. 'It would be nice to have some company.'

At breakfast Ella met Mrs Harris, a solid, smiling woman in an enormous paisley apron, with iron grey hair pulled severely back into a bun. Mrs Harris, she was told, cycled here every morning from the Parkway Council Estate and her duties as the family's daily included the provision of breakfast, general cleaning, laundry and preparation of the evening meal before she pedalled back each afternoon.

Ella wondered why her mother, who did not work, needed a woman to look after a house half the size of Mary's old place, Paddocks Farm. But then Mary didn't have the committees and ladies lunches and beauty appointments her mother had been telling her about. They, apparently, took up a huge amount of her time.

Seated for their very first breakfast together, Liam, opposite her, had buried his nose in a copy of the *Guardian* while her mother sat making notes on a small pad. As Mrs Harris finished pouring tea and left the room, Liam folded his paper and set it to one side.

'So,' He looked over his glasses at Ella. 'What are you up to today?'

'I'm meeting the girls at Cleo's. Issy put a note in my birthday card; she says they've got some surprise news for me.'

'Cleo's.' Mel looked up thoughtfully from her writing. 'Is that that coffee bar place in the High Street with the dreadful red front?'

'That's the one.'

'I'm not sure I approve of you in a place like that Ella.'

'Mother, don't be so stuffy, it's just somewhere where young people meet for a Coke or a coffee, that's all. Granddad wouldn't have objected.'

Mel frowned at her daughter. 'I don't doubt that. He probably didn't care about anything you got up to. He was more interested in chasing after that O'Farrell woman.'

Ella looked at her mother, annoyed at her pettiness.

'That is so untrue.' She protested. 'It wasn't like that at all. He treated me like an adult. He trusted me, and I never abused that trust. I did think the same rules would apply here, but now it's obvious to me they don't. You just think I'm some silly child.' She glared at her mother and pulling a piece of toast from the rack began to butter it vigorously.

'Ella.' Liam's gentle tone joined the conversation. 'We don't think that at all. We've really been looking forward to having you here to live and we want you to enjoy your stay with us. But you have to realise you're eighteen and until you're twenty one and an adult we're responsible for you. This isn't Meridan

Cross village, it's a sizeable town. You can't just come and go as you please. By this time next week, if your interview goes well, you'll be integrating into student life, meeting new friends, going out and enjoying yourself. And like any other responsible parents we'll need to know where you are, who you're with....'

'I'm sorry, I don't understand.' Ella's knife hovered over the marmalade jar. 'Interview? Student life? What are you talking about?'

'Your interview at Abbotsbridge Tech, you're seeing the Head of Business Studies at two thirty on Thursday.' He turned a puzzled face towards his wife. 'I'm sorry; I understood Mel had told you about the course.'

'What course?' Ella stared at her mother.

'Well, darling.' Mel gave a bright smile. 'It's a formality really. With your O levels they're bound to accept you for the Diploma.'

'What Diploma Mother?'

'Business Studies, with secretarial training. Two years. It's the *best* course there. It will give you an excellent commercial grounding. You'll be able to get a really good job as a secretary when you leave.'

'But I'm going back to Kingsford High in two days time.'

'Actually darling,' Mel cleared her throat uncomfortably, 'you aren't. I had a chat to your headmistress Miss Cameron, you see. She confirmed just as you said, that your interim exam grades weren't quite as good as they might have been, so I said under the circumstances it would probably be better to channel your energies elsewhere.'

'You said what!' Ella lowered her knife to her plate.

'Well.' Mel shook her head patronisingly. 'All that silly nonsense about becoming a vet. Your grandfather and old Bembridge may have indulged your fantasies but now you're here with us we have to be a little more realistic about your future.'

'Fine,' Ella got to her feet angrily and dropped her napkin onto the table, 'Well you can just stay here and be realistic, I'm going home!'

'This is your home Ella.' Mel sat watching her daughter, tapping her pen slowly against the pad. 'And as Liam said a few moments ago, you're eighteen, a minor and until you're twenty one, legally you're my responsibility.'

'Since when?' Ella said indignantly.

'Since always.' Mel gave a frosty smile. 'I'm your mother, your legal guardian, I always have been. Anyway, do you honestly think your grandfather will welcome you back? After deliberately going against his wishes and coming here? I think not.'

'I'm not going back to Willowbrook.' Ella said obstinately. 'I shall live with Grandma.'

'So you've changed your mind?'

'What do you mean?'

'Well I understood Little Court was short term. That you didn't want to stay there because of the wedge it might drive between your grandmother and grandfather. Is that no longer an issue? Or don't you care?'

Mel's words, hard but true, hit home. Ella knew that although Laura would welcome her with open arms, it would make things very difficult between her and Richard. And then there was Willowbrook. Mary was now Richard's wife. The whole pattern of things had changed in Meridan Cross. Her old life no longer existed. Her A level studies had taken a nosedive since her grandmother's accident. Could she guarantee she could pick them up again and get the grades she needed in an environment as uncertain as the one she was currently in? She could get a flat, but her weekly allowance was no longer in the hands of her grandparents, it had been taken over by Mel and Liam. Leaving school and getting a job was also a non starter. The weekly wage for an eighteen year old might cover the rent, but she had to live as well. And so, she realised, she was stuck. There was no alternative. She would have to remain here for the time being.

Seeing defeat in her daughter's face, Mel patted Ella's seat. 'Now, please darling, come back to the table,' She smiled, 'let's discuss this sensibly.'

Issy and Jenny sat side by side at a grey Formica topped table in Cleo's Coffee Bar waiting for Ella. Jenny looked at her watch.

'For goodness sake stop it, will you? That must be the twentieth time you've looked at that damn thing.' Issy frowned irritably.

'She's late.' Jenny said, turning her attention to the black plastic wall clock instead.

The waitress, tall and intimidating in a pink and navy tabard, a black velvet bow clipped to the back of her gravity defying hairdo arrived with her pad and a small sub of pencil.

'Are you two ready to order?' She asked, looking at them as if she suspected they were time wasters.

'Not yet.' Issy, pushing the condiments around like chess pieces, gave an indifferent shrug. 'We're waiting for someone.'

The woman eyed them suspiciously. Jenny gave her a weak smile and asked for two frothy coffees which seemed to pacify her. Stuffing the pad and pencil into the front of her tabard, she stalked back to the counter on her three inch stilettos. Returning she placed the coffee before them. As she turned to go Jenny saw Ella in the open doorway. Waving out to her, she beamed at the stony faced waitress and ordered another coffee and three doughnuts.

'You're late.' Issy grumbled as Ella sat down opposite them both. 'We were about to send out a search party.'

'Issy!' Jenny scolded. 'Sorry,' she said to Ella. 'She doesn't mean to be so abrupt; she's been in this bad mood all day!'

'It's that stupid brother of hers! He started it!' Issy retaliated. 'Came into the kitchen looking for Dad this morning to talk to him about some painting job he wanted doing and tripped over the doormat. Nearly put his head through the glass in the back door!'

'It wasn't deliberate.' Jenny protested. 'He's just a bit accident prone!'

'He's an idiot!' Issy was scathing.

'Not now Is.' Jenny said gently, glancing at Ella. 'Ella, what is the matter?'

'It's my mother.' Ella said quietly, pushing her dark hair behind her ears, still shaken from her recent confrontation. 'I was so looking forward to coming here, starting a new life. But I've been here twenty four hours and already she's showing me a side of her which I had no idea existed. She accused granddad of interfering and trying to control her life when she was young. But now she's doing exactly the same thing with me'

'Why?' Jenny asked. 'What's happened?'

'Well, first she banned me from any contact with Niall and now she's only gone behind my back and told the school I won't be returning. She won't allow me to train as a vet, says it's not a woman's job.'

'Unbelievable!' Jenny rolled her eyes.

'Ella that is awful!' Forgetting her own grievances, Issy added her indignation.

'Can't you just leave, go back to Meridan Cross?' Jenny said, leaning across the table.

'No.' Ella shook her head despondently.

'Yes you can.' Issy argued. 'It's simple. Just go home and pack your case.'

'That was my first reaction, but it's not as easy as that.' She shrugged miserably. 'You see Granddad warned me about her and said if anything went wrong he wouldn't have me back. And I can't impose on Grandma because it would cause a rift between her and Granddad. Mother's very clever; she's worked it all out too. She took great pleasure in telling me she's my legal guardian and until I'm twenty one she calls the shots. So I guess for the moment I'm stuck here without a boyfriend, doing a secretarial course at Tech.'

'You're going to Tech?' Issy looked at Jenny. They both smiled.

'Yes, why?'

'So are we.' Issy said as the waitress appeared with the third coffee and the doughnuts. 'That was our surprise news. You see Dad feels I need some commercial training if I'm going to be of any proper use in the business and Jen decided the bank wasn't for her. So we're both taking the two year Business Diploma and Secretarial training.'

'Me too!' Ella's spirits lifted. 'That means we'll all be together again. Just like old times!'

The doughnuts were warm and sugary. Ella picked hers up and bit into it, finding the jam straight away. She licked her fingers with relish and smiled at them both. Perhaps things weren't going to be as bad as she thought after all.

'You know,' She said, 'On my way here when I'd eventually calmed down I started to think. And I decided O.K. it's not what I want, but I'll do it and I'll make a success of it. I'll let her think she's won. But when I finish the course, I'm not going to get a job in an office like she wants me to. Oh no.' she looked at them both and smiled. 'I'm going to run my own business.'

97

'But what kind of business Ella?' Jenny frowned as she wiped sugar from her mouth with her finger. 'What could you do?'

'I haven't got a clue at the moment.' Ella said with a shrug as she finished her doughnut. 'But.' she added determinedly. 'Something will turn up, I know I will.'

NINE

Monday 4th September

'You should have said something before, Mel. You should have told her.'

Returning home for lunch, Liam sat beside his wife at the kitchen breakfast bar, a half eaten plate of ham salad and boiled potatoes in front of him.

'I told her when the time was right.' Mel said, settling her knife and fork together on her empty plate. 'She's very head strong. Doing it my way nips any arguments in the bud. I can't....won't have her arguing with me. Besides, the tactic worked with banning her seeing the O'Farrell boy didn't it? She protested then accepted the situation, just like she has now. It's all going to plan. Two down one to go.'

'What do you mean?'

'Clothes, Liam. Have you seen the length of her skirts? Simply appalling!' She shook her head. 'I've already had words. Father has been so lax with her! It's about time she learnt how to dress respectably.'

Liam put down his knife and fork and picked up his tea cup. 'Like you, you mean?'

'Well I have to do something. I can't have her walking round like that. It's disgusting.'

'It's what every other young woman is wearing Mel. It's youthful fashion. Personally I've got no problem with it. I think she looks great.'

Mel eyed him severely. 'What a typical male response.'

'But isn't that the point? Aren't you hoping for big things on the romantic front now she's here?'

Mel thought for a moment. 'I suppose I am.'

'Well take my advice then.'

'What?'

'Leave well enough alone.'

Thursday 7th September

Abbotsbridge Technical College had been built in the early sixties. It was a three storey flat roofed red brick building whose main entrance was fronted by lawns and shrubs. On the other three sides of the building there was a jumble of huts, a bicycle shed and a rough car park of half tarmac, half rubble. The late sixties had brought a huge increase in the demand for further education and to accommodate this a new extension was planned. Excavations for the foundations of the new building were now well underway.

Don Lattimer, Head of Business Studies, sat at his desk, his interest briefly caught by the activity below him as hard hatted workmen went about their business. After a moment's contemplation he turned back to the matter in hand, a late application from someone who wanted to take up a secretarial course place for the coming autumn term.

How further education had grown during the past five years and it wasn't only full time vocational courses which had increased in demand. Block, day release and evening classes were on the up too. And so were the applications. He stared at the one which currently sat on his blotter, wondering why someone with ten 'O' levels would contemplate secretarial training? A sudden knock at the door told him he was about to find out.

'Come in.'

Joan Trimble, his secretary hovered in the doorway

'Miss Kendrick's here, shall I show her in?'

'If you would Joan,' Don smiled back. Joan was a rare treasure. Competent and organised her quiet manner hid her true character. 'The Lioness' the other lecturers had nicknamed her. No one got past her to Don's office unless they had an appointment or a worthy excuse. Other Departmental Heads were not so well guarded and complained of always falling prey to the interruption of others. Don's working day was totally organised by Joan and most importantly his illegible scribble was turned very professionally into neatly typed reports and letters at the speed of light. Joan's presence made him feel his department ran like a well oiled machine.

He stood up as Joan ushered a pretty dark haired girl into the room, shook hands and indicated the seat on the other side of his desk.

'Miss Kendrick. Take a seat.' He said, watching her settle herself into the chair. 'May I call you Ella?'

She nodded.

'Now,' Don picked up her application form, flicked through it, and then dropped it back on his desk and sat back comfortably. 'Exactly why are you here'

'To apply for a secretarial course Mr Lattimer,' she said with a smile.

'With ten 'O' levels, three of them sciences at grade one, I don't believe it. No one would make this sort of effort with their GCEs unless they had a University career in mind; why the change of direction?'

'It wasn't my decision, it was my mother's.' Ella said quietly. 'She feels office work is more appropriate.'

'More appropriate than what?'

'Becoming a vet.'

'I see.' He could see from the expression on her face as she answered that the decision had not been accepted willingly. Ah well, he would pry no further. His prime job was to assess her suitability for training. Keep to the point of the interview he told himself as he smiled encouragingly at her.

'The name Kendrick's not familiar.' He stared at the application form curiously. 'Are you new to the area?'

'Yes, I've recently moved here to live with my mother and stepfather; Mel and Liam Carpenter. They returned here from abroad last year.'

'Ah yes, I know Liam, from way back.' He nodded. And Mel his silent self added. He knew very little about her other than she'd married Liam and gone abroad, returning to Abbotsbridge last year and causing a stir ever since. Blonde, brash and opinionated, he now understood exactly why Ella was here. He could see it was just Mel Carpenter's style to want to meddle in her daughter's life; she was so good at meddling in everyone else's.

'I forgot to say.' She interrupted his thoughts. 'It's the two year diploma course I'm interested in.'

'I see.' He nodded. 'Well, I can't see any problems in accepting you. Although if you want my truthful opinion, you're totally wasted here Ella, totally wasted.'

'Not for what I have in mind. I want to run my own business. And I think secretarial training will come in very useful.'

'What sort of business had you in mind?'

'I haven't a clue at the moment.' She shrugged then laughed. 'I'm still waiting for that flash of inspiration.'

'And it will come, I'm sure. Now then, where was I? Ah yes, I think we'll have some tea then I'll discuss the syllabus with you. How does that suit you?'

'That would be great. Thank you.'

Later, after Ella had left, Don Lattimer turned in his chair to gaze out of the window, his thoughts far away. The whole area knew of Mel Carpenter. People crossed the road to avoid her; she was an embarrassment to her husband and a complete bitch to everyone else. He remembered only six months ago at a dinner dance when on his way to the bar he had accidentally brushed against her, immaculately groomed and cobra deadly. Apologising, he moved on, only to hear her say in a very loud voice to the woman she was with. 'Isn't that Don Lattimer? Thought so. Do you know his wife? Such a drab little thing!' As he walked away he could hear her spiteful laughter.

At the time he had wished there was something he could have done to get back at her for her small mind and nasty tongue. And now suddenly, there was, for Ella he decided, was not only going to be his star pupil, he was also going to do everything he could to help her achieve her dream.

Friday 8th September

'Ella, are you still interested in learning to drive?'

Liam, alone with Ella in the breakfast room, was keen to build bridges and make up for yesterday morning's bad start.

'Yes.' Ella nodded, realising driving was going to be necessary part of her plan for self employment. 'And I'd like to start as soon as possible if that's O.K. with you.'

'Excellent.' He said as he eased the lid off the marmalade. 'I have a friend, Keith Manning, who owns a school; he'd be pleased to take you.'

'Great, I could pay him from my allowance.'

'There's no need for that, I'll be more than happy to cover the cost myself.' Liam smiled as he dropped a generous spoonful of marmalade onto his plate.

'Are you sure?'

'Positive. Besides it's the least I can do. I still feel bad about putting my foot in it yesterday.'

'You weren't to know.'

'All the same, I feel awful.' He looked at her thoughtfully. 'You really did have your heart set on being a vet didn't you?'

'Yes. But as Grandma always says, it's no use crying over spilt milk. Don Lattimer has offered me a place at Tech., so I'll be throwing myself into that when I start next week.'

'I'm sure you'll enjoy it.' He tried to sound comforting. 'And I'd be very pleased to employ you during the holidays. It would be good practical experience for you.'

'Yes it would, wouldn't it?' Her bright smile made him feel much better. 'Thank you.'

'Now, about the lessons.....'

'And what lessons are these?' Mel interrupted as she came into the room carrying a fresh pot of tea she had just prised from the clutches of Mrs Harris.

'Driving lessons for Ella.'

'Whatever for? She has no car of her own. I hope you haven't told her she can use mine!' Mel said peevishly as she sat down and pulled Liam's cup towards her.

'I wouldn't dream of asking you to put yourself out Mel.' Liam countered. 'She's quite welcome to use my Rover any time she wants. And don't be so negative. Don't you realise driving is as much a social skill as a practical one? It's the in thing at the moment for people who count in the town. Annabel Langley had her first lesson on her seventeenth birthday.'

Mel stopped pouring and looked thoughtfully at her husband. 'Did she really? Oh well, if the Langleys are doing it for Annabel, we'd better do it for Ella I suppose.'

'Who is Annabel Langley?' Ella frowned.

'Minor royalty as far as your mother is concerned.' Liam gave her a sly wink.

'Her father owns Langley's Department Store, among other things.' Mel added. 'They are top drawer. *Old* Abbotsbridge money, very well respected.'

'When do you think I'll be able to have my first lesson?' Ella asked, noting with interest how things could be turned completely around with a little pandering to her mother's snobbishness.

'I'll give Keith a call after breakfast; try and get you booked in for this coming Sunday afternoon.' Liam replied, retrieving his cup and reaching for the sugar. 'It will be quiet then, just the right sort of time to start.'

Sunday 10th September

Rachel rode Buster out of the trees and pulled him to a halt. She smiled as she took in the view below her. Autumn was already here; the hedges bright with berries, early morning mist hanging over the river. The evenings were drawing in too, casting long shadows across the landscape above which birds flew in great Vee formations, heading south.

Looking across to her right she noticed ploughing was already well underway in the barley field and in the distance she could see the solitary figure of Neil, walking Merlin along the boundary between Hundred Acre and the south west pasture. He had looked so miserable last Sunday. She wondered whether Ella had contacted him yet. She hoped so, not just for his sake, but because she was eager to hear any news he might have. Her phone had remained silent all week. The promised call had not arrived and it made her feel uneasy.

She had been so busy watching his progress around the field that the sudden plunging of the landscape into shade took her by surprise. She looked towards the west, noticing that the sun had disappeared completely behind a huge mountain of black cloud blowing in from the direction of the Brendon Hills. The wind strengthened suddenly, loosening dying leaves from nearby trees and Buster's ears went back and he chewed his bit nervously as thunder rumbled ominously in the distance.

'It's OK boy, don't fret.' She said to him soothingly, judging the speed it was approaching. 'No point trying to get back to the farm, we'll get soaked. Come on, we'll stay under the trees till it's over.'

The sky seemed to be overrun with storm clouds now and Rachel took Buster well back into the wood, taking shelter under the boughs of a large oak tree, hoping its huge canopy and the cleft in its trunk would offer sufficient cover. Dismounting she tied him to a low branch and pulled her green waterproof cape from the saddle bag, slipping it over her head and settling herself as far back into the tree as she could. The thunder was nearer now, growling ominously and then all at once the wood was lit by a brilliant flash of lightning. Buster moved closer to her, nuzzling his brown velvet nose into her face.

'Hey now,' She gave him a reassuring pat, 'don't worry, we'll be fine.'

The rain began almost immediately, heavy drops at first, which gradually gathered in intensity, until they became a ferocious force, drumming on the ground around her, soaking the grass and turning the exposed earth into a quagmire. Then the wind arrived, moving through the wood like a giant, shaking the first fading leaves from the trees like golden confetti. She pushed herself further into the gnarled old trunk of the tree and closed her eyes, tugging the hood of her cape tightly over her head, willing it to be over, as more thunder crashed around her.

She remained where she was, checking her watch regularly. After thirty minutes the thunder gradually receded and the flashes diminished, leaving an eerie stillness around her, broken only by the soft dripping of water onto the already soaked ground. The sun came out again bringing a jewelled brilliance to the rain soaked trees and undergrowth around her. Pushing her hood from her head and loosening her cape she untied Buster and picked her way carefully across the waterlogged ground towards the edge of the wood. Remounting she turned him downhill towards the lane where Fox Cottage stood. There was no sign of Niall and she wondered if he had managed to get home before the storm hit.

'Hi Rachel, bit of a drencher eh?'

She had reached the cottage and was surprised to find him sheltering in the porch. Merlin in the shelter of a cluster of lilac trees was nibbling lawn, steam beginning to rise from his rain soaked coat.

'Certainly was.' She reined Buster in. 'I had to shelter in the wood; I'd never have made it back to the farm in time.'

'Old Doggy Barker predicted this you know.'

'Did he?' Rachel looked amazed.

'Yes. He was rambling on this morning about some sort of funnel between the Quantocks and the Brendon Hills which can cause extreme weather conditions.'

'What did he mean, funnel?'

'Oh it's all about the contours of the land and what effect they can have if multiple weather fronts meet up there at the wrong time.' He grinned. 'Bit of a weather expert our Doggy. Says it doesn't happen very often, but when it does, you'me in for one hell of a lot of rain.' He mimicked Doggy's familiar growl.

Rachel laughed. 'You sound just like him.'

'Do I?' He stared at her.

'Is something the matter?' She frowned.

'No.' He shook his head. 'You heading back to the farm now?'

She nodded.

'Mind if I ride with you?'

''Course not.'

She waited while he untied Merlin and swung himself up into the saddle.

'I'm glad I've seen you.' She said as they turned their horses down the track towards the main road. 'Have you heard from Ella yet?'

'No.' He shook his head. 'I contacted her for the first time last Wednesday and who do I get? Her mother.' He made a face. 'She told me she doesn't want me hanging around Ella any more. Told me I'd be better off finding someone else. Ella's not for me apparently. There are young men with much better prospects in Abbotsbridge. I knew this would happen!' he said angrily. 'She said Ella has been told and has accepted that it is for the best.'

'Well I don't believe that for a start!' Rachel said indignantly. 'You have to fight it Niall.'

'How do I do that? Her mother is one determined woman. If I turn up she'll shut the door in my face. If I try phoning again I'm bound to get her. She's going to make sure I don't get anywhere near Ella'

'Of course,' Rachel said thoughtfully, 'You could ring the school and leave a message. Get Ella to call you back.'

'Rachel you are brilliant!' Niall pulled Merlin to a halt, a broad smile on his face. 'Why didn't I think of that? I'll phone first thing tomorrow, after breakfast.'

Wednesday 13th September

It was one fifteen when Ella, Jenny and Issy arrived at the second floor classroom well ahead of time for their first lesson of the afternoon. The Typing Room was large and square and decorated in the College's regulation magnolia. It was filled with twenty desks and typists chairs. On each desk sat a blue Imperial 70 typewriter. From the ceiling hung an intricate web of wiring, a single strand of wire suspended over each desk; connections for headphones, used in audio typing tuition.

While Jenny and Ella chose where they wanted to sit, Issy drifted towards the window where she leaned on the ledge, watching passers by below.

'Do you think we'll ever master this?' Jenny asked running her fingers over the keyboard. 'It still seems so complicated to me. How can you type out words with these jumbled up letters at any sort of speed. It's impossible.' She shook her head.

'Actually it's not as difficult as it looks.' Issy said still with her back to them, continuing to watch the road outside. 'Mum taught me the basics years ago and eventually it becomes second nature and then you can't imagine how you ever found it so.......Hey girls, there's this gorgeous man outside, getting out of a car. I'm sure I've seen him somewhere before. It gets better!' She turned round excitedly, 'He's coming into college.'

'Where?' Jenny got up to take a look, joining Issy at the window. 'Oh my God Ella, it's Niall.'

'*That* is Niall?' Issy looked at Ella in amazement. 'Well all I can say is his photo doesn't do him justice.'

'No it doesn't.' Ella replied, a huge smile on her face as she ran from the room.

He was just outside the main entrance when she intercepted him. Ignoring passers by she threw herself into his arms and kissed him.

'I'm *so* pleased to see you!' She said hugging him tightly.

'Are you?' He broke away from her, his face solemn. 'It's been over a week. Even though I'm banned from seeing you, I thought you'd try some way to make contact.'

'I'm sorry. It's so difficult. Everything's gone crazy since I arrived.'

'So I gather,' He said, irritably. 'I phoned the school, thought I could get a message to you there. They told me you'd left, that you were here now.' he looked up at the college building. 'What's going on Ella?'

'It's a long story Niall. Can you stay? I'll try and get off after the next lesson, around two thirty. Please, will you wait?'

He nodded silently.

'I have missed you terribly, you know.' She looked at him wistfully. 'I've been quite miserable without you.'

He took her hand and squeezed it tightly. 'I'll wait in the car.'

Rachel was hanging glasses up behind the bar when she saw Niall come in, order a half pint from Tom and join the Miller boys over by the fireplace. They hung together for a while, muted voices, and the odd laugh. Men's talk she guessed. Eventually Ash and Rowan left and Niall joined her at the bar where he asked for another half.

'Seems funny having you here during the week.' She said as she slipped the glass under nozzle. 'Bet you'll be glad to get back to Cirencester once the honeymooners are back.'

'Nonsense, I'm having a great time.' He forced a smile. 'Everything's going extremely well. Well almost everything. I saw Ella today.' he said glumly as he watched her refill his glass.

'And?' Rachel's face lit up.

'Don't ask....'

'Why?' Rachel set the full glass on the counter and took his money. 'Didn't run into Cruella did you?' she said, with her back to him as she rang it into the till.

'No, nothing like that.' He took a mouthful of beer and leaned on the bar. 'I phoned Kingsford High just like you suggested. They told me she'd left, that she was now at Abbotsbridge College.'

'At college? Doing what?' Rachel screwed up her face in a frown as she handed him his change.

'A Secretarial course.'

'You're joking!'

'I'm deadly serious.'

'So what did you do?'

'I drove out there this afternoon. Awful place, full of yobs with long hair. Scruffy lot! She saw me arrive, didn't seem to be in the least bit upset. Apparently Issy and Jenny are on the same course. Now how's that for coincidence?'

'Niall are you suggesting she's deliberately blown the career she's always wanted just to be with her friends?'

'No, of course not!' He shrugged moodily. 'I'm just so wound up, that's all!'

'But what about Ella?' Rachel was anxious for news. 'Did you see her? Did you talk?'

'Yes, she managed to get out early and I took her for a drive. She told me all about it then....' he made a face.

'What? What is it?'

'She said her mother had taken her out of school because being a vet is a silly idea. She has put her on this two year secretarial course instead. She thought about packing and coming back here but says she can't. There were various reasons, none of them which seemed credible. Let's face it, if Ella really wants to do something she does it and to hell with the consequences!' He took a mouthful of beer. 'And it doesn't end there. Not only has dear Mama banned her from seeing me, she's not allowed to come back to the village until Christmas now!'

'Oh dear,' Rachel said sympathetically, 'Poor Ella....'

'Poor Ella, it's me you should be sorry for!' He protested. 'She wasn't at all upset. In fact, she was very upbeat about the whole thing. Her latest plan is that when she leaves college she's going to run her own business. Doing what she hasn't a clue at the moment. In the end I lost track of it all, I was too upset.'

'But what about the two of you, have you worked out any way around this problem of not being able to see each other?'

'Not really. She did try to persuade me to visit this club place they're planning to go to this weekend, the Mill. But I could see it would be full of the same scruffy sorts she's with at college.' He looked horrified. 'In the end I agreed to contact her at Jenny's on Tuesdays or Thursdays when they do their homework together. My relationship has been reduced to a weekly phone call, great isn't it?'

'Oh Niall, I wish there was something I could do to help.'

'You can.'

'What?'

'*Casino Royale's* on at the Odeon in Kingsford. Do you fancy going to see it with me?'

Rachel hesitated. 'I'm not sure I should.'

'Oh please Rach,' Niall switched on an expression guaranteed to get him the sympathy vote. 'I'm so miserable and you really are just the tonic I need to cheer me up.'

She thought for a moment, then remembering her promise to Ella, said. 'Well, O.K.'

Thursday 14th September

'I'm glad you've sorted things out with Niall.' Issy said as she sat down opposite Ella in the college refectory. 'He's too gorgeous to be angry with for long.'

'That's how he gets away with so much.' Ella said, stirring her coffee. 'Good job you're not going out with him, you'd be a frayed doormat by now.'

'Don't be too hard on him.' Issy said, spooning sugar into her coffee. 'He's like me, a bad influence as far as your mother is concerned. It must have been a shock to find you weren't in school any more.'

'It was. The secretarial course went down particularly badly too. But at least we've sorted out a method of keeping in touch, although I'm a bit sad that he didn't want to join us at The Mill on Friday. I can't understand him passing up the opportunity for us to be together.'

'Perhaps it's not his scene.'

'Maybe not,' Ella said thoughtfully, 'Never mind, he's calling tonight, I've got that to look forward to. Hey' she nodded in the direction of the counter. 'Who's that girl? Don't I know her from somewhere?'

Since arriving at college Ella constantly asked questions about people she saw. Through Liam she already knew about the small clique of moneyed people in the town. Bryan Tate, whose Ford dealership Liam was redesigning. Miles Anderson, local councillor and businessman with influence in a great many places. Oliver Knight, who had married Winston Stewart's only daughter and got himself not only a beautiful wife, but half of his father-in-law's engineering company when he died. And right at the top of the heap there was the very old Abbotsbridge money, those whose ancestors were the bedrock of the town. People like Gerald Langley and Alex Nicholson whose families had built their businesses on wool and cloth. Gerald had many diverse business interests including Langleys, the town's biggest department store and Alex was in property, developing land and selling beautiful town and country houses at the top end of the market.

Here at college, Ella's queries were also endless when she saw someone of interest in the corridor or in the Refectory. Already friendly with Zoë, Mary, Teresa, Anne and Jackie, the five other girls on their course, at lunch or mid morning breaks there was always someone she wanted to know about. And today was no exception.

'Oh that's Nina Harrison.' Issy said watching the girl pass by. 'She works in the college office.'

'She must have a good job. That's a Mary Quant dress she's wearing. And the boots are Biba.'

'Are they?' Issy gazed at the camel wool mini dress and the shiny brown knee length boots.

Ella nodded. 'They were both featured in last month's *Honey*.'

'Ah, I expect Andy bought them for her. He's always taking her up to London shopping.'

'Andy who?'

'Andy Macayne.'

'Macayne?' Ella thought for a moment. 'That's the surname of Jenny's dad's business partner isn't it? Have I met him?'

'Yes, a long time ago. Do you remember the day we were down at the Bridge Coffee Bar? When Mick turned up? Andy was the one waiting in the van.'

Ella frowned. 'Was he?' She said eventually, shaking her head. 'No, I don't remember him.'

'He leered out of Mick's van at you.' Issy reminded her.

'Oh, the pretty one with the beauty spot on the corner of his upper lip.'

'That's right! Well, Nina is his girlfriend.' Issy explained. 'They've been together about year now.'

'Really?'

'It's not serious though. Never is with Andy. He'll two time her if he gets a chance.'

'Why doesn't she just ditch him and find someone else?'

Ella watched Nina settle herself down at an empty table. She had a sulky look about her, Ella thought, but she had unusual slanting eyes which gave her an exotic quality and pretty hair, thick and straight, the colour of gingerbread.

Issy smiled. 'Money. He keeps her in the latest London fashions, holidays her in the Med and pays for her to have her hair cut at one of the top London salons.'

'A kept woman eh?' Ella watched, fascinated, as the girl began her lunch.

'Time to go.' Issy stood up.

'What have we got this afternoon?'

'A double shot of shorthand.' Issy made a face, 'then Accounts - why do I put myself through this torture?'

Ella smiled as she got to her feet and gathered her things, aware that Issy was finding shorthand in particular something of a black art at the moment. As she slung her bag over her shoulder and pulled her jacket from the back of the chair she looked up and unexpectedly found herself under dark eyed surveillance.

'Well I never, look who's at the counter.' She said, as she swung her coat over her shoulders

Issy laughed as she pulled on her jacket. 'He remembers you.' She grinned as they left, passing the long line of students still queuing for their lunch.

'Ella,' Andy was all smiles as she reached him, greeting her like an old friend, 'Fancy seeing you here!'

Ella glanced briefly at him as she passed. 'Hello Andy.' She said pleasantly and walked on.

'Who's that girl?' Nina asked as Andy eventually joined her at the table with his lunch.

'Which girl?' He looked around the room before turning back to look at her with an innocent shrug.

'The one you spoke to just now.' She said irritably. 'Long, black hair, beige suede jacket.'

Pulling the tray from under the plate Andy slid it against the leg of the table, noting the suspicion in Nina's voice.

'Oh her,' He gave a casual shrug as he picked up his knife and fork and began his lunch. 'I think she's called Ella; she's one of Mick's Taylor's sister's friends.'

'How do you know her?'

'I met her once when I was with Mick. She was with his sister and Issy Llewellyn; they were all at school together.'

'When was that, last year?'

'No.' He shook his head. 'Must have been a couple of years ago.'

'She must have created an impression then,' Nina's green cat's eyes fixed themselves on him. 'you remembering her after all this time after one meeting.'

'Nina, why the third degree? I was only being polite that's all. Now please, stop this or I might just change my mind about London next weekend.'

Nina went back to her meal. She knew better than to argue with him when a shopping trip to the Kings Road and Carnaby Street was imminent. Silently she made a mental note to find out more about the mysterious Ella. Polite indeed! He'd looked positively over the moon to see her. All the signs were there again and while she normally knew how to handle his romantic detours, there was something different about this girl. Something quite worrying.

TEN

Friday 15th September

Ella joined Issy and Jenny as they queued to get into The Mill. It was Friday evening, college was over for the week and all three girls were looking forward to a good night out. Max, the club's resident bouncer, a blond giant with a crew cut, smiled warmly at the three of them as one by one they signed in. Behind him, in a basket, curled up and snoring loudly, lay the club's ultimate riot deterrent, Bruce the cross bred Alsatian.

In the main dance area, people were on the floor, the place already pulsating to the Foundations *'Baby, Now that I've Found You.'* Standing at the bar Ella swayed to the beat of the music as Issy ordered three glasses of brandy and Babycham. She had been in Abbotsbridge for three weeks and far from being the happy experience she had expected, she now found herself constantly at odds with her mother, who seemed to want to interfere in every aspect of her life. Currently it was what she wore. Too short, too tight. Everything, it seemed, was disapproved of. Well not everything perhaps. Andy Macayne had certainly become a favourite conversation topic. Mel name dropped continuously, full of praise for the son of one of Liam's major clients. Ella trod a wary path. Yes she had met him, yes he was very pleasant. No she was not interested, besides didn't he already have a girlfriend? This last piece of information should have ended the whole affair, but not where her mother was concerned. Andy's present relationship, disapproved of by his father, was thankfully all but over she was told. He was on the verge of being very much available.

Ella sighed wearily. She had no interest in Andy. Her mind was fixed on more important things like Niall. She knew he had taken things badly; he had been angry on the day they met, unable to believe her education had taken such a downturn; horrified that her future now lay in something as lowly as office work. He did not seem to be listening when she told him she was going to turn the whole thing around, work for herself, be her own boss. He had agreed to phone her, but wouldn't entertain the thought of coming to The Mill. It was all very disappointing and when they had said all they had to say, he dropped her at the bottom of Cambridge Crescent, where she had kissed him and reminded him about the little gold heart and her promise to him. She watched his car until it disappeared out of sight, hoping it was enough to put his mind at rest. He had left her promising he would call her at Jenny's on Thursday evening around seven. But last night seven o'clock came and went and the phone remained ominously silent.

The buzz of the club was distracting and last night's disappointment and all the associated worries began to fade as thoughts of the coming evening filled her mind. As the three girls made their way to an empty table, Ella caught the mood of the evening, the movement of bodies on the dance floor, the laughter, the music. The weekend was here at last, time to dance, have a good time, and enjoy the moment. Tuesday would come soon enough and if the phone still didn't ring she'd simply have to take the bull by the horns and find some way of getting in touch him. Whatever the problem, she was determined to overcome it. After all, she loved him and love conquered all didn't it?

It was the end of another Friday evening's drinking at the Somerset Arms and Rachel was about to go home. As usual, she had gone through her normal routine of cleaning ashtrays, wiping table tops and making sure everything was clean and ready for opening the next day. 'I'll be off now then.' she called out as she pulled on her coat. 'See you tomorrow.'

Cheerful responses came from the back of the bar where Tom and Lily were busy filling the large commercial dishwasher with glasses, and then Tom appeared, wiping his hands on a towel before crossing to the front door to let Rachel out.

She stepped out into the chilliness of an early autumn evening, a hint of frost in the air. Above a full moon hung in the sky, ready to light her way back through the village to the shop. As she crossed the small car park which fronted the pub she saw him standing there under the inn sign, hands buried in the pockets of his flying jacket.

'What are you doing here?'

'I've come to walk you home.'

'There's no need.'

'Yes there is. Doggy said there's a tramp living rough up in Hundred Acre, comes down into the village at night to scavenge. I didn't want you running into him.'

'Well that's very chivalrous of you,' she smiled. 'Thank you.'

'It's no problem. Besides I enjoy your company, because I think you are......' He searched for the words. 'A breath of fresh air.'

'A breath of fresh air?' Her eyebrows lifted in surprise. 'Really?'

'Really.' He nodded, then sliding his arm around her shoulder he said. 'Come on, let's get you home.'

Friday 6th October

'What's the matter Ella?' Jenny said, as they made their way down the stairs towards the refectory for lunch. 'You look really fed up.'

112

'I am.' Ella sighed.

'Oh dear, was it that ticking off old Jonesy gave us all for handing in our Commerce essays late? Went on a bit didn't he?'

'He always does. It *was* the 9th though, I wrote it down, although I don't think it would have done much good arguing the point with him.'

'So what is bugging you?'

'Niall,' she said quietly. 'Something's wrong.'

They joined the queue, avoiding the day's hot menu, opting instead for sandwiches and coffee which they took to a quiet table in the far corner of the room.

'We got off to a bad start with the phone calls. He missed his first promised call and didn't apologise or give any reason when he eventually did ring. But since it's become a regular thing I've noticed this gradual change,' Ella said as they settled themselves down. 'It's as if he's taken a step back from me. There are these horrible silences when I mention things about Meridan Cross or Cirencester. He doesn't seem to want to say very much.'

'I expect he's beginning to feel the strain.' Jenny said after a mouthful of sandwich. 'It must be difficult trying to have a long distance relationship anyway, but when your girlfriend's mother's made it very clear you're not wanted.......'

'But surely that should make him more determined. I am!' Ella argued.

'If you want my advice,' Jenny replied, sugaring her coffee. 'I think you need to see each other, have a really good talk. Why don't you just take a day out of college? I'm sure he could do the same. No one would know....'

'You're right.' Ella cheered up considerably. 'I'll suggest it to him next week.'

Tuesday 10th October

'I'm sorry Ella I can't, it's impossible.'

'But Niall,' Ella said miserably, clasping the receiver tightly as she sat in Jenny's father Jack's study, 'We need some time together. We need to talk.'

'Come back for the weekend then.'

'I can't.' She said painfully. 'Not before Christmas. She'll have no excuse to stop me then.'

'Ella since when has anyone ever stopped you doing what you want to do?'

'It's different here Niall, you have no idea.'

'Don't tell me you're scared of her.' The sarcastic edge to his tone annoyed her.

'No, but if I have to live here I'd like it to be as peaceful an experience as possible. She has the habit of making life very difficult if she wants to......'

'Well, it's your own fault! You were the one who was so keen to go there in the first place!'

'I know. I've made a terrible mistake.' She said, feeling tears creeping into her voice at his harsh remarks. 'But the one thing that kept me going was knowing that despite it all I still had you. Now I'm not so sure....'

'Ella. Please. Don't cry.' His tone softened.

'I can't help it.' She blinked back her tears. 'I just have this feeling that maybe you're tired of me, that there's someone else you'd rather be with....'

'Ella!'

'Well, is there? Is that why you've lost interest in us?'

'Ella, no that's not it at all. I'm a bit low that's all.' He paused for a moment. 'You remember I told you we would be off on six weeks work placement soon? Well the allocations came through last week and guess where they're sending me? East bloody Anglia! Miles away from anywhere!' It was his turn to sound upset now. 'I leave on Saturday and I'm really depressed. I'm sorry; I didn't want to worry you about it because I know how things are with your mother. The thing is I don't know how frequently I'll be able to phone while I'm there and I know how you rely on my calls.'

'Is that all?' She gave a small sigh of relief. 'Oh Niall, please,' she was laughing and crying at the same time. 'Don't worry, I'll give you Jenny's address. A letter will be fine.'

Saturday 14th October

Mary O'Farrell stood at the gate with Richard, watching Niall load his suitcase into the back of the E-type.

'Did you remember to pack the two extra sweaters I put out?' She called out. 'I left them on the spare bed.'

'Yes, yes, I've got the lot.' He said slamming the boot before returning to where she stood.

'You take care now.' She whispered, cupping his face in her hands and giving him a farewell kiss. 'And don't forget to keep in touch with Ella. You have got Jenny's address haven't you?'

'Tucked safely into my wallet.' He patted his flying jacket, 'I'll ring you as soon as I get there.' He said moving towards the car. 'I know how you worry....'

Standing in the road just outside the shop, Rachel watched her mother driving off into the distance in her Morris Minor Traveller, en route for the cash and carry. This morning, in her absence she had been left to mind the shop and she knew most of her time would be taken up with making up orders for collection later on in the day. As soon as the car disappeared from sight she turned back towards the shop, knowing the Robinsons at Field Way had left a particularly large order which Mrs Robinson wanted made up by lunch time so she could collect it after she had collected her family allowance from the Post Office at Morden.

As she reached the top of the steps she heard the blare of a car horn and turned to see the white E-type pull in below her. Niall got out, zipping up his flying jacket. He was smiling.

'Oh.' She put her hand to her mouth. 'I completely forgot, you're off today aren't you?'

'Yep!' He joined her at the top of the steps. 'Six weeks in the wilds of East Anglia. However am I going to cope?'

'Oh you'll be fine, I know you will.'

'I like your confidence.' He laughed. 'Personally I'm not so sure.'

'So, what brings you here? Something to keep you going on the journey?'

'Mmm.' His blue eyes held hers, his smile as wicked as ever.

'What can I get you?' She turned towards the shop. 'Pastie? Mars Bar?'

'Not even close.' He caught her by the shoulders and spun her lightly round into his arms.

'Niall!' She gasped. 'What are you doing? Let go of me!'

'Not before you kiss me goodbye.'

'What?' She laughed. 'You're crazy, do you know that?'

'Rachel.' He said, pressing his lips against her forehead. 'I don't know what I'd have done without you during the past few weeks. 'You're a wonderful girl!'

'And you're a wonderful man.' She looked at him seriously. 'Ella's very lucky.'

'Rachel.' He whispered, brushing his finger gently across her lips. 'Be quiet.' And then slowly and very deliberately he lifted her chin and kissed her mouth.

Thursday 26th October

Rachel was glued to the television watching *The Defenders*, when the phone rang. She wrinkled her nose; her mother was out playing whist which meant she would not only have to leave the warmth of the sitting room to answer the phone but also drag herself away from the gorgeous Robert Reed, who with his father was poised to win yet another court battle.

With a groan of annoyance she left the room and took herself off to the small linoleum covered passageway where the phone hung on the wall. Settling herself against the lukewarm radiator, she lifted the receiver.

'Meridan Cross 469.'

'Rach?'

'Ella, Oh Ella.' She cheered up immediately. 'Hello, how are you?'

'I'm fine. Can you chat?'

'Yes, Mum's out at a whist drive in the Hall, she won't be back for ages.'

'Rach it's so good to hear your voice. Much better than letters eh?'

'Yes, are you ringing from Jenny's?'

'Where else? There's a total ban on everything to do with Meridan Cross at my mother's house.'

'I know, it must be awful for you. But you're OK aren't you? You've got Jenny and Issy, and you're still going to that club at weekends.'

'Yes, and Jenny's mum's been great. I get to use Jenny dad's study so I can talk to Niall privately. And how are things with you?'

'Fine, I'm still enjoying the pub work and I passed my driving test on Tuesday.'

'Rachel that's fantastic!'

'How are your lessons going?'

'Very well, I'm really enjoying it. I'm having two lessons a week; Liam said it should speed things up. I hope to take my test before Christmas.'

There was a short pause then Ella said. 'Rach, do you know if Mary's heard from Niall yet? I did try ringing, but I guess they must be at the same whist drive.'

The mention of Niall's name made Rachel bite her lip guiltily. 'I think they are,' she said, and then added. 'And the answer to your question is yes she has and he's fine. Hasn't he been in touch then?'

'No. I knew he probably wouldn't be able to ring, but I did give him Jenny's address and I thought by now, well, that I'd have had at least one letter.'

'Maybe it's gone astray in the post.'

'Yes, maybe it has.'

'Shall I get Mary to call you?'

'No, it's OK, I'll try and contact her at the weekend.'

'I'll tell her, though, shall I, that you've not heard from him yet?'

'If you could, thanks.' Ella's voice sounded flat, full of disappointment. 'I'd better go, these calls cost me a small fortune. Take care.'

'You too.' Rachel said and hung up.

She returned to the front room; the programme was ending. Robert Reed was standing outside the court shaking hands with the glamorous young widow he'd just successfully defended. Rachel put a shovel full of coal on the fire then reached up, pulling out the envelope sitting on the mantelpiece behind the clock and stood there looking at it for a moment.

Arriving two days ago, it had been a complete surprise. He had not mentioned anything about keeping in touch when he left her that day standing in the road watching him drive away that day. Her fingers went to her lips, remembering his kiss. She had planned to write back, to tell him how empty the village was without him and how much she was looking forward to his return. But Ella's call now made that impossible. It was dangerous, she thought, so very dangerous. His flirtatious way had aroused old feelings in her; feelings that had no place in her life, not when he belonged to her best friend. Taking a last look at the letter she leaned forward and threw it gently into the flames.

Friday 3rd November

Mary was on the phone in the hall talking to Niall when Richard came in.

'Well I wonder where her letters are going then. Is the address written clearly? What? Check with her? I'd better write it down then. Yes, I have a pen and paper.' She scribbled down the address, repeating each line as he said it. 'Great, I'll check with her when she calls next week. It's got to be that, hasn't it? What? Yes I will remember you to her when I speak to her. O.K. Take care then. Bye.'

'Problems?' Richard eyed her curiously.

'Niall's letters haven't been getting through to Ella. She was having them sent to Jenny's house, but none of them have arrived. Niall says he's not surprised really. The nearest post box is a two miles away on a long stretch of deserted road. I expect the postman only collects once a month, they're probably still there!'

'I don't think so.' Richard shook his head. 'Margaret told me the other day that Rachel had got a letter from him.'

'Rachel?' Mary gave a puzzled frown. 'What's he doing writing to Rachel?'

'They have been seen in each other's company rather a lot lately.' Richard hesitated. 'You don't think....'

'What are you trying to say?' She rounded on him sharply. 'That he's got something going on with Rachel behind Ella's back? Never! I know he's a born flirt but now he's with Ella, it's different. Oh, I know her being in Abbotsbridge has made life difficult for him, but please be assured, there's no room for anyone else in his heart. I'm his mother. I know these things.'

Thursday 9th November

'Rachel. Hi, it's me.'

Rachel held the receiver tightly, butterflies in her stomach as she heard Ella's voice on the other end of the phone.

'Ella. Hello. Have you had a letter yet?' She crossed her fingers, remembering the three others she'd had since, each one of them and their talk of missing her, consigned to the fire.

'Yes, yes, he got the address wrong. Totally mad isn't he? He wrote it down as Westhill Road. No wonder they never reached Jenny.' She giggled. 'Goodness knows who ended up with them. He says he didn't get them back.'

'Well at least you've heard now.' Rachel said, feeling a little less guilty.

'He'll be home soon. On the 29th.' Ella said. 'Rach I've made an important decision. I'm coming back to Meridan Cross that weekend. Jenny and I have worked out a plan. I've already spoken to Grandma about it and she says I can stay at Little Court. I love him so much, all I want is to be with him!'

Wednesday 22nd November

Mel looked up from the beef casserole she had been pushing around her plate.

'Have you got your dress yet?'

Ella frowned.

'The Rotary Dance at the Forum on Friday.'

'Oh, yes.' Ella nodded. 'I bought it last weekend.'

'What colour? Not blue I hope.' Mel added tetchily.

'Pink, actually.' Ella finished her meal and pushed her plate to one side. 'We won't be too late will we? I have to be up early the next day to pack. Jenny's father is picking me up at ten thirty.'

'It finishes around midnight.' Liam said wiping his mouth with his napkin. 'Remind me, what exactly is it you're up to with Jenny this weekend?'

'Chaperoning!' Mel said fiercely. 'I'm not having that girl and my son sleeping together!'

Ella glared at her mother. 'We're going to Bristol to see Nick. And *nothing* will be going on!'

'I had high hopes that that postage stamp relationship would fizzle out, just like yours.' Mel sniffed disdainfully.

'Well it hasn't.' Ella said getting up from the table. 'And it's not long distance, you know he comes back to Abbotsbridge at least once a month and stays with the Taylors.'

'Yes, my own son keeping the company of strangers in preference to his own family.' Reminded, Mel felt a familiar stab of outrage. 'Goodness knows what everyone must think!'

'I doubt most people are even aware.' Liam said with a tired sigh as he folded his napkin. 'They're far too concerned with the problems going on in their own lives.'

'Well that's all you know!' Mel snapped. 'Only last week Sheila said to me.....'

'I'm in my room doing homework.' Ella was at the door, eager to get away from her mother's moans and groans.

'And I've got a layout to finish off.' Liam pushed back his chair and rose to his feet, also keen to be away. 'I'll be in my den for most of the evening.'

Left alone, Mel sat there looking at the after dinner clutter. She felt irritable and upset. Indifference was something she expected from Ella; under all sorts of influences from the people she mixed with – bad ones, she expected, if they came from the likes of the Taylor girl and that awful Issy Llewellyn with her sing-song Welsh voice. But now Liam, cutting her off mid sentence; retreating to his den as if she was making a great fuss about nothing. It was deeply upsetting. Of course, it hadn't always been like that.

She closed her eyes, seeing him again for the first time at the party, a lean handsome man with green eyes and light brown hair. Leaning against the door jamb, he had been deep in conversation with a small group of men in her boss Malcolm Davidson's kitchen. The occasion was a party at the Davidson's to celebrate their 25th wedding anniversary.

'Who's that?' She whispered to her friend Diana as they squeezed through to refill their glasses.

'Liam Carpenter. He's an architect; does the occasional sub contract job for the council. He's very clever apparently and still single too. Bit of a catch eh?'

He looked up then, almost as if he'd heard them speaking, giving Mel a warm smile before returning to his conversation.

'It seems he likes the look of you too.' Diana was amused.

Mel had no idea exactly what it was about him that attracted her so much, the way he moved, the leanness of his body or the intenseness of his green eyes. He just seemed perfect in every way and the voice when he was eventually introduced to her, deep and masculine sent shivers through her. He invited her to dinner and she accepted, aware that he was the most attractive man she had encountered for some time.

At work she had deliberately created a new identity for herself, a young childless widow living with her only relative, an elderly aunt, in nearby Kingsford. The last thing she wanted them all knowing was the mundane details of her true identity. The story she told was that her aunt had brought her up after her entire family had been killed during an air raid over Bristol in 1944. She had returned to the city after the war to work and later married her childhood sweetheart, but tragically lost him when he was killed in a car accident just eighteen months after their wedding. She had now moved back to Meridan Cross to keep her ageing aunt company. The identity pleased her; it omitted the most depressing and irritating areas of her life, her children and her father. In an ideal world this creation was the person she would have been and this status, she knew, was just right for the eligible Liam Carpenter.

In the months that followed she continued with her deception; her aunt's failing health being her excuse not to take him back to Kingsford. She enjoyed every moment spent with this handsome, educated man, encouraged to take time away from her family by her mother who thought she was out enjoying herself with Diana. She now ignored the constant criticism from her father about her extended absences from the children. She didn't care any more, because when she was with Liam she escaped into another place; a world where she was truly happy. And being there made her cope with what she now saw as an increasingly miserable existence in Meridan Cross.

It was nine months later when Liam dropped his bombshell. A job offer with a large multi national construction company working abroad for a few years. It was a golden opportunity, he said, to do the job he loved and see something of the world. His first project would take him to Australia to work on a new marina development and he would be leaving in six weeks' time As she looked at him, her whole world falling apart, he reached across the table and took her by the hand.

'Marry me Mel.'

Of course she had to accept. She had walked away from her home and her family without a backward glance. No feelings, no guilt. After all she had one life and she owed it to herself to make the most of it. And it had been wonderful; seeing the world, moving in glamorous circles, being the centre of attention and adored by her husband.

Oh how he'd loved her then, she thought as she got up and began clearing the plates away. But time had changed everything. Of course there were still traces of his affection - surprise meals out, or perfume. Or delicate pieces of jewellery - he had excellent taste. But she knew she was no longer the centre of his life. His work came first, it's what drove him, maybe it always had and she had just failed to notice. The sex too had become disappointing, infrequent and functional. There was no excitement any more. Standing at the sink, she pulled on her rubber gloves and ran hot water into the bowl, adding a squirt of Fairy Liquid. The man she married had changed. She didn't like it and she was determined to do something about it. But exactly what that something was right now she had no idea.

Thursday 23rd November

It was dark when the white E-type pulled up outside Willowbrook. Mary, keeping vigil at the window, was at the front door immediately to help her weary son in with his luggage.

'Welcome home.' She hugged him tightly. 'I expect you're pleased to be back.'

'Too right, I'll sleep like the dead tonight. The bed was diabolical and the room they gave me.' He gave a shiver. 'Freezing.'

'Come on through to the kitchen.' She said as he pulled off his coat in the hall. 'I've kept supper for you.'

'Was it really that bad? 'She asked, watching him as he sat at the table tucking into steak and kidney pie and vegetables.

'Not really, just miles from anywhere. And so flat. I really missed Meridan Cross. The valley, Hundred Acre.'

'And Ella?'

'What?'

'Well I hope you have missed her. She's taking a chance coming here to see you. If her mother finds out...'

'What are you talking about?'

'Ella's coming to Meridan Cross this weekend!' Mary clasped her hands in excitement. 'She's defying her mother to be with you. Isn't that romantic?' She stared at his blank expression. 'Well look pleased for heaven's sake. How many weeks have you spent moping about with a long face trying to think of a way to see her? And now she's solved your problem. You're a lucky young man; she must love you very much.'

Friday 24th November

Ella do come on, we're all waiting!' Mel stood at the bottom of the stairs tapping her foot irritably.

Liam, in dinner jacket and bow tie checked his watch. 'Don't panic, we've plenty of time, it doesn't start 'till eight.'

Mel rounded on him impatiently. 'And what sort of seats will be left then? We need to be there at least twenty minutes earlier, it's very important we're seated in the right place. You of all people should know that!' She turned her attention to the stairs once more. 'Ella! If you don't come down in the next thirty seconds I will come up and get you!'

A door slammed and they both looked up. Ella appeared at the top of the stairs looking down at them, smiling. She was wearing a tight shocking pink silk dress with long sleeves and deep cuffs punctuated with small pearl buttons. Her evening bag and high heeled shoes were a contrasting pale pink and her dark curly hair had been pinned up, small corkscrew tendrils escaping prettily around a face expertly applied with make up.

'Did you have a hand in this?' Liam looked his wife.

Mel shook her head silently, watching Ella descend the stairs. She looked fantastic. Heads were certainly going to turn tonight.

'You look stunning darling.' She smiled with approval as Liam helped Ella on with her coat. 'Absolutely stunning!'

Niall left Meridan Cross at 8.00 making the excuse that he was going over to Saddlers End for a reunion with the Miller Boys. His true destination, however, was somewhere quite different. As he drove his thoughts were on the coming evening and what he had to do. This was going to be one of the most difficult days of his life, but he couldn't just put it in a letter, or do it by phone. No, this had to be face to face and it had to be now. He had spent the last six weeks agonising over the direction his life should take, where he wanted to be and who with. On bitter evenings in his cold little room he would look out at the stars and think about the one person he was missing. And it hadn't been Ella. How this had come about he had no idea. In fact six months ago if someone had suggested he could form any emotional attachment to Rachel he would have laughed out loud. He had always found her attractive but thought of her as quiet and dull, a complete antithesis to the lively, outgoing Ella. Until now she had held no interest for him. But since Ella's departure he'd got to know her properly and had discovered he was wrong. She was bright and fun to be with. Her calm and gentle way made him feel happy and relaxed, while Ella's strong will and focussed determination only seemed to make him frustrated and irritable. When he heard Ella was coming to the village for the weekend, panic seized him. There was no way he could let that happen. He had to finish with her and to do that he knew he would have to travel out to Abbotsbridge to see her. Because if he did it in Meridan Cross, he risked losing Rachel and he couldn't allow that to happen.

Of course, he knew tonight wouldn't be easy. First he had to get past her mother - although he guessed if she knew his reason for being there he'd be welcomed in. But exactly what was he going to tell Ella? Sorry I don't love you any more because I've fallen in love with your best friend? That seemed blunt and heartless. But there was no easy way to let girls go was there? He'd done it many times before and Ella like the others, who had also been special once, was special no more. Besides, Abbotsbridge was her life now and no doubt there were young men her mother did approve of already queuing up to go out with her. There'd be a few tears but he was convinced she would soon forget him.'

Liam swung the car into a vacant space at the back of the Forum, now ablaze with light. As they made their way towards the rear entrance Mel felt pleased. Everything was going well; with Ella looking like a million dollars, she'd have all the eligible young men dancing attendance on her tonight. But none of them mattered because she'd already organised Ella a partner for the evening: Andy Macayne.

Thinking about Andy made her automatically think of his father and a small tremor of pleasure run through her. She had known of Bob Macayne through Liam's dealings with Taylor Macayne, the construction company Bob owned with Jack Taylor, but had only been introduced to him properly a month ago at a dinner party. Something about the way his dark eyes kept watching her across the table that evening had left a strange, fluttery feeling in her stomach. A week later they met in the doorway of Lloyds Bank and the way he smiled and said hello took her breath away. Although Liam had told her that Bob was single and celibate by choice - devoted to the memory of his dead wife Lucia - Mel was of the opinion that reputations, especially ones like that, were just asking to be broken. Well, if not broken, then perhaps bent a little. Bob, she considered, might be just what she was looking for to bring a little excitement into her life.

'They're out.'

Niall took his finger off the doorbell and turned to see the shadowy figure of a woman and a dog hovering by the front gate.

'Do you happen to know where they've gone?'

'Some dinner dance at the Forum. Mr Carpenter mentioned it when I saw him last Sunday. Shouldn't think they'd be back until well after midnight.'

'Was Ella with them?'

'Yes.' The woman smiled. 'Looked lovely; all in pink she was. Saw them leave as I came out with Jess here.' She studied him for a moment. 'They won't let you in like that you know. It's a black tie do.'

'Is it?' He surveyed his jeans.

'Shame you missed them.' The woman smiled and walked on, her footsteps receding into the distance.

'Bugger!'

He returned to the car, sitting for a moment, trying to work out a new strategy. He should go home, he knew that. Confronting her in a public place was a crazy thing to do, but he had no choice. If he didn't bring things to an end tonight, tomorrow she would be in Meridan Cross. And that would be far worse. Turning the key in the ignition, he heard the engine fire. He remembered the Forum. It used to be a cinema. It was just off Bridge Street and there was a car park, he recalled, at the rear.

ELEVEN

Friday 24th November

Despite her initial misgivings, Ella found she was actually enjoying the evening so far. Sparkling wine was on offer as they arrived and everyone gathered there seemed very friendly, asking her questions about college and how she was finding life in Abbotsbridge. Liam was the perfect gentleman, introducing her to everybody; her mother, however, was conspicuous by her absence.

She found herself meeting people she knew by sight from evenings at the Mill. There was blond Justin Langley and his fair haired sister Annabel, engaged to Bryan Tate's son Rich. And Rich's older sister, the kohl eyed hippie Bryony, arty jewellery designer, recently married to Gareth Knight, heir apparent to Stewart's Engineering. They all greeted her warmly, Bryony admiring her dress and saying it was just the colour she was looking for to incorporate into a necklace design she was working on. At the same time Ella made a note of those sharing their table for the evening; the Fitzallyns, the Websters and the Morris's, all three wives part of her mother's Rotary ladies' circle.

At seven forty five they were called in to be seated for dinner. By nine thirty this was over and the tables were being pulled to the edge of the room, ready for the dancing to begin. The MC moved out onto the stage, cracked a few jokes and then introduced the programme for the evening. As he left the curtains parted to loud applause and the Carltons, a six piece band started off the evening with a tango. Liam drew Ella to her feet.

'You do dance I hope?'

'Properly? Of course! It wasn't all barn dancing in Meridan Cross.' She said making him laugh.

'In that case, shall we?'

The floor was packed, a whirl of multi coloured ladies and dark suited men. Across the floor Ella saw her mother dancing with a handsome rugged looking man with a halo of black hair.

'Who's that?' She asked Liam.

'Bob Macayne.'

'Andy's father?'

He nodded.

'Why is she dancing with him?'

'When the music started your mother made a bee line for him. Said she wanted to dance with someone who didn't trample on her feet.'

'You haven't trodden on mine yet.'

'I'm obviously having a good evening. Usually I'm hopeless.'

'Not as hopeless as you think!'

'You're just being kind.'

'I'm not. Look, he's just trodden on her foot!'

'Has he?' They pulled to a stop so Liam could take a look.

'Yes, there!' Ella grimaced. 'He's done it again.'

'Nice to know there's a fellow carthorse in the room. 'Liam said, giving Ella a satisfied smile.

Later, as Ella was partnering Charles Fitzallyn in a waltz one of the waiters interrupted them.

'Sorry Sir.' He said to Charles, 'I'm looking for Miss Kendrick.' He smiled at Ella. 'And that must be you, because they told me to look for someone dressed in pink.'

'Yes, this is indeed the lady.' Charles replied with an admiring glance. 'Is there a problem?'

'A gentleman is in the foyer asking for her.'

Ella looked bemused. 'Why didn't you bring him in?'

'I'm afraid he wasn't dressed appropriately.'

'How not appropriately?'

The waiter considered the question then said. 'Jeans, flying jacket.'

'It's Niall.' She gave a gasp of delight. 'Niall's come to see me!' She put her hands to her face, filled with excitement. 'I'm so sorry Mr Fitzallyn, it's my boyfriend. He's been away for six weeks and I just have to see him. Will you excuse me please?'

'Of course my dear,' Charles released her with an indulgent smile.

Ella pushed through the crowds and climbed the steps which led out of the ballroom into the main foyer. She saw him immediately, sitting on one of the long benches by the big double front doors, his hands resting on his knees.

'Niall.' She ran to him throwing her arms around him as he got to his feet. 'Niall this is wonderful!'

'Ella, please.' He disentangled himself from her instantly as if embarrassed by her behaviour. As he looked down into her face she realised something was different. There was a serious set to his mouth. She knew then he'd come with bad news.

'What is it?' She asked hesitantly. 'Has something dreadful happened?'

'No, but there's something I need to talk to you about urgently. Can we go somewhere quiet? Perhaps over there?' He indicated a small half curtained alcove.

Andy Macayne was running late. Earlier that week he had been press ganged into attending the Rotary Ball at the Forum this evening. His father had said it was important to put in an appearance now that he was working in the company as these sorts of local events were a useful opportunity to develop new business contacts. Of course he had no problems with that at all. His first working event, just the chance he was looking for to show Nina off. However, when he mentioned bringing her along, Bob was insistent that a girl from the Parkway Council Estate with a drunk for a father was the last person he wanted partnering his son to such a function. And so caught between a rock and a hard place, Andy found himself lying. Well it wasn't really a lie, more a half truth. He told Nina he had an urgent business commitment which he couldn't get out of. His father was adamant, he had no choice. Understandably Nina was unhappy. Originally they had been due to see *Barbarella* at the Odeon and then go on to Ronaldo's for dinner afterwards. Now he was expected to be at the Forum for the evening knew he'd have to make up big time and he realised that would mean a visit to Kendal's jewellers in the morning.

Arriving at the Forum he found the car park full and had to leave his TR4 a couple of streets away and walk. Now only yards from his destination the sound of music and laughter were clearly audible. It sounded as if a good evening was well under way.

As he came through the big double doors he heard the sound of raised voices. A young couple were arguing in a half screened alcove off to the left. The girl, shaking her head, was obviously upset.

'Lover's tiff,' The cloakroom attendant said as he took his overcoat from him and wrapped it around a hanger. 'Been at it a while. Think he's giving her the elbow. Must be mad, she's a cracker.'

Andy stared across at them again and realised he was looking at Ella. The man she was with, tall, broad shouldered and blond, he concluded, must be Niall, the boyfriend she'd left behind in Meridan Cross. The one Mick told him Mel Carpenter had banned from seeing her. Taking his ticket from the attendant he moved across the foyer slowly, towards the edge of the alcove to eavesdrop.

'Ella, I've said all I came to say, I must go.' He heard Niall say as he turned away from her.

'No!' Ella grabbed his arm 'You can't! We need to talk this through properly. You're not being fair!'

'Fair!' He rounded on her. 'Were you fair with me when you decided to move here? Did you bother to discuss it? No, you just did what you wanted and left me to accept your decision. Well now you're just going to have to accept mine!' He said pushing her away.

'Niall listen!' She blocked his path. 'I'm really sorry. I know you're angry and you have every right to be. But wait until tomorrow, until I'm in Meridan Cross. I'm sure we can sort things out then.'

He grabbed her by the shoulders, pushing his face close to hers. 'No Ella,' he said very slowly. 'Once you're there you'll be having everybody gang up on me. I won't have that. We're doing this my way and we're doing it here. It's over. We're finished.'

'What's going on?' With Ella near to tears Andy decided to intervene.

Niall looked at him frostily. 'It's private.'

'Rather a public place to choose for a private conversation.' He looked around the room then at Ella. 'Are you OK Ella?'

She nodded, blinking back the tears.

'You two know each other?' Niall looked at both of them suspiciously.

'Yes, of course.' Andy said calmly. 'My father does business with Ella's stepfather.'

'Does he? How very cosy.'

'Don't be so childish Niall!' Forgetting her tears Ella turned on him angrily.

'Childish am I?' His voice was mocking. 'Seems I've made the right decision. New boyfriend is he?'

'No he's not!' She protested.

'Don't be stupid!' Andy waved the cloakroom ticket he was still holding. 'I'm not with Ella, I've only just arrived.'

'Don't call me stupid!' Niall's finger went out towards Andy's face.

'Well you are!' Andy challenged. 'There's nothing going on between us! I know what your game is.'

'What!?'

'You're dumping her aren't you? And you're feeling guilty about the whole thing so you've decided to use me to shift the blame. Now I call that really cowardly!'

'A coward am I!' Anger flooded into Niall's face as he made a grab for Andy, catching him by the lapels of his suit and propelling him towards the far wall.

'For goodness sake Niall, leave him alone!' Ella shouted at him, fearful of what he was about to do.

'No one speaks to me like that! Apologise!' Niall said through gritted teeth. Now he had Andy pinned up against the wall, he leaned his arm heavily against his throat. 'Come on, say sorry!'

'No!' Andy remained defiant.

'Gentlemen, that's enough! Come on now, break it up!'

Ella turned. A tall man in evening dress was standing there watching them.

Niall turned to look at him. 'This has nothing to do with you.' He said insolently. 'Just go away and mind your own business.'

'As you're on my premises,' the stranger said softly. 'I'm afraid it is my business. So let him go or I'm afraid I'll have to call the police and I'm sure you don't want that to happen.'

Niall stared at the man for a moment then reluctantly released Andy and with one last contemptuous look at all of them he pushed through the curtain and was gone.

'Niall!' Ella rushed forward, intending to go after him, but a firm hand caught her, pulling her back.

'He's best left.' The man was looking at her. A handsome face, she thought through her tears, with warm, kind eyes. 'He needs to cool off.' Then turning to Andy who was still rubbing his throat, he said. 'So, what did you do that upset him so much?'

'Nothing!' Andy looked offended. 'He was arguing with Ella when I arrived. Looked like it was about to get nasty so I came over to try and calm things down.' He rubbed his throat again. 'As you can see, I wasn't very successful.'

'Andy's telling the truth.' Ella said, dabbing at her eyes with a tissue. 'Niall was being really horrible.'

'Did he hurt you?' The man turned concerned eyes towards her.

'No. I only got upset when he started picking on Andy.' She managed a small smile. 'Thank you for intervening Mr....'

'Benedict.' The man said with a smile. 'Tad Benedict. Come along now; let's get you back to your table.'

Niall, behind the wheel of the Jaguar braked heavily on a right hand bend, accelerating out of it with a scream of tyres. The lights of Abbotsbridge had been left behind now and he was travelling the darkness of the B road which covered the twelve miles to Meridan Cross. As he left the town behind his thoughts returned to the events of the last half hour. It had seemed so straightforward, so simple to set someone free. A veteran of broken relationships, he had anticipated the tears and tantrums that were sure to follow. But Ella hadn't reacted like that at all. Instead she'd tried to reason with him. She was tough and tenacious and when he found his resolve beginning to slip, he had to bring in the only weapon left to him; his anger.

He took a bend on the wrong side, the Jaguar started to slide and he tugged on the wheel, taking the car back onto the left hand side of the road. He tore through Upton Gifford then out onto a roller coaster of open road which stretched out towards the top of Hundred Acre, dipping and rising in a straight grey ribbon under the light of the full moon. As soon as he reached the top of Sedgewick Hill he could see the lights of Meridan Cross spread out along the valley.

If only Mr Smooth hadn't poked his nose in. His arrival had changed everything, put a different perspective on the whole matter. Seeing them together he smelled a rat. All the time he had been struggling with his conscience over his feelings for Rachel, he was now sure Ella had been seeing him. Guilty as hell he was too, even though he denied it. Why else would he have become so protective of her?

What he really needed now was a drink to blot out the anger and humiliation he felt. He checked his watch. Just after ten. Tomorrow he would be fine, put it all behind him, get things going with Rachel. But tonight he was at the mercy of his emotions, and right now all he wanted to do was to get very drunk.

Mel emerged from the ladies toilet feeling better for a reapplication of make up and spray of her favourite Dior perfume. She stared into the ballroom. The lights were dimmed, the last waltz playing, time to go home. She gave a thoughtful smile. Left to her own devices, she'd had quite an interesting evening with Bob Macayne. She had completely broken with convention and asked him to dance. He had taken her out onto the floor, holding her in a formal, uncomfortable way. She had tried to liven things up by pulling him closer to her and smiling up at him provocatively from under her false eye lashes. This had caused him to tread on her feet a couple of times and collide with other couples as they danced round. A bit of a let down really, she thought as she watched him walk off to talk to Liam, feeling disappointed that he had not turned out to be the cool, confident man she'd imagined.

She decided not to go back to the table straight away, instead she made her way upstairs to the small enclosed first floor balcony which overlooked the gardens to have a last cigarette before finding Liam and the others. She climbed the stone staircase to the landing and opened the door. The night air was chilly as it touched her face and came into contact with the skin beneath the thin material of her blue cocktail dress. She opened her bag, took out a packet of Senior Service and opened them, putting a cigarette in her mouth before continuing to search for her lighter.

In the dimness of the balcony someone stepped forward and a flame flared. Shocked and surprised she took the cigarette from her mouth, reaching for the wrist of the shadowy figure behind the lighter and pushing it down in an attempt to identify who was behind it. Bob Macayne stood there smiling.

'Well, Mrs Carpenter.' He said, dark eyes glittering in the half light. 'Come up here for a breather have you?'

'I'm sorry?' She experienced a rush of nervousness as she looked at him, feeling strangely vulnerable under his cool, appraising gaze.

'You know, I'm intrigued by your activities.' He laughed sarcastically as he lit her cigarette. 'All that teasing. The innuendo, the closeness, the touching. Is it attention you seek because Liam spends all the evening talking business or are you just out to shock all those prim matrons?'

'A bit of both really.' She said with a simple shrug of her shoulders. 'Liam is a workaholic, he never turns off. I'm left to make my own amusement. And when I see all those po-faced wives in their drab little outfits trying to keep up appearances and having their doting husbands dance attendance on them something in me wants to provoke, shock even.' She blew smoke into the air.

'Well I certainly think you achieved that this evening.' He gave a slow smile. 'Barbara Morris's face was bright puce seeing you out on the floor with her Douglas for such a long time.'

'Douglas is my favourite partner; I could dance with him all evening. He is so light on his feet.'

'Which is more than you can say for me.'

'You just need to brush up.' Holding the cigarette away from her face she tilted her head and looked at him thoughtfully. 'You have good balance; I felt the rhythm in you. Your feet were in the wrong place at the wrong time that was all.'

'No one's ever complained before.'

'I doubt they dared.' She laughed and blew more smoke into the air.

'Are you saying I'm intimidating?' He looked hurt.

'You're a powerful man. That's something that attracts women, but it also scares them. Therefore they probably prefer to humour you and set the bones later rather than tell the truth.'

'And what do *you* think of me Mrs Carpenter?' The dark eyes gleamed.

'I think,' she said stubbing out her cigarette with her shoe and looking into his eyes. 'That you're a man who knows he's extremely attractive to women.'

'Are you attracted to me?'

'Maybe, but I am sensible enough to know that the way I see you is my fantasy.' She regarded him carefully. 'I wouldn't mind betting if you kissed me now I'd probably find you quite disappointing.'

'Well,' He said, slowly pulling her into his arms. 'Let's find out, shall we?'

Ella had lost count of the time she had circled the hall. *Blue Moon* had become *Smoke Gets in Your Eyes* and now *Moon River*. As soon as Tad Benedict returned them safely to the ballroom she had fallen gratefully into Andy's arms, wanting dancing and the music to distract her. Andy too was feeling down he told her, brought here tonight by his father wishes, having to break a date, unable to bring Nina with him because his father had forbidden it. Ella knew exactly how he felt; she sensed a kindred spirit as he talked of Nina and his father's disapproval of the relationship.

As they continued to dance she thought about Niall; banned by her mother, unable to have any contact with her other than secretly by phone or letter. He was right, of course, she had completely excluded him when making the decision to come to Abbotsbridge to live. But at the time she had felt rejected by those who loved her, the same kind of rejection, she reflected, that he was probably feeling now. Rejection that had made him make wild accusations about Andy and herself. How could she have been so selfish, so insensitive to his feelings? Tomorrow she decided, she would phone him first thing after breakfast. Hopefully he would have calmed down by then, might even be regretting the hastiness of his actions. They would talk and then she would ask Jack Taylor to drive her to Meridan Cross to be with him for the whole weekend. It would be an emotional reunion; she smiled to herself, picturing the scene. Of course she would apologise, try to make it up to him any way she could. I love him, she thought, what else can I do?

Across the dance floor Tad Benedict was sitting with his wife Faye watching as the dancers passed their table.

'The poor girl was clearly upset.' He was saying. 'Don't know what it was all about. When I interrupted her boyfriend had Macayne pinned against the wall, trying to choke him. Of course seeing Andy there I automatically thought he was the troublemaker. Well with his reputation what else was I to think? But seems I was wrong. The girl confirmed he'd arrived just as the argument was getting nasty.'

'Andy? A hero?' Glass in hand, Faye eyed her husband suspiciously. 'Not unless there's something on the end of it for him Tad. Did he know her?

'Yes, he called her Ella.'

'Ella?'

'Yes.' Tad looked out amongst the dancers. 'Look here she comes now.'

Faye watched as Andy Macayne and his brunette partner in shocking pink passed by.

'Ah *Ella*.'

'You know her?'

'Of her. She moved here in September.' Faye watched the couple's progress around the room. 'You know I was curious. When Sheila Fitzallyn told me about her I wondered whether she'd look anything like that mother of hers. And she doesn't. Not at all.'

Faye what are you talking about?' Tad watched as the couple disappeared among the other dancers before turning back to his wife. 'Who is she?'

'Ella Kendrick. Mel Carpenter's daughter.'

'I didn't know she had a daughter.'

'She has a son too, so Sheila said. Both from a previous marriage which no one knew about. Not even Liam, apparently.'

'Well, well. So Mel has a secret past.' Tad smiled. 'I bet she's lapping up all this attention, especially with a daughter like that to show off. You have to admit she's a real head turner.'

'Yes, she is.' Faye glanced across to where Ella had now left the dance floor and was being returned to her seat. 'And if tonight's anything to go by, a magnet for trouble too, just like her mother.'

Friday 24th November

'I think you've had enough my lad.' Tom Bennett, serving the Miller brothers with two halves of best bitter frowned at a grinning Niall O'Farrell standing beside them at the bar waving a five pound note at Rachel. 'Rachel no! No more, he's had enough.'

'Tom!' Niall protested as he looked at the heavy set publican. 'Don't be a spoil sport!' He continued to wave the note in the air. 'Just one more for the road eh?'

'No!' Tom shook his head. 'And I'm not a spoil sport. I'm the voice of reason. You've a car outside.'

'Yeah? So?'

'In your condition you're not in a fit state to drive a milk float.'

'Fair enough, I'll go somewhere where they will serve me then.' Piqued, Niall pocketed the money and looked down the bar towards Ash and Rowan. 'Where did you two say you were off to?'

'The Capricorn Club.' Rowan replied. wiping the froth from his mouth with the back of his hand. 'on the B3564 just outside Higher Padbury. It's open till two. No membership needed, you can pay on the door.'

'Great!'

He looked along the bar where Rachel was polishing beer glasses and hanging them up. 'Want to come along Rach?'

Rachel looked at Tom who shrugged. 'Up to you,' he said. 'But you'd better do the driving; he really is not in a fit state, despite all he says.'

'I'd love to. Better phone mum first though,' Rachel said with a quiet smile. 'Just to let her know where I'm going, otherwise she'll only worry.'

'Great!' Niall smiled at Tom. 'Be nice if Tom would let you off a bit earlier too,' he looked up at the clock then to the only other occupants of the bar, Doggy Barker and Jake Carr playing dominoes. 'seeing as it's almost closing time and the pub's nearly empty.

'You're a cheeky sod O'Farrell.' Tom Bennett laughed at him. 'Go on Rachel, Lily and I can manage.'

'We'll make a move then Niall.' Finishing his beer Ash and his brother left.

'See you there.' Niall called after them, remaining perched on the bar stool, waiting for Rachel. Anaesthetised by the alcohol, he now felt strangely relaxed and when thoughts of Ella crept into his mind again he realised he really didn't give a damn. If she was seeing someone else then who cared? What did it matter? Their final moments together had been a real pig's breakfast, but now it was over. He could move on. Rachel. He felt strangely aroused at the thought of her huge blue eyes and silver blonde hair and her constant air of calmness. Of course Ella had been lovely, but she was too independent, too free thinking. He should have known she'd be trouble in the beginning when she was playing hard to get. And, of course, falling for Rachel hadn't just happened overnight. He'd really grappled with his conscience about that, tried his best to resist temptation. But she was so warm and sweet and caring it was something that was bound to have happened in the long run, with or without Ella present. Now he was free, he was going to tell her exactly how he felt.

After ringing her mother, Rachel retrieved her coat and handbag and paid a quick visit to the ladies toilet to brush her hair and check her make up. As she put on her lipstick she tried not to feel guilty about the lie she'd just told. Well it wasn't really a lie, saying she was going to a club with some of the Young Farmers' group. After all, the Miller Boys and Niall were members. It was a sort of half truth. Still, what option had she given her mother's attitude towards Niall? When it came to Margaret's ears that they had been seen together, she had waved a cautionary finger at her daughter. He made a fool of you once before, she said. He'll do it again. He's that type. But Rachel had seen her mother's objections as merely another aspect of her narrow outlook on life. As far as she was concerned she was now eighteen and what had happened last year had no bearing on what was going on now. He belonged to Ella. All he was looking for was a kindred spirit to fill the empty weekends until she came back to Meridan Cross again. So she simply ignored Margaret's dire warnings and went on seeing him.

Of course, she thought as she returned her brush and lipstick to her handbag, deep down she still adored Niall. There was no one quite like him. She laughed when she remembered the lengths she had gone to just over a year ago to make him notice her. Childish things, she reflected, things she wouldn't dream of doing now. No, now was different, she was glad to be his friend. The guardian angel to watch over him for Ella. Tonight he had come into the Arms just after ten clearly rattled. Something was the matter. Perhaps she would be able to get some answers from him on their drive out to the Capricorn Club.

The night was clear, the sky peppered with stars as they left the Arms and crossed the car park.

'Will you be OK driving this thing?' Niall pointed at the Jaguar.

'We're not going in that.'

'Aren't we?' He looked at the Morris Minor Countryman parked next to it then at her and saw her nod. 'You're joking.'

'There nothing wrong with my mother's car. Come on, hop in.'

The road to Higher Padbury was long and straight, three miles across open country side and Rachel held the Morris at a steady forty miles an hour, heeding her mother's warning about speeding. Niall sat beside her, a silent figure who had not spoken since he had got into the car, his head resting against the window of the passenger door.

'Niall?' She said as the lights of Meridan Cross disappeared in her rear view mirror.

'Yes?'

'Sorry, I thought you'd dozed off.'

'I was thinking.'

'Something happened hasn't it? All that whisky, that's not you. What is it?'

'I saw Ella tonight.' He said in a calm, quiet voice. 'It's over between us.'

'No!' Shocked at his revelation, Rachel lost control for a moment, the car clipping the grass verge, throwing out into the road. Quickly she pulled hard on the wheel and straightened up.

'I don't understand. Why?'

'Because over the last three months we've gradually grown apart.' He gave a heavy sigh. 'It hasn't helped that her mother won't let me see her. Oh I know we talked regularly on the phone, but it wasn't really the same. The college thing upset me too. She had a great career opportunity in front of her. That's all gone now. And is she upset? Who knows? All she talks about is running a business when she finishes this course she's on. In fact all she seems to talk about is *her* damn future, there's no *us* anymore. She made me feel like second best and I couldn't live like that. But there's an added complication.' He looked at her in the darkness. 'I've met someone else.'

'What!' Rachel braked violently and pulled the car to a halt. Turning off the engine she faced him in the darkness. 'Niall, how could you do that to her? Breaking up is one thing, but sneaking around behind her back with another girl! It's unforgivable. And you're so wrong, I know she loves you very much. All her letters say so. Every single one said she couldn't wait until Christmas when she could be with you again.'

'It's all lies, Rachel.' He shook his head. 'I went over to Abbotsbridge tonight to see her and what did I find? All of them at a dinner dance, with Ella in the arms of some smooth looking bastard in a dinner jacket.' He paused for a moment. 'Somehow it made it so much easier then. To make the break, to tell her that I'm in love someone else.'

'This new girlfriend of yours,' She glared at him angrily. 'Does she know about Ella?'

He nodded.

'That's awful, how could she go with you behind Ella's back?'

'She doesn't know how I feel, I haven't told her yet.'

'You say you love someone and they don't know about it? That doesn't make sense.'

'Yes it does, because it's you Rachel.' He said quietly, reaching out to stroke her face. 'I've fallen in love with you.'

'Me? No!' She pushed his hand away. 'That's impossible. We're friends.'

'*Were* friends. Now I'm free I want more than that.'

'I can't,' She said frostily. 'I just can't.'

'Listen to me. She's betrayed me. With someone else.' His voice was gentle, mesmerising. 'He's dark. Handsome. She doesn't care about me any more. So I've let her go, and I'm glad because now I've got to know you I realise I want you more than anyone else in the world.' He leaned closer to her, tilting her chin with the tip of his finger, his lips seeking hers.

She let him kiss her gently on the mouth, closing her eyes, her mind filled with conflicting thoughts. She really didn't think she should be letting him do this, but if what he said was true? Could she have betrayed him like that? It was possible, after all she was always at that club with Issy and Jenny; there was plenty of opportunity to meet someone else. Poor Niall, she was beginning to feel sorry for him now. She felt his arms around her. His breath sounded deep in his throat as he broke away and looked at her in the darkness for a moment, and then slowly he began to pull her coat from her shoulders.

'Niall I don't really think I......' She began, knowing exactly what he was intending, but he kissed away her protests and casually disposed of her coat in the back of the car.

She sat there paralysed, feeling his lips soft in the base of her neck, working their way downwards as he unbuttoned her blouse and ran his fingers under the silky material. For a second she thought about trying to stop him, but then realised she didn't want to. So many times she had played out this role through the romantic paperbacks she read; dreamed of a moment just like this. And now it was here. I love him, she told herself. And now he loves me. That makes what we're doing the most natural thing in the world doesn't it?

'Let's move into the back.' She heard him whisper in her ear.

Kicking off her shoes she clambered through the gap between the seats. Her mother always kept the back seats folded down as the main use of the vehicle was to ferry stock for the shop from the cash and carry. On her hands and knees Rachel pushed a couple of small empty boxes back towards the doors and felt for the big heavy tartan car rug which was kept folded up against the back of the driver's seat. Together they spread it over the folded down seats. Niall laid her coat on top of it and suddenly they were kneeling facing each other in the darkness, the car windows thick with condensation and their breath visible in the car's cold interior.

Gently his arms went round her, his mouth soft on her own as he removed her blouse then felt at her back, unclipping her bra, freeing her breasts. He bent his head, slowly sucking each nipple in turn which made her gasp as a ripple of pleasure ran through her. His hands moved to her skirt, which he unzipped, sliding the garment slowly down over her hips together with her tights and pants. She lay back against the smooth nylon lining of her coat, propped up on one elbow, watching him silently as he took his own clothes off and tossed them into the front of the car. Then he knelt beside her looking at her in the blackness.

'Rachel, before we go any farther, there's something I need to know. Are you...?.'

'Niall, please....' She reached out and placed her hand on the smoothness of his chest. 'It's all right. I know what you're going to say, and the answer's yes. Yes, yes I am.'

135

TWELVE

Saturday 25th November

'Mel, are you listening? I said is there any more toast?' Liam, irritated by the distracted state of his wife, set his paper to one side and stared at her.

'What? Oh sorry.' She took a deep breath, making a pathetic face at him. 'I'm not feeling too good this morning.'

Ella looked at her mother as she returned from the kitchen with a replenished toast rack and set it beside her stepfather. She really did look odd, not her usual scissor-sharp self. 'I thought you looked a bit strange last night.' She commented as she reached for a piece of newly arrived toast and began to butter it.

'Strange! What do you mean by strange?' Mel snapped.

'I don't know really.' Ella held the toast to her mouth, trying to put a name to what she had seen. 'I suppose it was the fall you had. You looked a bit shaken and your hair was all over the place. You were lucky not to have broken something.'

'Too many gins.' Liam muttered from behind his paper.

'I was *not* drunk.' She looked at them both irritably. 'I was not! Haven't you both anything better to do than sit in judgement over my supposed behaviour.'

'Yes I have as a matter of fact.' Ella got up from the table. 'I'm going out for a walk.'

'A walk?' Mel frowned. 'But I thought you were off to Bristol with the Taylor girl.'

'It's been cancelled.'

'But I thought....' Mel's voice trailed away as she heard the front door slam. She looked at Liam, puzzled. 'When was that cancelled then? That's the first I've heard of it.'

'I shouldn't worry about it Mel.' He said folding the paper and getting to his feet. 'I'm in my den if you want me. Going over some plans for Bob.'

Bob. She heard the name echo silently off the walls of the room as she watched Liam leave. Alone with the clutter of the breakfast table she found the aftershocks of the night before were still causing tremors through her body as she thought about Bob Macayne. How could this be happening? All she'd done was let him kiss her. She was so sure she knew what she was doing, that just like on the dance floor he would be a disappointment. But he wasn't, he was just the opposite. It was like nothing she had ever experienced before, his mouth hot on hers, his hands everywhere, stroking, caressing; silky smooth arousal wherever they touched her. For one brief moment she had felt totally under his spell, something that both frightened and excited her.

When he had finished he had looked at her, his eyes dark and sensuous.

'Thank you Mrs Carpenter,' He smiled. 'That was quite an interesting experiment. We must repeat it again sometime.' Then he was gone, the door closing behind him, leaving her emotions in tatters. She stood there trying to compose herself, aware that in the heat of their passionate embrace her hair had escaped from its elaborate setting and loose tendrils now fell untidily around her face. Her mind raced, how was she going to explain? Then she had it. A fall - that was it. She had tripped over a step.

She smiled, remembering how easy it had been to lie and be believed and how relieved she felt with Liam's comforting arms around her, back within the safe walls of her marriage. Still, the thought of Bob and what could happen between them gave her a strange prickle of excitement. It was wonderful to be attractive to someone again, to break free from her role of suburban housewife. The elation lasted only moments however, quickly replaced by cold, hard reality. Of course, it was just a few moments madness, she told herself disappointedly. It was the drink talking; he hadn't meant what he'd said at all. He was just out to prove a point and he had. And when they met again he probably wouldn't even remember.

Ella walked along the street, wrapped against the coldness of the bright frosty morning. The nearest phone box was outside Crombie's newsagents in Crossley Street, about five minutes walk away. How she wished she had passed her driving test so she could borrow Liam's car and drive to Meridan Cross. She had a test date now but that was two weeks away in mid-December. Unfortunately that didn't help her present situation. Everything, she sighed, seemed to be against her.

When she reached the phone box it was already occupied and she filled in time by going into the shop and changing a pound note. She wanted to make sure she had a good supply of change as she had no idea how long her conversation would take. After a few minutes pacing up and down to keep warm, the middle aged woman occupant who seemed to have taken root in the box, emerged with a smile and walked off down the road. Ella dived in and fed her change into the slot. Heart in her mouth she began dialling.

Mary Evas walked into the hall, drawn away from the magazine she was reading by the persistence of the phone. 'Meridan Cross 254. Ella! Hello, how are you?

I'm told you're coming back for the weekend! You aren't?' She frowned into the phone. 'But I thought you wanted to see Niall. You've already seen him!' She frowned again. 'Where? Abbotsbridge? Ella none of this is making sense. I thought Niall was with the Miller boys last night.'

She stood for a moment, listening, then with a sharp intake of breath she placed the receiver on the hall table and climbed the narrow twisting stairs to the landing. Knocking on Niall's bedroom door she looked around it. He was sitting up in bed, his face serious.

'Ella's on the phone. What in heaven's name have you been up to?'

'I've finished with her.'

'Niall, have you gone completely mad?'

'No. It was a perfectly rational decision.'

'Rational? And how have you come to that conclusion?'

Niall gave a silent shrug, unwilling to be drawn into an argument.

'Niall!' Mary said, losing her patience. 'I don't know what's happened between the two of you, but I would like you to come down and sort it out at once!'

With a grunt of annoyance Niall got out of bed and pulled his dressing gown from the back of the door. Taking the stairs two at a time he reached the hall and picked up the receiver.

'Hello....Ella. What do you want? Yes, I did mean what I said. Yes, it's over. Why? Because I don't fit into your life any more, I'm surplus to requirements. Well I am aren't I? You've already got someone else. Yes you have, don't give me that friends rubbish. What? No, I don't want to meet you! What's the point? It's over. I don't want you any more, now please.......leave me alone will you?' He put the phone down heavily and turned to see his mother standing there, her arms folded an angry flush on her cheeks.

'Oh you are one pigheaded young man Niall O'Farrell!'

'Mum.' He walked over to his mother and gave her shoulder a reassuring squeeze. 'I know you liked her, but these six weeks away have given me time to think about our relationship. It wasn't working. Honestly it wasn't.' He looked down into her face, his eyes very blue. 'It was the distance....her mother.' he gave a sad shake of his head. 'But you know what the worst thing was? Turning up to see her last night and finding her with someone else. I knew then it really *was* all over.'

'I can't believe this Niall, I really can't.' Mary shook her head. 'I know Ella. She's not the sort of girl who'd two-time you. There's been some terrible misunderstanding. You need talk to her.'

Niall's expression hardened. 'There's no point.'

Mary watched him turn and run up the stairs, heard his bedroom door close and with a tired sigh went back to the sitting room and her magazine. Twenty minutes later the front door slammed and she heard the sound of car engine. Crossing to the window she saw the E-type disappearing down the lane.

'Oh Niall!' She said impatiently. 'Please, don't do this.'

Rachel was pulling lunch time pints for the Miller boys when Niall walked into the Somerset Arms. He had been in her thoughts ever since she had dropped him off at the pub to collect his car in the early hours of this morning. Returning home, she had let herself into the shop quietly, careful not to wake her mother. However, once in bed she found sleep impossible; memories of their earlier passionate encounter constantly replaying in her mind. But as daylight began to filter through the thin curtains covering her bedroom window, she had her first moment of doubt, wondering if she'd done the right thing letting him 'go all the way' as the girls at school used to call it. She couldn't bear him thinking she was easy or cheap, like Sheila Jenkins who lived in Field Way and walked around with a neck covered in love bites. But now all that worry was over; he was here and he was smiling.

'Hi,' she said. 'Can I get you a drink?'

'Thanks.' He pulled a handful of change from his jacket pocket. 'Just a half, please.'

She pulled a glass from the rack, pushed it under the nozzle and slowly eased back the pump handle.

He smiled at her and leaned across the bar. 'I can't stop thinking about you,' he whispered.

'Me too.' She felt colour filling her cheeks.

'Are you free tonight?' He asked as he picked up the glass and handed her the money.

'Oh Niall.' She said her heart pounding. 'Of course! Yes! Where? What time?

'The lane at the side of the pub. I'll pick you up at closing time.'

After phoning Jenny to let her know what had happened, Ella collected up the change carefully arranged in the phone box and put it back into her purse feeling miserable. How could he have been so rude to her? If he was feeling so bad about their relationship why hadn't he talked to her about it before? Not dump her like this without any warning. She pushed out of the phone box and began to walk back to Cambridge Crescent, determined that when she arrived she'd have a smile on her face. The last thing she wanted right now was her mother knowing what had happened.

'Ella! Wait!'

She turned at the sound of her name and saw Liam. Wrapped in a grey cashmere coat and black scarf, he ran the last few yards to catch her up.

'How is Niall?' He said as he reached her. 'Did you speak to him?'

'How do you know about Niall?' Ella eyed him warily.

'I ran into Tad Benedict. He was concerned about you.'

'I suppose that means Mother knows?'

He shook his head. 'Your secret's safe with me.'

'Thank you.'

'I gather the news isn't good?'

'I thought it was just temper last night.' She shook her head. 'But it wasn't. I don't understand why, but he simply doesn't want me around any more.'

Liam looked up at the deep blueness of the sky then at his stepdaughter. 'Look I know maybe it's easier said than done, but perhaps you should just back off for a while. Go out and enjoy yourself, have a good time. Leave him to kick his heels. Christmas is only a few weeks away.' He smiled. 'And as we all know, the festive season is a great time for kissing and making up.'

Ella gave a weak smile.

'Now then,' He gave her shoulder a comforting squeeze. 'Would you care to join me for a walk? I know a brilliant coffee shop where they do the most amazing Danish pastries. We could stop there afterwards. Discuss tactics over coffee and cake!'

'Tactics? What sort of tactics?'

'Ones to help you cope with your mother. I think you need some expert advice.'

'I do?'

'Yes. And I'm the expert.'

Saturday 25th November

Sheila Jenkins was standing in the bus shelter opposite Ross's garage waiting for the 239 to take her into Kingsford where she worked as an assistant on the Electrical Department in the local Woolworth. Since the station had closed she had been forced to get up twenty minutes earlier each morning to catch the bus. This change might have been most inconvenient had it not been for the arrival a month ago of David Sears, the new Assistant Store Manager. Twenty three, attractive, unattached. Now each working day was greeted with enthusiasm, the change to the pattern of her morning's journey into work a minor issue in comparison to the thrill of working alongside the irresistible David.

She was woken from her daydreams of passionate encounters in the stock room by the sound of hooves as a horse and rider approached slowly along the High Street. As they got closer she recognised Rachel Sylvester her fair hair tied back under her riding hat, the collar of her wax jacket turned up against the coldness of the morning.

'Morning Rach.' She called out as the rider passed. 'Bloody awful weather eh?'

On seeing her Rachel pulled the horse up and dismounted.

'Sheila!' She looked both surprised and pleased as she crossed over to the bus shelter. 'Just the person I wanted to see.'

'Me?' Sheila looked puzzled.

'Yes. Can I have a quick word?'

'What about?

'Family planning.' Rachel said quietly. 'I need some advice. For a friend.'

Saturday 2nd December

Richard Evas sat by the fire relaxing after his lunch. After spending all morning out in the cold with George Wootton looking over the bay gelding he had for sale and chatting generally about farming matters, the Lancashire hot pot awaiting him on his return had gone down very well.

He looked up as the sitting room door opened and Mary came in carrying a small tray of tea, which she set on a nearby table before sitting down to pour. Handing him a cup, she poured out one for herself.

'Guess what?' She said, offering him the sugar basin. 'Cousin Eric phoned this morning. He knows its short notice but he wondered whether we'd like to join him and Jeanette for Christmas, seeing they couldn't make the wedding. We'd go up on Christmas Eve and come back Boxing Day so you wouldn't be away from the farm too long.'

'Great idea.' Richard replied as he took a sip of his tea. 'I've never been away from Willowbrook at Christmas before, but, well, there's always a first time for everything and it should be fairly quiet here. Jake won't mind looking after things and I'm sure Niall will give him a hand.'

'Of course he will.' Mary looked delighted. 'Excellent! I'll call Eric back this evening.'

'But I might not be here.' Niall said bluntly when, on his return from the pub, his mother told him about their arrangements for Christmas.

'Oh? And why not?'

'Because I might be doing other things.'

'Such as?'

'Skiing.'

'Skiing.' She laughed. 'You can't ski.'

'That's the whole reason for going Mother. To learn. The Miller boys were talking in the pub at lunch time. They asked me if I'd like to spend Christmas in Austria. I said I might.' He shrugged. 'Not much to stay around here for is there, especially now you two will be sneaking off to Evesham.'

'Please don't take that tone with me Niall.' Mary looked offended.

'I'm sorry.' He apologised, stroking her shoulder with the kind of expression that was normally reserved for younger, more impressionable women. 'It's just things have been a bit stressful lately.'

'And whose fault is that? I had rather hoped you'd have come to your senses by now and patched things up with Ella.'

'Well you thought wrong.' He said stubbornly. 'Look, I know you mean well, but Ella and me, we really are over.'

'You can't be serious.'

'Sorry, I am.'

'Niall!'

'Mother!' He turned, his eyes challenging her as he reached the door, and then he smiled. 'Look, I'll be back late tonight. 'Don't wait up.' He disappeared into the hall.

'Are you seeing someone else?' Her suspicions aroused, Mary followed him.

'What if I am?' He gave a teasing grin as he pulled his jacket from the peg.

'Then,' Mary said icily. 'I would not approve and I would do everything in my power to discourage her, whoever she was.'

'You don't mean that.' He hesitated, his jacket half on.

'Yes I do. You've treated Ella very shabbily. In fact I think you've been an absolute pig! You didn't even stop to talk to her properly when you did it and now twenty four hours later you're busy chasing after some other little floozie who's taken your fancy!'

'Floozie? Shame on you Mum, making assumptions about people you have never seen.'

'Ah, so there is someone. Well, as I said before, I don't want her here. What you do out of this house is your own business, but I'll not have her under this roof. Whoever she is, she's not welcome!' She waved a cautionary finger at him. 'And woe betide you if I do find out her identity for I shall not hesitate to tell her about your appalling behaviour!'

Sunday 3rd December

Nina Harrison lay in bed thinking of Andy. It had been a dreadful night; she had said some awful things. Things she now regretted. She had also slapped his face. She regretted that too. But at the time she felt he deserved it, two timing her like that with Ella Kendrick. She looked at the luminous hands of her alarm clock. One thirty. She closed her eyes tightly, praying for unconsciousness. But all that came flooding into her mind were the events of Wednesday 15th September, 1966. The day they first met.

'Hey, it's him again.' Janet Moore nodded excitedly in the direction of the main foyer. 'That's the second time we've seen him today. Real dish isn't he?'

Nina looked up from her typewriter. From where she sat she had a clear view over the top of the counter and through the window of their office to the main hall, where two young men stood in front of the vending machine checking through the change they had just pulled from their pockets. She knew the object of Janet's attention was the darker of the two and that he was Bob Macayne's son Andy, at college on day release. She smiled to herself and turned her concentration to the invoice in front of her. If Janet thought she stood anything of a chance with someone like him she had to be mad. Hadn't anyone told her rich men's sons didn't date fat typists with peroxide hair from the college office?

'He's coming this way!' Janet's excited voice brought Nina's invoice typing to a halt. She watched as the older girl scuttled across to the rear of the office to check her mascara and tease out her bleach blonde shoulder length hair.

Tugging at her mini skirt she wiggled back to the counter to shuffle through some papers as she waited.

The office door opened and in walked Mick Taylor, Andy's stocky sandy haired companion. Nina knew him from the Mill where on several occasions he had bought her a drink and asked her to dance. She had a feeling he would like to ask her out but didn't see any point. She didn't fancy him even with his flash car and money, although looking at him now she decided with his build he'd suit the chunky Janet quite nicely.

Andy walked up to the counter, smiling at both of them. A half crown clattered onto its surface. 'Sorry to bother you girls, but have either of you got change for the coffee machine?'

Janet gave a silly grin and went in search of her purse. Ignoring him, Nina pulled out the completed invoice from her typewriter and began checking through it.

'I'm sure I've got loads of change in my purse.' She heard Janet say in an eager-to-please voice as she rummaged in her handbag. 'It's here somewhere!' As she spilled the contents of her handbag onto her desk Nina pulled her purse from her desk drawer and stood up.

'Change of half a crown is it?' She stared at him blatantly.

'Yes.' His eyes locked onto hers, then wandered down her body. He smiled slowly.

'Think I might be able to help then.' She walked slowly to the counter and unzipped the purse, pulling out four sixpences and two three-penny pieces. 'That do you?'

'Nicely thank you.' He picked up the money slowly. As Nina retrieved the half crown from the counter, Andy reached out and caught the ends of her pale ginger hair. 'Beautiful hair,' he said admiringly. 'Reminds me of Jane Asher's. Doing anything Saturday?'

'Might be.' Her eyes caught his again. She smiled.

'Come on...' He stared at her name badge. 'Nina. Stop playing hard to get. I'll be waiting for you outside the Town Hall. Saturday night, eight o'clock.' he hesitated as he reached the door. Oh, I hope you like Italian; we're eating at Ronaldo's.'

'Ronaldo's?' Janet stared opened mouthed as the door closed. 'That's the most expensive place in town!'

'Don't worry.' Nina looked at her with a sly smirk. 'I'm worth it.'

'I hope you realise that could have been me if you hadn't interfered!' Janet complained.

'He wanted change you couldn't find your purse. I was just being helpful.' Nina said with an innocent shrug.

'Helping yourself more like!' Janet replied sourly. 'Well I give you a week before he dumps you! Girls like you are ten a penny as far as he's concerned!'

'Is that so?' Nina stared at the plain overweight twenty one year old. 'Well we'll see about that won't we?'

The challenge which had come out of Janet's sour grape attitude was too much for Nina. Secretly she'd always fancied Andy Macayne. He'd been in college on day release for over a year now, but their paths had never crossed. She knew any girl he took out didn't stay with him for very long. He enjoyed the chase maybe? Or was he looking for something he hadn't yet found? She thought of some of his ex's. Julia Maynard, Felicity Hope, Shirley Reynolds, Marcia O'Dell. All nice girls from smart suburban homes. Girls who didn't have a clue about........she smiled.

She was right, of course. Sex had been the answer. The honeyed trap to catch and hold Andy Macayne. Of course he was still attracted to pretty women, even strayed occasionally, but she was always able to bring him back into line. A few anonymous threats would soon send any competition on its way. She had even punched one girl, although she was careful to cover her tracks to make sure Andy knew nothing. She was proud of her reputation, knowing it was the key to getting her exactly what she wanted in life.

Six months passed and she was still there, a permanent fixture in his life. He bought her expensive clothes, took her abroad on holiday. She ignored the jibes from her older sister Elaine, putting it down to envy. And she was going to be even more envious. Because if things went the way she hoped they would, Andy was going to be her passport out of the Parkway Estate

A year on she was dreaming of engagement rings. Of becoming Mrs Andrew Macayne. She visualised the beautiful house with her own car and a monthly clothes allowance. A far cry from her ordinary life on a run down council estate. Of course, the one big stumbling block was Andy's father. He did not approve of their relationship. Her father was one of his employees. She knew what that meant. But she could wait. After his twenty-first birthday in October Andy would not only come into money, he would be able to make his own choices.

Then Ella Kendrick arrived at college. A pretty girl, irritatingly calm and confident. Someone from Andy's world. She had known right from the start when she'd seen the expression on Andy's face as he greeted her that day in the refectory she had a problem on her hands. Every other girl who'd threatened her relationship with Andy had been easy to defeat. They'd come from the present. Ella, however, was different; she came from the past, from a time Nina knew nothing about. So her relationship with Andy was an unknown quantity and that made her feel decidedly edgy. The added problem was Ella's mother. If she so much as laid a finger on her she knew she would end up having to deal with Mel Carpenter. And she was not the sort of woman you crossed without getting into big trouble.

Of course Andy had been quick to calm her fears, to assure her it was the briefest of meetings that she meant nothing. In fact he seemed to go out of his way to reinforce his commitment to her with flowers and a long weekend in London. And last week when he had to cancel their cinema date because of a last minute work commitment he'd been press ganged into by his father, he'd presented her with a beautiful gold bracelet.

Admiring it as she stood queuing for coffee in the refectory a few days later she felt just a little embarrassed about her paranoia. Until, that was, she heard someone behind her talking about the incident at the Forum. It made her feel sick and angry knowing her fears had been justified after all. Worse still, he had not only two timed her, he had lied to her as well.

She knew he was having a drink at the Red Lion with the boys this evening and made her way there determined to confront him and show him up for the liar he was. The mistake she made was deciding to make that argument public. Frustratingly, Andy simply sat there surrounded by his friends calmly listening as she faced him with her accusations. As she spoke, she noticed gathering amusement in the faces of those around him, most of whom she knew disliked her, and realised she couldn't stay there any more. She had to make one last gesture and leave quickly. So she pulled the gold bracelet from her wrist, threw it in his face and ran out of the pub.

He caught up with her in the car park, gripping her arm tightly as he tried to reason with her. Frustrated by her inability to free herself from him, she lashed out, shouting that she hated him and never wanted to see him again. Her hand connected in a violent slap with the side of his face just as a car turned into the car park, catching them both in the blaze of its headlights. Andy let go of her. 'You've got it all wrong Nina, all wrong,' was all he had said before walking away with his hand pressed against his left cheek. As he reached the door of the Red Lion, Mick Taylor came out. Giving them both a puzzled look Mick zipped up his jacket and crossed over to the waiting car. It was only then she realised Jack Taylor was behind the wheel with Jenny sitting in the back. By Monday everyone in college would know what had happened, including Ella Kendrick.

She sat up in bed, held her head in her hands and groaned. How could she have been so stupid, so impulsive? In a moment's madness she had let her temper get the better of her and wrecked everything she had been working for. She didn't know how she was going to do it, but she had to get him back somehow because if she lost him she also lost her dream. And without that her life meant nothing.

Monday 4th December

The next morning at breakfast Nina put her problems on hold as she ate her cereal and toast and chatted to her older sister Elaine, who had called in to drop her baby off on her way to work at Turners, the haberdashery in Kingsford. Since husband Barry had been sacked from Stewarts Engineering works recently she had become the main breadwinner. This morning she wanted to speak to her father, hoping he might be able to put in a good word for him at Taylor Macayne.

Elsie Harrison, a small, thin, anxious looking woman wrapped in a green apron was busy frying bread and tomatoes in a battered, blackened frying pan. She turned her head towards the door at the sound of approaching footsteps and flipped over the two slices of bread as her husband Ron entered the room. He was a short barrel-chested man with well Brylcreemed ginger hair, a coating of stubble gracing his chin. He wore brown twill trousers and black braces, his shirt open at the neck. Bleary from a night's drinking at the Bunch of Grapes, he gazed at them all; his wife at the cooker, the two girls sitting opposite each other, heads together talking. His eyes fixed on Nina wearing a black and camel roll neck dress which he knew probably cost more than he earned in a week. The thought of how she came by it irritated him intensely.

'I want a word with you!' He said curtly, looking at her as he took his place at the table. 'What time did you call that last night?'

'Half eleven.' Nina answered carelessly, stuffing the last piece of toast into her mouth. 'Is there a problem?'

'Dad can I talk to you about Barry?' Elaine interrupted, looking at her watch and realising she had to be going soon.

'There is when you're making enough noise to wake the bloody dead!' Ron said angrily, ignoring his elder daughter. 'No consideration for others, that's you! Treat this house like a blasted hotel!'

'I do not!' Nina protested. 'I do my share.'

'She does too.' Elsie came to her daughter's rescue as she left her frying pan to dump a cup of tea in front of him. 'She washes up and irons sometimes.'

'Does she now!' He sniffed disbelievingly. 'Never noticed it myself!' He glared at Nina. 'All I've seen is the mess she leaves behind her when she's tarting herself up to go out! Bloody bathroom was in a right state the other night. All damp towels and steam running down the walls! You could open a window you know!'

'Oh give it a rest Dad!' Get off me back! If you want to do something useful, talk to our Elaine.' Nina nodded towards her sister, eager to distract her father. 'She wants to ask you about Barry'.

'Does she now?' He said with a disinterested glance, reaching across the table to help himself to sugar.

'Ron! Listen, will you!' Elsie Harrison turned away from the frying pan to glare at her husband.'Our Elaine's hung on specially to see you this morning. She'll have to be off in a minute!'

Elaine nodded and encouraged by her mother opened her mouth to begin her well rehearsed plea on her husband's behalf.

'I'll do no such thing woman!' Ron growled. 'I'm dealing with this one at the minute.' He stabbed his teaspoon at his younger daughter. 'It seems to me Miss that you've been getting a bit above yourself since you've been going with that waste of space old man Macayne calls a son. There's rules on behaviour in this house. And slamming in at half past eleven isn't one of them.'

Elaine closed her eyes, trying to suppress the frustration she was feeling. Wearily she got to her feet. 'I have to go Mum or I'll be late.'

'What?' Ron looked at her as if he hadn't a clue what she was talking about.

'I came to see you about Barry, Dad.'

'Barry? I'm not interested in bloody Barry.' His heavy eyebrows knitted together in a frown. 'There's another great waste of space!'

'Oh for goodness sake!' Elaine snatched up her bag, gesturing hopelessly at her mother. 'What's the use?'

'None at all,' Nina said smirking at her sister, 'when you're dealing with someone like old Adolph Hitler here!'

'Don't you dare speak to me like that!' Ron lunged across the table at his daughter. 'You little cow!'

Nina jumped to her feet laughing, kissed her mother and went to collect her coat from the hall. Elaine followed.

'See you tonight Mum.' Elaine said, glancing at her father's angry red face as she left.

'You'll get yourself into serious trouble one day.' She said as she caught Nina up. 'Don't you realise that now you've hopped it he'll only take it out on Mum?'

'I'm already in serious trouble.'

'Oh what now?'

'Andy. He did something awful and I lost my temper and slapped him. I wish I hadn't. I think it might have finished things between us.' She bit her lip. 'The thing is, I want him back but I haven't got a clue what to do.'

'For goodness sake, ditch him Nina.' Elaine shook her head impatiently. 'Can't you see? He's just using you.'

'No he isn't. He's going to propose soon.' Nina said confidently.

'You can't marry *him*!'

'Why not?' Nina bristled.

'He's not our sort!'

'Well he's my sort!'

'Don't tell me you're in *love*?'

'What if I am.'

'With his money more like and the flash clothes he buys you.'

'So, what's wrong with that? Loads of people marry for money.' Nina shrugged. 'Better than marrying for love and ending up in a two up two down with a washed up failure like your Barry!'

'How dare you say that!' Elaine grabbed her sister by the arm. 'You spiteful little cow! Apologise at once!'

'I will not! I don't say sorry to anyone!' Nina sneered at her sister, wrenching herself free. 'Never have, never will!'

'Well,' Elaine said backing away an unpleasant smirk on her face. 'With an attitude like that little sister, I'd say you haven't got a hope in hell of getting him back' And catching sight of the approaching bus she headed for the stop leaving Nina standing there alone on the pavement.

On the other side of town Bob Macayne sat at the heavy oak dining room table stirring his coffee. Taking a sip he replaced the cup in the saucer, shook out the folds of the *Abbotsbridge News* and began searching for the planning applications. He looked casually over the top of his glasses, half his attention still on the paper, as the door opened and his son came into the room.

Andy walked over to the dresser, lifting the lids on the serving dishes, helping himself to bacon, scrambled egg and fried bread. Then crossing to the table he sat down opposite his father.

Bob picked up his cup again, frowning in concentration at the paper. 'It says here Stewarts are planning to build a technical lab by the river, I must give Gerald a ring,' He said, glancing up at Andy. 'Christ who did that to you!'

'It's nothing.' Andy shrugged.

'First nothing I've ever known to have fingers.' Bob said looking at his son's cheek. 'She did that didn't she? She's got the same damned evil temper as that father of hers.'

'I told you it's nothing.' Andy insisted, pouring himself coffee.

'Well I hope you finished with her.' Bob said, folding his paper and laying it on the table. 'I wouldn't let any woman do that to me.'

'Actually if it makes you feel any better she finished with me. She's convinced I'm having a thing with Ella Kendrick, because of what happened at the Rotary Ball.'

'And are you?'

'No, she's just a friend that's all.'

Bob drained his coffee cup and returned it to its saucer. 'Personally I think someone like Ella would be very good for you Andy.'

'She already has a boyfriend Dad.'

'*Had* a boyfriend Andy. Past tense.' Bob pulled off his glasses and looked at his son intently. 'After what you told me about the other night I would think that relationship is now well and truly over.'

'Yes, well I saw Ella at college this week and she says it isn't. And after this bust up with Nina, I think it's probably best if I keep out of the way for a while.'

'On the contrary, I think sending a nice bouquet of flowers to Ella and inviting her to dinner is what you should be doing.' Bob said, putting his glasses away. 'Fate has offered you a golden opportunity lad, grab it with both hands.' He stood up, ready to leave. 'Andy, Nina Harrison is bad news. That mark on your face constitutes common assault, don't you realise that? As I said, she's just like her old man. His filthy temper has got him into a lot of trouble over the years. Take my advice; get her out of your life once and for all. She's not for you, never has been and never will be!'

Mary was sitting at the breakfast table buttering toast when Niall walked into the kitchen.

'Good morning.'

She looked at him, noting the pale growth of stubble on his chin. 'Why do I get the funniest feeling that you've just got in?'

'Probably because I have.'

As she helped herself to marmalade he pulled out a chair and sat down opposite her. 'Where've you been all night? With your new girlfriend?'

'Mum! Please don't.' He shook his head. 'If you must know there is no one, I was winding you up. I know I shouldn't have and I'm sorry. Actually I went out with the Miller Boys to a new club they've found.' he grabbed a spare cup and saucer and pulled the cosy off the teapot. 'We were late back so I decided maybe it was best to crash out at Saddlers End. Save disturbing you and Richard.'

'Why the sudden thoughtfulness?' Mary eyed him warily.

'It's the least I could do.' He shrugged as he poured the tea. 'In fact I've been thinking maybe I should get out from under your feet, leave you and Richard in peace. Become a bit more responsible for myself.'

'And how do you intend to do that?'

'Fox Cottage is empty.' He pushed the cosy over the teapot and reached for the milk jug. 'I don't suppose Richard would consider letting it out to me would he?'

'I don't know.' Mary frowned, trying to visualise a life without her son under the same roof.

'I think it would be a good move.'

'How's that?'

'Well, beside the independence, there's the security angle. Doggy said he caught the tramp who's been living in Hundred Acre trying the front door the other day. Sent him packing,' He smiled as he stirred his tea, 'With Toby's teeth in seat of his trousers.'

Mary considered his words as she offered him toast and pushed the marmalade in his direction. 'You could be right,' she said, after a moment's silence. 'From what you're saying it does look as though having someone living there would be useful. Although I take it I'd still be expected to supply your meals and do your laundry.'

'Why break the habits of a lifetime?' He gave her a heart breaking smile.

'To be sure,' she said, infuriated yet amused by his cheek. 'You're as full of the blarney as your Grandfather O'Malley was!'

'Is that a yes then?'

She hesitated, her eyes meeting his. He was so like Sam in every way and because of that she found it hard to deny him anything. 'Oh all right! I'll talk to Richard about it this evening.'

THIRTEEN

Tuesday 5th December

Mick and Andy had come to Sutton's Builders Merchants that morning with a list of items needed for work being carried out on four town houses in Gladstone Terrace.

Leaving Andy to load the van, Mick had gone back inside for a quick word with the owner, Rick Sutton. As he was securing the tailgate of the flatbed Andy suddenly heard a familiar voice behind him.

'Hello Andy, can we talk?'

He turned around to see Nina standing there, hands pushed into the pockets of her navy reefer jacket.

'There's nothing to say.' He said abruptly, ramming the bolt home and securing the tarpaulin.

'Your face!' Her eyes opened wide with surprise.

She closed the gap between them, reaching out to touch the bruising around his eye.

'Just piss off Nina!' He said angrily, knocking her hand away.

'Please,' she stopped, watching him warily. 'I came to apologise. I was crazy, out of my head; I didn't know what I was doing. I'm truly sorry.'

'It's too late.'

'But you know I love you Andy, I really do.'

'This is love?' He pointed to his cheek.

'I was angry. I thought you didn't want me any more.'

'I don't! Not after this.' He looked at her for a moment, pausing to gather his thoughts then gave a careless shrug. 'You've only got yourself to blame.'

Turning his back on her, he walked around to the front of the flat bed and tugged open the cab door.

'You don't mean that!' She trailed after him, unease in her eyes. 'You need me, I know you do. I admit I over-reacted but I realise now you'll soon tire of Ella Kendrick, just like you have all the rest.'

'Nina!' He turned on her angrily. 'There is no me and Ella Kendrick. And if you are prepared to do this,' he pointed to his face. 'On the strength of rumour

150

and gossip then I'm well rid of you! I've put up with your aggressiveness in the past, but no more! It's finished!' And hauling himself behind the wheel he slammed the door firmly shut.

'You can't do this to me!' She shouted angrily, banging her fist against the glass. 'You have to take me back!'

Winding down the window he looked at her, his eyes cold and hard. 'Wrong. I don't have to do anything. Just look at you, standing there, threatening me again. You're unstable.'

'I'm not. Andy.....please.....' Nina stood there shaking her head, her hand at her face, tears brimming in her eyes. 'All I want is another chance.'

Just at that moment the main doors of Sutton's opened and Mick walked out whistling. When he saw Nina he hesitated for a moment, his gaze going from her to the van and then back to her again.

'Come on!' Andy leaned out of the window and shouted at him. 'They're waiting for this stuff back on site. We're late already!'

Mick ran to the van stopping for a moment as he reached Nina. 'Are you OK?' He said, touching her shoulder gently.

'Leave her Mick!'

Mick hovered for a second, torn between comfort and abandonment. Another shout from Andy, threatening to drive off without him stirred him into action. He ran to the van, pulled open the door and climbed in. Within seconds the vehicle was gone, leaving Nina standing in the car park, alone with her misery. Elaine's words, although making her realise what she needed to do to get him back, had come too late.

Wednesday 6th December

Liam arrived home at his usual time of 5.30 p.m., turned his key in the front door and walked in. The hall welcomed him, well furnished and comforting, his cocoon from the daily grind of work. He set his briefcase beside the telephone table and took off his coat and scarf.

From the kitchen a delicious smell of cooking wafted. He inhaled deeply. The unmistakeable smell of beef casserole - Mrs Harris had been working her magic again. At once the day's problems dissolved; the drawings which had arrived late, the cancelled meeting, all were pushed aside as he entered the lounge, looking forward to a delicious meal followed by comfortable evening by the fire.

He could hear the raised voices as soon as he opened the door and sighed inwardly, wondering what had caused mother and daughter to clash yet again.

Mel was in the kitchen, a flowery apron wrapped around her waist, presiding over pans of vegetables bubbling away on the cooker. Ella was leaning in the dining room doorway, her back to him. They were arguing. Mel suddenly saw Liam and smiled.

'Hello darling, dinner won't be long.'

Ella turned and smiled too but he could see she was upset.

He looked at them both. 'Would you like me to go out and come in again?'

Ella opened her mouth but Mel squeezed past her into the dining room. 'Darling we were discussing Christmas arrangements that's all.'

'I didn't realise we'd made any.'

'We have now. Mrs Harris won't be here so I thought it would be nice to get away to a hotel. With roaring fires, good food, comfortable surroundings and just relax for three or four days. I've managed to book us in to a hotel in the Cotswolds. The White Hart, near Moreton in Marsh. It's just the thing you need.' She enthused. 'A break away from Abbotsbridge and the business.'

'Great! I'm all for that.' Liam nodded amicably. He turned to look at Ella. 'What's the problem? Don't you think you'd enjoy the break? I'm sure there would be local stables where you could hire a horse and go riding if you wanted to get out from under our feet.'

Ella shook her head.

Liam sighed. 'Oh Ella, come on, it's our first Christmas together as a family, you must come.'

'I haven't been invited. Apparently it's just you and mother.'

'Mel?' Liam turned to look at his wife.

Mel, eyes wide with innocence, offered upturned palms in a placatory gesture. 'It's not my fault. I thought she was off to Meridan Cross. How was I to know Laura was going to Madeira?'

'Well just phone the hotel and book an extra room.'

'I can't. It's full.'

'Right,' Liam took a deep breath. 'If we all can't go then we'll just have to book somewhere else.'

'What! Ten days before Christmas!' Mel stood there indignantly. 'I was lucky to get our room! You can't make me cancel! You just can't! I work hard all year! I deserve this! I really do!'

Ella saw the change begin almost instantly. The trembling lip, the loud sniffs, the merest hint of tears in the corners of her mother's eyes. This was Mel at her very best. An Oscar winning performance which would guarantee to get her what she wanted.

But Liam was having none of it. He raised a warning hand towards his wife. 'Mel, please. No tears. This is outrageous. You can't leave Ella alone at Christmas and that is that!'

'Liam.' Mel gave an indignant sniff. 'I'm not quite as brutal as you seem to think. Ella won't be alone, I've made separate arrangements for her. We just hadn't got around to discussing them.'

'What arrangements?' Liam and Ella said in one voice.

'I've spoken to Bob. He says he'd be very happy for Ella to spend Christmas at Everdene.'

'Bob Macayne?' Liam said angrily. 'Ella's not some pet Labrador you can farm out for the holiday. What if she doesn't want to go?'

'Of course she wants to go!'

'No I don't.' Ella joined the argument.

'But Bob would love to have you darling and be sensible, there isn't anywhere else.'

'Yes there is.' Ella replied defiantly. 'I can go to the Taylors.'

'The Taylors?' Disapproval settled itself stiffly on Mel's face. 'I don't think so Ella!'

'Well Nick's going to be there....'

'Nick is spending Christmas with the Taylors? But you told me he was going to be in North Wales with friends.'

'Did I? I meant before Christmas. He's back here for Christmas Day. You must have misunderstood.'

'But I could have sworn you said...' Mel looked at Liam then back at Ella, her powerful stance diminishing suddenly. Her son was spending Christmas in the Taylor household and she knew nothing about it. It was unthinkable and she knew all too well he'd done it deliberately to upset her.

'It doesn't matter!' She said with an aggrieved wave of her hand. 'Nothing matters. You can all spend Christmas where you like! I really don't care.' And with a huge gasp of indignation she disappeared back into the kitchen closing the door behind her.

'You didn't have to do this you know.'

'Nonsense, I wanted to, I'm enjoying myself. Honestly.'

Mick grinned happily as he put the drinks on the table and sat down opposite Nina. 'Well,' he said after taking a mouthful of beer and setting his glass down. 'it's nice to see you looking more like your old self.'

'I've you to thank for that.' She gave him a grateful smile. 'Asking me out for a drink. It's cheered me up no end.'

'Good.' Mick felt his face colouring with embarrassment under her gaze. 'Personally I think you've had a pretty raw deal Nina, I've known Andy for years; he always been easy come easy go with people's feelings.'

'None of this would have happened if he hadn't got involved with that......witch.'

'It's nothing to do with Ella.' Mick said gently. 'He wasn't with her. He went on his own at his father's request, arrived late and walked into a full scale row going on between Ella and her boyfriend. He was only trying to help her. I don't think for a moment it was anything more than that. You and Andy have just had another of your spats that's all, give it a few days, he'll come back.'

'I don't know whether I want him back.' She gave a sigh and looked at him from under her long lashes. 'The more I think about it the more convinced I am that I might be happier with someone like you Mick.'

'Me?' Mick said, with a nervous laugh, embarrassment reddening his face again. 'You can't be serious.'

'Mick Taylor,' She laughed, slipping her hand over his. 'I've never been more serious about anything. I'd be really proud to go out with someone like you.'

'You're joking!' Mick swallowed hard, aware she had moved herself closer to him and the air was now filled with the heady fragrance of her perfume.

'No I mean it!' She nodded enthusiastically. 'You know I've always admired you. I could never understand why girls weren't falling all over themselves to go out with you. You're such a good sort, honest, reliable....'

'You left out boring.' Mick added with a laugh as he brought his glass to his lips.

'Don't be like that.' She looked offended. 'You should be proud of what you are. Look at Andy, selfish, spoilt, arrogant.'

'Also handsome, sexy and fun to be with.' Mick offered.

'See, you're doing it again. Putting yourself down. I bet you'd be just as much fun on a date.'

Mick shook his head and laughed. 'No chance. I wouldn't even come close.'

'Let me be the judge of that.'

'What do you mean?'

'You can take me out tomorrow night and we'll find out just how boring you really are, or aren't as the case may be.'

'But where would we go?'

'Anywhere. Cinema, a meal. Or just a drink. Haven't you dated girls before?'

'Of course I have.'

'Well then.' She gave a flirtatious laugh. 'I'm a girl, use your imagination.'

Saturday 16th December

'I'm not sure about this Niall. Are you sure no one will find out?' Rachel asked following cautiously behind Niall as he groped for the light switch. He stood there smiling at her as the room was bathed in a warm light.

'Of course not. Fox Cottage is far enough off the beaten track. We're quite private up here. Do you like it?' He laughed. 'It's a damned sight more comfortable than your Mum's Morris Minor.'

'It's wonderful.' Rachel nodded as she gazed around the room; colourful rugs, comfy settees, pictures on the wall and a welcoming fire in the hearth.

'How much longer are we going to have to keep this secret from your mother?' she said, unbuttoning her coat, 'You really should tell her about us. Or are you ashamed of me?'

'Of course not, my darling.' Niall replied, taking her coat and draping it over one of the settees. 'It's just that mother hasn't taken my split with Ella very well. She still thinks it's all a silly storm in a teacup. She's convinced herself that we'll get back together again. Not a day goes by without it being mentioned and with Richard being Ella's grandfather it puts me in a very difficult position. The worst thing I can do at the moment is tell her about us. Give her a little time to adjust. Another month should do it.' He touched her cheek gently. 'I promise faithfully that as soon as the time's right I'll be proud to take you home, but until then it's still going to have to stay our secret, I'm afraid.'

Rachel looked disappointed.

'Look cheer up, there's something I want to ask you.'

'What?' She gave him a half interested frown.

'Will you come away with me at Christmas?'

'Where?'

'Lyme Regis. I thought it would be wonderful, just the two of us in a small romantic hotel, waking up in together in a big bed. Please, say yes.'

'I'd really love to.' She made a face. 'But we're going to Auntie Ethel's.'

'Sounds like fun.'

'It is if you're their age. They talk about the War mostly and get squiffy on cheap sherry.' She smiled. 'I really want to be with you, but....'

'You just leave things to me. I've an idea.'

'Have you? What?'

'How about if I organised an invitation for you, to a party held by someone very important. Someone that would impress your mother so much she'd have no trouble letting you off Christmas in Taunton.'

'Niall.' She looked at him uncomfortably. 'What are you up to?'

'Wait and see.'

'You won't get into any trouble will you?'

'Rachel.' Niall silenced her, placing a finger gently against her lips. 'Stop worrying, just be ready to pack your case.'

'I'm sorry, I can't help it.' She smiled up at him, her eyes blue, her hair a pale blonde cloud around her shoulders. 'I love you so much, I really do.'

'Come here.' He said, pulling her to him and kissing her mouth gently as his fingers unzipped her dress. 'Do you know what I've been thinking about all day?'

She shook her head, feeling a tingle of anticipation as the dress fell to the floor and she felt his fingers at her back, releasing the clasp of her bra.

'Making love to you.' He said huskily as he bent his head to her breasts and ran his tongue tantalisingly over each nipple. 'Right here, in front of the fire.'

Tuesday 19th December

Liam Carpenter walked through to the kitchen carrying a tray with the remnants of the lunch which Mrs Harris had prepared for him. As he deposited it on the draining board the back door opened and Mel walked in, carrying the results of her morning's shopping trip. Liam looked over the top of his glasses at her purchases.

'More necessary items?' He asked, wondering what she could possibly need when she had a wardrobe bursting at the seams with fashionable clothes.

'Everything's necessary Liam!' She eyed him severely. 'You do want me to look my best I hope?'

'Of course, Mel.'

Dropping the bags in one corner of the kitchen she pulled her gloves off, looking at him in a speculative manner, wondering at the reason behind the sudden need to query her spending.

'Is there a problem? Do I detect a need for the tightening of belts?   Is business bad? Have your father's care bills become even more extortionate?'

'Just having a joke with you that's all.' He said, deliberately ignoring the jibe about his father as he homed in on the carriers and boxes.

'What have you bought then? Come on, let me see.'

She snatched them up defensively. 'You are querying my spending aren't you?'

'No I'm not, I'm taking an interest. Christmas is coming and I don't want to go out and buy you something you already have.'

The thought of elegantly wrapped gifts melted her resistance and she hastily began to pull various items out of their bags. A new dress for the New Year's Ball, shoes to match, various items of underwear, make up and perfume.

'Very nice.' He said as she held the green chiffon against herself.

They were interrupted suddenly by the banging of the side gate into the rear garden. Ella came through the back door, breathless and smiling.

'You're early.' Mel said looking up at the kitchen clock.

'I took the afternoon off.' Ella stood there, leaning against the back door still out of breath from her run.

'Well?' Liam looked at her inquisitively.

Mel noted the conspiratorial glances which passed between her husband and daughter and felt a stab of annoyance. Something was going on, something she had been excluded from. And like their united fronts during arguments, this sort of thing seemed to be happening all too frequently lately. Irritably, she gathered up her shopping and left the kitchen.

Liam, his eyes fixed on Ella, did not even seem to notice his wife's departure. 'Is it good news?'

Ella nodded, reaching into her jacket pocket, producing a folded piece of paper.

'Yes, I've done it! I've passed my driving test!'

'Right, let me get my coat.' He walked briskly into the hall. 'Mel!' he shouted up the stairs, 'Ella's passed her test, isn't that good news? We're just going out for a short spin in the Rover.'

When there was no response, he shrugged and smiled to himself. Too busy putting all that shopping away he decided as he came back into the kitchen, tossing the car keys to Ella.

As she stood at the bedroom window, watching the Rover move carefully down the road Mel's resentfulness grew. How dare Liam do this! Why couldn't he have told her that Ella was taking her test today? In fact why couldn't Ella have mentioned it herself? She still hadn't got over the fact she hadn't known about Nick's Christmas plans. More and more she realised things weren't going at all the way she had thought they would. Her children were selfish and uncaring, thinking only of themselves. Unhappily she turned from the window and looked at the dress which lay in its open box nestling among the soft sheets of tissue. Picking it up carefully she walked over to her mirror and held it up against herself, dreaming not only of being out on the dance floor but having the comforting feel of Bob Macayne's arms around her.

Margaret Sylvester picked up the phone, silencing the ring which had pulled her from the top of her step ladder where she had been stacking boxes of Corn Flakes.

'Meridan Cross 469.'

'Mrs Sylvester?' A well educated young female voice responded.

'Yes.' She answered cautiously.

'It's Natasha, Brigadier Hesketh-Maurice's daughter from Higher Padbury. I know Rachel through Young Farmers.'

'Oh hello,' Margaret immediately remembered the attractive young redhead who sometimes came into the shop.

'Look I know it's short notice Mrs Sylvester, but we're having a bit of a do here at the Manor on Christmas Day, starting around four. Daddy said to invite all the YF members so I'm ringing to ask whether Rachel would like to come.'

'Oh dear,' Margaret hesitated. 'She won't be here.'

'That is a shame.' The voice carried a ring of disappointment. 'We're having a buffet and fireworks and there's dancing too. She's would be more than welcome to stay over, I could run her back home on Boxing Day.'

'The problem is, we're in Taunton over Christmas with my sister.' As soon as she'd said it, Margaret felt pathetic. How could she possibly turn down an opportunity like this? A chance for Rachel to mix with people who mattered. To have a taste of the high life. It could only do her good.

'Oh well. Never mind.'

'No! Wait. It's fine. She'd love to come.'

'Are you sure?'

'Yes, positive. She's only young once after all, and I'm sure she won't miss our company. Not when she'll be having such a good time.'

'That's wonderful, you're so kind Mrs Sylvester. Tell her I'll be in touch later in the week to finalise the details will you?'

'Yes, of course. Goodbye. And thank you.' Margaret put down the phone feeling breathless and excited. Christmas with the Hesketh-Maurice's. Just wait until Rachel came home.

Natasha Hesketh-Maurice, sitting in the window of Fox Cottage, replaced the telephone receiver.

'She's agreed.' She said with a smile. 'In fact she's over the moon. Now the rest is up to you.'

'Thanks 'Tash.' Niall, sitting next to her, gave her a hug. 'I owe you one!'

Friday 22nd December

Tad Benedict was discovered in the early fifties. Billed as Britain's answer to Guy Mitchell, he spent two weeks at number one with *The Londonderry Air* in the summer of 1954. But by 1956 Bill Hayley was in the charts, rock and roll had arrived and everything was changing. Realising he wasn't a well known household name like Jimmy Young or Dickie Valentine who would sustain their careers alongside the new arrivals, he knew he needed to move on; to diversify. And so, with the money he had earned from his stage performances and chart successes he moved first into the hotel business, buying up property and renovating. His hotels were comfortable and informal, each with a small, intimate lounge bar where live music would entertain guests for the evening. Occasionally, when he visited, he would be persuaded to sing, but normally he just loved to sit and listen; jazz and blues his favourite.

His next venture was the Mill. His first idea for the old stone building's use was as tea rooms, attracting tourists and locals who wanted a light snack in a pleasant environment with the additional option of taking a rowing boat out on the river. But it was a seasonal business, packed in summer and virtually empty in the winter. When the numbers dwindled he looked at the building again and wondered what he could do to generate more permanent income.

About that time he had gone into entertainment management in a small way. One of the bands on his books were a local group called the Bus Stops and although Tad was realistic enough to know he had not got star quality on his hands, they were competent musicians and had been invited on several occasions to support front page names headlining at the Winter Gardens in Weston Super Mare. It was when Tad travelled with them on one occasion and saw the energy and enthusiasm in an audience full of young people obviously hooked on popular music that he realised where the Mill's future lay.

He had heard about the clubs in London; places where people could come to dance and drink. Abbotsbridge had nothing like this, nor was there anything resembling it for at least a thirty mile radius. Weekend dances in local town or village halls with a band and mobile disco was the extent of provincial entertainment. There was a gap in the market and a youth culture out there with money burning a hole in its pocket. And so The Mill was born.

It was essentially a club for the young, a place with good music, food and alcohol. Tad spent time in London, visiting the clubs, looking at décor and lighting and listening to the kind of music played. All this research was used to make the Mill a completely unique venue. He managed to entice a young, ambitious DJ from Bristol with a competitive salary and the offer of a chance to lead the field in a new club which he was confident was set to be the talk of the area. After delays created by the local planners and the hospitalisation of his electrical contractor with a broken leg, the club eventually opened to the public in the summer of 1965.

It was an instant success. As he had predicted, people flocked there, there was nothing like it anywhere in the area. It became the in place. The club everyone wanted membership of; famous for its welcome, easy atmosphere and good music.

Jenny, Issy and Ella were part of the regular Friday and Saturday night crowd. Tonight, however, was a little more special than usual as Issy had insisted they had to celebrate Ella passing her driving test. However, for Ella the celebrations were overshadowed by the fact that she had still not resolved her problems with Niall. Secretly keeping in touch with Mary she had learned that he had decided to go to Austria with the Miller boys over Christmas, ruining any plans she'd had for reconciliation.

Things appeared to have gone rapidly downhill from that moment. Her mother's decision about Christmas had come as a complete bombshell. This coupled with Willowbrook being off limits and her grandmother flying out to Madeira made her feel she'd have no option but spend Christmas with the Macaynes after all. The last thing she wanted to do. However, when she told Jenny her rash comments about spending Christmas with her family, Jenny had simply smiled and said that was OK, her mum and dad wouldn't mind and she would be more than welcome. 'Besides, you don't want to go up to Everdene for Christmas.' She'd added. 'It's the most miserable place on earth!'

They found a table near the stage. Issy bought three vodka and tonics. They touched glasses, toasted Ella's success behind the wheel. They discussed the week at college. Whether they liked the colour of Annabel Langley's dress. Gave their usual marks out of ten to the group of young men leaning on the bar. By her third vodka Ella was starting to relax, and then.

'Would you like to dance?' A touch on her left shoulder caused her to turn around. A young fresh faced man in his early twenties wearing a grey button down shirt and black cords was hovering. He was the one Issy had given a nine out of ten to only moments ago.

'Sure.' Aware of Issy's amused eyes on her she smiled and got up.

The club had now come alive to Martha Reeves and the Vandellas *'Jimmy Mack'* and it seemed as if almost everyone was on the floor. Ella's partner told her, as best he could above all the noise, that his name was Dave and that he lived in Abbotsbridge and worked as a draughtsman at Stewarts. Ella smiled and nodded, trying to show an interest and then the beat caught her and without warning she found her feet moving and her spirits lifting. When the music eventually stopped she thanked him and was about to return to her table when a strong arm caught her and pulled her back.

'Not so fast darling.'

The young man, with long dark hair and sideboards pulled her roughly to him, his arms tightening around her like a vice, his breath smelling heavily of alcohol. The tempo had slowed suddenly and the first chords of Long John

Baldry's *'Let the Heartaches Begin'* came through the speakers. He looked down into Ella's face, his smile revealing uneven teeth as his grip tightened. Ella pulled against him, angry at his rudeness and casual treatment of her.

'Let me go!' She said trying to break his grip.

'God you're a stroppy bird!' The stranger said impatiently. 'All I asked for was a bloody dance.'

'I don't recall you asking for anything!' Ella reacted angrily. 'You just grabbed me; no one treats me like that.'

'Oh well just hark at you! And just who do you think you are?' He threw back his head and began to laugh loudly as they circled the dance floor, Ella imprisoned tightly in his grip.

'Come on Pete, that's enough.'

Someone appeared beside them, his face obscured by darkness. Pete released her immediately, muttering something under his breath as he walked away.

'Sorry about that, are you all right?' As the music stopped and the lights went up she found herself face to face with Andy Macayne sporting the black eye all of Abbotsbridge Tech. was talking about.

'Fine, thank you.'

'Pete's one of Dad's brickies.' Andy said, watching him walking back to the bar. 'Likes his drink. Trouble is when he's had a few he thinks he's God's gift to women.' he smiled. 'Unfortunately, like you, most women don't share that view.'

'No,' Ella smiled back. 'He really scared me.' The music started again. The Small Faces *'Tin Soldier.'*

'I, however,' He said, looking at her with eyes like melted chocolate, as his hand reached for hers. 'am a complete gentleman. Will you dance with me?'

When the music had finished he took her by the hand and guided her back to her table where an astonished Issy and Jenny sat. 'Take care, see you again soon.' He said, squeezing her hand and with a wave disappeared back into the crowd.

'Well, what was all that about?' Issy frowned.

'Oh I had a bit of bother with someone. Your three out of ten.' She said to Jenny. 'He grabbed me, wouldn't let me go. Luckily Andy intervened.'

'Set the whole thing up, more like it,' Issy replied, staring after him.

'I don't think for a moment he'd do something that childish.' Ella was keen to rush to his defence.

'You would be surprised what he's capable of if it gets him what he wants.'

'Issy stop it!' Jenny scolded.

'Stop what?' Issy was all wide eyed innocence.

'The character assassination.'

'He deserves it. I wouldn't trust him as far as I could throw him.' Issy shook her head. 'His name's been linked with yours already.'

'Has it? How?'

'That big bust up he had with Nina. It was because she found out he'd been to the Rotary Ball with you.'

'But I wasn't with Andy, he was with his father!' Ella protested. She closed her eyes and let out a groan of annoyance.

'Sorry Ella.' Jenny made a face. 'Mick told me the very same thing.'

'And where is Igor tonight?' Issy asked, scanning the room. 'He's usually close behind his master.'

'I don't know.' Jenny peered into the dimness of the club, searching for her brother's familiar face. 'He left the house as I was getting ready. Said he might not be at the Mill tonight because he had other things to do.'

'What sort of other things?'

'Haven't a clue Iz.' Jenny shrugged. 'But he's been having them rather a lot lately.'

FOURTEEN

Saturday 23rd December

Meridan Cross lay under a blanket of white frost as the Rover approached the village, nosing its way down the hill under a canopy of leafless trees.

Ella smiled. Her time away from Meridan Cross had made her forget how beautiful it could look in winter. Of course she knew she would miss being here for Christmas but at least now she would be spending it with the Taylors and not Bob.

'Nearly there.' Liam's voice interrupted her thoughts.

'So we are.' She replied, as they passed the Somerset Arms. 'Thanks for running me out here. Lucky you had a business appointment in the area wasn't it?'

'Yes, very fortunate.'

'Anyone I know?'

'I don't think so. Ken and Beryl Grant? They've just bought the Old Vicarage at Morden.'

'Yes, Grandma did mention it had been sold when I spoke to her last. Put a good word in for you did she?'

'She certainly did.'

They reached the gates of Little Court and Liam took the Rover at a gentle pace down its gravelled driveway towards the grand red bricked Elizabethan manor house.

'Would you mind if I drove back?' Ella asked as they pulled up outside the front door.

'If that's what you want.' He gave her a funny sideways smile.

'What is it?'

'Nothing.' A strange mischief danced in his eyes.

'I can do it you know!' She protested, sensing his amusement. 'You don't think I can do you? Not without crashing the gears like mother does. Well I'm not like mother, not at all!'

'Hey, calm down.' He patted her shoulder reassuringly. 'I'm very impressed with you so far.'

'Then why are you laughing?'

'I'm not.'

'Yes you are.'

'Ella please, I am not laughing at you. Look, your grandmother's at the door, off you go now. I'll be back in an hour and I promise, you'll be driving home.'

Laura was delighted to see Ella and sad that she would not be there for Christmas. 'It's all been rather a mess hasn't it?' She said as she poured Ella coffee in her sitting room. 'My dear cousin Lottie lost her beloved Harry a few months ago and asked specially that I fly out to Madeira to spend Christmas with her. You didn't mention Christmas arrangements during our phone conversations and I took it for granted that you were doing something with Niall but then Mary told me you and Niall had fallen out and were spending Christmas apart.'

'It's a stupid misunderstanding really.' Ella said accepting the offered cup. 'And he's being his usual difficult self. I did think Christmas might be a good time to sort ourselves out, but apparently he's decided to go to Austria instead.'

'With the Miller boys I gather.'

'He's being so childish!' She shook her head. 'You know he hasn't even bothered to send me a Christmas card!'

'Never mind, perhaps when he comes back he'll see sense.' Laura said helpfully. 'What exactly happened anyway?'

Ella sat sipping her coffee and relating the events in November which had triggered the trouble.

'If only I'd learned to drive earlier I would have come up here myself and made him see me.' Ella said, placing her empty cup on the tray. 'It's so frustrating!'

'I know.' Laura sympathised. 'He drives Mary mad with his stubbornness. But I'm sure he'll come round, it's just going to take a little time that's all.'

'I do hope so!' Ella sighed, and then catching sight of the tree in the corner with presents piled beneath it, turned to her bag. 'Before I forget.' she pulled out a prettily wrapped box. 'Not to be opened before Christmas Day.'

'Thank you my darling.' Laura kissed her. 'At this rate I shall need a separate suitcase for just presents, everyone is leaving them early.'

'And I've a huge favour to ask.' Ella said, pulling three more brightly wrapped parcels from her carrier bag. 'I don't suppose you could deliver these to Willowbrook for me, could you?'

'Ella,' Laura's expression became serious. 'You could do it yourself you know. I know Niall's not there but it would be a good opportunity to see your grandfather.'

'I'm not sure.' Ella was hesitant. 'He was so angry with me. I think he hates me nearly as much as he does Mother.'

'Nonsense! That was just his bluster darling. Mary says he misses you terribly.'

'I miss him too.' Ella hung her head. 'But at the moment all I can think about is sorting out my problems with Niall. And now for some reason Rachel's stopped writing and doesn't return my phone calls.'

'Ah Rachel,' Laura smiled as she took the presents. 'She's working with Mary at the stables part time and Margaret tells me she's become involved with Meridan Cross Young Farmers, out most evenings in fact. So with the pub and the shop as well I doubt she has time to draw breath let alone write letters or make phone calls. But if I see her I promise I'll have word. And what about you? How's college going?'

'Very well, I'm really enjoying it.' Ella brightened. 'And I've made a very important decision. I'm going to run my own business when I leave.'

'What kind of business?' Laura looked intrigued.

'I have no idea yet, but I just know something will come up,' Ella said positively.

'Well when it does I want you to let me know.'

'Of course. You'll be the first, I promise.'

'And I'd like to help financially.'

'That's very generous,' Ella shook her head. 'But I have to learn to stand on my own two feet.'

'I know that, my darling girl, but a little help will go a long way in getting you started.'

'Only on one condition then.' Ella relented. 'That I pay you back, with interest.'

'There really is no need.'

'Maybe not, but it's the way I want it.' Ella was insistent.

'You're just like your father you know, so independent.' Laura smiled as she got to her feet. 'Now, I've something to show you. I'll just get my coat.'

Intrigued, Ella followed her grandmother through the house and out towards the stables.

'What have you been buying now?'

Laura didn't reply, but walked silently ahead until they reached the old coach house. Inserting a key in the lock, she slid back the heavy green doors, revealing a brand new red and white Mini Cooper.

Laura looked at Ella. 'Do you like it?'

'You're replacing the Bentley with *this*?'

'No, I've still got the Bentley.'

'So what's this, your fun car?' Ella began to smile as she imagined her grandmother racing around the lanes between the villages.

'No it's *your* fun car. It's your Christmas present from all of us Ella. I hope you like it.'

Stunned, Ella ran her fingertips over the bonnet of the car. 'I can't possibly accept this.' She said as she admired the gleaming paintwork. 'It's far too expensive.'

'Nonsense.' Laura looked at her seriously. 'We all felt you needed your own car. It will mean that you'll be able to come and go as you please and more importantly you can come here whenever you want. You'll be totally independent. Please, say that you'll accept it. It would make your grandfather and me extremely happy. Here,' she produced the keys from her coat pocket. 'Go on, get in.'

Ella took the keys, put her arms around Laura and kissed her cheek. 'Thank you *so* much and please thank grandfather for me.'

'The best thanks you could give him would be to turn up on his doorstep. I know that's difficult for you at the moment, but please Ella,' Laura took Ella's hands in hers. 'Promise me you'll think about making that journey after Christmas.'

Ella nodded. She knew her grandmother was right, but currently Niall was her main concern. Once things were back to normal with him she promised herself that her grandfather would take priority. As she unlocked the car, Liam appeared

'You knew didn't you?' Ella looked firstly at him then at her grandmother. 'That's why you were laughing when I asked about driving home.'

'I have to confess,' he said with a smile. 'that I was indeed in on this.'

'So you didn't have an appointment after all.'

'No. I've been in the Somerset Arms playing dominoes with Doggy. Needless to say he thrashed me.'

Liam looked at the delighted expression on Ella's face. He thought of their journey home, of Mel's hostile reaction to Laura and Richard's generosity, the echoes of which would almost certainly carry over into their four days away. But all that was somehow irrelevant. Ella was happy and as far as he was concerned that was all that mattered.

Comfortably settled in a window seat of The Golden Fleece on the edge of town, Mick and Nina were having what had now become their usual weekend drink. The pub, bright with the festive sparkle of decorations, was full of people enjoying a pre-Christmas drink. Mick had chosen the location carefully, within easy reach, but far enough away to afford them total privacy. It had become their regular meeting place. Mick watched Nina as her fingers fished out the orange slice from her glass and she brought it to her mouth nibbling the flesh eagerly. She had always fascinated him; the way the thick torrent of tawny hair fell around her shoulders, her buttock skimming mini skirts which got all the guys drooling. And those legs! He understood why Andy held onto her. She was gorgeous, but more than that, she was totally faithful. The only problem was that Andy was a flirt and Nina possessive, it was a volatile combination and he wasn't surprised that it had eventually ended. But it would be different with him, he decided, because he could give her all the things a woman needed in a man. Love, stability, fidelity.

Of course she had given him something too; confidence. A fortnight with her had made him realise that he wasn't a bore that he could be fun, entertaining, someone a girl like her wanted to be with. In the short time they had been dating she had turned his world into a warmer, brighter place. For the first time in his life he felt really happy and he knew the last thing he wanted was for that to change. And there was a possibility it could if the ever fickle Andy decided he wanted her back. So there was only one course of action to take. Something rash and impulsive, totally alien to his normally sensible way of doing things.

'You're quiet this evening.' She looked at him curiously.

'I was just thinking about Christmas.'

'Oh yeah, inviting me over to meet your folks are you?'

'Yes, as a matter of fact.'

'You're kidding!' She began to laugh. 'Me? Meet your mum and dad?'

'Why not? You're going to be part of the family anyway.'

'Come again? Mick, what exactly have you been drinking?' She picked up his empty glass and sniffed it suspiciously.

'It's Watney's, and I've only had the one. Listen to me Nina Harrison.' He took her by the hand. 'I'm deadly serious about this. I know we've only been going out for a couple of weeks but I've known you for a long time as Andy's girlfriend. I always wanted the chance to be with you and now it's come, well, I realise it's become such a special thing I couldn't bear losing you. So I know the only way to keep you here for ever is to make a proper commitment and ask you to marry me.'

Nina's eyes widened. 'Are you serious?'

'Totally.'

'Mick, I don't know what to say.'

'Please, just say yes Nina.'

Monday 25th December

The church was packed. The cold stone interior decorated in the rich reds and golds of Christmas, with large bunches of bright berried holly set in brass vases and a colourful nativity scene created at the foot of the pulpit.

Standing between Jenny and her father Jack, Ella lowered her hymn book as *'Oh Come All Ye Faithful'* came to its conclusion. As the Reverend Hubbard climbed into the pulpit to give the congregation his Christmas address she sat down amazed that in just twenty four hours she could feel as happy as this. Of course, poor Liam was probably having a dreadful time of it in the Cotswolds. Her mother had gone into a massive sulk as soon as she'd seen the Mini and her annoyance had still been in evidence as she flounced out to the car yesterday afternoon without even saying goodbye. Liam, however, had thrown his arms around Ella and given her a big hug before picking up the two large suitcases Mel had spent hours packing. 'All this for four days,' he said with a grin. 'It's like travelling with royalty.'

Around five she drove across town to the Taylor home, an elegant red brick

166

Georgian house with pale colonnades, whose navy front door was decorated with a huge holly wreath.   Lights blazed in the downstairs rooms and once inside Ella found herself immediately immersed in the atmosphere of a warm, comfortable house readying itself for Christmas.   Delicious aromas drifted from the kitchen, a huge tree covered in baubles and garlands, presents at its feet stood in the opening between the dining room and the lounge where there was a roaring log fire and comfortable soft sofas.   This how home should be she thought and it's something my mother could never achieve. Never in a million years.

'Has Nick phoned?' She asked Jenny as they were getting ready to go out.

'No, still halfway up Snowdon I expect.   Said he'd be here tea-time tomorrow.'

'My mad brother.' Ella laughed. 'Nearly as bad as yours. Where is Mick by the way? Surely he's not working this late on Christmas Eve.'

'He left before you arrived,' Jenny replied.   'Another of his 'things to do' moments.'

As the Mill was closed, the Red Lion in the High Street with it's festive decorations, old beams and open fire became the next best alternative. At 8.30 it was smoky, noisy and almost full. Once inside the door Jenny spotted an empty table and grabbed it, leaving Ella to queue at the bar for drinks. Issy arrived just after nine thirty, squeezing through the crowded bar to join them, her work in the hotel finished for the evening. Back in Kingsford her parents were now well into their festive meet and greet with their guests, serving a lavish Christmas Eve buffet and mulled wine.

At half ten Annabel, Rich, Gareth and Bryony looked in for a drink en route to a party somewhere in Kingsford. Annabel looked wonderful in a red wool mini dress, her thick fair caught in a French pleat. 'Ossie Clarke darlings.' she said to the girls' admiring stare. 'An early Christmas present from Daddy.'

Bryony, dark to Annabel's fair, wore her hair loose around her shoulders, her eyes heavily lined with kohl. Her dress was crushed purple velvet, long and low cut. Bought in the Portobello Road she said. But as always it was her jewellery which stole the show. Geometric earrings made from gilt and black glass and a finely braided silver chain round her neck from which a small silver key could just be seen dangling invitingly between the softness of her breasts.

'It's a great talking point.' She said, fishing it from her cleavage. 'Annabel wants me to make her one in gold set with diamonds, don't you darling?'

'Mmm,' Annabel nodded, 'but I have to confess what I really would like is a Mini.' She looked enviously at Ella. 'You are so lucky Ella! Anyone who's anyone owns one now don't they? Rock stars, photographers, even royalty! You've started something you know! It's definitely my next must have.'

'A very Merry Christmas to all of you.'

Ella, roused from her daydream of the last twenty four hours, realised the

Revered Hubbard's sermon had come to an end. He announced the last hymn and stepped slowly down from the pulpit. The service came to a conclusion with *'Christians Awake Salute the Happy Morn'*.

A weak sun was trying to break through a light grey sky as Ella joined the Taylors afterwards to shake the vicar's hand at the church door and chat briefly to other familiar faces. She remembered how old Doggy always said he could smell snow. It occurred to her it was usually on days such as this when the sky held a pink tinge and the wind was raw and easterly. She thought of Meridan Cross then with its colourless fields. The barren blackness of the wood as it sprawled over Sedgewick Hill and the icy grey slick of river running through the valley below. In contrast, there was nothing remarkable about Abbotsbridge she reflected, watching the streets slip by from the back of Jack Taylor's Mercedes as they drove home. Here there were just buildings, pigeons and a few bald lime trees circling the fountain in the town square.

Lunch at the Taylors was a real family event, with delicious food and lots of laughter. Afterwards the doors to the lounge were pushed back to enable them all to watch the Queen's Speech. Mick seemed quiet and preoccupied and once lunch was over and the table cleared he made his excuses and disappeared, saying he would be back later.

'There he goes, off again.' Jenny nudged Ella.

His departure coincided with the arrival of Nick in a taxi. Jenny and Ella ran out to meet him, hugging him ferociously, both pleased and surprised to see him a day earlier than planned.

Peeling off his coat and leaving his case in the hall, Nick was soon stretching his legs out in front of the warm fire in the lounge and drink in hand was subjected to a barrage of questions about his activities during the last twenty four hours. The weather, he told them had been responsible for terminating their small expedition before it had even really got started. As the snow began to fall, all five decided they had no wish to spend Christmas stranded in a B & B in Llanberris. So they were soon heading south, eager to be with their families.

At six thirty when Betty called them into the dining room for a tea of cold turkey and ham with salad there was no sign of Mick, his place at the table remained ominously vacant. Although nothing was said, Ella did not miss the unspoken messages between Jack and Betty; expressions that said they were not happy.

He appeared in the doorway just before eight. They had all just settled down to watch the Morecambe and Wise Christmas Special. A box of Black Magic was being handed round. Jack Taylor turned from the comfort of his chair to look at his son.

'Mick, where've you been? We've visitors; how could you just slope off like that? You didn't even turn in for tea. Where are your manners?'

'Sorry.' Mick looked embarrassed for a moment, and then the smile returned. 'I didn't mean to be rude Dad, but there is a reason.' He moved forward slightly so he was in full view of them all. 'You see I've been seeing someone. And, well, I thought Christmas might be the ideal time to bring her here to meet the family.'

'Well, don't keep the poor girl standing there, for heaven's sake!' Betty scolded. 'Bring her in!'

'Yes.' Jack echoed. 'Come on Mick, introduce her properly.'

Mick smiled and disappeared, returning hand in hand with a young woman wearing a black mini dress and white tights who stood smiling nervously at everyone in the room. 'Mum and Dad, everyone, I'd like you all to meet Nina, the dearest, most special girl in the world.' he looked at her adoringly and then back to the stunned group.

Clearing his throat nervously, he continued. 'And, um, well the thing is, she's not just my girlfriend any more, because I proposed to her on Friday. And she accepted!' He gently lifted her left hand to show off the ruby and diamond cluster which sparkled on her finger and with a hopeful grin announced. 'We're engaged!'

Nina Harrison watched the stunned expressions on the faces of the assembled Taylor family and their guests. For her Mick's proposal had come as a shock too, but she'd had accepted without hesitation. It was just the bait she needed, because once Andy heard about the engagement, she was sure he'd be falling over himself to get her back.

Two figures stood at the end of The Cob, watching the swell of the sea against its base. The day was cold, a leaden sky meeting the vast emptiness of steely grey sea. A lonely tanker crept by on the horizon, while overhead gulls wheeled, battling against the wind with pitiful cries. Niall wrapped a protective arm around Rachel. Both wore winter coats and scarves swathed around their necks to protect them from the biting wind. They had left the hotel to walk off the enormous lunch they had just eaten and the journey around Lyme now brought them to the end of the famous breakwater, where they stood, breathing in the salt air.

'Happy?'

'Absolutely,' She looked up at him, pushing wind lashed tendrils of hair from her face. 'Lunch was wonderful.' Her hand went to her face and she hiccoughed. 'I think I might have drunk rather too much wine though.'

'So, how does this rate against Christmas at Aunt Ethel's?'

'You don't really want me to answer that do you?'

He kissed her nose. 'Failed miserably haven't I?'

'Don't be silly.' She gave him a playful punch. 'I've had the most wonderful Christmas ever. And I will always remember.' She screwed up her eyes and thought for a moment. 'Our lovely room at the Marine Hotel and the log fire and all the other guests who thought it was so romantic because they were convinced we were Christmas honeymooners.' She giggled. 'But most of all, I shall remember it for this.' She pulled off her glove and showed him the gold band set with a solitary pearl which sat on the third finger of her right hand. 'It's lovely. Thank you.'

'Oh Rachel.' He tenderly stroked her face with the back of his hand.

She shivered slightly at his touch.

'Cold?'

She nodded.

He pulled her to him, wrapping both arms around her in a tight hug. 'I've got just the remedy for that.' he whispered in her ear. 'A big soft bed, my warm body to keep you company and plenty of....'

'Niall!' She laughed, embarrassed.

Gently he reached out and cupped her face in his hands and brought his lips to hers. The taste of her mouth, cold and salty, was strangely arousing.

'I do love you, you know.' She looked up into his face, her eyes blue and trusting.

'And I love you too.' He whispered as he rested his forehead against her shoulder. God if he'd had a pound for every time he'd said that to someone he'd be a millionaire by now. He raised his head to look at her, realising that this time it was different; that for the first time in his life he really meant it.

Sunday 31st December

'He's been going out with her for two weeks!' Issy Llewlleyn commented as she sat watching Mick and Nina on the dance floor wrapped in each others arms. 'Now I know he's totally mad.'

'Dad says he's taken leave of his senses.' Jenny said despondently, watching the same scene with dismay. 'And Mum, well, she won't talk about it, she's too upset. She says Nina is going to be nothing but trouble.'

It was New Year's Eve at the Mill and the three girls were sitting at the bar on high stools drinking brandy and Babycham. The events of Christmas Day had cast a shadow over the Taylor family, leaving them shell shocked and at a loss to know what to do for the best. Jack had tried to reason with his son, to get him to hold off the engagement, saying they had not known each other long enough to make such a serious commitment but Mick would have none of it. As far as he was concerned he was in love and all he saw in dissenting voices was prejudice. Determined to have his own way, he was now deliberately avoiding the family as much as possible.

Although she was trying not to show it, Jenny knew her mother was upset and felt frustrated that there was nothing she could do about it. To be dating Nina was bad enough, to propose marriage within fourteen days, total madness.

'She's using him,' Issy said watching as Nina nuzzled into Mick's neck, 'to get Andy back.'

'But Andy's not interested in her any more. ' Ella commented as she paid the barman for the latest round of drinks.

'Isn't he?' Issy frowned, wondering why the sight of Mick and his fiancée wrapped in each others arms was making her feel intensely irritable. 'Well we shall see won't we?'

Ella looked up at the clock. 'Three minutes of the old year left girls, time to get on the floor.'

They slid from their seats and joined the jostle of people waiting for the countdown into 1968. Big Ben's boom echoed over the speakers then everyone joined hands for *Auld Lang Syne*. As this finished a great cheer went up from the crowd and a large net full of multicoloured balloons was released from the ceiling.

As Ella stood alone, parted from her friends by the push and shove of bodies, she contemplated her New Years' resolution to resolve her problems with Niall. All thoughts of this disappeared however when she felt someone touch her arm and turned to find Andy beside her.

'I came to wish you a Happy New Year.' He said putting his arms around her as the Beatles' *'Hello Goodbye'* began.

'Happy New Year, Andy.' She laughed up at him and tilted her head back to let him kiss her.

Strangely enjoying the pressure of his mouth on hers Ella soon found herself responding. She closed her eyes, her arms snaking slowly around his neck. Eventually he broke away and looked at her with a shake of his head.

'It's such a shame.' He said quietly. 'Such an awful shame.'

'What is?'

'A girl like you chasing after a man who obviously doesn't give a damn.' He gently touched her cheek.

'I love him.'

'Do you Ella? That's not what it felt like just now.'

'I'm sorry.' Ella hung her head guilty, knowing her kiss had been perhaps a little too enthusiastic. 'New Year's Eve, I got a bit carried away.'

'Niall doesn't want you any more; I would have thought that was obvious.'

'I don't believe that...'

'What do you believe?'

'That he's still being pig headed. Refusing to see me is his way of getting even. It's typical Niall.'

'So what will you do?'

'I'm going to drive out to talk to him next week and try to make him see sense.'

'You must really love him.'

'I do. Very much. And deep down I know he loves me, that's why I can't give up on him.'

'He's a lucky man, your Niall, I envy him such devotion.'

'Don't patronise Andy, please.'

'That was not my intention Ella, honestly.' He looked hurt.

'Andy, I'm sorry....'

'Don't be sorry,' He stroked her face. 'Just be ready.'

'Ready? What for?'

'For me, to catch you when you fall of course.' He replied and with a light brush of his lips against her cheek he turned and walked away into the crowd.

Across town, the New Year was being celebrated in a far more genteel manner. In the Masonic Hall *Auld Lang Syne* had been sung, people had embraced and faces had been pressed chastely against each other. Mel, radiant in her green chiffon, had just returned to her seat, her gaze fixing itself once more on Bob Macayne.

Bob was currently partnering Sheila Fitzallyn. He was making her laugh as they circled the floor energetically in time to the bands *'Dancing Cheek to Cheek.'* When the music came to an end he returned her to her seat and unexpectedly extended a hand in invitation to Mel.

'I haven't seen you around lately.' She said once she was in his arms, trying to sound as casual as she could. 'Have you been away?'

'Yes, as a matter of fact I have.' He did not look at her as they danced around the room.

'Anywhere exciting?'

'Oh, nowhere you'd be interested in.'

'Try me.'

She heard him draw in his breath as if he was finding her irritating.

'I'm sorry; I didn't mean to be tiresome Bob. None of my business really.'

'Actually,' He looked down at her, with eyes as dark as coal, and smiled. 'Someone just caught the back of my heel as they passed. As to where I've been, well if you must know, it's Leeds. On business.'

'Leeds?' She made a face.

'See.' He said. 'I knew you wouldn't find it interesting and not only that, you haven't noticed have you?'

'Noticed what?'

'That I've been brushing up on my dancing. So far I've managed to avoid your feet.'

'Congratulations, so you have.' She smiled back.

'Please, don't do that.'

'What?'

'Smile like that; it makes you look very kissable.'

'Kissable?'

'Yes. Sorry, I didn't mean to embarrass you.'

'You haven't.' She looked at him thoughtfully. 'I was just under the impression that our last encounter was an amusing interlude fuelled by rather too much alcohol.'

'Oh no, I wanted us to meet. You're an intriguing woman. In fact I find myself so fascinated that you must join me for dinner one evening so I can learn more about you.'

'I don't think Liam would be too keen about that.'

'That's OK we'll do it while he's away.'

'Away? Where?'

'In Harrogate, there's a Town Planning conference coming up in February. I'm funding Liam; it will be very useful for our future plans.'

'And what plans are these?'

'Redeveloping the centre of Abbotsbridge.'

'Tell me more.'

'You don't want to hear about boring things like that,' He smiled. 'Let's talk about dinner. Have you any particular preference, or would you like to leave the booking to me?'

'Surprise me Bob.' Mel smiled, suddenly thrilled by the invitation and the chance of some excitement in her life. 'I just love surprises!'

1968

FIFTEEN

Saturday 6th January

Ella left for Meridan Cross after breakfast. As far as her mother and Liam were
concerned she was spending the day with Issy and Jenny. She had spent most of
the night lying awake thinking about Niall.   Going away with the Miller boys
had, she knew, been an act of defiance. It was childish and pointless but it was
typical of Niall.   She knew today was not going to be easy, but she was
determined that at the end of it she would be back in his arms again. And to
ensure the best possible chance of success for her mission, she was going with
the element of surprise. No one in Meridan Cross, not even her grandmother,
had any idea she was coming.

As she came over Sedgewick Hill and dropped down through the wood she
felt strangely calm. Glimpsing the village through the trees, its houses and
cottages sprawled out along the valley floor she experienced the usual warm,
emotional pull. Home; this was still her home, a place where she felt safe – even
if she was at odds with the two most important men in her life.

At the entrance to Saddlers End she saw Rowan Miller in his father's battered
old Land Rover, waiting to pull out into the road. She waved out and then
pulled in a few yards ahead of the junction, stopped and got out.

'Rowan!' She threw herself into his arms, giving him a tight hug. 'Happy
New Year!'

'And you Ella.' He gave her a brotherly kiss on the cheek. 'Nice car.' He
grinned, looking at the Mini. 'No need to ask who gave you that.' Then holding
her out at arms length he said with a smile. 'You look well.' his dark eyes
glittered, full of mischief. 'Your romantic Christmas away obviously did you
good!'

'What?' She stared at him.

'You and Niall, Lyme Regis.' He said with a smile. 'Oh it's OK, your secret's safe with us. Ash and I were quite happy to provide an alibi for you both. As far as Mary's concerned, Niall had a wonderful holiday with us.' then seeing her shocked expression he touched her shoulder awkwardly. 'Sorry, I didn't mean to embarrass you.'

'It's O.K., you haven't.' She forced a laugh. 'Well,' she broke away from him with a smile. 'Guess I'd better get moving, mustn't keep him waiting eh?'

'Going up to the cottage are you?'

'The cottage?'

'Yeah, Fox Cottage, where Niall lives.' He grinned. 'You *are* in a bad way aren't you?'

After leaving Rowan, Ella drove slowly towards the village. Lyme Regis for Christmas? What was going on? Well, there was only one way she was going to find out. As she came to the track which led up to Fox Cottage she slowed the car down and turned left. Niall's E-type was parked in a newly built rough stone pull in just below the cottage and she parked up behind it. She got out of the Mini, pulling the collar of her jacket around her face to protect her from the cold easterly wind which teased her hair. It seemed a fit companion for the bleakness of the barley field and the wood, harsh and unwelcoming in their winter black. As she reached the cottage, she glimpsed a fire burning brightly through the front window. She thought about knocking, but decided she'd surprise him instead. Finding the front door locked she went around to the rear where the door stood slightly ajar.

In the kitchen the remnants of breakfast lay everywhere; the battered shell of a boiled egg, half eaten toast, a jar of marmalade with the lid removed. Typical male chaos she thought with a smile, moving forward into the lounge, finding it furnished comfortably with some of the surplus furniture from Paddocks, a real home from home. Realising he must be upstairs and still intent on surprise she crossed the lounge silently and stood at the foot of the stairs. Placing one hand on the newel post, she began to climb. Halfway up she stopped abruptly as she heard the unmistakable sound of music and a woman's laughter coming from above.

Curiosity urged her forward, step by step until she had reached the top of the stairs. Gingerly she tiptoed along the landing with a feeling of unease; her heart thudding, her breath tight in her throat. The voices were clearer now, louder than the music which was coming from a radio. She could hear everything that was being said.

'Niall stop it! I have to go, I'm late already.'

'Oh come on, just once more.'

'No!'

'You don't mean that, you know you like it.'

'Yes, I do but.......ooh, don't do that!'

'See, you can't resist me, you like it as much as I do!'

There was silence then, followed by girlish giggles and a creak of bedsprings. Ella realised the voices were coming from the room which used to be her mother's bedroom; a pretty, light room which looked out over the barley field towards the village. She crept forward, placed the flat of her hand against the roughness of the door and eased it open. It looked so different now, painted pale lemon; all the old dark furniture gone. The double bed was in disarray, the eiderdown spilling from it onto the floor, joining clothes which lay strewn untidily across the carpet. Niall and a woman lay facing each other. Niall, with his back to the door, was running his hand gently down the paleness of the woman's arm, the only part of her on view, as the morning sun spilled in over them through partially drawn curtains. Stunned with shock, Ella simply stood there gazing at them.

'Do you know Rachel,' She heard him say softly. 'You're such a tease.' Then he bent his head and kissed her.

Rachel! He was with Rachel! Ella turned from the door immediately, cupping her hand firmly over her mouth to stifle the sound which rose in her throat as she turned and fled back down the landing towards the stairs.

Niall raised his head as he heard the bang of a door below and quickly heaved himself out of bed. 'There's someone downstairs!' He whispered, reaching for his shirt and jeans. Quickly Rachel sank down into the bed retrieving the covers from the floor and pulling them round her.

Cautiously Niall left the bedroom and crept slowly down the landing. At the top of the stairs he paused for a moment, and then descended carefully, taking one tread at a time, his hand skimming the banister as he went. Reaching the bottom, he hesitated, listening for a moment before making his way cautiously towards the kitchen. As he reached the door one of his bare feet came into contact with something cold and metallic embedded in the carpet. He stepped back frowning and squatting down picked up the small heart on its fine gold chain.

'Ella!' He said under his breath. 'Oh shit!'

As he stood up he heard the sound of a car engine in the lane. Finding his shoes he pulled them on and ran to the front door, pulling it open. He reached the gate in time to see a red Mini bumping crazily down the track. On reaching the main road it turned right and accelerated away with a squeal of tyres. Returning to the cottage he found Rachel standing at the top of the stairs wrapped in the eiderdown.

'Who was it?' She asked nervously as she slowly descended the stairs.

'Nobody,' He replied, shoving the heart into the pocket of his jeans. 'Front door wasn't shut properly. A draught must have caught it.'

'Thank goodness.' With a relieved smile she came down the stairs and wrapped him in the eiderdown, covering his worried face with kisses. 'Come on; let's go back to bed....'

'I can't.' He shook his head. 'I've suddenly remembered there's something I have to do.'

'Well there's a sudden change Niall O'Farrell!' She pouted. 'You couldn't resist me just now. What's the matter?'

'Nothing,' He looked down at her, his smile returning as he kissed her gently. 'Nothing at all, just go back to bed and wait. I won't be long.'

Ella got to Abbotsbridge thirty minutes later. She had no idea how she had managed the drive there without having an accident. She had let the Mini scream in second all the way back up Sedgewick Hill as she sobbed loudly, clinging to the steering wheel, her vision blurred by tears. Stopping at the top by a clump of Douglas Firs she dried her eyes and tried to compose herself. As she put away her handkerchief she wondered how he could be so cruel to have done this when he knew she was still trying to talk to him to sort things out. And what of Rachel? She had always wanted him, made a fool of herself trying to attract him when she was younger. She remembered the last night she was in Meridan Cross, when she'd asked Rachel to look after him. Well she'd done that all right. No wonder she'd stopped writing to her. She'd been betrayed by two of the people she'd believed closest to her. The thought stabbed painfully through her and a fresh rush of tears overcame her. She wondered if she would ever be able to forgive them for what they had done. By the time she had reached the centre of Abbotsbridge, she knew going home was impossible and Jenny's would be the best place to head for to find someone to talk to.

Betty Taylor opened the door to her, her eyes widening with surprise as she saw her tearstained face. 'Ella, love, whatever's wrong? Come in, come in!' She quickly ushered her into the hall.

'Jenny!' She shouted up the stairs. 'Come quickly, it's Ella!'

Jenny appeared immediately and seeing Ella's face, descended the stairs two at a time.

'Ella! What's happened?'

'I've just come from Meridan Cross.' Ella looked at them both and then pulled out her handkerchief. 'I know now why Niall's been avoiding me.' she gave a huge choking sob. 'I found him in bed with Rachel!'

Betty showed them both into the lounge. 'I'll put the kettle on.' she said and left, closing the door quietly behind her.

With her arm around Ella's shoulder Jenny gently eased her onto the settee.

'Come on then,' Jenny's dark eyes were calm and comforting. 'Tell me everything.'

Ella blew her nose and began. When she had finished she looked across at Jenny, her eyes brimming with tears once more. 'What am I going to do, Jen?' 'I'll never be able to go back to Meridan Cross again. Not after this. How could he? I feel so foolish, so humiliated.'

Beyond the door the phone rang in the hall and they both heard Betty answer it. She appeared moments later.

'It's Niall.' She said to Ella. 'He wants to speak to you.'

'How did he know I was here?' Ella frowned.

Betty shrugged. 'Would you like me to tell him I haven't seen you?'

'No,' Ella wiped away her tears, her face tight and angry. 'It's all right Mrs Taylor, I'll speak to him.'

'Are you sure dear?'

Ella nodded. Taking a deep breath she walked calmly into the hall and picked up the phone.

'Yes?'

'Ella, Ella.' His voice was very emotional. 'I'm *so* sorry.'

'Are you?'

'Of course I am. This is the last thing I wanted to happen. But I did try to tell you, didn't I? Back in November?'

'Did you?' Her voice was icy. 'I don't recall Rachel's name being mentioned that night, do you? In fact, you made it sound as if I was the one responsible for our break up. And then when Andy turned up you made some nasty accusations. All of which were totally untrue.'

'I know, I'm sorry.'

'No you're not!' She said coldly. 'I don't think you've ever been sorry for anything in your life! You're selfish! You use people! I expect once you're tired of Rachel you'll dump her, just like you've dumped me.'

'No, it's different this time. I think I'm in love Ella. Really in love, I.....'

'Oh shut up!' She interrupted angrily.

'But Ella, you must listen. I need to explain. To make you understand just how it all happened.'

She gave a harsh laugh. 'You really have got a nerve!'

Ella,' The placating tone was there again. 'Don't be like that. I just don't want you thinking.....'

'Niall,' She interrupted, keeping her voice light. 'It doesn't really matter what I think any more. The people you should worry about are Margaret and Mary and what's going to happen when they find out what's been going on at Fox Cottage.'

'And who's going to tell them!?' It was his turn to be angry now. 'You?'

'In the mood I'm in I just might!' Ella replied and slammed the phone down.

Niall pushed angrily out of the phone box. Was that a threat? No, Ella was upset, that was all. In a day or two things would be different. She'd come to terms with it all. But what was she doing in Meridan Cross? And how did she know he was at Fox Cottage? Someone must have told her. But who? It couldn't have been his mother, she'd have mentioned it. Laura perhaps? No. Otherwise she'd have headed straight for Little Court. But why had she come at all? It was over, wasn't it? Hadn't he made that clear enough? He had completely avoided her since November. No card or present at Christmas. He thought she'd got the message that he wanted rid of her and she was out of his life for good. Why then had she still hung on?

Reaching the Jaguar he pulled the car keys from his pocket only to find the gold heart and its fine chain wrapped around them. He untangled the keys and got into the car where he sat for a moment behind the wheel, studying the heart as it nestled in his open palm. When he had originally picked it up from the carpet, he thought it had been dropped by accident, that there had been a break in the chain, or the clasp had been faulty. Examining it now, he knew now that was not the case. She must have taken it off deliberately and thrown it down. As he draped it over the edge of his hand he saw them both standing in the paleness of the September moonlight and heard the words of her promise as clearly as if she was with him now.

This heart is a symbol of our love. As long as I wear it, it will show the world that we belong together.'

'She really loved me.' He said quietly. 'She really did.' He pressed his face into his hands. 'And now….Oh God what a mess!'

'How do you think she's feeling?'

'Don't know.' Jenny shook her head. 'She's been pretty calm since she spoke to him, but you never know with Ella. There's a very private part of her no one gets to, not even Nick.'

It was Saturday night and the two girls were sitting at the bar of the Mill. Ella had just gone to the ladies and Issy was using her absence as an opportunity to mull over the events of the day.

'Total bastard wasn't he?' She said thoughtfully. 'Pity, he was a real dish.'

'Looks aren't everything Iz.' Jenny answered. She tapped the side of her forehead with her finger. 'It's what goes on in here that counts.'

'I suppose you're right.' Issy conceded. 'I bet her mother is over the moon though. She's been praying for this.'

'Hey, here she comes.' Jenny hissed. 'Change the subject quickly.'

Issy watched as Ella appeared, cutting a swathe through the crowd, turning male heads as she passed.

'You know,' She said, fishing the cherry out of her Babycham. 'What she needs is a decent man. Someone who'll treat her right, won't let her down.'

'Got any one in mind?'

'Not specifically.' Issy replied thoughtfully. 'But, he's just got to be out there somewhere, hasn't he?'

Wednesday 10th January

Ella had just finished her breakfast when she heard the sound of the phone in the hall.

'I'll get it.' Putting down his paper Liam left the room.

'Who can that can be at this time of the morning?' Mel frowned before going back to her copy of *Vogue*.

'It's for you Ella.' Liam said as he returned to the breakfast table.

'Who is it?' Ella looked up at him, puzzled.

'Jenny I think.' He shrugged. 'Sorry, forgot to ask.'

In the hall, Ella picked up the receiver and seated herself at the bottom of the stairs.

'Hello. Ella?'

She recognised the voice immediately.

'What do you want Rachel?' She heard the abruptness in her own voice.

'To talk to you.' The voice sounded hesitant. 'About last Saturday. Niall's very upset you know.'

'And so he should be after the way he's treated me.'

'I didn't know it was you at the cottage. He didn't tell me until he came back from phoning you. He was in a right old state.'

'So he asked you to phone me did he? To try to smooth things out.'

'No, he didn't. I decided to phone because there's something I want you to understand.'

'I understand very well thank you. About betrayal.'

'Betrayal? *I* haven't betrayed anyone!'

'Haven't you? You knew exactly how difficult it was for me here. You knew Niall and I were going through a bad patch and you took advantage of it. You always wanted him didn't you?'

'Don't be like that.'

'Like what?'

'Dog in a manager. You're the one who finished with him to go out with that Andy what's-his-name!'

'Is that what he told you? God you are a mug!'

'Don't call me that!'

'Well you are! I'm not going out with anyone, I've been trying to talk to him for months now but he's been deliberately avoiding me. Even Mary couldn't get any sense out of him. And now I know why. Because all the time he's been messing about with you!'

'He's not messing about. We're in love.' Rachel said defiantly. 'He bought me a ring! It's a pearl and it's beautiful.'

'You are the most gullible person I know Rachel Sylvester!' Ella said, the thought of the ring making her even angrier. 'And you deserve everything that's going to happen to you!'

'What do you mean by that?'

'Once he gets bored or things don't go his way he's going to dump you, just like he dumped me and it will serve you right!' Ella replied before hanging up.

As she got to her feet to replace the telephone on the hall table, she was aware of someone standing behind her in the open doorway leading to the kitchen.

'Do you normally eavesdrop on other people's phone calls?' She turned on her mother savagely.

'I didn't eavesdrop!' Mel said indignantly. 'I just happened to be in the kitchen. Your voice was rather loud. You were drowning out Jimmy Young!' She folded her arms with just a hint of smugness. 'I gather it's all over then.'

Ella ignored her mother. Gathering her coat and bag from the hall floor she opened the front door. She stopped, turning to look at Mel for a moment, her face calm. 'As a matter of fact it is. Happy now?'

'Oh much more than happy.' Mel said as the front door slammed shut. 'Absolutely ecstatic!'

Monday 22nd January

Ella kicked the tyre. A flat; that was all she needed. Bending down she ran her hand around the tread, her fingers eventually coming into contact with the smooth, flat head of a nail. With a tired sigh she unlocked the boot, removing the floor and pulling out the black plastic bundle containing the jack and wheel brace. Then she released the spare wheel and heaved it out onto the tarmac, resting it against the side of the car. With the jack inserted she began to raise the car slightly until the wheel just made contact with the ground. How glad she was that she had read her instruction book and that she had spent a lifetime on a farm where tyre changing of one sort or another was a regular occurrence.

The first three wheel nuts came off with no trouble, but predictably the fourth did not. She tried all sorts of angles to get leverage but with no success. Exhausted, she squatted on her haunches cursing her bad luck. The pale grey sky which had hung over Abbotsbridge the whole day was gradually darkening and an accompanying cold wind made her shiver as she wondered how she was going to get around this problem.

'Damn!' She said out loud, getting to her feet and banging the roof of the car with the flat of her hand. Being self sufficient was one thing, but brute strength was something she did not have.

'Oh hell!' She ran her fingers through her hair. What was she going to do now? She checked her watch. 'I'm going to be late home, she'll kill me,' she said to herself. 'Damn....damn....'

'Are you OK?'

Coming out of the darkness, the voice took her by surprise and she spun around quickly, wheel brace in hand.

A tall, thin faced young man, wearing a leather jacket, jeans and a green polo neck sweater, stood looking at her, the smile on his face evaporating rapidly as his eyes caught sight of the potential weapon being brandished in her right hand.

'That's supposed to be for undoing wheel nuts.' He said eyeing it warily.

'I'm *so* sorry!' She lowered the wheel brace, horrified at what she had nearly done. 'I didn't hear you come up behind me, you gave me a real fright.'

She stared at him, there was a familiarity about the shaggy brown hair with its auburn highlights and the light brown eyes which she judged were the best feature in an otherwise fairly ordinary face.

'Guess it's me who should be sorry for scaring you then.' The smile surfaced again, lifting the corners of his mouth slightly. Ella stood there transfixed as he spoke. He wasn't conventionally handsome like Niall or Andy but for some reason that smile was having a very strange affect on her.

'What is it? A puncture?'

She nodded, emerging from her trance. 'I've managed to get three of the wheel nuts off but the last one just won't budge. Typical isn't it?'

She watched him as he squatted down beside the tyre.

'It's a nail.' She said helpfully.

'So it is.' He nodded, running his hand over the tread. 'A big one too by the feel of it.'

'Right,' He got to his feet. 'let's see what I can do for you.....'

'Sorry. I'm Ella.'

'Pleased to meet you Ella. I'm Matt.' He took the wheel brace gently from her.

Within five minutes the new tyre was on and the old one returned to the boot.

'Thank you so much.' Ella felt relieved that the hassle she expected from her mother for being late had now been averted. 'Can I give you a lift anywhere?'

He shook his head. 'No thanks, I've got my own transport.' he indicated the green Mini Pickup parked in the corner of the car park. 'Not quite as glamorous as yours but it gets me from A to B.'

Ella stared at him thoughtfully. 'Have we met before?'

'Don't think so.' He shook his head.

'I know.' It came to her. 'It was at the Forum. Tad Benedict. You remind me of him. Is he a relative of yours?'

Matt grinned as he picked up the jack and began to repack it. 'You could say that. He's my father.'

'Really?' She smiled back in surprise. 'He was very kind. I don't know what would have happened if he hadn't turned up.'

Matt's warm eyes were fixed on her again. 'He told me about it. Here.' he placed the wheel brace and jack gently in her hands. 'So, is it all sorted now, you and your boyfriend?'

'No.' She said as she tucked them back into the boot floor and looked at him again. 'Actually it's all over.'

'I'm sorry.'

'I'm not.' Staring into his eyes, she realised she really meant it.

'Plenty more fish in the sea eh?' The smile was there again, making her insides feel like melted butter.

'Something like that.' She answered breathlessly.

'Well.' He hesitated, looking at his watch as if he had to be somewhere. 'Must go, nice to have met you Ella. Oh, and don't forget.' He pointed at the boot. 'Get that to a garage as soon as possible - it's illegal not to have a roadworthy spare.'

The wind had dropped slightly and as he spoke his breath hung visibly in the cold evening air. Shadows played across his face, darkening his eyes, giving them an almost hypnotic quality as he looked at her. There was something about his closeness that totally overwhelmed her and suddenly she was overtaken by a strange impulse to draw him into her arms and kiss him. Quickly she came to her senses. This was stupid. Very stupid. She managed a weak smile as he turned to go; then all of a sudden she knew couldn't leave it like this, she just had to see him again.

'Matt!' She called after him.

He stopped and turned to look at her, the keys to his car in his hand.

'I'd like to buy you a drink to say thank you. For this.' She pointed at the tyre.

'There's no need, really. I was more than happy to help.'

'I insist.'

'O.K.' He nodded. 'Where?'

'You choose.'

'The Mill. Saturday?'

She nodded. 'What time?'

He thought for a moment. 'Catch you around ten.' And turning up his collar against the chill of the winter's evening, he ran to the Pickup.

'Ah there you are, I was beginning to give up on you!' Mel looked up irritably as Ella came through the kitchen door. With Mrs Harris off with flu and unable to assist, she was finding the food preparation for her ladies evening a bit of a struggle.

'Sorry, I had a puncture; it took a time to get the wheel off.' Ella dropped her folders onto the kitchen worktop. 'When did you say your ladies were arriving?'

'Seven thirty.'

'Mother, there's tons of time yet.'

'That's as maybe, but you know I like these things done properly, now do go up and change please, I need some vol-au-vents filling.' Mel picked up her daughter's files pushed them to her chest and pointed towards the hall door.

'Can I just ask a quick question before I go?'

'If you must.' Mel said impatiently, turning her attention to cutting up a quiche.

'What do you know about the Benedict family?'

'Why do you wish to know?' Mel stopped suddenly, pulling the knife from the quiche and turning to face Ella.

'I met Matt Benedict today. He helped me with the puncture.'

Mel stood there with an expression Ella had grown to recognise as disapproval.

'Well I'm sure it was very kind of him but, well let's put it this way, there are some people in this town who are really not our sort.'

'The Benedicts by any chance?'

'The Benedicts in particular.' Mel replied curtly. 'Now go up and change please!'

Tuesday 23rd January

'Jen.' Ella looked at her friend across the table where they sat facing each other in one of the quieter corners of the College Refectory. 'What do you know about Matt Benedict?'

It was Issy's turn to queue for the coffees that morning and Ella had seized the moment, now they were out of the classroom to get an answer to the question which had been bothering her since the previous evening. Jenny's dark eyes looked puzzled as they scanned Ella's face. 'Matt Benedict?'

'Mmm. I asked Mother. She wasn't very enthusiastic.' Ella looked worried. 'Exactly what have the family done wrong, are they criminals or something?'

'Of course not!' Jenny looked amused. 'Tad used to be a singer before he opened the Mill. Had several big hits in the fifties. He's a highly respected business man.' She laughed. 'And not short of a bob or two as Dad would say.'

'So why did my mother make such a fuss?' Ella frowned. 'She wouldn't talk about them, said they were...what was it she called them? Not our sort of people. '

The mention of Matt's name had triggered off the memory of the wonderful smile and those tawny eyes. A slight tremor ran down her spine.

'I don't think many people in this town are your mother's sort of people. She thinks my Dad's common because he started out driving a lorry for a living.' Jenny replied tartly as she watched Issy's progress in the queue. 'Why this sudden interest in Matt?'

'I met him in the car park last night. I had a puncture, couldn't get the wheel off. He came along and sorted it all out.' She laughed.'I liked him. He was....different.'

'Different.' Jenny looked thoughtful. 'Let's say he's not your average red blooded Abbotsbridge College male.'

'He's not...you know.....queer is he?'

'No!' Jenny shook her head and laughed. 'He's just...well, a bit serious. I guess he has a lot of responsibility. He's an only son working in a large business he'll probably end up running.' She laughed. 'Just like Issy.'

'What about me?' Issy asked as she arrived with a tray of coffee and three small packs of digestive biscuits.

'Jen was just comparing you to Matt Benedict.' Ella said, helping herself to a mug.

'I'm nothing like him.' Issy said sitting down. 'He's a guy, I'm a girl. His dad's loaded, mine's not. I'm cute and fun to be with. He's dull and boring.'

'He is not!' Ella protested. 'I liked him. He helped me with a puncture last night and I'm going to buy him a drink at the Mill tomorrow night to say thank you.'

184

'Bad move Ella!' Issy made a face as she broke open a packet of biscuits. 'Didn't anyone tell you, he doesn't do girls. He's heavily into music, a real anorak. Believe me he won't even remember you by tomorrow night. I bet you a double vodka he doesn't even bother turning up!'

'Issy, why are you being so horrible?' Jenny glared at her.

'She deserves better Jen.' Issy gave Ella's shoulder a comforting pat. 'Sorry Ella, I didn't mean to be so blunt, but honestly Matt Benedict's just not your sort.'

'Funnily enough, my mother said that too.' Ella replied with a defiant glint in her grey eyes, even more determined to prove them all wrong.

Saturday 27th January

'You're looking especially nice tonight.' Liam ran an appreciative eye over Ella as she came downstairs wearing a long sleeved green and black mini dress. Her mass of dark hair was caught up with two shiny black combs, a few loose tendrils escaping prettily around her face.

'Thank you.' She smiled as she pulled on her coat. 'I'm off to meet the girls at the Mill, tell Mother not to wait up.'

'I've not seen that dress before have I? Special occasion?'

'Maybe.'

'A date?'

'Not really.' She shook her head. 'But I am meeting someone for a drink.'

'It's not Andy is it? You know how your mother is hopeful you two will get together.'

'Then I'm afraid she's in for a big disappointment,' Ella said with a laugh. 'See you later.'

Liam watched her go. The old sparkle was back. Who was it, he wondered? Who it could be who had brought about this change in her? He couldn't wait to find out.

Mel arrived home earlier than usual that evening. Predictably it had been a boring round of chit chat with the Ladies Circle which she was chairing for the year. They had talked about various charity raising schemes, a Summer Fair in the Park to raise money for the local hospice, a ball at the Masonic Hall to raise funds for a mini bus to take members of the local Over Sixties Club on outings. How she hated this pathetic little group of affluent women handing out their patronage to the less well off, smugly thinking they were doing their bit for society. It was so Laura Kendrick.

She felt a discontentment seeping through her. Irritably, she twisted the key in the front door and pushed it open. She had worked so hard behind the scenes to help Liam's career over the years. The business had thrived, why therefore were they stuck in this unfashionable part of town? Surely she deserved a new home, preferably somewhere in the Portway area where those who mattered lived. Of course, the answer always came back the same: Liam's father's care bills, they alone were responsible for the heavy drain on his income she thought resentfully.

What she needed right now, she decided as she pulled off her coat and hung it in the hall, was distraction, something to lift her spirits. Instantly Bob floated through her thoughts. He was the one who just might make the difference, save her from the dissatisfaction and boredom of her marriage. But he was a let down too, conspicuous by his absence. She had not seen him since the New Year's Eve Ball. He'd mentioned a dinner date in February. Well February was nearly here, so why hadn't he got in touch again? She considered the situation for a moment then decided maybe he, like everything else in her life, was just a bitter disappointment.

'My round I think.' Issy announced, rummaging in her handbag for her purse as Jenny disappeared through the crowds to the ladies cloakroom. Ella handed Issy her glass, her gaze sweeping the interior of the club for the umpteenth time. Where was he?

'Shan't be long!' Issy said as she scooped up Jenny's empty glass and left, dodging round the dancers as she made her way to the bar.

After she had gone, Ella watched the dance floor as couples smooched to Gene Pitney. Everyone was here tonight; a big crowd from college, Mick up at the bar, Nina on the dance floor, Andy with Gareth, Bryony, Annabel and Rich. Only Matt Benedict was conspicuous by his absence. A small niggle in the back of her mind had begun to tell her that maybe Issy's predictions were right.

Across the room Jenny, returning from the cloakroom, saw her brother sitting up at the bar. Changing direction she went to join him.

'Hi Sis.' He greeted her with a grin. 'Can I get you a drink?'

'Thanks but I'm think I'm about to get one.' She nodded across to the other side of the bar where Issy was paying the barman, three brandy and Babychams on a tray in front of her.

'She's in a good mood for a change.' Mick said, noticing the smile on Issy's face as she took her change and continued to chat to the barman.

'She's celebrating.'

'The banqueting suite?'

'You know about it?'

He nodded. 'It seems to have taken ages to get off the ground, but the good news is we've got the contract.'

'Thought you might.' She smiled, her gaze trawling the dance floor. 'I see Nina's dancing with Tony.'

'Yeah.' He grinned, his eyes bright with happiness as he looked out into the darkness and saw her.

Jenny watched them swaying to the music. 'Don't you mind that?' she said, noting the way Nina was moulding herself quite intimately to Tony.

Mick took a mouthful of his beer looking at her reproachfully. 'What's to mind? Nina's mine. She knows that. He knows that. You know, none of you know the person she really is. Warm. Gentle.'

'Aren't you forgetting what she did to Andy's face!'

Mick bristled. 'She's different with me!'

'Oh Mick!' She snapped; her brother's blind adoration was beginning to get to her.

'Well she is.' He said, seeing her exasperated look. 'I bring out the best in her because I treat her the way a woman should be treated.'

Jenny slid off the stool, wanting to end the conversation. She reluctantly had to admit that Issy was right, Mick was impossible. He couldn't be persuaded; in fact he seemed to have lost all powers of reasoning or logic.

'Where are you going?'

'Back to my seat, you know Dad's right about you!'

'Oh yeah what's he said now?' It was Mick's turn to be angry now. No one understood Nina. Saw the person he saw. They were all prejudiced and he hated it.

'That you keep your brain in your pants. You can't see it can you? She'll never marry you, she doesn't really want you at all. You're being used in some game she's playing to get Andy back.'

'You've been listening to Issy haven't you? I'm well aware of what she thinks!' His grey-blue eyes surveyed her sadly as she slid off the stool, about to leave. 'Why can't you just be happy for me? I'm not a fool; I know what I'm doing.'

'That's the problem big brother,' Jenny said looping her bag over her shoulder and moving away. 'I don't think you do.'

Issy set the drinks down on the table, disturbing Ella's daydream. 'Welcome back.' she said tucking the tray under the table. 'You were miles away.'

'I know.'

'Thinking about Matt?' She pushed Ella's glass towards her.

'Yes, you were right; he's not going to show is he?'

'Doesn't look like it.' Issy said as she scanned the room. Her gaze stopped just past Ella's left shoulder. She frowned.

'Is it him?' Ella turned eagerly.

'No, it's Jen.' Issy nodded to where a straight faced Jenny was still talking to her brother. 'That Mick! He needs a good shake not a talking to!'

'Tut, tut Issy Llewellyn, such uncharitable comments!'

They both looked up to find themselves under the dark eyed scrutiny of Andy Macayne who pulled up a seat, slotting himself between them.

'We don't welcome gatecrashers.' Issy said peevishly.

'Don't worry my little Welsh dragon; I haven't come to upset your evening, only to relieve you of your friend here for a dance. Ella?'

Ella got to her feet and followed him out onto the dimness of the dance floor. They came together, his embrace light, his eyes dark, unfathomable. Of course, she thought as they circled the floor, it would have been so much better if she'd been in Matt's arms. But now she thought with a stab of disappointment, there was very little chance of that happening.

'Fancy her do you?'

'What?'

'That girl down there in the green dress, you've been watching her all night.'

'Have I?' Matt replied, his face feeling hot with embarrassment. He was suddenly glad of the dimness and his half hidden position, tucked in behind Mark Maddison, the club's resident DJ.

'Yes you have Matty and the question is what are you going to do about it?'

Mark loved to tease Matt. To him it was pure irony that every night of the week available women flocked to his father's club and yet he was too shy to ask any one of them to dance. Mark had set himself the task of match maker, determined to pair him off with someone. Tonight, as every other night, was an uphill struggle.

'Not a lot.' Matt made a face.

'You're hopeless, you. Would it help if I gave you one or two good introductory chat up lines to get you going?'

'I've already spoken to her.'

'When?'

'Earlier in the week.' Matt bit his tongue then, stopping himself from telling Mark about their arranged drink, knowing it would only add fuel to the fire.

'Well there's your ice breaker, what are you waiting for? Go on, get out there!'

'Too late,' Matt nodded to where Andy Macayne was now hovering at the girls' table.

'Macayne, he's everywhere! Like the local tom cat!' Mark's brows creased irritably as he keyed in the next record, opening up the microphone to announce it. As the dancers settled down to a slower tempo he pulled off his headphones and slid out of his seat.

'Right,' He looked at Matt. 'Watch things here for a minute, can you?'

'Where are you going?'

'Outside, there's something I gotta do. Won't take long. If the record ends before I get back just flick the tape on.' He nodded towards the tape deck, and then disappeared.

Left on his own, Matt watched as Andy brought Ella out onto the floor. There was possessiveness in the way he held her, as if he was making a statement to everyone there that she was off limits to anybody but him. Matt sighed. It was over. He'd blown it. And yet he had been so full of confidence, standing there in that empty car park, agreeing to meet her here tonight. But there was a reason for that; at the time he had been on a high, unable to believe his luck. Of course he'd lied about not seeing her before. He had, on many occasions. He remembered the first time she had walked into the club. Sitting with Mark he had been unable to take his eyes off her. He quite honestly had never seen anyone quite so beautiful. And as if in silent agreement with him, every male head in the room had turned to watch her as she passed. Later he learned she already had a boyfriend. The news, although no more than he expected, left him feeling strangely deflated but then he realised at least it kept her out of reach and inaccessible to anyone else in Abbotsbridge. Then his father told him about the incident at the Forum; about Andy Macayne. This news caused him to give up his foolish daydreams and push her completely from his mind. If Macayne had a foot in the door, no one else stood a chance. Then quite unexpectedly on a cold January evening in the college car park, fate had delivered her right into his hands.

He watched Andy smiling, chatting. Tonight was to have been his golden moment, an opportunity to perhaps begin something wonderful. But when the crowds began to arrive, he had started to feel uneasy about being thrust into the limelight with Ella, the girl every guy in the club would give anything to be with. Doubts niggled at him. What if she hadn't meant what she said? What if he went out there and spoke to her and she didn't want to know? Faced with the fear of rejection he bottled out, hanging around backstage, hovering in the darkness, watching her every move. He saw her take her attention away from Andy for a moment and stare around the dance floor. Was she looking for him? If so he'd really blown it hadn't he?

'Still want a dance with her?' Mark reappeared suddenly, a wicked expression on his face, just as '*Words*' came to an end.

'No chance now.' Matt nodded towards Andy, who had now secured his arms firmly around Ella waiting for the next track to start. 'He's there to stay.'

'Not for long.' Mark grinned and opened up the mike.

'That's my car!' Irritably Andy turned to look up at the podium where Mark was sitting. "I didn't think I'd blocked anyone in. Stay there.' he ordered. 'Don't move.'

Ella watched him leave and then as *'Nights in White Satin'* began to drift through the speakers she carefully edged her way around the perimeter of the dance floor, looking for Issy and Jenny. If he wanted to dance with her again he could come and ask, she wasn't prepared to hang around for anyone, especially when his request had sounded more like an order.

'Hello.' He appeared out of nowhere, and she felt her breath catch in her throat as she looked up into those wonderful eyes.

'I was beginning to think you weren't coming,' She said, unable to disguise the pleasure she felt at having him here with her at last.

'Sorry, I got held up.' He said with an embarrassed heave of his shoulders. She was even lovelier than he remembered and she really seemed pleased to see him. All at once the only thing he wanted to do was hold her.

'Can I get you that drink now?'

'Id rather dance with you first, if you don't mind.'

189

'Of course I don't mind.' She laughed, amused and closed in on him, reaching up to rest her hands gently on his shoulders.

Matt took her in his arms, felt the softness of her hair against his face, the warmth of her body against his and knew without hesitation he never wanted this wonderful feeling to end.

SIXTEEN

Friday 2nd February

Laura's monthly letter was lying amongst the other post on the hall floor which Ella picked up on her way to breakfast. Recognising her grandmother's neat handwriting she tucked it into her bag, knowing just the sight of it would be enough to bring a sour expression to her mother's face. She decided she would read it later, somewhere quiet.

The morning was busy. They had a shorthand test first period and then double English, during which they were asked to put down their thoughts on pop music and its influence on modern life. Ella was so busy concentrating that it wasn't until lunch when Jenny and Issy left her to search for text books in the library for their economic geography assignment, that she realised she still had the letter. And so with a coffee and a doughnut she found a quiet corner table in the refectory, opened it and began to read.

Grandma was well, although just getting over a cold. She said Sid Jenkins from Field Way was coming in to decorate the Lodge for Ettie and Ted - something that was long overdue - and she had been into Kingsford to choose wallpaper with Ettie. Richard and Mary were well. Mary's stables continued to thrive and she had bought four more ponies. She said that Rachel was now dividing her time between the shop in the morning, the stables in the afternoon and the pub three evenings a week. On her spare nights she was involved with Meridan Cross Young Farmers, often staying over at the Hesketh-Maurice's - a strange pairing Laura thought, unable to see Natasha and Rachel as friends. Did she also know that Niall had moved out of Willowbrook and was now living in Fox Cottage at weekends? Laura confessed to finding this strange given the fact that he still had his meals at the farm and Mary did his washing and ironing. Ella saw it all clearly then. Niall must have set up an alibi with Natasha Hesketh-Maurice so Rachel could sleep with him at Fox Cottage. No wonder no one had suspected anything. Then she looked at the next paragraph and gave a groan.

'As you know, next month is my birthday which I usually celebrate with an 'At Home' for family and friends. This year I've decided to let Ettie put her feet *up for a change and have booked the Royal Hotel at Great Morden for lunch instead. Mary and Richard have been invited which also means that Niall will be there too. Maybe my celebrations will give you both an opportunity to sort yourselves out. I saw Niall last weekend and I have to say he does look miserable. Male pride is such a silly thing don't you think? Darling all I want is for you to be happy and if he's the one you want, despite the fact he's being difficult at the moment, wouldn't it be a super thing for me to play some part in helping bring you together again?*

Oh by the way, Mary suggested it might be nice to invite Rachel too. Of course I agreed immediately. It's a grand idea, I think she'll enjoy our company and I'm sure you'll both have such a lot to talk about..

Ella placed the letter on the table and picked up her coffee cup. 'Oh,' she said out loud. 'I don't believe this.'

'Ella? Are you all right?'

She looked up to find Matt standing over her. She smiled, remembering Saturday night, the dance, the drink afterwards and way they'd been together chatting about anything and everything until the club closed, oblivious of anyone around them. It had been a wonderful evening, he was easy to talk to, comfortable to be with - it was as if she'd known him for years. He'd promised to catch up with her at college in the week and now here he was.

'Sorry, yes, I'm fine.' She noticed the tray he was carrying. 'Please.' She indicated the seat opposite.

He settled himself down, arranging a plate of sandwiches and a cup of coffee in front of him, his gaze drifting between her and the letter.

'What's that you're reading? He asked, picking up a sandwich. 'Has Niall written to say sorry?'

She looked at him and laughed. 'Niall,' she said, 'has never apologised for anything in his life.'

'Perhaps it's time he made a start then.' He replied, taking a bite out of the first sandwich.

'It's a bit late for that.' She shook her head. 'It's over. He's with my ex-best friend.' she made a face. 'Actually she's welcome to him.' She waved the letter at him. 'No, this is a letter from my grandmother. She's invited me to her birthday lunch.'

'So why the long face?

'Because they've been invited too.' She gave a helpless shrug. 'I'm stuck. I can't possibly let my grandmother down, but I just can't see me sitting down to lunch with *them*, especially when my grandmother thinks it's going to be an opportunity to get Niall and me back together. She doesn't know you see.'

He looked at her over the top of his cup. 'Couldn't just call your grandmother and tell her what's happened? That would take all the pressure off. And, if as you told me, you no longer care about either of them, sitting down to lunch with them would no longer be a problem, would it?'

Ella thought for a moment. 'Apart from dented pride I suppose not.'

'I think, Miss Kendrick that you can cope with a little dented pride.'

'You're right.' She said as she folded up the letter and pushed it back into the envelope, giving him a radiant smile. 'I can!'

She looked at him for a moment, drawn by the clearness of his eyes and the way just a smile could turn him from Mr Average into something really special. Then she noticed the refectory clock 'Oh no is that the time?' She gave a groan. 'Sorry, I have to go.'

She scooped up her coat and bag and stood up quickly. 'I didn't realise it was so late. I've got three minutes to get to the third floor and the lift's out of order.'

'Will you be at the Mill tomorrow night?'

She nodded. 'You?'

'Yeah. I was thinking, maybe we could get together again.'

She nodded. 'I'd like that.'

'Let's make it a date then.'

The power of his smile robbed her of speech for a moment.

'Is that a yes or a no?'

'Sorry!' She found her voice. 'It's a yes, a definite yes!'

Friday 9th February

Joan Trimble in her grey suit and pearls intercepted Ella just as her class was finishing for the afternoon. 'Ah Ella, just the person. Mr Lattimer asked me to find you. Could you spare him a few minutes before you go home?'

'Yes, of course.' Ella nodded, wondering whatever he could want to see her about.

'Don't look so worried.' Joan reassured her. 'He's got some important news and I think when you hear it you'll be extremely pleased.'

Niall's white E-type reached the outskirts of Meridan Cross at 4.30. Rain had begun to fall during his drive home, heavy at first, turning to a light mizzle, blurring the landscape into indistinct shades of grey. But as he topped Sedgewick Hill and began his descent into the valley, everything miraculously cleared and he could see the village lights twinkling welcomingly as dusk crept into the valley.

A chilly wind blew out of the damp, dark wood and down the track as he got out of the car and retrieved his holdall from the boot. He ran quickly to the cottage, eager to reach its shelter. Searching the pockets of his sheepskin he retrieved his key and inserted it in the lock. As he opened the door he saw the fire burning brightly in the hearth, felt the warmth and smiled. She had been here today as she did every Friday, setting the fire and lighting it so that the cottage was warm and cosy for his return. His nose caught the smell of cooking food coming from the kitchen. There was no denying it; Rachel took care of all his creature comforts. By seven thirty she'd be here and then.......

He'd been thinking about her for most of the journey home. It was always like this on Friday afternoons. An hour and a half alone in the car with the radio on, dreaming of the weekend, looking forward to seeing her, being with her, making love to her. She was wonderful. Sweet, loving and fun to be with. He adored her body. Her small round breasts crowned with huge pink nipples and the softest, smoothest skin he'd ever touched. She was everything he wanted. For the first time in his life he was in love. He should be happy, but he wasn't. For two dark shadows hung over the relationship. Shadows which refused to go away. His mother, who even after all this time, was still arguing the case for making up with Ella and worse still, believed it was going to happen. And Ella herself; out there somewhere, angry, humiliated and probably waiting for the right moment to expose him for what he knew he was. A liar and a coward.

'What do you think of the idea then?'

'I think,' Ella nodded enthusiastically, 'it's wonderful.'

Don Lattimer smiled. 'I spent the last few months asking around town, getting feedback from business colleagues, seeing exactly how the community is served at the moment. It's all here in these notes.' He handed her a flat folder. 'Even better, I actually ran into Mollie Flanagan. She's the owner of Workshop in Grove Street. She tells me she's looking to retire in eighteen month's time. If you play your cards right, you could pick up a nice little established business. I'd go and have a chat to her if I were you. Get a feel for what she does.'

'Thank you I will.' Ella said as she tucked the folder under her arm. An employment agency, it could be just what she was looking for.

Tuesday 13th February

Rachel got off the 6.00 bus from Morden, pulling her navy coat together against the chill of the February evening. The night air was icy against her face as she began the five minute walk from the bus stop outside the pub to her mother's shop. Rain was forecast; she hoped she would get home before it started as she had no umbrella. The street lights through the village shone brightly, their yellow halos shimmering in the darkness, turning the pink washed walls of the cottages in the High Street pale orange.

As she walked she had time to think. To lay out her thoughts in a clear and concise way, without the continuous distraction of other peoples' conversations which she had experienced on the bus.

That very first time with Niall, that's when it had happened. Bad luck some would have said. But it had nothing to do with luck. It was gross stupidity. How could she have misunderstood what he was asking her? By the time she realised what he really meant, it was too late, his mouth was on hers, his hands everywhere and her resistance in tatters. And so she pushed her fears of the inevitable away, her mind instead on how she had been longing for this moment and now it was here, how wonderful and natural it felt to be doing this with him. Tomorrow she promised herself she would arrange to see Dr Beckwith and get herself on the pill. She remembered someone at school saying it was impossible to get pregnant the first time. It was going to be all right, it really was.

She caught up with Sheila Jenkins the following Monday, with the excuse she was asking for a friend. Shelia, worldly wise and with a reputation, knew everything there was to know about sex. She told Rachel about the clinic in Kingsford. Dr Beckwith would be no good because he would only prescribe for girls under twenty one who were about to get married. So Rachel had taken the bus to Kingsford the next morning, on the pretence that she wanted to do some Christmas shopping.

The clinic was a long, low modern building with a beige pebble dashed façade and large windows, with a waiting room full of young girls her around her own age. A lady doctor with a kind face had seen her, taking all her details, asking her questions about her own and her immediate family's health. The pill was extremely reliable she was told, but there were side effects, and people with a family history of certain diseases were advised against taking it. The doctor explained how it worked and that it would take two months to become effective in her system. During that time she advised her to use some other form of contraception as well.

Rachel left the clinic with six packets of Norinyl feeling things were worse rather than better. For how could she persuade Niall either not to have sex with her or to use condoms for two months without letting him know she had lied to him? It was impossible. She took the first tablet that evening and when Niall returned the following weekend, told him she had her period, hoping that by the time they got together again she'd have at least a week's supply in her system and some immunity from pregnancy. The missed periods to begin with had not worried her because the doctor had said that on the pill her cycle would change. It was, however, the sudden advent of nausea each morning which had set alarm bells ringing, and today's trip to Dr Beckwith had confirmed her worst suspicions.

She had now reached the steps. Almost home. And as if on cue a light drizzle began to fall. Opening the back door she took a deep breath. She was nearly three months pregnant and somehow she had to find a way to tell her mother.

Wednesday 14th February

Mary Evas was nearly at the end of her journey. She had taken Merlin for his regular daily outing, following the railway line out of the village towards the flood plain. It was a direction she had not taken before and she found it flat and easy, giving Merlin his head on occasions, letting him gallop along stretches of field which formed the extreme western boundary of Willowbrook.

On her way back she had called in to see how the Williamsons were getting on. They were a young couple with two small children and out of all the potential tenants she had interviewed for Paddocks Farm she had immediately warmed to Steven Williamson's love of farming and country life. Tania Williamson had been pleased to see her and had encouraged Mary to stay for a coffee, wanting to discuss several things, including some final adjustments to the food arrangements for the forthcoming Valentine's Dance in the Village Hall the following Saturday, which she was helping with.

At 11.30 she resumed her journey down the long twisting driveway from Paddocks and back into the road which would take her through the village and eastwards back towards the farm. The day was cold, grey and damp and she was glad she had decided to put an Arran sweater on under her wax jacket. Fingers of low cloud wove themselves through the dark, lifeless trees in Hundred Acre like wisps of smoke and a black scattering of rooks was suspended on the air above its summit, circling monotonously.

She was so busy looking at the wood that she did not notice the figure in front of her until the last minute. She pulled Merlin up sharply, her path blocked by Margaret Sylvester, her expression even more sour than usual. Hands pushed deep into the brown coat which hung open over her pink nylon overall, slippers on her feet, she made a strange picture.

'Margaret.' Mary forced a smile. 'Is something wrong?'

'You could say that.' Margaret looked at her with a hard but unfathomable expression. 'Got a minute?'

Mary checked her watch. 'Yes, I suppose so, but not long, I have to get back. Richard will be home for lunch. Is it important?'

'Oh yes.' Margaret's thin mouth pushed itself into a tight line. 'It's about your boy and my Rachel.'

Niall was in the kitchen filling the kettle at the sink when Mary walked in and laid her riding crop and gloves on the table.

'Good timing,' He turned with a smile. 'I'm just about to make some tea.'

She stood looking at him for a moment, her calm expression hiding the turmoil she was feeling inside.

'Is something wrong?' He asked as he plugged the kettle in and turned it on.

'Yes.' Mary placed her palms on the blue Formica surface of the kitchen table. 'I've just been waylaid by Margaret Sylvester.'

'Road testing her broomstick no doubt.' Niall smirked. 'What did she want?'

'Well, she seems to have this strange idea that you've been seeing Rachel these past few months. Is that true?'

'Yes.' He said cautiously, pulling two mugs down from the dresser. 'I've been out with her a couple of times. Why?'

'She's pregnant.'

'Pregnant!?' He turned to stare blankly at his mother.

196

'Yes,' Mary nodded. 'And apparently she's saying it's yours.'

Niall stood there looking at his mother as if she had said something he did not quite understand.

'Well?' Mary broke the silence. 'Say something Niall for goodness sake, preferably that the woman's talking complete rubbish.'

Niall put the mugs down next to the kettle and turned his back on his mother. Leaning on the sink he gazed out of the window. She heard him swear softly and in that moment realised that the hope she'd held onto all the way home that Margaret's words had been from malicious spite was dead in the water.

'So it is true.' Her voice came out in almost a whisper. Her youngest son, beautiful and golden. Brought up to be sensible. To know right from wrong. How could this have happened?

'Yes.' He turned to look at her, stunned. 'But she told me she was on the pill..........'

'So, how did you arrange all this deceit behind my back?' Mary reacted angrily. 'Where did you go?' Then suddenly it came to her. 'Fox Cottage.' she pointed an accusing finger at him. 'That's why you wanted to rent it!'

'There was no other way for us to be together.' He said defensively. 'I couldn't tell you about her because you were still so full of Ella and me getting back together. I didn't want to upset you.'

'Well I think you've managed that quite nicely now, don't you?'

'I'm sorry.' He looked across the room at her. 'I never take chances, I'm always so careful. I really believed her when she said she was on the pill........'

'Well she wasn't. Apparently she went on it after she started seeing you but of course by then it was too late.'

'Then why didn't she say something, for God's sake? Why didn't she tell me?' Anger was in his eyes now as he pushed his fingers through his hair.

'Niall, the girl's completely besotted with you! She told her mother that you said it was over with Ella and it was her you were in love with.'

'Yes, that's right, I did.'

'So why didn't you tell me?'

'Because you wouldn't listen!'

'What's all the shouting about?' Richard appeared in the doorway, pulling off his jacket as he came into the kitchen.

Mary took a step backwards and leaned against the dresser, her head bowed, her hand against her mouth, trying to get rid of the feeling that the whole world had suddenly gone mad.

Richard hung his coat on the back of the kitchen door, looked at mother and son and frowned deeply. 'Mary? What's happened?'

'Rachel Sylvester is three months pregnant and this is the culprit.' She said nodding tiredly towards her son.

'And how's this come about?' Richard asked, looking at Niall, his blue eyes hardening.

'I've been seeing her since I broke up with Ella.'

'More than just seeing her I'd say if she's pregnant.' Richard said scornfully. He stared angrily at his stepson. 'Hey, I hope you weren't up to your tricks with Ella, because if I find out you've touched her I'll deal with you personally!'

'No of course I wasn't. Things were different between me and Ella.'

'Oh I see, girls like Rachel are fair game are they?'

'No! Ella wanted us to wait, that was all. After she'd gone to Abbotsbridge I became friends with Rachel.....yes friends,' he said looking at their doubting faces. 'But I soon realised my feelings were changing.' He looked at them again. 'I didn't touch her then though. And I tried so hard to fight it, honestly I did.'

He paused for a moment as if trying to collect his thoughts then continued.

'The trouble was the more I thought about Rachel the more I began to realise that it wasn't going to work with Ella. She's so strong, so committed to what she's doing, where she wants to go. I realised she'd changed. She wasn't the same girl I'd been with here. In fact, she'd almost become a stranger. I knew then I had to end it. I told myself once I done that I'd be free to tell Rachel how I felt about her.' He looked up at Mary, frowned and shook his head. 'Of course it all went wrong. I went to see Ella. She was out and I rather stupidly followed her to the dance she'd gone to with her parents. We argued, this guy poked his nose in and I ended up being asked to leave. That was the night that finally pushed Rachel and me together. Once that had happened I knew there was no turning back. I haven't seen Ella since. I know I've done wrong, but I do love Rachel so much. I've never been so happy.' He screwed his face up painfully. 'But a baby - this is the last thing I wanted.'

'Margaret wants to see you.' Mary said quietly. 'Tonight.'

'Yes, yes of course.' He looked up at his mother, nodding in agreement.

'Niall...' She looked at him seriously. 'I think I ought to warn you.........'

'It's OK Mum.' He waved a dismissing hand at her. 'I can handle her. I love Rachel and I intend to marry her, what more can she want?'

When Niall knocked on the back door of the shop that evening he was greeted by a sour faced Margaret who stood back almost grudgingly to let him in. Closing the door behind him she led him down a badly lit linoleum covered passageway into her front room; a colourless place, with faded cream walls and dark furniture. Indicating a seat next to a struggling fire, she closed the door.

'Where's Rachel?' He frowned as she sat down opposite him. 'Shouldn't she be here?'

'She's away at her Aunt Ethel's, till I sort this fiasco out.' Margaret said bluntly. 'Having her here would only make matters worse.'

'I don't agree.......'

'I don't care what you think young man.' Margaret's lips tightened. 'After what you've done to my daughter.........'

'Mrs Sylvester.' He interrupted, looking at her fearlessly. 'I know what you must be thinking, but the thing is, I love Rachel very much and there's no question of me not wanting to marry her. The baby's just brought things forward. You needn't worry, she'll be well looked after.'

'I see.' Margaret Sylvester pursed her lips thoughtfully. 'Perhaps you'd like to enlighten me on just how you propose to do that?'

'Well,' He leaned forward, his hands clasped. 'I'm already living in Fox Cottage, so we have a home and I finish college this summer, so I'll be here all the time, working at Willowbrook.'

'And you're happy with those arrangements are you?'

'Well, yes.' He looked up with a puzzled frown. 'Aren't you?'

'Far from it.' Margaret gave a cold smile. 'Let me tell you what I think about your so called arrangements. Firstly, there is no way my daughter is going to live in a dump like Fox Cottage. It's damp, gloomy and certainly not the place to bring up a baby.'

'But you're wrong. Richard had it decorated last summer and Mum furnished it for me when I moved in. Rachel loves it. I'm sure you'll agree once you've seen it.'

'I don't want to see it.' She said awkwardly. 'She's not living there and that's that.'

'Well there isn't anywhere else.' He protested. 'We can't possibly live at Willowbrook.'

'You don't need to live at Willowbrook. There's plenty of room here.'

'Here?' Niall surveyed the drab poverty of the room. 'I couldn't live here!'

'That's fine, I don't mind,' Margaret said with an indifferent shrug. 'As far as I'm concerned *you* can go where you please! As long as Rachel and the baby stay here that's all that matters.'

'But she'll be my wife; she won't belong here any more.'

'Rachel will always belong here. She's my daughter,' Margaret said icily. 'You're not going to take her from me just because you've got her in the family way. You can marry her, provide for her, but she will remain here with or without you.'

'And what does Rachel have to say about this?'

'Rachel is a child. She'll do as she's told.'

'But she loves me and she knows I love her. You have to let her go, let her make her own way in the world.'

'I don't have to do anything.' Margaret replied. 'And if it comes to a choice between you and me young man, let me warn you, you'll be the loser. She knows where her duty lies. It's to her mother. So,' She gave a malicious smile, 'Will you be moving in here or not?'

Niall got to his feet, feeling the anger bubble up inside him. He had never struck a woman in his life, but he knew this moment was as near to it as he would ever be.

'No!' He said looking down at her angrily. 'I won't.'

'Nothing more to be said then is there?' Margaret shrugged as she shuffled towards the door and threw it open. 'Good night Mr O'Farrell.'

SEVENTEEN

Friday 16th February

Octagon Motors, in a blaze of light, stood beckoning like a bright beacon at the end of the dual carriageway leading out of Abbotsbridge. On the brightly lit forecourt vehicles were arriving, guests alighting. It was owner Bryan Tate's opening night, after a close down and a complete refurbishment and all of Abbotsbridge were there. Liam, as designer of the new octagonal building being dubbed 'the Polo mint' was one of the guests of honour, Mel by his side, stunning in a tight apple green dress, her hair immaculately smooth, cut shorter to jaw length in a new style especially for the occasion.

Clutching her wine glass, she viewed the showroom, where people milled around the display vehicles like visitors at the Earls Court Motor Show. Liam had been approached by Bryan, eager to introduce him to Ford's Regional Manager Bernie Carter. Bernie had been very taken with the radical new style of Bryan's showroom and was talking enthusiastically about adopting its style as new build for other dealers. Bored with a conversation that did not include her, she had drifted away to the edge of the gathering and was looking out of the window into the darkness when she felt the pressure of a hand in the middle of her back and caught the familiar scent of cologne.

'Good evening Mrs Carpenter.' She felt his warm breath on the back of her neck.

'Mr Macayne.' She turned with a smile, all politeness. 'How nice to see you.'

'It seems Liam's done it again.' He said, gesturing towards the atrium above them with his glass. 'It's an unusual design, very futuristic don't you think?'

'Yes.' Mel replied as she discarded her glass on the tray of a passing waiter. 'He is very gifted. He has great vision and an appreciation of beautiful things.'

'And does that include you?' He said with a smile that made her weak. 'He seems to spend so much of his time at work.'

'He has commitments.' She said defensively.

'Commitments?' The smile was there again.

'A sick father and expensive American hospital bills.'

'Still, all work and no play…' He shrugged and drank back the last of his wine.

'It's not that bad. We do have fun occasionally.'

'Not often enough though, I would guess.' He said his voice dark and smooth, 'For a woman like you.'

'And what would you know about a woman like me Mr Macayne?' Her smile was slightly aloof, she was enjoying the sparring session they were having.

The eyebrows arched. Mesmerising dark eyes held hers. 'Very little at the moment, but I intend finding out more. On that dinner date we spoke of.'

'Dinner date? Oh yes, that.' She gave a half interested smile. 'Were you serious? I thought it was just small talk.'

'Small talk?' He began to laugh. 'Oh dear Mrs Carpenter, you don't know me at all do you?' And without another word he turned and walked away.

Monday 19th February

'I'm not happy Tad.' Faye Benedict took off her glasses and pinched the bridge of her nose. She had been sitting at the large, heavy oak desk in the office above the Mill, working on the accounts for several hours now. The heat and brightness of the desk lamp had taken its toll; she was beginning to feel tired. Her mind had wandered during the hours she had been going through the figures in front of her, only half of it concentrating on the job in hand. The other half had been on a constant replay of events two weeks ago when Matt had come home.

She had noticed the change then, insignificant to most. He hadn't just been happy, there had been a definite glow about him. Tad had dismissed the whole thing as an over reaction on her part. His studies were going well; he was enjoying working at the club. He had every right to be happy about life, but Faye knew it was more than that, no one knew Matt like she did. She was like a barometer; when he was a small boy she always knew when he was about to go down with any illness even before symptoms manifested themselves. He was her only child; he was precious, more precious than most. Hadn't she almost lost her own life bringing him into the world? That had made her closer than most mothers; although she had always made sure it had never been in a way which would smother him. She was merely there for him, to give encouragement when he needed it and to be concerned when she saw trouble looming ahead which his youth and inexperience might not recognise. It was concern for his welfare which hung over her now and which had caused her to find a voice when her husband had entered her small office.

'What's the problem?' Tad, looking weary, took off his sports jacket, loosened his tie and sat down opposite her. He leaned his elbows gently on the high polish of a desk strewn with ledgers and rested his chin on his knuckles, looking closely into her face.

'Is it the club? Surely not, I thought takings were up. Those Bristol lads went down a storm last week.'

'No, far from it,' She shook her head. 'The figures are very healthy; we're doing better than ever - Tad.' She reached out and touched his arm. 'It's about Matt. And don't laugh or say I'm just being silly like you usually do. This time I do think we have a problem.'

'What sort of problem? He's doing well at college, isn't he? And I'm impressed with the way he's coming on at the club too! He's got great potential as a manager, you know.' He smiled, 'Must be in the blood.'

'It's nothing to do with work.' Faye bit her lip. 'It's that girl.'

'You mean Ella?'

She nodded. 'I expect you think I'm crazy but, you've just said how well he's doing and I don't want anything ruining that.'

'Anybody, you mean.' Tad got up and walked over to a small bar set in the far corner of the room. Selecting two whisky tumblers he poured a generous measure of malt whisky into each of them. Returning to the desk he sat down, handing one of them to his wife.

'It's not like that.' She took the glass with a smile. 'I'm a reasonable woman, desperately trying not to have any prejudices, but why out of all the possible girls he could have got involved with did it have to be Mel Carpenter's daughter?'

Tad took a mouthful of whisky; it warmed the back of his throat. He was caught between two camps. He loved his wife and wanted no more than to run his businesses and live happily in Abbotsbridge with his son eventually taking over everything and leaving him to a comfortable retirement. However, he had met Ella, and he liked her. It was difficult to accept she was Mel's daughter. There was nothing about her which was remotely like her mother. 'Actually Faye,' He said slowly. 'She's a nice girl.'

Faye raised eyebrows as she brought her glass to her lips. 'What about that rumpus she caused at the Forum last November?'

'A storm in a teacup,' The gold flecked eyes inherited by Matt looked directly into hers. 'None of which was her fault.'

Faye held his gaze. He was a good judge of character, rarely wrong about anyone. He had founded a successful business by involving himself with the right people, keeping away from any shady deals or illegal practices. Perhaps he was right.

'I think you should invite her to lunch. That way you can meet her properly. Dispel the myths. What about next Sunday?'

'Daisy's coming.'

'Well, one extra won't make much difference will it?'

She turned his words over for a moment and then shook her head. 'I'm not sure.'

'Oh Faye, come on. Matt is twenty years old, he's a man. With not much experience of life as yet, I grant you, but I think we've done a good job so far. We've brought him up well. He's a strong individual.'

'But is he strong enough to cope with having his heart broken?'

'It's a friendship, that's all; they're having fun together, enjoying each other's company.'

'You obviously didn't see what I've been seeing the last few Saturdays on the dance floor. The way they were looking at each other. The way they were dancing together.'

Tad laughed. 'You're showing your age Faye.'

'Well it has certainly upset Andy Macayne. You should have seen his face the other night.'

'Andy's just like his father,' Tad finished off his whisky, 'Thinks money gives him an automatic right to everything.'

Faye stared into her empty glass. The room fell silent. They had appeared to have reached an impasse.

Tad looked at her. She was the centre of his life; he had never loved anyone so much. First their inability to conceive a child had brought them closer together during those first years of marriage. During that time he had concentrated on his career, then when he realised his life in showbiz would never be a golden one he had wisely started the business, putting his money into something he could fall back on. One by one he had bought and refurbished the hotels and Faye was always there, an anchor in stormy seas when the businesses were growing, bringing her own brand of magic with her hotel management skills. Everything seemed to fall into place so well and then the biggest surprise of all. She was pregnant.

The memory was warm, it made him smile, but then there had been complications with the birth. God what an awful moment that had been, when he thought he might lose both of them. All the hard work had been for Faye and then for the new baby. He had thought of a life without them and realised how little it would mean. He'd prayed on his knees that night for God to save them and his prayers had been answered. After twenty four hours of uncertainty they were suddenly both out of danger. They had christened him Matthew meaning 'Gift of God', for that is indeed what he had been.

Looking at Faye now, still slim and youthful, he felt thankful for all he had. He reached across the table and touched her face gently with his fingers.

'Faye,' He said quietly. 'Matt's as important to me as he is to you, you know that, and there's no way I'll ever put his future in jeopardy. As I said before, invite her to lunch, see what you think. You may be pleasantly surprised.'

She stood up, leaned over the desk and kissed him gently on the cheek.

'Do I take it that means yes?' He asked, getting to his feet.

She nodded, smiling as she closed the heavy ledgers, pushing them to one side of the desk. It never ceased to amaze her how Tad could turn things around, he was so calm and logical and suddenly she felt foolish at the time she had wasted worrying about Matt.

'Come on.' Tad picked up his coat and reached for her hand. 'Let's go home.'

Thursday 22nd February

Jenny Taylor dropped her college folders onto the back seat of Ella's Mini and eased herself into the passenger seat.

'You're looking very pleased with yourself.' She said as Ella started the engine.

'I have an appointment to see someone this afternoon.' Ella replied, as they left the car park, 'About starting my business.'

'You kept that quiet.' Jenny said, waving out as they passed Zoë and Teresa standing on the college steps talking to two boys in motorbike gear.

'I wanted to surprise everyone once I'd completed the deal.'

'So who is it?' Jenny said as they joined the flow of traffic into the High Street. 'Anyone I know?'

'Mollie Flanagan?'

Jenny nodded. 'She runs an employment agency in Grove Street.'

'That's the one. Well, I'm meeting her there at four thirty. Don Lattimer set it up for me.'

Jenny frowned. 'I thought you said you were going to work for yourself.'

'I am. Mollie's all set to retire in the summer of '69, just when we finish. If everything turns out the way I hope it will, I will be buying her business.'

Jenny thought for a moment. 'Everyone knows Mollie, she's been here years. Are you sure it's what you want to do Ella?'

'Yes. ' Ella nodded positively. 'It's perfect. An established business so I don't have to start from scratch and hopefully there'll be potential to expand. If we can come to an agreement on price, Molly's offered to give me guidance on the day-to-day running. Of course I'll need someone to look after the financial side of things. I won't have time to do everything. My priority will be marketing the business, building a reputation.'

'Ella.'

'What?'

'Stop the car please. Just here.'

'What is it? ' Ella shot a worried glance at Jenny as she tucked the Mini in behind a navy Cortina. 'Aren't you feeling very well?'

'Yes, I'm fine. Look, I could do the finance.'

'You could?'

'Yes, you'll need someone you can trust, why not me?'

'Well if you're really interested. I'd be more than willing to hire you.'

'Oh I don't want to be an employee Ella, I want to be a partner.'

'A partner?'

'Why not?' Jenny wrinkled her nose. To be truthful, I'm feeling a bit left out. Issy's full of her plans for the new banqueting suite. I want something too and I'm sure Dad would be willing to loan me the money. *Please* say you'll think about it.'

'OK, I'll think about it.'

Ella considered the offer. For something as sensitive as accounts Jenny was right, she would need someone she could trust. And although lacking in experience Jen was exceptionally good with figures. It was the perfect solution. She gave her a smile as she indicated, pulled out and swung the Mini round in the road.

'Hey, I thought you were taking me home?'

'No, I'm taking you to my meeting at Workshop. Partner.'

The premises looked very dated Ella thought as she took in the grey façade and off white Venetian blinds at the window. The half glass front door declared *'Workshop, Agency for Temporary and Permanent Employment.* 'This opened into a plain and functional reception area which contained several easy chairs, a metal four drawer filing cabinet and reception desk.

Mollie Flanagan, a small, neat woman with a warm smile greeted them and made them coffee. She told the girls she was ready to call it a day. She showed Ella an impressive list of local clients she was actively doing business with. She was looking to close in the Summer of '69 with or without a buyer, her life savings sunk into a pretty cottage in the Lake District.

Ella looked around; the furniture would need replacing and every room redecorating. She also thought about location, tucked out of the way down a side street. Molly was known by reputation, people sought her out. A new untried owner would need to be very visual to pull business in.

At the end of a very amicable meeting and agreement on a price, Ella and Jenny left saying they would get back to Mollie in forty eight hours with their final decision.

After sorting out their finances they met with Mollie again. Yes they would buy the business, funds were now in place. However they had decided not to take up an option on the existing premises. Workshop would be starting under new ownership elsewhere.

Sunday 25th February

'It's lunch with the Benedicts today then is it?' Liam asked looking over the top of his Sunday paper at Ella.

'Yes, Matt's picking me up at 12.30.'

Ella pushed away her cereal bowl and began helping herself to toast.

'Parents inviting you over, sounds like it's getting serious.' He teased. Whether this was true or not, he thought, Matt had definitely made a difference to Ella's life in the short time she had been seeing him. She now seemed completely over Niall.

'I do hope not.' Mel joined the conversation, casting a cool eye over her daughter as she brought a fresh pot of tea to the breakfast table. 'I want Ella married into a respectable family thank you.'

'There's nothing wrong with the Benedicts Mel.' Liam folded his paper noisily and pushed his cup to the middle of the table. 'They're one of the wealthiest families in East Portway.'

'And where's their money come from do tell me?' Mel gave an arrogant snort as she poured tea into his cup. 'A few shabby hotels, the Forum and a second rate club that keeps teenagers off the streets. Big deal Liam!'

'That's a very spiteful and unnecessary way to describe his business.' Liam said chastisingly. 'Tad is honest and well respected, which is more than can be said for some others in this town.'

'And who exactly are these others!?' Mel bristled, thinking immediately of Bob. Since his reappearance at the opening of Octagon Motors he filled her every waking moment. But again he appeared to have disappeared without trace. She found it very frustrating.

'Hey you two, stop it.' Ella returned her half eaten piece of toast to the plate and wiped her mouth on her napkin. 'I've accepted a lunch invitation that's all. Matt and I are friends; I have no intention of getting myself tied up with him or anyone else in the immediate future. I have my career to think of.'

Mel laughed. 'I'd hardly call secretarial work a career Ella.'

'I'm not going to be a secretary.'

'You're doing a secretarial course!' Mel said impatiently as she finished pouring into the three cups. 'What else do you expect to be?'

'Self employed.' Ella smiled, eager to break the news she had been keeping secret. 'I'm starting my own business.'

'Ella that's excellent news!' Liam said, opening out his paper again. 'What are you going to do?'

'Run a recruitment agency. I'm buying Workshop from Mollie Flanagan. She's retiring next year. At exactly the same time I finish college. It's perfect.'

'What would you know about employment!?' Mel said sarcastically, returning the tea pot to the table and covering it with the cosy. 'You're just an inexperienced child.'

'I've arranged to meet with Mollie every week to learn her skills. And she's promised to stay around for the first month, just to make sure things go smoothly.'

'And what exactly are you going to buy this business with?' Mel looked amused. 'Shirt buttons? You need capital to start a business Ella and at your age banks will laugh at you and show you the door.'

'I don't need a bank.' Ella smiled pleasantly. 'Grandma agreed to loan me the money to get started.'

Mel closed her eyes. 'I might have known Laura Kendrick would be poking her nose in with her charitable hand outs!'

'Mel, don't be so hostile.' Liam frowned as he stirred his tea and picked up his paper again. 'Laura is Ella's grandmother, it's only natural she wants to help out.'

'It's not charity either, it's a loan!' Ella said defensively, annoyed that her mother was being so bitchy about the whole thing. 'We've drawn up a proper contract and I'm paying her back with interest. Jenny's coming in with me too; she's going to look after all the finance.'

'The Taylor girl. Ella are you completely stupid?' Mel seated herself back at the breakfast table with an exasperated sigh. 'Has it not crossed your mind that any partner you take on should be making a financial contribution towards a business? That little witch is taking you and your brother for a ride. How can you both be so gullible!?'

'I'm not gullible.' Ella glared at her mother. 'And if you must know, Jack Taylor is putting up the money Jenny needs for her share of the business. Satisfied?'

'I suppose so.' Mel eyed her resentfully. Ella seemed to have an answer for everything these days. 'But there's still this business with Nick. I'm not happy about that at all.'

'She really loves him. You should be happy for them both.'

'Nick is a very good catch for anyone. Like you he will eventually inherit a great deal of money. Don't you think she's aware of that? For goodness sake, wake up!'

'I am awake.' Ella got to her feet angrily, tossing her napkin onto the table. 'And I don't think I want to listen to any more of this. If you'll excuse me...........'

'Now see what you've done!' Mel directed her anger towards Liam as Ella left the room.

'Me?' He put his paper down once more, puzzled at the aggressive stance his wife had taken towards him.

'Yes you, encouraging her in all these hare brained schemes. Business indeed!'

'It's not that hare brained Mel, in fact, it's quite a sensible move.' He said folding up his paper and getting up from his chair. 'Despite what you might think.' He eased himself towards the door, eager to take shelter in his studio, where all was peace and tranquillity. 'Ella has an old head on those shoulders of hers. And given time, I think she'll surprise us all!'

EIGHTEEN

Sunday 25th February

'It's unbelievable!' Ella gazed around Matt's bedroom with awe. 'Are those guitars real?'

Matt nodded. 'They're Dad's. He can play as well as sing. The blue one's a Gibson.' He indicated with a wave of his hand. 'the red's a Fender. The brown and cream one's a Rickenbacker. He got that in an auction. Rumour had it that it once belonged to Buddy Holly.'

'Really?'

'Maybe not.' Matt shook his head and grinned. 'But the money went to a good cause.'

As lunch was not quite ready, Faye had suggested he keep Ella entertained for a while and what better place than his room, full of music memorabilia, including his father's prized gold disc for *'The Londonderry Air.'*

'Are these all yours too?' She ran her fingers along the racks of LPs and singles. 'There must be hundreds of pounds worth here.'

'You're probably right,' He smiled. 'I've been collecting since 1960. My very first single 'he reached over and pulled out a light blue Warner Brothers sleeve. 'Was this - *Cathy's Clown* by the Everley Brothers.'

'Yes, I remember them.' She laughed as she took it from him and looked at it. 'My grandfather used to say they sounded like a couple of drunken women.'

'Well I guess to the older ear they were different; not crooners like Frank Sinatra or Dean Martin. I've been lucky having a father who's been in show business. While he doesn't necessarily like modern music, he does understand why we do.'

'Wish my mother was like that, she hates all modern music.' She smiled and handed him back the record, turning her attention to his wall full of posters. 'I just love Tony Hicks of the Hollies.' She sighed, reaching up to touch the face which stared down at her. 'He's really good looking, oh and you've got one of the Beatles too. Now Paul McCartney's my favourite. He's got such soulful eyes.' She turned to look at Matt. 'Yours are like that.' She stared at him for a moment then back at the poster. 'And his voice,' she traced a finger around his dark hair. 'When I first heard '*Yesterday*' it made me feel so sad, I wanted to cry.'

'It's a great song. Simple, yet very soulful. 'Matt agreed, taking a quick look at his face in a nearby mirror to see if he could see any resemblance. 'Do you know he reckons he woke up one morning with the tune in his head?'

'Amazing.' Ella turned from her contemplation of the Beatles. 'Still, I suppose it comes to you in all ways, doesn't it?' She said, her eyes fixed on him. 'When you're a musical genius, I mean.'

Matt stared at her. Beautiful, he thought, and so close. For a moment he was tempted to reach out, pull her into his arms and kiss her but unexpectedly a strange paralysis gripped him. Fear of failure, of rejection, of making a fool of himself came from out of nowhere and collided in his head. Rescue came in the form of a voice calling from somewhere below. His mother announcing lunch was ready. With a nervous smile he quickly moved away from Ella, throwing the bedroom door open, feeling relieved and safe in the space now created between them. 'Come on.' he said ushering her out onto the landing and towards the stairs. 'I'm starving.'

Aunt Daisy was seventy nine years old. She was Tad's only living relative and occupied a Victorian bay windowed terraced house on the south side of Abbotsbridge. An assorted menagerie also resided at 42 Dorchester Road - four cats, two budgies and a small Jack Russell terrier called Winston. The latter was now curled up on the cushions of the settee in the drawing room, eyeing Matt and Ella with canine suspicion as they passed through to the dining room.

A small bespectacled woman in navy crimplene, her hair a halo of white around a time etched face sat at the large circular table in the middle of a room furnished with dark Regency style furniture. Inquisitive blue eyes fixed their gaze on Ella as Matt showed her to her seat.

Faye was back and forth with hot dishes of vegetables which she laid on the table while Tad had begun to carve an enormous joint of beef, setting slices onto plates with generous sized Yorkshire puddings.

'Aunt Daisy, this is Ella, a friend of mine.' Matt made the introductions as he and Ella sat down.

Aunt Daisy nodded silently, eyes still fixed on Ella. 'Pleased to meet you,' she said in a little old lady voice and then her attention was drawn to the plate of food which Faye put in front of her.

'Help yourself to vegetables Daisy.' Faye pushed the dish towards her, slipping a serving spoon under the lid. Aunt Daisy, served first, obviously considered herself the guest of honour and smiled graciously before spooning onto her plate what Ella thought were quite substantial helpings for such a small elderly lady.

Plates were placed before Matt and Ella and in no time the whole family were seated and eating. Tad opened a bottle of Claret and circled the table, filling glasses. Aunt Daisy stared at her glass for a moment before raising it to her lips and taking a huge gulp. She made a face and putting her hand to her mouth, belched loudly. Faye frowned across the table at her then looked at Tad who just shrugged. Ella looked at Matt, suppressing a smile, aware that he had said his great aunt was a bit of a turn and could come out with some real howlers if imbibed with too much alcohol. But today, she decided, that wasn't going to happen, not if Faye had anything to do with it.

Conversation was varied as they ate. Tad and Matt discussed the pros and cons of holding a talent night at the Mill. Faye mentioned she was looking at brochures but there was so much choice she was still undecided where the best location was for their next holiday. Ella talked about her upbringing in Meridan Cross and how much she loved and missed the countryside. Only Aunt Daisy sat silently, eating her lunch, her eyes fixed on her plate. After a second gulp of wine which drained the glass, she gave a loud hiccough and fixed her gaze on Ella.

'I've been watching you.' She said with a nod. 'You're not like the last one he brought here. What was her name? Caroline something or other? Asthmatic you know.' She shook her head seriously. 'Had to blow into one of those things to get her breath back. Well, of course, we couldn't have her. Can't have defective people marrying into the family can we? That would never do. But you're different, dear. Isn't she Tad?' All smiles, she looked to her nephew for confirmation. 'I think I like this one!'

'Yes, she's very nice!' Tad agreed.

'Yes, I think she'll do very....'

'Come along Auntie!' Faye interrupted, nodding towards Daisy's plate. 'Get on with your lunch.'

'Oh and now you're angry with me Faye. Isn't she Tad? And all I'm doing is being honest!'

Ella picked up her wine glass, watching the small tableau. The unrepentant look on Aunt Daisy's face, the embarrassment which crackled between Tad and Faye and the suppressed amusement in Matt's eyes as he gazed across the table at her.

'Auntie if you want to talk to Ella.' Faye said breaking the silence. 'I'm sure you can find less embarrassing topics.'

Aunt Daisy smiled mischievously and fixed her bright eyes on Ella again.

'So how long have you been living in Abbotsbridge then dear?'

'Six months.' Ella finished her meal and set her knife and fork together.

'And are you still at school?'

'College - I'm doing a secretarial course.'

'A secretary eh? Take a letter Miss Smith.' She chuckled at her own joke.

'Actually I'm not going to be a secretary,' She said quietly. 'I'm going to run an employment agency.'

'Yes.' Tad gave her an encouraging smile as he wiped his mouth on his napkin. 'Matt told me you were hoping to go into business. So you've finally found something.'

'Yes, I'm buying Workshop.'

'Mollie Flanagan's business, well, well. Where's she off to?'

'The Lake District. She's retiring. We've decided to move out of Grove Street though; we need to be more central.'

'We?' Faye frowned and shot a suspicious glance at Matt.

'Jenny Taylor.' Ella smiled, aware of the direction Faye's thoughts were taking. 'Well someone has to do the books. I'm absolutely hopeless at accounts.'

'And what do your parents do?' Aunt Daisy chirped up suddenly.

'My father's dead. My mother remarried. My stepfather's an architect. Mother doesn't work,' Ella laughed. 'She just enjoys spending his money.'

The old lady nodded and went back to her meal as if she had suddenly lost interest.

'More wine?' Tad circled the table again, refilling glasses, this time offering a freshly opened bottle of white as well as the remnants of the red.

Aunt Daisy thrust her glass forward as he passed behind her.

'I think you'd be better with a soft drink Auntie.' Tad said gently in her ear. 'Lemonade, or perhaps some orange.'

'I'll try some of the white Tad dear, no more red for me thank you.' She said, ignoring him completely. Reluctantly Tad poured her half a glass, aware of Faye's frown.

'Ella?' Tad offered the bottles.

'White, please.'

'Ella. You know that is an unusual name.' Aunt Daisy was off again. 'Who decided to call you that then?'

'Aunt Daisy, that's enough. Ella's a guest; she doesn't need the Spanish inquisition.' Faye scolded as she reached across the table to collect up the plates.

'It's not a problem Mrs Benedict.' Ella said handing her plate to Faye. 'It was my Father.' she said turning back to the old lady, 'After his grandmother. My full name is Marcella, but everyone calls me Ella.'

The old lady nodded then turned her attention to Faye. 'I'm only being polite Faye, taking an interest. Just like you told me to!'

Ignoring her, Faye, assisted by Tad carried out plates and dishes into the kitchen, reappearing with pudding plates and a large jug of cream. She took a bowl of fruit salad and a strawberry pavlova from the sideboard and placed them on the table.

'Now then, who would like what?'

The arrival of pudding silenced Aunt Daisy for a while and the conversation moved on to the council's ambitious plans to revamp the centre of Abbotsbridge with a new shopping centre and multi-storey car park.

'Do you think Liam will get a look in on the design?' Tad asked.

'I do hope so.' Ella was hopeful. 'I don't know much about architecture but from what I've seen of his work, especially Bryan Tate's new garage design, I'm sure he stands a very good chance.'

Aunt Daisy raised her spoon and smiled at Ella. 'You two are talking about that Liam Carpenter aren't you? He designed the big extension Tad and Faye had built recently. It's got a heated swimming pool in it and plants growing. It's an amazing place. Such a clever man!'

'One thing Liam has is wonderful eye for design.' Tad nodded in agreement.

'Such a shame, though.' Aunt Daisy leaned across the table towards Ella and lowered her voice. 'He has a dreadful wife, you know. A real bitch apparently!' she hissed through her false teeth. 'Everyone says he should have left her years ago. Still, I suppose one man's meat.....'

Matt drove Ella home in a silence broken only by the intermittent squeak of the wipers shifting rain from the windscreen of his father's BMW. His hope of detatching Ella from her awful mother and persuading his parents she was someone in her own right had been torpedoed by Aunt Daisy's tactless remarks, drawing attention to the fact that Mel Carpenter had a reputation which even little old ladies knew about. He blamed everyone - his mother for inviting her, his father for giving her too much wine and Aunt Daisy herself for never knowing when to shut up.

Immediately the words were out of her mouth Faye and Tad had simultaneously raised their eyes towards Ella to see her reaction. What had been expected or anticipated he had no idea. What actually happened was that Ella finished off the last mouthful of her pudding, placed her spoon gently down on her plate and looking across the table at Faye said very coolly and calmly. 'Delicious pavlova, did you make it yourself?'

Faye nodded, looking both shocked and relieved. 'I don't cook as often as I'd like to.' She forced a smile. 'The club and hotel accounts take up a lot of my time.'

Quite cleverly he thought Ella had used this opening to ask his mother about her work, thereby rescuing them all from a very difficult situation and moving the conversation on and away from the embarrassment of Aunt Daisy who, almost as soon as her pudding was finished, tucked her head onto her chest and started to nod off.

Coffee followed and they moved into the lounge where Aunt Daisy was made comfortable on the settee and guarded by Winston soon began to snore softly. Everything had been calm and civilised; they had watched T.V. but as he sat there observing his parents and Ella he wondered what was really going on behind the polite masks they wore. Then it was eight thirty and time to take Ella home. His mother and father had made a great fuss of her as Matt helped her on with her coat, even waving her off at the front door.

Once in the car he decided to apologise, to tell her that he wouldn't blame her if she never wanted to see him again. But he found that once he was alone with her he was struck dumb, frightened to open his mouth in case he made things much worse. So the journey home progressed in silence and although words swam around in his head somehow he did not trust them to come out in any sensible order. So instead he concentrated on the road ahead, turning the radio on half way through the journey in an attempt to break the great gulf of stillness between them.

Cambridge Crescent arrived ahead of him all too quickly; red brick houses and wrought iron gates passing until finally he pulled up outside No 33. In his mind's eye he visualised what was to come. Saw her reaching for the door once the car had stopped. Pushing it open, escaping without a backward glance, putting as much distance as she could between him and herself, never wanting to see him again after such an embarrassing experience. Instead however, as the car came to a stop she simply turned and looked at him, her eyes shining in the yellow reflection of the street light.

'Thank you for today, I really enjoyed it.' She said quietly. 'And you were right about one thing.'

'What?'

'Aunt Daisy putting her foot in it.'

'Ella,' He gave an embarrassed shake of his head before turning to meet her gaze. 'I'm so ashamed.'

'Well don't be. It's true. My mother *is* awful. I don't know how Liam puts up with her sometimes.' Ella shrugged matter-of-factly as she lifted her handbag into her lap. 'And,' the beginnings of a smile lifted the corners of her mouth. 'Daisy did have an excuse. At the time she was well under the influence of your dad's best claret!'

Matt sat back; looking at the roof lining of the BMW he closed his eyes and began to laugh quietly.

'It wasn't that funny Matt.'

'Sorry, I'm feeling relieved that's all. After what Aunt Daisy said I thought you'd be so upset, you wouldn't want to see me again.'

'Honestly?' Now it was her turn to laugh.

'Yep, I thought that's it, she'll never speak to me again. It's all over.'

'Well it isn't, far from it.' She gave him a wonderful smile. 'I was hoping you'd tell me where we're going next week. Didn't you mention something about the cinema?'

'Yes, *'Bonnie and Clyde'* is on at the Odeon.' He replied, his heart pounding. 'If we catch the early house at six fifteen we could go for a drink afterwards.'

'Great, I'm free Tuesday.'

'Sorry,' He shook his head. 'Tuesday is out, Friday too. I've got other things on.'

'Sounds very mysterious.' Ella looked at him inquisitively as her hand released the door catch.

'Oh it's nothing, just stuff.' He said as she got out of the car.

'Not seeing someone else are you?' There was a hint of teasing curiosity in her voice as she propped open the door.

'Jealous?'

'Of course, I enjoy having you all to myself.'

'I like being with you too.'

'Do you?'

He nodded.

'Matt...' She hung on the door looking in at him.

'Yes?'

The porch light came on at No 33, illuminating the driveway and bathing the BMW in its icy brilliance. It flashed on and off impatiently half a dozen times then stopped. With a sigh of annoyance, Ella turned to look at the house.

'Sorry, better go, that's mother's semaphore for come in at once.' She leaned into the car with a smile. 'What do you want to do about *Bonnie and Clyde*?'

'Let's make it Wednesday. Six o'clock outside the Odeon.'

Friday 1st March

Rachel got out of the car and stood looking at the austere brown pebble dash of the shop front.

'Come along, don't stand there dawdling!' Margaret was behind her at once, pushing her forward, her voice harsh and uncaring. Pulling her coat around her she walked slowly up the steps and stood waiting while her mother searched her handbag for the door key. The house struck cold as she entered; the narrowness of the hall claustrophobic.

'Let's have that off you.' Margaret pulled the coat roughly from her shoulders. 'Go on, in there.' She pointed to the living room as she hung Rachel's coat up with her own. 'I'll put the kettle on.'

It was barely warm, the fire a feeble flicker behind the fireguard. Rachel took it away and threw on a generous sized log. Flames appeared from nowhere, licking greedily around the wood, bringing a sudden burst of warmth to the room.

She retreated to a nearby chair where she sat trying to come to terms with the misery of the past fortnight. The news that she was pregnant and Niall was responsible had brought an almost hysterical reaction from her mother. Niall, she had screamed at her, was nothing but a chancer, in the same mould as her own father with his looks and his golden tongue. For the first time in her life Rachel had argued with her mother. Niall loved her, he would marry her. She showed her mother the pearl ring he had bought her. The punishment for her outspokenness had been a slapped face and its immediate confiscation.

'He won't marry you, you stupid girl.' Margaret shouted. 'He's practically engaged to Ella Kendrick.'

'But that's over. He's finished with her.'

'That's not what his mother told me when she came in the shop the other day.'

'She doesn't know about us. Niall said we should keep it secret for a while because his mother still wanted him to get back with Ella. We were going to leave it for a while, till it all blew over.'

'And you believe that?' Margaret shook her head slowly. 'God girl you're dimmer than I thought. Don't you understand? It's all lies. They tell you that to get what they want from you.' She closed her eyes tightly. 'I thought you had more sense than that to let a man do that to you!'

'I love him. I'd do anything for him.' Rachel blurted out, tears stinging her eyes.

'Such devotion!' Margaret said savagely. 'Pity he's not going to feel the same way when he hears the news.'

'Yes he will, he loves me!'

'Rubbish!' Margaret shook her head irritably. 'You're dreaming girl! You just wait.....'

'What are you going to do?' Rachel looked at her mother fearfully, wiping her tears away with the back of her hand.

'I'm going to break the news to his mother and ask her to send him down here to see me. I'll talk to him.'

'It will be all right Mum.' Rachel said meekly. 'You'll see. Once he's here, once I tell him, I know he'll want to marry me.'

'Ah, but you're not going to be here my lady. I'm sending you to Ethel for a couple of weeks. I'll deal with this.'

And now, Rachel thought, the two weeks have gone and I'm home. Back from that awful house in Taunton, with its musty smells where I've been a virtual prisoner, press ganged into cleaning and cooking. And I have sat in the car for almost an hour, waiting for her to say something and no word has passed her lips. She's being deliberately spiteful and cruel, but I know that's because it hasn't gone her way. He *is* going to marry me and she can't stand being wrong.

Margaret appeared at that moment, carrying two cups of tea. She handed one to Rachel and sat down opposite, pulling her cardigan across her thin body.

'He said yes didn't he?' Rachel said eagerly, trying not to feel to smug about the answer she knew almost certain was coming.

Margaret stirred her tea, her expression stony. 'As a matter of fact he didn't.'

'I don't believe you.' The cup and saucer wobbled in Rachel's hand.

'It's true. He didn't want to know.'

'No!' Rachel's face crumpled, her voice became a wail of despair. 'No!' She fumbled blindly through her tears to find somewhere to put her cup and saucer.

'Rachel.' Margaret went to her daughter, taking the cup from her, kneeling beside her, her voice soothing. 'I know you think I'm hard and uncaring, but I'm not really. Your father got me pregnant, married me and ran off with someone else a month after you were born. I didn't want that happening to you. Think of this as a blessing in disguise. At least we know exactly where we stand before the baby's born.' she smoothed Rachel's hair back from her face. 'You don't need him. You've got me. We can look after the baby together. We're all the family it needs.'

NINETEEN

Friday 1st March

The red Massey Ferguson tractor made a neat path across the open field, the seed drill behind it releasing barley into the fresh blackness of the soil. The landscape was empty with the exception of the cloud of lapwing which hung in the air a little way behind the tractor, settling and re-settling over the furrows as it laboured its way back and forth. The weather was exceptionally mild. A bright sun hung in a vivid blue sky full of fat clouds, while over Hundred Acre, bursts of green were beginning to show through the subdued darkness of the wood. The warmth of the day had caused Niall to discard his jacket halfway through his morning's work, rolling the sleeves of his thick Aran jumper up to his elbows.

He came to the end of a row and turned, killing the engine for a moment to relax, his thoughts turning to Rachel. Since his original meeting with Margaret Sylvester he had on three occasions been accosted by her and threatened with all sorts of dire consequences if he didn't meet her demands to marry Rachel and live at the shop. Such aggressive threats, he knew, meant she was feeling the pressure of having an unmarried pregnant daughter on her hands without a solution in sight. He smiled to himself, knowing he had her just where he wanted her. A couple more weeks should do it, he could sense by then she'd be ready to change her mind. Do it his way.

He was still deep in thought when a peppering of rooks burst from the trees and into the air. He noticed movement where the wood ended and the field began and saw a horse and rider emerge from the trees, immediately recognising Merlin's silver grey coat.

'Ella.' He gave a groan. 'Shit!' He frowned; the rider was clearly visible to him now and it wasn't Ella at all. He jumped from the tractor and stood there watching them approach. It was Rachel; she had come looking for him, everything was going to be all right.

She pulled Merlin up as she reached him.

'Rachel, oh Rachel! I'm so glad to see you.'

'Are you?' Her expression was hard, her blue eyes frosty.

'Well, yes, of course I am. I've been so worried about you. I had no idea where you were, how you were feeling.'

'Well as you can see, I'm fine.' She replied, pulling Merlin's head round. 'In fact we're both fine, me and the baby.'

'Darling,' He reached up for her. 'Let me help you down. We have to talk....'

'Do we? I thought you'd already said everything there was to say to Mum.' She tightened her grip on the reins. 'How could you Niall?'

'What are you talking about?'

'You said you loved me!'

'I do.' His blue eyes widened in amazement. 'I want to marry you! What's she been saying?'

'Who?'

'Your poisonous mother!'

'Don't you talk about her like that!' She spat at him. 'She's been wonderful!'

'Rachel please,' He put a steadying hand on Merlin's bridle, 'I need to talk to you.'

'No! You listen!' She shouted, tears welling up in her eyes. 'It's too late to come creeping round me. Mum said you'd do this. Well, I don't want anything more to do with you! I'm going to have this baby and I don't want a penny from you! I'll bring it up myself. Mum's going to help me.' Her face twisted hatefully. 'I don't need you Niall; in fact I wonder what ever I saw in you in the first place!'

'Rachel, you've got this all wrong. I went to see your mother and she...'

'Shut up!' She yelled at him. 'I don't want to hear your lies...'

'I'm not lying!' He tugged at the bridle. 'For God's sake will you just calm down and listen!'

'No! Let go.' She thrashed at him with her riding crop, stinging blows across his head and arm. He cried out in pain and released the bridle in an effort to protect himself from her sudden savage attack.

Rachel saw her moment and took it, turning Merlin back towards Hundred Acre, digging her heels into his flanks and galloping off. He took the boundary of the field, a dry stone wall, with ease and automatically headed west along a path covered in the soft mulch of last year's leaves. Brushing her tears away angrily as she rode, Rachel knew she had made a complete fool of herself. Of course she should never have ridden out there. She should have given him a wide berth just as her mother had advised. But she had been angry and determined to tell him what she thought of him.

The path dipped slightly, taking her into a small clearing carpeted in early primroses. She was so busy thinking that she didn't see the overhanging branch. It caught her in the side of the head, knocking her off balance and out of the saddle. Stunned, she landed helplessly on her back in the softness of the pale yellow and green carpet. Merlin, who had come to a halt on the far side of the clearing, turned to look at her, giving a snort of amusement. Slowly Rachel got to her feet, brushed herself off and picked up her riding crop.

'Are you laughing at me boy?' She said as she walked over and retrieved his reins. He snorted loudly again and she laughed, giving his velvet muzzle a rub before pulling herself into the saddle once more.

She continued her journey, erasing her encounter with Niall from her mind. He didn't matter any more, she didn't need him. He was shallow, despicable. Ella had been right about him dumping her. It was easy to hate him now. The hate gave her the strength and determination she needed. Suddenly she felt clearer about her future. It wasn't what she wanted, but then, she wouldn't be the first girl in the village to have a baby without being married. Trish Robinson had a little girl and she was doing all right. Her mother was looking after it while she had gone back to her job at the mushroom factory in Higher Padbury.

The beginnings of a dull ache in her back made her pull herself upright and square her shoulders. She halted Merlin and stretched. She must have pulled a muscle in the fall. A hot bath once she got home should help. The shop had a new range of bath salts, she was sure her mother wouldn't miss one packet. She rode on, dreaming of sinking into the relaxing depths of rose scented water. It was as she reached the edge of the wood and headed down the track past Fox Cottage that out of nowhere came the first sharp, grabbing pain in her stomach.

Four miles away Ella was approaching the village in her red Mini Cooper. Having got special permission for an afternoon off from college, she was looking forward to her weekend, staying at Little Court for Laura's birthday celebrations. This was her first return to Meridan Cross since that awful day in January when - she blotted the images from her mind immediately. It really was over. They were welcome to each other. She didn't care. For someone far more important now occupied her thoughts. Matt.

Farther down the valley, Laura was in the garden cutting daffodils from the great golden clumps in the flowerbeds below the kitchen window. Three weeks ago Ella had phoned her to accept her invitation and to give her some surprising news.

'Grandma I think you ought to know. It's about Niall.' Ella had said, 'We're not seeing each other any more. But please don't worry about me,' she added, 'I'm fine.'

She sounded bright and Laura, who had always been able to detect any cover up where Ella's emotions were concerned, knew she was telling the truth. Although anxious to know more about what exactly had brought Niall and Ella's relationship to an end, Laura was to be denied this as the rest of the conversation centred on things going on in Abbotsbridge and someone called Matt who she said had helped her get over Niall.

'You two sound very close.' Laura said, wondering whether he was the cause of it all.

'Matt's a really good friend,' Ella replied. 'He's only twenty, but he's so mature about everything. I've learned to let go and see Niall as just part of the past now.'

But the past that Ella was coming back to wasn't going to be quite as easy as she imagined it would be. Things Ella knew nothing of had happened since that phone call. News of Rachel being pregnant and Niall being responsible had come to Laura's ears earlier in the week, something which a subdued Mary had subsequently confirmed. Three days later when visiting the village shop, Laura then found herself forced to listen to an outraged Margaret declaring that Niall was refusing to marry her daughter. Was Rachel the reason he and Ella had finished and not this Matt, Laura wondered? Maybe he'd tired of Ella. And now that things had gone badly wrong with Rachel he was abandoning her too, quite cruelly in fact. Poor Mary, Laura thought as she picked up her basket of flowers, having a son who had turned out to be a complete cad.

Ella's car had reached the western edge of Sedgewick Hill from where the road ran out of the wood and down into the valley. Ahead of her in the distance, the river meandered into the flood plain. There the starkness of winter was gradually being replaced by the fresh colours of early spring. Rounding a bend in the road, she caught her first glimpse of Meridan Cross. The cottages of the village tucked comfortably under the edge of Hundred Acre to her left, the mellow stone of Willowbrook Farm facing the village on the opposite side of the valley to her right and Little Court with its tall chimneys sitting majestically between them. On the outskirts of the village she slowed the car. Before arriving at Little Court there was someone she had to see, someone very important. With a flip of the indicator, she turned the Mini up the track towards the farm.

When she eventually pulled up outside the farmhouse she noticed both Land Rovers were missing. Hopes of finally clearing the air with her grandfather and Mary faded and then she thought of Merlin; maybe she could saddle him up, take him out for a short run to kill time while she waited for their return. She crossed the yard towards the stable. As she pushed open the heavy wooden door she heard a low moan of pain and in the dimness could just make out the figure of Rachel lying in the straw, her knees drawn up into her stomach, her hands between her legs.

'Rachel?' Ella went over and knelt beside her. 'Rachel what is it? Are you hurt?'

'It's the baby.' There was fear in Rachel's eyes. 'I think I'm losing the baby.'

'Baby?' Ella frowned, trying to pull Rachel to her feet. 'What are you talking about? Oh my goodness!' she put her hand to her mouth as she saw the blood seeping into the straw.

'Ella?' Richard Evas's head appeared around the stable door.

'Granddad!' Ella swung around, relieved. 'Thank goodness you're here. It's Rachel, she's bleeding. She keeps talking about a baby.'

Richard Evas stepped forward, peering into the dim interior. Seeing Rachel lying there he turned quickly to Ella. 'You'd better run and phone for an ambulance.'

'Is she pregnant?'

'Yes she is, now please....quickly, get to a phone!'

Ella dashed out of the barn and headed for the farmhouse.

Turning Rachel slowly onto her back, Richard bunched up some straw for a pillow and dragged a bale across to support her legs.

'It hurts Mr Evas, it really hurts.' Rachel looked up at him, eyes enormous in the paleness of her face as she cradled her stomach. 'Am I really going to lose my baby?'

'I don't know my dear.' Richard shook his head. 'I really don't know.'

Saturday 2nd March

Despite the traumatic events of Friday, Ella reflected, the meal at the Royal Hotel had been quite an enjoyable affair. Richard and Mary were absent, but those who did attend had thoroughly enjoyed the lunch and Laura's old friend and bridge partner, retired artist Hugo Munroe-Black, sartorially elegant in his green velvet jacket and yellow patterned cravat, had proposed the toast and amused the guests with stories from Laura's past. Presents were opened; pearl earrings from Ella, champagne, cut glass, a cashmere wrap, more champagne. And then finally a cake appeared, all white icing and cascading pastel flowers, a surprise from Winnie. At three thirty the small group left the hotel, sheltering from the rainy afternoon under a multitude of umbrellas, tugged at mercilessly by a rough wind as they made a dash for their cars.

And now they were home and Ella, who had changed into a comfortable sweater and jeans and woven her hair into a thick plait, was sitting warming her hands by the fire in her grandmother's small private sitting room, waiting for Ettie to arrive with a tray of tea.

The door opened suddenly and Laura came in, heading immediately for the window to pull the curtains. She too had changed, swapping her smart red wool dress and black jacket for a green jumper and brown slacks.

'It really is a nasty old day out there.' She shivered slightly and rubbed her hands together as she crossed the room to join Ella beside the fire.

Ella watched her grandmother settle herself in the chair opposite. 'Thank you for a lovely lunch,' she said. 'I was fascinated by some of the stories Hugo told us. Did you really beat that American Colonel in a shooting match during the war?'

'I did.' Laura said with a wicked smile. 'Erwin Bloomberg was his name. Here with the Americans on the run up to D-Day. Thought we British and our fête were a bit of a joke. Fête worse than death he called it.' she pulled a face. 'The home guard had set up a shooting contest. It was when he started cat calling and making fun of them that I thought, I'm not having this. So I challenged him. Five shots each. He took one look at me and I knew what he was thinking. Silly little English woman, I'll soon put her in her place. Little did he know that I'd handled a gun since I was nine years old. I was a crack shot. I got five bulls eyes to his three. His face was a picture. It certainly shut him up!'

'You're so cool and calm about everything.' Ella said, looking at her grandmother with admiration. 'Nothing fazes you does it?'

'I could say the same about you.' Laura said with an amused smile.

'Do you think so?'

'Indeed yes. Today at the lunch there you were chatting away as if you hadn't a care in the world and yet it's been a terrible weekend for you. Your Grandfather's appalling outburst for a start! So unfair! If he's going to start blaming someone he should perhaps be looking a little closer to home!'

Ella nodded still feeling the sting of his words, his face red and angry as they watched the ambulance moving down the track on its way to the hospital.

'I hope you realise that if you hadn't gone running off to Abbotsbridge to live,' He shouted at her. 'none of this would be happening.'

'Then there was the shock of finding out what had been going on behind your back.' Laura continued.

'I already knew Grandma.'

'You did?' Laura looked surprised.

Ella nodded. 'I came back to the village just after Christmas. I wanted to see Niall. I was fed up with him avoiding me. Thought it was time we sorted things out once and for all.'

'And?'

'I met Rowan Miller on my way here. Stopped to talk to him. He was saying some really odd things, about us going away for Christmas together to Lyme Regis. He mentioned that Niall was living in Fox Cottage, something else he thought I already knew! When I went up there, hoping to get some answers, I found them there together.' She gave a sigh. 'Suddenly everything fell into place.'

'Oh my dear, how simply awful!' Laura's hand went to her face. 'Whatever did you do?'

'I left, very quickly. I was in a dreadful state. I don't know how I managed to drive back to Abbotsbridge, but I did. I couldn't believe he'd blamed me for the break-up when all the time Rachel was the reason he didn't want me any more. He lied and he was such a coward.' She looked at her grandmother. 'I was so upset and angry. I felt humiliated too and knew it would be a long time before I could ever come back here again, that's why I kept making excuses not to visit. Then, when you wrote to me about your birthday, I didn't know what to do. It was Matt who said I should come.' She smiled again as she thought of Matt's words. 'He's been such a good friend.'

'I'd love to meet him one day.' Laura said as Ettie appeared with the tea.

'You will.' Ella nodded. 'I promise.'

Down the valley at Willowbrook, Niall had just returned from yet another attempt to visit Rachel in hospital. 'Here, you'd better put these in water.' He said dumping a large bouquet of flowers on the draining board as he came into the kitchen.

'Still no joy then?' Mary turned from the cooker where she was stirring gravy.

'No.' He hung his coat on the back door before pulling out a chair and sitting himself down. 'Margaret won't let me anywhere near her.'

'Oh dear,' Mary said wearily retrieving the pot and pouring him and herself a mug of tea each. 'Still,' she gave a thoughtful smile. 'Margaret can't hide her for ever. Once she's back here working, I'll make sure you get to talk to her.'

'Rachel isn't coming back,' Niall replied. 'Margaret told me she's sending her back to her Aunt. Says with her arthritis her sister needs someone to look after her and keep the place clean.'

'And she was doing so well here at the stables!' Mary drew her breath in sharply. 'So, what happens now?'

Cradling the mug he regarded her quietly. 'Well, I can only speak for myself. As far as I'm concerned I have only one option. Leave Meridan Cross. I can't go on living here any more, not after this.'

'Leave the village!' Mary looked taken aback. She had always believed them close; that no matter what troubles there were, as mother and son they would always be there for each other. The thought of him leaving was too painful to contemplate. Her mind scrabbled around for reasons to make him stay.

'What about College? You can't just walk out on your studies.'

'I've no intention of doing that.' He looked at her calmly. 'I'm going to work for Cousin Eric. You remember mentioning that he was looking for someone when he phoned last week? I decided to call him after I left the hospital. We had a good chat. He's keen to take me on as soon as possible.' He said cheerfully. 'I can travel to Cirencester and back from there. Of course he did say it had to be on one condition.'

'And what was that?'

'That you approved.'

He's sorted it all out, without even discussing it with me, she thought. All I'm needed for is to rubber stamp his actions. So he can go with a clear conscience. How could he do this to me?

'Well Mum?' His voice broke into her thoughts. 'If you agree I can be there by late evening.'

'You're going today?'

'Yes, don't look so upset, the sooner I start getting on with my new life the better.'

222

'I see.' She said, the lump in her throat reducing her voice to a whisper. 'Well I suppose if that's how you feel......'

'Great, thanks.' He looked relieved as he got to his feet and pulled his coat from the back door. 'I knew you'd agree.' He came to stand beside her, bending to brush his lips against her hair. 'Now, I suppose I'd better join the others in the milking parlour for the last time. Wouldn't do to let them down on my final day would it?'

'No Niall.' She looked up at him, feeling the prickle of tears in her eyes. 'Heaven forbid you should do that.'

Sunday 3rd March

Ella sat watching her grandmother. Amazingly, twenty four hours had seen a complete change in the weather, bringing back the warmth and sunshine once more. With the French doors wide open, from the breakfast table Ella could see the river teasing the tendrils of the huge white willows which sat high on its banks at the end of the garden. Just below this, Laura stood on the small jetty, throwing food for the ducks, her back to her granddaughter. Eventually she finished and dusting the crumbs from her hands began to walk back towards the house.

'I often think,' she said as she reached Ella and sat down beside her, 'that your grandfather would turn in his grave if he could see me feeding those birds.' She laughed out loud. 'As far as he was concerned, anything with feathers needed a gun taking to it. We used to have regular shooting parties here between the wars you know. They were the talk of the county.'

'Excuse me Mrs Kendrick.' Ettie appeared in the doorway. 'Mrs Evas is here.'

'Perhaps with news do you think?' Laura looked expectantly at Ella. 'Bring her through Ettie. Oh and can you organise an extra cup and saucer please?'

'Certainly Mrs Kendrick,' Ettie nodded and left, returning minutes later with Mary who was carrying a long flat box wrapped in silver paper.

'Sorry we missed the meal yesterday.' She gave an apologetic smile. 'This is for you.....' she handed Laura the box. 'We hope you like it. The colour was Richard's choice.'

'Do sit.' Laura took the gift and indicated the chair next to her. 'Ella, would you do the honours dear?' she indicated the coffee pot.

As Ella began to pour, Laura unwrapped her gift, revealing a beautiful blue and gold Hermès scarf. 'It's beautiful. Thank you.' She looked across at Mary, her smile turning quickly to a frown. 'Mary, are you all right? You look pale.'

'I haven't slept very well I'm afraid.'

'Yes.' Laura replied. 'It's a bad business. Not helped by Richard's outburst I have to say.'

'Said in the heat of the moment Laura,' Mary turned to Ella, accepting the coffee. 'He really is very sorry.'

'And how about Rachel?' Laura enquired as Ettie arrived with the extra cup and saucer. 'Is there any news?'

'None,' Mary said spooning sugar into her coffee cup and beginning to stir. 'Margaret won't let anyone near her.'

'Not even Niall?'

'Especially not Niall, he…' Mary stopped abruptly, her gaze drifting to Ella then back to Laura.

'Don't look so concerned, Ella is fine.' Laura said reassuringly. 'You can speak quite freely about him and Rachel in front of her.'

'That's right,' Ella nodded. 'I don't have a problem Mary.'

'Oh dear,' the spoon clattered into the saucer and Mary's eyes began to cloud with tears as her hand went unsteadily to her face. 'It's all such a mess, it really is.'

'Oh, my dear,' Laura set her present to one side and moved next to Mary slipping a comforting arm around her shoulder. 'You've been through so much lately.'

Mary sniffed and nodded, pulling a handkerchief from her pocket and blowing her nose. 'Niall's gone.' she said quietly. 'Yesterday, to work for my cousin in Evesham. A new start he said. I was so angry with him. For the first time the veil's been lifted from my eyes. I can see him for what he really is. Selfish. Heartless. Escaping to Eric's. Leaving everyone else to sort out the awful mess here.' She leaned to one side, her hand going into her jacket pocket. 'And this morning when I went into his room to pull the curtains, I found this.' She pulled a folded cream envelope from her pocket and handed it to Ella. 'It's for you.'

'Me?' Ella looked puzzled as she took the envelope and opened it. Inside were two sheets of neatly folded vellum.

'I can't believe he's done this.' Mary continued with a shake of her head. 'How could he just leave? We were always so close. And then there's poor little Rachel. How can he abandon her? If he really loved her he'd never have let Margaret stand in his way.' She stopped for a moment to dab at her eyes with the handkerchief. 'He really is the most incredibly selfish person I know!'

'Oh Mary!' Laura's comforting arm was there once more. 'I am *so* sorry.'

Ella rested the letter on her lap. It was all there. All his feelings from the moment he had stepped out of the woods on that September afternoon, right up until yesterday when he had left to start his new life.

He spoke of the changes her move to Abbotsbridge had brought. He talked of the enormous strength she had, the single minded determination to find success from failure, something which had both fascinated and frightened him. Being apart from each other hadn't brought him closer to her he said, it had made him realise he wasn't in love at all.

Of course, in the beginning Rachel had simply been a friend. Someone to talk to about the problems he was having. And then he found the more he saw her, the more she got under his skin. It was the night he had come to Abbotsbridge that was the turning point.

'Looking back, I feel no pride in how I went about persuading Rachel to sleep with me.' He wrote. *'It seemed so easy gaining her sympathy, telling her you had left me for someone else. That you didn't care. I wanted her so much I wasn't concerned about the real truth. In fact it didn't seem like a lie at all. I saw you and Andy together and that was all the excuse I needed to legitimise what I wanted to do. I convinced myself that you were having such a good time in Abbotsbridge it would all be OK and that you'd soon forget about me. But that didn't happen. You know, I never imagined you'd hold on the way you did. I underestimated how much you really loved me. It was when I found the heart I'd given you for your birthday that I realised. That was the day you found us together. Of course, I was scared at first, but then I thought maybe things weren't so bad after all. You'd tell my mother, there would be a big row, it would all be out in the open and I'd be a free agent again. Unfortunately that didn't happen and what made matters worse was that I realised I really had fallen in love with Rachel. I knew I needed to come clean, to face my mother but somehow I just couldn't tell her. Coward that I am, I kept hoping you'd do that for me.*

When Mum told me Rachel was pregnant, although it wasn't what I really wanted for us both, I thought everything had worked out and at last we could be together. But her mother had other ideas. She asked to see me and I was told that if I married Rachel I would have to come and live with them. I couldn't do that Ella, sharing her shabby world, handing over my money at the end of the week like a lodger handing over rent. She made me so angry with her demands. I could see the way she manipulated Rachel and she thought she could do that with me because she had me in a corner. So I stood up to her, said I wouldn't marry Rachel on those terms. I thought she would come to her senses and let us set up home in Fox Cottage. But she didn't and to make matters worse, she twisted the situation, so it looked as if I'd abandoned Rachel. I don't think she ever wanted us to be together. Rachel's the ultimate insurance policy for her old age. She's a wicked woman! And now Rachel hates me, won't even see me. I can't explain, tell her the truth. I long to hold her in my arms, tell her I love her, but I know it's impossible.

When I saw Margaret at the hospital she told me that when Rachel is discharged she plans to send her away to Taunton to live with her Aunt. She'll be employed as her housekeeper. Reading between the lines you know what that means don't you? So I've really no choice. I have to leave Meridan Cross so that Rachel will be able to stay in the village and keep her freedom. Cousin Eric and his wife are good people; they'll see I'm all right.

I only hope in time that Mum will forgive me. She has to live in the same village as Margaret and I know what damage that vindictive woman can do. In some ways therefore, I'm making this sacrifice for her too, although she'll probably think as always I'm shirking my responsibilities. I know I've upset her by leaving so soon and giving the impression that I couldn't give a damn, but I had to be hard. I just couldn't have coped with her tears. It was as much as I could do to hold back my own.

Well, time to get on the road. They are expecting me around eight this evening. Ella, I'd like to end this letter by saying that I'm so sorry for what I did to you, and I know you'll find some of what I've had to say to you painful. But I need you to see that I haven't got off lightly. Far from it. I've lost not only the woman I love but also the love and respect of those I care about most. I'm being paid back now for all the times I took everyone and everything for granted. Serves me right eh? I only hope that in years to come you and all the others I've hurt so badly will find it in their hearts to forgive me. I'm hopeful that Evesham will turn me into a better man. One Mum can be proud of.

Take care. Be happy. I hope you find the love you deserve.

Niall.'

Ella was suddenly aware of the conversation going on around her; Mary's tearful anger and Laura's soothing tone. 'Before you say anything else,' she leaned across the table and offered Mary the letter. 'I think you ought to read this.'

TWENTY

Monday 4th March

Hands deep in his jacket pockets, Matt stood alone outside the Odeon. Ella was very late. And she'd been so keen to see this Bond film. The queue had now gone. Their tickets purchased, their seats taken. *You Only Live Twice* had started five minutes ago. So where was she? What had kept her? And then he realised these were foolish questions. He already knew. She'd been to Meridan Cross at the weekend for her grandmother's birthday. She'd seen Niall and they had made up. He had already told himself this might happen. Being aware of it, however, did not make things any less painful.

And then he saw her, hurrying towards him, clutching at her leather coat, her hair loose around her shoulders. Catching sight of him she waved and smiled and began to run.

'I forgot the time! Then I couldn't find a parking space anywhere!' There was genuine concern in her face. 'Are we too late?'

'Fraid so.' He indicated the empty foyer.

'Matt I am sorry.' She squeezed his arm. 'Blame it on the weekend. You'll never believe what's happened!'

He'd dreaded this moment, but smiled bravely.

'Something to do with Niall I guess.'

She nodded. 'He's gone. Left Meridan Cross to work for relatives just outside Evesham.'

'Gone?' Relief washed over him. 'Why?'

'It's complicated and best explained over a vodka and tonic.'

'Come on.' He slipped his arm around her shoulder. 'I know just the place.'

'I must say, you look positively radiant this evening.' Bob Macayne watched Mel across the table in the restaurant of the Ragbourne Grove Hotel just east of Kingsford where they were finishing their coffee.

'Well.' Mel smiled. 'It's lovely to be wined and dined like this. I feel really pampered. And of course today I've received the news I've been expecting for a while now.'

She smiled at Bob. After all the weeks of waiting they were here at last, having dinner, getting to know each other as he had promised. He was charming, witty and very sexy and she felt herself drawn even more under his spell. He made her feel special; listened to what she had to say, laughed at her jokes. She now how realised through someone like him it would be possible to escape the tedium and disappointment of her life in Cambridge Crescent.

'Oh?' Bob raised inquisitive eyebrows as he drew his wine glass to his lips. 'And what's that?'

'My daughter and that dreadful Niall O'Farrell really are no more. I can't tell you just how happy that makes me.'

'Ah yes, your father's stepson.'

'That's right. I'm so pleased. I want the best for my daughter Bob. I want her to marry into a good Abbotsbridge family. Now someone like Andy would be just right for her.'

'Funnily enough I was saying much the same thing to him quite recently.'

'You were?'

'Yes. He needs to take life more seriously. Stop all this running around, breaking hearts and settle down.' He shrugged. 'Ella is just the type of girl that would suit him.'

He reached for the bottle of Chablis sitting in the middle of the table.

'More wine?'

She nodded, offering him her glass.

'I agree. I know I'm her mother and rather biased but from what she says I think he does like her.' She said enthusiastically. 'Couldn't we build on this? It's a good start, surely?'

Bob gave a quiet sigh as he returned the bottle to its silver ice bucket.

'Unfortunately Mel, Andy's full of good starts. It's the finishes that are the problem.'

'And so that's about it.' Ella finished, looking out of the window of the Valley View Pub which overlooked the river below and the Kington district of Abbotsbridge, where large expensive houses hugged the hillside, their gardens running all the way to the water's edge. 'Of course I had to tell my mother. I didn't want to but as soon as I got home she pounced on me. You can imagine how gleeful she was about it all.'

Matt watched her sympathetically. He couldn't believe what she'd just told him. He felt sure that when she returned to Meridan Cross, Niall would take her back; that his wise words telling her to go back for her Grandmother's birthday would mean the end of everything. But now the impossible had happened. Niall had gone for good. She was free at last. But the quiet elation he had felt at her news was quickly dampened when he realised that he would only have her to himself until the next good looking man came along. And with a girl like Ella he knew that wouldn't take long.

'So what are you going to do now?' He asked, looking at her as he raised his half empty glass to his lips, his mind on Andy and how he would react when this news reached him.

'I don't know.' She shrugged. 'I haven't really thought about it. I'm just so relieved it's finally over.   I realise now that we were finished weeks ago. Anyway, things have been different for me ever since I met....' she hesitated.

'Andy.' The name was out before he could stop himself.

'Andy?' She looked puzzled.

'Well, I thought.......'

'Matt he's not my type.' She stared into her empty glass, rotating its stem back and forth between her thumb and finger. 'Although my mother would have everyone believing otherwise. 'If only she knew.' She laughed, her eyes meeting his. 'Matt....' she said after a moment's silence, 'I....well...there's something you need to know....' she moved her head towards his and without warning leaned over and kissed him softly on the lips.

After the initial shock of what she had done, his first instinct was to kiss her back but he hesitated. She was obviously still upset. What other reason could there be behind this crazy, irrational thing she had just done. But she was so close and the temptation to abandon himself to his feelings was almost irresistible. His mind was made up for him by the song playing on the pub's juke box. *And a taste of honey's worse than none at all* - Smokey Robinson was giving him a warning to step back from the brink. Ella was just a dream; a crazy, irrational dream. It could never be real. Not for someone like him. So he simply gave her an awkward smile and said. 'What was all that about then?'

'Oh!' She looked flustered.' Sorry!

'It's O.K.,' Matt gave her a bemused look. 'I guess everyone's allowed at least one impulsive moment in their lives.'

'*Impulsive moment.*' Was that how he saw it? She looked away, letting her gaze drift out of the window into the darkness, trying to hide her disappointment. She was free. She knew now that she loved him, really loved him. But he didn't feel the same way.

'Another drink?'   Matt picked up her glass, wanting to break the uncomfortable silence which had settled itself between them

'Better not.' She shook her head as she looked at her watch. 'It's ten thirty. Time I was making a move. Liam's away and mother is out for the evening. I want to get back before she does. I can't bear any more gloating.'

The last thing Mel was thinking about at that moment was going home. In fact she was finding it difficult to believe what was happening to her. She remembered getting up from the table and feeling dizzy. Bob called a waiter over and together they had helped her into the lounge where she had rested for a while on one of the couches. Then Bob was helping her to her feet again. He had booked a room for her. She was in no state to go home. Better that she stayed there the night. She vaguely remembered the lift, then the few steps along the corridor and a door being unlocked. The bed was so soft, she lay back thankfully. Bob pulled off her shoes and settled her back comfortably. He removed his jacket and pulled off his tie before coming to sit beside her, his face creased with concern.

'Too much wine?'

'I think so.' She placed her palm against her forehead, her mouth tasted awful. 'Is there any water?'

He went to the bathroom, returning with a glass.

She pushed herself into a sitting position and took it from him, drinking it back, enjoying the cool bland taste.

'Thanks.' She handed him the glass and lay back staring up at him, the dizziness retreating, a warm, mellow feeling taking its place. 'You're a gentleman and I'm an embarrassment.'

'No you're not. It's my fault. I shouldn't have taken so many liberties with your glass.'

She smiled at him, reaching up, gently touching the cleft in his chin. 'Don't argue, with me Mr Macayne, I say you're a gentleman.'

His fingers closed over hers, he pulled her hand away and leaned forward, his eyes dark, his expression thoughtful. She closed her eyes, waiting for moment she would feel the brush of his lips against her forehead. They touched her mouth instead, a soft pressure at first, then stronger, more insistent. She opened her eyes wide and pulled back, startled by this sudden and unexpected act of intimacy

'Forgive me,' He sat back. 'I shouldn't have.......'

'On the contrary,' She pushed herself up onto one elbow with a slow smile, her head clearing miraculously. 'I've been waiting for you to do that all evening.'

Friday 15th March

'You wanted to see me Mrs Evas?'

Rachel hovered in the doorway of the stables where Mary was busy grooming Buster.

'Ah Rachel, yes. Have you got a minute?'

Rachel nodded and moved into the barn, seating herself on a hay bale.

'How are you feeling now?' Mary asked as she moved Buster back into his stall.

'Much better, thank you.'

'You've had a nasty time of it, I'm so sorry.'

'It's O.K. Mrs Evas.' Rachel pushed her hands in her jeans and looked at the floor. 'It's not your fault.'

'Rachel, I've something for you.' Mary pulled an envelope from the pocket of her green quilted body warmer and handed it to Rachel.

'What is it?'

'It's a letter. From Niall.'

'I'm sorry Mrs Evas.' Rachel said, pushing it back at Mary. 'I'm not interested.'

'My dear, Niall wrote this letter to Ella before he left. After reading it she gave it to me. She said it was important you should have it as soon as you were back at work.'

'Have you read it?'

Mary nodded.

'So what's in it?'

'The truth Rachel.' She said offering the envelope to her once more. 'Simply the truth. Please, just see for yourself.'

Matt found Ella sitting under a tree in a quiet corner of the College gardens. She was thumbing through a buff folder and making notes on a shorthand pad.

'Revision?' He asked, smiling as he reached her.

'Yes, Law.' She made a face. 'I'm just brushing up on the Law of Contract. We have a test tomorrow.'

It was over a week since the kiss in the Valley View Inn. She'd been very quiet for a few days afterwards. Only natural he supposed after all the drama of miscarriages and departures. But now she was back to being her normal self. It was back to being warm and platonic; back to being safe.

'Cheer up,' He said. 'I've come to ask you something.'

'What?' She was curious now, closing the folder and looking up at him, full of interest.

'Well.' He said, standing over her in his button down Ben Sherman shirt and black leather jacket, hands stuffed in the pockets of his jeans. 'I want you to come somewhere with me tonight.'

'But I thought Fridays were off limits to me.'

'Tonight's an exception. There's something I want to you to see. A surprise.'

'What sort of surprise?' Quickly Ella pushed pad and folder into her holdall and got to her feet.

'Can't say.'

'Oh come on!' Ella closed in on him.' At least give me a clue.'

'Sorry, can't do that, Ella. You'll just have to wait.'

Matt was enjoying teasing her; it put him in the rare position of having her undivided attention. 'Look, I need you to give me an honest unbiased opinion and you can't do that unless it's a complete surprise.' He turned to go. 'I'll pick you up at eight, it's casual dress.' he said over his shoulder, and then turned and laughed. 'Oh and do tell your mother it will be the BMW, I won't embarrass her by arriving in the Pick Up.'

Ella was ready by seven thirty and watching by the window much to her mother's annoyance.

'I don't know why you insist in hanging around that Benedict boy Ella, he's most unsuitable.' Mel said as she sat thumbing through a magazine.

'He's a friend, that's all. A really good friend.'

'He's such an unappealing looking boy! Hasn't got anything going for him at all!' Mel made face. 'I can never imagine how an attractive woman like Faye Benedict with a husband as good looking as Tad ended up with a freak like him.'

'He's not a freak!' Ella replied, annoyed at her mother's criticism. 'He's…he's…' she searched for the right word. The arrival of the BMW saved her the bother and she vacated her perch on the arm of the chair and left the room without as much as a goodbye.

The arrogance of the young, Mel sighed as she moved to the window to watch her daughter's departure. Well, at least he had brought a decent car this time and not that dreadful little green van thing he usually collected her in.

'It's all Liam's fault.' She said out loud as she watched them go. 'I shouldn't have let him talk me into allowing her to wear those dreadful clothes. I should have known short skirts would only encourage undesirables.'

'Where are we going?' Ella asked as Matt nosed the BMW out of Cambridge Crescent.

'Wait and see.'

'Oh Matt, that's not fair, you can at least tell me where you're taking me.'

'The Unicorn.'

'A pub?'

He nodded, changing down as they approached the traffic lights in the High Street.

'Never heard of it.' Ella tried to draw her own conclusions. A pub? What could he possibly have to show her in a pub?

During the rest of the journey she continued to prod but found him deliberately evasive. He was determined to remain secretive so she contented herself with looking out of the window, watching houses slip by until they were in open countryside.

The Unicorn appeared suddenly up ahead on a right hand bend. Brightly lit, it shone like a beacon in the gathering gloom of a dull Friday evening. Although fairly early in the evening, the car park was packed with a mixture of cars and motor cycles.

'Is this a biker's pub?' Ella asked suspiciously, looking at the collection of parked motorbikes as she got out of the car. Her mother had warned her about such places as being the haunt of Hells Angels, scruffy men in leather gear who never washed and smelled like No 40's tom cat.

'Yes, bikers come here.' Matt replied, picking up on the disapproval in her tone. 'Ella they're people like you and me who happen to ride motorbikes instead of driving cars. The reason they wear leather is for warmth and protection. There are no Hells Angels in Abbotsbridge, despite what your mother might tell you.'

Looking suitably chastised, Ella mumbled an apology.

She could hear it almost as soon as they left the car. Above the sound of voices, laughter and the chink of glasses from the open windows of the skittle alley there was music.

'A band,' She said excitedly, standing for a moment to listen. 'You've brought me here to listen to a band.'

'Not *a* band Ella.' Matt corrected. '*My* band - that's where I've been on Tuesdays and Fridays.'

'Your other woman.' She smiled, relieved now she knew now it wasn't.

'What?'

'I thought you were seeing someone else.'

'Did you really?' He laughed. 'No. Tuesday is practice night and on Fridays we've been doing gigs in pubs and clubs within a twenty mile radius. Tonight I thought as they're playing locally you might like to see them.' He checked his watch. 'They're on in twenty minutes, come on; let me get you a drink.'

The bar was packed. Cigarette smoke hung thickly in the air above a sea of bodies. In one corner a crowd of young men were gathered together clapping and singing along to the four piece group on a small stage at the end of the room.

Ella looked around. Plain white washed walls similar to the pub's exterior with posters of current idols like the Rolling Stones, the Bee Gees, the Hollies and Manfred Mann. This was so different from the Mill, everyone was casual, some in full bike leathers, others in jeans and sweaters or open necked shirts. Matt arrived with her vodka and she sipped it slowly, taking in the atmosphere. The place was a goldmine. The landlord, a heavy florid faced man with a moustache worked alongside two barmaids, serving a constant press of people at the bar, exchanging banter with each and every customer. Instinctively something told her what was going to happen this evening would be worth waiting for.

Matt drew her over to a group of bikers she had seen when she first arrived, introducing them to her. They were a lively, good humoured lot; just as Matt had said, ordinary people enjoying a drink and the music. After a short chat he guided her through the crowd to find space nearer the front of the room where a four piece called the White Diamonds had finished and were unplugging amplifiers and packing away their gear.

'Do you help your band set up?' She asked, thinking how complicated it all looked.

'No.' Matt shook his head, pulling an empty beer barrel over and inviting her to sit down. 'I sometimes give them a hand to load the van then they're on their own. I'm no nursemaid, they sort themselves out. They're the musicians after all. Baz, the big guy on lead guitar is in charge, he sorts all the technical stuff out.'

'What's the band called? Can I meet them?'

'They call themselves The Attitude, and they've got plenty of that I can tell you. I'll introduce you after the session. Ah, here they are.'

As the outgoing group departed, five young men arrived carrying their equipment and began setting up. Matt identified each one in turn - drummer Todd Graham with his baby face and wild bleach blond hair; bass guitarist Paddy Patrick, tall and thin with a mass of unruly ginger hair; singer and rhythm guitarist Jeff Turner with his deep blue eyed come-to-bed stare; solid six footer Baz Young, playing lead guitar and finally organist Paul Fussell, with his straight, black shoulder length hair. All were clad in denim with the exception of Paul who was in black, hippie beads at his throat.

'Where did you find them?'

'Oh they were already working round the pubs in Kingsford. I heard about them from a mate who reckoned they had potential but needed a bit of tweaking.'

'Tweaking?'

'Teaching them a bit of discipline for a start. They were a real mob when I first got to know them. Todd's still a bit of a maniac, but the rest tend to pull him into line when he gets out of hand. Their choice of music was a bit iffy too. I pushed them into harder stuff, like the Stones, Spencer Davis and Cliff Bennett and the Rebel Rousers. What I think they'd be good at is rock with a bit of melody, you know something with a hook that everyone remembers, but with a bit of guts about it. I've started writing my own stuff.' He gave an optimistic smile. 'I'm quite pleased with the results so far.'

'Songs?' Ella was impressed. 'I had no idea Matt.'

'Dad taught me to read music. I started composing when I was ten. Writing lyrics came a few years afterwards.'

'Are you any good?'

'You'll be able to make your own mind up about that soon, but not tonight, it's too early. Hang on, I think they're ready, yep, Baz is nodding.'

The publican was up on the makeshift stage now, pulling the microphone from its stand.

'Ladies and gentlemen, for the very first time at the Unicorn and hopefully not the last, please put your hands together for The Attitude.'

Some time later as the groups rendition of Spencer Davis Group's '*Gimme Some Loving*' came to it's conclusion and the room erupted with applause and whistles, Ella looked at Matt and squeezed his hand tightly. 'They're good,' she said, transferring her gaze from him to the stage.' In fact they're amazing!'

TWENTY ONE

Saturday 20th April

The three girls had arrived at the Mill and were going through their usual make up check in the ladies which always preceded the start of a night out.

'You're looking especially glamorous this evening, anything we should know about?' Issy, applying pale pink frost to her lips, cast a suspicious eye on the bright red and black check mini dress Ella was wearing.

'Looks expensive, I bet it came from Christiana's.' Jenny said, gazing at Ella and wishing for just one night she too could look as glamorous.

'Actually I got it in Annabel's Boutique.'

'Annabel's? Where's that?' Jenny frowned.

'In Langley's.'

'Langley's?' Issy pulled a face. 'They don't do young stuff.'

'They do now. The boutique is Annabel Langley's twenty first birthday present.' Ella did a slow three sixty degree turn to show off her new dress. 'The launch party is next week but I had a sneak preview Thursday. I liked this and she let me buy it.'

'Friends in high places eh.' Issy couldn't resist a good-natured dig. 'But whose benefit is it for Ella? Please don't tell me it's for Andy.'

'Certainly not!' Ella finished checking her face in the mirror and turned around to face them both. 'Matt's showing a band here tonight. It's a special night for him, so I wanted to look my best.'

'What band's this then?' Issy produced a small bottle of Goya *Timeless* from her bag and gave her neck and wrists a liberal dousing.

'It's a project he's been working on for a few months. Tad's agreed they can do tonight's spot at the club.'

'Have you seen them?' Jenny asked. 'Are they any good?'

'Yes I have and I think they are brilliant,' Ella replied confidently. 'As good as anything in the charts at the moment.'

'Ah you're just saying that because it's Matty and you don't want to hurt his feelings.' Issy teased, collecting up her make up and putting it back into her handbag.

'No I'm not. They are good. But you make your own mind up Issy Llewellyn.'

'I will do too Ella Kendrick, and if they're rubbish you can buy the drinks for the rest of the evening.'

'Done!' Ella accepted, 'And if they aren't. You can!' She smiled slyly. 'And I hope you've brought plenty of money, because you're going to need it!'

As on all Saturday nights the club was packed, Ella saw familiar faces from Abbotsbridge Tech among the crowds. She spotted Nina sitting up at the bar with Mick, a bored look on her face. Mick was talking to her, his head quite close to hers, but her gaze was somewhere out in the distance and as Ella followed it she spotted Andy Macayne and his usual crowd at a corner table. It wasn't long before tiring of their company he had wandered over, drink in hand, for a chat.

'You're looking stunning tonight Ella. There was no need to go to all this trouble for me.' He greeted her with a smile.

'Don't flatter yourself, she hasn't.' Issy was quick to respond.

'Fancy a dance?' He said, ignoring Issy's remark.

Ella nodded, feeling sorry that Issy couldn't see the side of Andy which she knew. He wasn't all that bad, just motherless and misunderstood; sometimes he could be quite good fun.

As they drifted onto the dance floor to the Isley's '*I Guess I'll Always Love You*', Ella took the opportunity to look around and see if she could see Matt anywhere. He had told her that unlike the night at the pub, tonight he would have to be backstage with them, making sure that everything was right before they came on. She knew they were due on when the D.J. took a break. The clock above the bar was nudging ten, it was almost time.

Moments later the music gradually faded, followed by a drum roll. The spotlight over the disco faded and the green velvet curtains shrouding the stage parted slightly and out stepped Tad, microphone in hand.

'Ladies and gentlemen, it's time for live music and you know the Mill brings you only the best. Tonight I am proud to be giving air time to a local five piece band from Kingsford. My son tells me they're very good; just how good we're about to find out. Ladies and gentlemen may I present The Attitude!'

He swung out his arm and left the stage, the curtain trailing back with him as he went, revealing Matt's protégés. Sound exploded into the club as they started up with The Stones' '*Paint It Black.*' Within seconds everyone was clapping and moving to the beat.

Ella watched, Andy by her side, caught by the band's energy and its impact on the audience. Someone touched her arm and she turned to see Matt beside her grinning. Tonight he had shed his baggy jumper and jeans for brown cords and a green shirt. He acknowledged Andy who gave him an abrupt nod.

'Hi, sorry I couldn't catch up with you before,' He shouted to her over the music.

'Don't worry, I was in safe hands.' Ella looked up at Andy then at the

crowd which surrounded her, moving and clapping as one to the music.
'They've done it again, haven't they?'

'Done what?' He leaned his head closer to hers to catch her words properly.

'Cast their spell over everyone. Just like at the Unicorn.'

They watched for a while, then the music came to an end with a moment of
heavy percussion from Todd followed by whistles and applause.

Matt looked pleased. 'It seems they have.' His voice returned to normality.
All of a sudden he wanted to get her away, to have her to himself. 'Come on,
let's watch them from the edge of the stage.'

'OK.' She turned to Andy and said something Matt couldn't quite hear
above the noise of the crowd.

Andy made a face then put an arm around Ella and pulled her tightly to him
and kissed her firmly on the lips. 'Catch you later, gorgeous,' he said as he
released her and with a passing glance at Matt wandered off into the crowd.

Ella watched him go, her fingers pressed against her mouth trying to wipe the
taste of him away, angry with his pathetically childish demonstration. 'Sorry,'
she looked up at Matt, feeling hot with embarrassment. 'I can't think what
possessed him to do that.'

Matt knew but he didn't care. Ella was with him, nothing else mattered. He
turned his attention to the stage and the group, waiting for their next number to
start. They announced *'Got to Get You Into My Life'* and filled the room with
their energy again. Bodies started to move as their performance spread through
the room, bringing people to their feet to dance to the beat. Soon the floor was
one huge mass of dancers.

'Come on, let's go.' Matt wore an expression of pure pleasure as he looked
down at Ella, closing his fingers around hers and drawing her away from the
crush of the dance floor and up a small flight of stairs to side of the stage where
they could watch in comfort.

Sonny Scott was impressed with what he had seen so far. Tad certainly had
done well for himself - a lovely home in one of the best parts of Abbotsbridge,
an attractive wife who also played an active part in his business and a son who
obviously shared his father's passion for music. All in all, he felt quite envious.

He had arrived quite by chance that afternoon on his way back from a
meeting in Plymouth with Harry Hartcliffe, the boss of one of Britain's smaller
holiday camp chains. Sonny had known Harry years ago when he had started
out with one ex-RAF camp on the south coast after the war. Things were
beginning to settle down and the holiday business starting to take off. Harry had
got on the bandwagon small time and grown steadily. He would never be up
with the big boys like Butlins and Pontins, but there was room for him. He gave
value for money; quality accommodation, good food and excellent
entertainment. His motto *'Hartcliffe Holidays - a Home from Home'* had
attracted many over the years who now returned, bringing their children and
their grandchildren.

Sonny had driven down to Plymouth, spending the morning sitting in the sun lounge of Harry's large white house overlooking The Sound, finalising contracts for the summer season for four of his sites. The meeting had ended with lunch and Sonny had left around two.

Just outside Exeter he remembered he was within twenty miles of Tad. He could drop in and see him for a few hours then travel back to London at a leisurely pace that evening. His wife Lorna's death two years ago from cancer meant there was no need to rush home any more. He loved the way Tad always remembered something from their chequered past, a tale or some small occurrence which they had both been involved in and on this particular day he was keen to see his old friend and relive his glory days in the fifties when they were younger and the world appeared to be at their feet. Of course Tad had always had the edge; the looks, the voice. In the end Sonny had turned to managing. He was good with people, he had a nose for talent and for a while things looked good. But times changed, the sixties arrived and with it the Beatles and Rolling Stones and their like, supported by younger, more ambitious men like Brian Epstein and Andrew Loog Oldham. He was a dying breed, so now he was out of the rat race and content to move keen semi-professionals around clubs and holiday camps like Hartcliffes.

Sitting in Tad's lounge with a glass of whisky in his hand and an invitation to stay over after a visit to his club, Sonny felt warm and comfortable. The outside world was a lonely place, but with old friends like Tad and Faye, there would always be these pleasant interludes.

'So what's new?' He asked. 'Faye mentioned you manage in a small way.'

'Oh nothing exciting, just a few local lads who want to supplement their daytime jobs. There's a market for it and I fill that need. People still like live music and if you have musicians who can duplicate current chart hits, they love it. I have one regular band which plays at the club at weekends plus a spot on Saturday nights for new talent. The disco fills in between.' He gave an enthusiastic smile. 'Works very well, it's always fairly busy in the week and full house Friday and Saturday nights. I've no complaints.'

He looked at Sonny, small and balding in a wide lapelled pinstriped suit which looked far too large for him. He looked like a pocket sized gangster. Other than time's gradual erosion of his hairline not a lot had changed about him.

'Actually,' He got to his feet, whisky decanter in hand, to refill his glass. 'My boy's showing a group tonight. He's been quite enthusiastic about them; been grooming them himself.' he laughed, 'Fancy taking a look?'

'Why not?' Sonny held out his glass and watched as Tad poured his best twelve year malt into it. 'Not that I'm into that end of things now. There's far too many younger, cleverer bastards out there now Tad. I'm quite happy looking after the middle of the road stuff. It brings in a steady income with less risk. Although I might be tempted out of retirement if a talent like the Beatles were to fall into my lap.'

They both laughed and raised their glasses. 'To old times.' Tad said, with just a hint of emotion in his voice.

That had been three hours ago, and now he stood next to Tad on the edge of the stage watching the five piece storming through Chris Farlowe's'*Out of Time'*. 'Bloody'ell Tad,' he said, mopping his perspiring forehead and looking at his old friend. 'Bloody'ell. Do you realise what you have here?'

'They're good aren't they?' Tad moved his feet to the beat. 'They've got the whole club going. It's brilliant.'

'It's more than brilliant.' Sonny's round face creased into a huge grin. 'This lot have the potential to be big.'

'Oh come on you old rogue!' Tad laughed out loud. 'That's my whisky talking.'

'Straight up Tad,' Sonny's face became serious. 'In the right hands this lot could really go places. The beauty of them is they may be playing other peoples' songs but it's an original interpretation. What you need is someone to come up with a cracker of a song for them.'

As if in answer, Jeff brought the song to a close, waited for the applause to die down then stepped up to the microphone.

'Ladies and Gentlemen, thank you. We've spent all evening entertaining you with everyone else's hits, now we'd like you to listen to something original. Written for us by Matt Benedict I'd like to present the first performance of '*Mr In-between.*'

It was Jeff who took centre stage, tapping his feet and moving his shoulders to the beat as the opening bars of the song began. Leaning into the microphone, his eyes firmly fixed on one of the girls in front row below him he began to sing.

There's something you just gotta know
Though you won't believe it's true
And that's how much you mean to me
And what you put me through
There's someone hovering in your past
You can't free from your mind
And then there is this new guy
With whom you're spending time
And me, I'm just a friend to you
Living on the edge of your scene
Loving a girl who sees me just as
Mr In-Between

******

I guess that you will never know
How I've longed to hold you tight
and tell you that I love you

But the time never seems right
Perhaps I'm scared that you might laugh
Or turn and walk away
So I guess for now I'll be content
My present role to play
By your side when times are bad
The one on whom you lean
A lover waiting in the wings
Your Mr In-Between

****

What can I do, I'm tied to you
So near and yet so far
Your confidant, confessor,
Adoring all you are
Believing that there'll come a day
When you will turn and see
The reality that is the man
And a love that's meant to be
  Then it will be the others' turn
To be the ones who're green
When I am your Forever Guy
Not Mr In-Between

'Matt it's brilliant!' Ella looked at him, her eyes full of admiration as the song moved into a guitar break. 'I had no idea you could write something like that! Have you written any more?'

'Five or six,' He felt himself blushing with embarrassment at the praise she was heaping on him. This very first song had been written just for her, to him it said everything about their relationship, it's words expressing what he didn't have the courage to tell her himself. He looked out into the club where a packed floor of couples were dancing together to the romantic rhythm of the music and smiled. He'd done it. He knew the group had potential; all it had needed was some hard work and perseverance. Tonight they could all leave with their heads held high and look forward to a good future with bookings elsewhere in the area. He'd achieved his ambition; it was a beginning for them. Tad appeared out of the darkness and threw his arms around his son and Ella's shoulders. He was smiling. Jeff was bringing the song to an end, wooing the audience with the rhythm of his body. Girls were congregating around the edge of the stage, reaching up to touch him as if he was already a star.

'Well done Matt! Brilliant! Your singer's a real ladies man.' He smiled down at them both, enjoying his son's moment of success. 'I think this calls for celebrations up in the office later on, bring the boys up too. There's someone I want you all to meet. An old friend of mine who dropped in tonight, he's very impressed.'

'Great!' Matt hugged Ella. 'We'll be there.'

The band ended their session to rapturous applause, stamping, whistles and shouts of 'More!' The disco started up as the curtains closed over the group and distracted by the heavy beat of Motown the crowds turned their attention to Stevie Wonder.

Matt left Ella for a moment to talk to the group then returned, slipped his arm around her waist and led her onto the dance floor where they spent the rest of the evening together. He became the target for much back slapping and compliments and Issy and Jenny came over to add their enthusiastic congratulations; Issy to tell them there was a drink waiting for them both at their table.

And at the end of the evening, Ella climbed the stairs with him to the room above the club. The group was already there stretched along two settees, all looking very pleased with themselves. Jeff watched Ella with heavy eyed interest as she walked in with Matt; the others nodded hello, remembering her from introductions at The Unicorn a few weeks before.

Tad, in the corner, was in the process of uncorking a second bottle of Moet which opened with a healthy pop. Once the bubbles had subsided he began to pour it into a collection of tall glasses on a nearby table.

Faye, sitting by the window was talking to a short, dark haired balding man with a shiny forehead which he was mopping at regular intervals with a large handkerchief. Turning as Faye noticed their arrival; he walked over to them, his grin as wide as the lapels of the suit he wore.

'Well, at last I get to meet the genius. Congratulations!' His face creased with pleasure as he reached out to shake Matt firmly by the hand. 'And you must be Ella.' Smelling strongly of Old Spice, he leaned across and kissed her cheek. 'I'm Sonny Scott; I expect Tad has told you about me.'

'Sure.' Matt returned his smile. 'You're Dad's old friend from the fifties.'

'That's right. And let me tell you I was really impressed with what I saw tonight.'

'Thank you, everyone worked hard and it paid off. I'm very proud of them.'

'So what happens now?' Sonny asked as Tad arrived and handed around the champagne. 'Have you got a manager lined up for these boys?'

'Manager?' Matt looked perplexed. 'Well I guess Baz is the nearest thing. He looks after the bookings and the money side of things.' He shook his head. 'But a proper manager would be overkill.'

'Not if they're planning to play the Hammersmith Odeon.'

'They aren't.'

'But they will be.' Sonny raised his glass, a glint in his brown eyes.

Ella looked at Matt questioningly. Was this little man serious or had he just had more than his fair share of Tad's alcoholic hospitality? Matt shrugged as if he had no idea what was going on.

Sonny turned to look at the five shaggy haired young men relaxing on Tad's settees. 'Lads.' He said in his clear cockney accent. 'You was bloody brilliant tonight, I really enjoyed your performance! Believe me, I've been in the business a long time, I know when I see special, and you're special. So I have a proposition to make, I'd like to sign you up.' He turned to Matt, 'with your songwriter here, of course.'

'Great.' Matt raised his glass. 'If you could get us a few spots up in the smoke we could make a killing.'

The others nodded their agreement, bringing their glasses together, toasting themselves and potential future success.

'No, you misunderstand me.' Sonny shook his head, moving over to pull up a stool and sit between the two couches, looking at them all intently. 'I'm talking big time boys. You see I think you have real talent. In fact, I'm so impressed that when I go back to town tomorrow I'm going to have words with a few of my contacts in the business. Could you come up to London at short notice?'

They all looked at each other in amazement then nodded enthusiastically.

Tad stepped forward. 'Sonny, I think we ought to slow things down a bit. We don't want to get these lads hopes up too early do we?'

'OK, OK!' The little man raised his hands in a gesture of pacification to his friend. 'Let me rephrase that. Boys I will definitely sign you up. I can get you work, a lot of it, mostly outside this area. However, I am of the opinion that you have the potential to become full time professionals and do well out of it, and to that end I am prepared to talk to a few friends in the business. If I can persuade them you're worth seeing I will send for you. There,' he looked at Tad. 'can't be fairer than that can I?'

'No.' Tad agreed, bottle in hand, offering Sonny a top up, glad that he had put the brakes on his friend's runaway enthusiasm. Signing them up was one thing, promising them overnight national fame was something entirely different. He could see the excitement in the faces of the five young men sitting there. They were keen, would give up their day jobs if the opportunity came to become full time musicians and big money beckoned. But in the past he had seen so many like them fed empty promises and left disillusioned. He had an interest in this band through Matt and he was going to make sure nothing went wrong. Sonny had a nose for talent, but he tended to get carried away, building dreams and sometimes those dreams didn't quite go to plan. Better to take things at a more realistic pace.

Faye too was watching the tableau in front of her. Sonny talking from the heart, gesturing enthusiastically, convinced he had star potential on his hands. Tad with his pragmatic outlook, trying to be encouraging but cautious. The five lads all looking just like the Beatles must have when they were on the verge of being discovered. Faces eager, dreaming of what fame and fortune could bring them. And Matt. If Sonny's predictions were right this had implications for her son too. It meant losing him. But she knew he needed to follow his destiny and somehow the pain of being parted from him was worth it because what she had seen take place tonight had made her feel uneasy. Just what was going on between Andy Macayne and Ella she wondered? She had been watching earlier that evening as Matt found Ella in the crowd and had witnessed the familiar way in which Andy had put his arm around Ella and kissed her before moving off to join his cronies. The gesture was giving Matt a definite if unspoken message that she was his property. As he walked away, she had caught Ella looking at Matt, saw her say something to him before turning away, anger in her face. Could it be that despite the likeable and friendly face she presented to everyone, there was a darker side to her personality which had the capacity to hurt people in the same way as her mother?

She focused on Sonny again, still talking to the band, very animated, full of enthusiasm. She prayed that his assessment of them had been right. Time away from Abbotsbridge would do Matt good. It would mature him and make him independent and hopefully by the time he returned Ella would have forgotten him completely and found someone else to play her games with.

TWENTY TWO

Wednesday 17th April

With the Easter holidays and college closed for a fortnight Ella, Issy and Jenny were spending the morning shopping; sheltering from the rain under Issy's father's large black golfing umbrella as they made their way from one store to another. They had tried on dresses in Annabel's, chosen perfume in Langley's main Department Store and bought underwear in Dorothy Perkins. By twelve the three were hungry and looking for somewhere to have lunch when Jenny spotted a Wimpy Bar.

'My mother would have a fit if she saw me in here.' Ella laughed, as they pulled themselves up onto high swivel stools in the window and waited for their order to arrive.

'Your mother is seriously weird.' Issy said, as she slipped out of her black and white wet look mac.

'It's not her fault.' Jenny leapt to Ella's defence. 'You can't choose your relatives. Hey! Isn't that Matt?'

'So it is.' Ella followed the direction of her gaze. 'I wonder if anything more has happened with the band.'

'I'll find out.' Issy banged hard on the window and waved.

Matt waved back, hovering at the edge of the pavement. When there was a gap in the traffic he crossed the road and pushing through the main door of the Wimpy Bar, he came over to join them. 'Hi.' he grinned, 'How are you all?'

'We're fine.' Issy took it upon herself to be spokeswoman. 'How about you, got that recording contract yet?'

'No, but we've been asked to go to London next week. Sonny's arranged for us to spend a day in the studio cutting a few tracks. I'm looking forward to it; it will be a completely new experience.'

'I bet the boys are excited.' Ella said, wishing she could go. She would have loved to be part of the music scene for a day, to see how Matt's lyrics were translated in the studio.

'Yes they are. It could be their big break; I hope they make the most of it.'

244

'You'll all be giving us autographed photographs for our bedroom walls soon.' Jenny teased.

'That's a long way off Jen, if ever.' Matt looked amused. 'They might think we're rubbish.'

'Of course they won't. They're brilliant! Aren't they?' Ella said turning to the other two for confirmation as the waitress arrived with their order.

'Yes, I think so,' Jenny agreed, 'Don't you Iz?' Issy nodded in silent agreement.

'Well thanks for the support.' He grinned, then with an eye on their food said, 'I'll leave you to your lunch then.'

'See you at the Club on Saturday night.' Ella called out to his retreating back.

'What time?' He turned and catching Issy's watchful eye coloured immediately.

'Nine thirty?'

'Nine thirty then.' With a final wave he stepped out into the street and was soon lost in the lunchtime crowd.

Watching him go, Ella felt uneasy. The kiss in the Valley View Inn back in March had been such a silly thing to do. She still cringed when she thought about it; impulse wasn't the way to go with Matt. She had been sitting back, carefully planning her next move, but she realised now that although he had played down the business of going to London with the group, things might just be on the verge of breaking for the band. And if that was the case, she would need to do something quickly or risk losing him completely.

Monday 22nd April

Ella looked at the clock. Twelve twenty five. Another five minutes to lunch. God this Law period was dragging this morning. They had been in the classroom since ten thirty. Mike Wearing their tutor had been in full flow, scribbling intensely on the black board. She now knew that leaving a dead cat in someone's garden constituted a trespass, something that left her wondering if she would ever find herself in a situation where such knowledge could be usefully employed.

She looked out of the window. Matt would be in London by now. He and the band had left at seven thirty in their black Transit van with all their equipment, Tad following in his BMW. She had got up early and driven around to Portway to wave them off, standing in the road beside his less-than-friendly mother until they had turned the corner and were out of sight. By now they would be in the studio. She hoped the day was going well. Matt's heart was in his music and he had worked so hard with The Attitude. She felt they deserved a chance and was confident Sonny's friends would appreciate what she and the audiences at the Unicorn and The Mill had seen and heard.

Matt had promised to call her that evening to let her know what was happening. She couldn't wait to hear his news. As the hands of the clock clicked onto half past the lunch bell sounded and Mike dismissed the class.

'I thought I would die of boredom.' Issy complained, as they made their way to the Refectory, Jenny having gone ahead to grab a table and organise lunch.

'It's just a process we have to go through.' Ella said, taking her seat and gazing at the limp looking lettuce on her plate. 'If it means a Diploma at the end then I'll just grin and bear it. Jen, this lettuce looks as though it needs resuscitation.'

'Sorry, it's all they had.' Jenny replied.

'How much do we owe you?'

'Two and six each.' Jenny pulled out her purse.

Ella handed over the right amount but Issy only had a ten shilling note. Jenny pulled out a handful of coins and handed them over to her.

'Hang on a minute,' Issy held up a silver coin. 'What's this Jenny Taylor? Trying to slip me your old holiday money?'

'I haven't got any foreign money.' Jenny protested.

'Well what do you call this?' Issy slapped two coins onto the table.

'It's two and six. I gave you two half crowns, two shillings and six pence.'

'This isn't two bob.' Issy pointed suspiciously. 'And this isn't six pence either!'

Ella picked up the coins and began to laugh. 'It's the new decimal stuff that's just come out. The value is the same it just looks different. Weird isn't it, to think we'll all have to get used to this soon.'

'Absolutely unnecessary if you ask me, just like learning Principles of English Law.' Issy said, sulkily. 'Uh oh, lover boy's coming over.'

Ella looked up to see Andy approaching with a broad smile on his face.

'Hi girls.' He looked pleased to see them all. Jenny acknowledged him with a silent nod and Issy, ignoring him completely, picked up her knife and fork and began to eat.

'I came to ask if you were going to be at the Club on Saturday, Ella.'

'Yes, I'll be there.' She nodded.

'With Matt.' Issy glared up at him.

'The King of Rock and Roll eh?' Andy gave a dry laugh. Issy gave him a cold stare.

'Don't be like that Andy.' Ella said, resting her knife and fork on her plate. 'Matt's worked hard; he deserves any rewards that come as a result of last Saturday. And you have to admit they were good.'

'Well, yes, I guess they were.' Andy agreed grudgingly. 'And I suppose if you've promised to meet him I'll have to play second fiddle for the evening.' A sulky little boy look appeared on his face.

'Oh for goodness sake, don't be such a martyr!' Ella said, irritated by his attitude. 'There's nothing to stop you dancing with me if you really want to. All you have to do is ask.'

'What? Permission from him! Forget it!'

'Andy, that's not what I meant!'

But he wasn't listening. He was already striding away towards the Refectory exit, aiming a kick at the waste bin in the doorway as he left.

It was eight thirty that evening when the phone rang. Ella rushed into the hall and lifted the receiver.

'Hi.' She recognised Matt's voice. 'How did it go?'

'Very well.'

'Good!'

'And guess what? They really liked *Mr In-Between* and wait for it....' He was laughing now. 'It's going to be released as a single!'

'Matt, that's wonderful! When?'

'This Friday. They're rushing it to the shops. Doing a lot of advanced plugging. The guys are booked in for a photo shoot early next week. There's going to be a big publicity thing. Honest Ella, everyone here seems really excited about us, I can't believe it.'

'Where are you?'

'We're still in London. Dad's coming back tomorrow but I'm staying on with the lads. It's a real roller coaster thing. New hair. New image. Lots of promotional stuff. I won't be back until next week. We're expecting to go up to Manchester to record *Top of the Pops* some time. Danny Donovan the Radio One DJ is having our record as his Tip for the Top.'

'I can't believe this, Matt. The group in the charts!'

'Don't get too enthusiastic, it could be a complete flop.'

'Oh come on, where's your confidence? I'm convinced you'll have a hit, even if you're not.'

'Well, let's hope so.'

In the silence that suddenly fell between them Ella realised the time had come. The fame thing had happened just like she thought it might and she couldn't leave it any longer.

'Matt....' She said, breathlessly. 'There's something very important I need to say to you. I...'

'Sorry Ella, Dad's calling.' All of a sudden he sounded very far away. 'The record company have booked us all a table for dinner. The car's just arrived to pick us up. Must go.'

'But Matt....'

'Ella, I'm sorry, I can't stop.'

'Can I phone you later then?'

'Sorry, no time. As I said, it's madness up here at the moment. Look, I'll see you at the Club Saturday week. You can have my undivided attention then, I promise.'

The phone went dead; he was gone. Ella looked unhappily at the receiver before replacing it. She sat on the stairs, cradling the phone, knowing she would now have to wait eleven days before she could tell him how much she loved him.

Thursday 2nd May

'Tell me you don't really want to see this rubbish Ella.'

'Mother, it's important. Matt's group are on tonight, we're all watching.'

'Oh well I'm off out anyway. Mel said, pulling on her raincoat. 'When Liam returns there's some cold meat in the fridge. Can you get some salad and potatoes organised?'

'Yes, yes I will!' The programme was just starting and Ella wished her mother would just go and leave her in peace.

'Right I'm going. I expect you'll be in bed when I get back.'

'Just go. Please?'

Mel left the room, annoyed at being turned out of the house by her daughter.

Ella heard her reverse out of the driveway then sat back and relaxed to watch the show.

Danny Donovan in his outrageous frills and shiny purple suit was talking into the microphone, announcing the first act of the evening, The Herd. This was followed by Gary Puckett and the Union Gap with 'Young Girl'. Dusty Springfield sang her latest release followed by the Foundations with 'Any Old Time Baby.' Englebert Humperdink came next and then the Love Affair.

Then the moment came as he stood in front of the camera smiling and announced that his Tip for the Top was going over the border. The Marmalade, a new band out of Scotland just bubbling under the Top Twenty with their first release Lovin' Things'.

Watching the group launch enthusiastically into their number, Ella sat back disappointed. Perhaps things hadn't happened as quickly as Matt had expected. Maybe the Attitude would be Tip for the Top next week.

As The Marmalade finished the camera panned across to Danny, mike in hand, looking really pleased with himself as the top ten count down ran behind him.

'Well now,' he shouted above the cheers of the crowd. 'I was intending to have this lot as my Tip for the Top this evening, but it seems you all beat me to it. Again I'm welcoming new talent, and these guys are going to be *so* big! The new number one is *Mr In-Between* by The Attitude!'

Ella gasped. There in front of her on the screen was Jeff, in tight trousers and paisley shirt, swaying his hips to the rhythm, seducing the microphone as he sang the lyrics to Matt's song.

She sat unable to move until the credits began to roll, then went out into the hall and picked up the phone. She rang Matt, intending to be the first to congratulate him, but got the frosty tones of Faye instead. She told her he was back but had gone to the club with Tad. There was going to be a party on

Saturday.   Nothing fancy, just something for club members and they had decided to get things underway as soon as possible. It would be ticket only and she would arrange to leave three with Issy.

'Matt will probably be too busy to see anyone between now and then, but I'm sure he'll catch up with you Saturday.' She assured Ella.

Thanking her and asking her to pass on her congratulations she then rang Issy.

'Who have you been talking to, I've been trying to phone you,' Issy said, all breathless excitement.

'Faye. Matt's out with Tad. There's going to be a party at The Mill on Saturday, Faye said she'd drop tickets in to you for the three of us.'

'Sounds great. I can't believe it Ella, Matty's hit the big time, who'd have thought it?'

'I'm so pleased for him, it's his dream come true. You don't realise how much he's always wanted this.'

'I wonder if he knows just what he's letting himself in for,' Issy said, with a giggle. 'He'll have women trying to tear his clothes off and get into bed with him. God, he colours up in our presence, how's he going to cope with all those groupies?'

'Don't be daft Iz, he's the songwriter. He's in the background.'

'You obviously didn't see the *Daily Mirror* earlier this week.' She giggled again. There was a big article about him, and a picture. They've signed a record deal and are going on tour this month. He's as famous as the band now.'

'Yes, I suppose he is.' Ella felt uneasy. 'Look, I must go, I haven't phoned Jen yet. I'll see you tomorrow.' As she began to dial Jenny's number she realised how important Saturday had become.   It looked as though it would be her last and only opportunity and she was determined there was no way he was going to leave Abbotsbridge without knowing exactly how she felt about him.

TWENTY THREE

Saturday 4th May

Jack Taylor dropped Issy, Jenny and Ella outside the Mill at seven thirty. It would be early enough, Issy said, to avoid any fans that might be there. As the white Mercedes crossed the river, however, a large crowd of girls were already there waiting.

As Jack pulled up to let the three of them out they found the car besieged by a screaming, shouting mob. Issy forced her way out of the car, followed by Ella and Jenny.

'For goodness sake!' She shouted at a girl with lank, greasy hair who was trying to cling to the open back door of the car. 'Get out of the way!'

With difficulty they made their way the front door where Max stood holding it open to let them in, ready to push out any unwanted guests.

'It's like a rugby scrum out there!' Issy said, as she took off her coat and handed it to the cloakroom attendant.

The bar, which had a few dozen people congregated around it, had been decorated with multicoloured balloons and streamers and the heavy green stage curtains were open to reveal a drum kit showing The Attitude's geometric Logo. The whole place had an air of celebration and as the three of them walked in, a waitress in formal black and white came forward to offer them a glass of champagne. Unobtrusive background music was playing, giving the feel that things at the club were waiting to get underway.

'Well,' Issy looked around, acknowledging a couple of familiar faces as Jenny spotted Mick and excused herself. 'They've certainly transformed this place in forty eight hours haven't they?' She turned to Ella. 'Have you seen Matt?'

Ella shook her head. 'Faye said he'd catch up with me tonight.' She looked around the room. 'I wonder where he is?'

Issy watched Ella as she sipped her champagne. Although she was doing her best to look cheerful, it was obvious something was worrying her.

'Cheer up,' She said, giving Ella a playful nudge. 'He'll be here. He's probably a bit tied up at the moment. You know, back stage making sure everything's OK.'

'Yes, you're probably right,' Ella replied. 'I expect you think I'm paranoid don't you?'

'No. Up until now you've been closely involved in everything he's been doing, it's only natural standing here like this you're feel a little left out.' Issy thought for a moment. 'I know who'll know what's going on. Here, hold this for a minute will you?' she handed her glass to Ella.

'Where are you going?' Ella frowned.

'To consult the Oracle.'

Waiting for Issy, Ella watched the entrance and people arriving while also trying to work out who exactly the Oracle was. The Tates and Knights drifted in; Annabel in French blue, her blonde hair pinned up and braided with ribbons, Bryony in white and gold like an Egyptian priestess. Seeing Ella they came over, staying for a brief chat before moving off to find a table. As they went she heard laughter from somewhere up above and her eyes were drawn towards the large picture window of Tad's first floor office which gave a panoramic view of the inside of the club. The curtains had been drawn back and she could see a large group of people gathered there. Men and women, drinking and chatting. Right in front of the window she noticed three women in tight shiny cocktail dresses. One she recognised as Faye, wearing fuchsia pink and talking to a tall blonde woman in gold. Beside her stood a thin, fair haired young woman in green, almost a replica of the older woman. As she watched she saw a young man join the group. It was Matt, in a dark suit and bow tie. She watched him hand glasses of champagne to Faye and the blonde woman. As he stepped back, the young blonde slid an arm around his waist pulled him tightly to her, looking up into his face with a smile. She saw him raise his arm towards someone in the room and a waitress appeared with more champagne. He took two glasses from the tray and handed one to the girl. She raised the flute, touching his in a toast.

Faye had lied to her she thought angrily; it wasn't a just quiet do for members at all. She wondered who could be so special to be invited up there before the evening started. And why had she suddenly been excluded? Was it possible that now Matt had found fame he was trying to distance himself from her? The thought of this rejection jabbed spitefully at her.

Intercepting a passing waitress, Ella commandeered two glasses of champagne. Moving over to the bar she eased herself up onto a high stool and sat there brooding. By the time Issy returned Ella had finished her second glass and was on her third.

'What's going on?' Issy looked suspiciously at the empty glasses on the bar as she pulled herself onto the stool next to Ella.

Ella raised her eyes towards the window above the club. 'That's going on,' she said, feeling stone cold sober despite the fire of the alcohol in her stomach.

Issy's gaze travelled upwards. 'Ah yes, I see.'

'Have you seen the blonde woman and the girl before?'

'That's Bernice Murphy and her daughter Cassandra.'

'Who?'

'She's the wife of the owner of Centaur Records, the label the band has signed to. The daughter's a model.'

'How do you know all this?'

Issy tapped her finger to her nose. 'Max the Oracle of course,' she whispered. 'Most people think he's as dumb as his canine friend Bruce but they're wrong. Max knows everything. There's a private party going on upstairs; Tad, Faye, Matt, the band, Sonny and a small delegation from the record company plus their respective partners.'

'Oh.' Ella took a deep breath.

Issy looked up again and saw the blonde reattached herself to Matt. 'Her father's the boss,' she tried to sound reassuring. 'Matt will be expected to be nice to her.'

Although Ella knew there was probably an element truth in what Issy was saying, it didn't make seeing them together any easier. As the girl pressed her face against Matt's and kissed his cheek she felt her pain turn to cold anger.

Faye Benedict looked down into the club but was unable to see much because of the reflection of the lights of Tad's office against the window. The party was becoming wearisome. While the men talked about music and money and the band were enjoying themselves with their girlfriends she had found herself with no alternative but to join Bernice Murphy and her offspring Cassandra. Bernice, it appeared, was the kind of rich wife who divided her time between shopping, beauty parlours and soaking up the sun on some far flung beach; she occupied another world which Faye knew nothing of and had little interest in.

This, thought Faye, is my punishment for trying to be devious and manipulative like Mel Carpenter. She knew she should have left well enough alone, but it had been so important to make sure that Matt was well and truly separated from Ella this evening. He was embarking on a new era of his life and she wanted Mel Carpenter's daughter left behind for ever. Looking across at Cassandra Murphy she now regretted her actions.

When the stunning blonde walked into the party with her mother and father, Faye was delighted. Pairing her off with Matt was just the thing she needed to do to ensure Ella got a clear message that he had moved on. Looking at her now, however, she realised she just might have made the biggest mistake of her life. For the last quarter of an hour she had lisped her way through a series of topics almost as mind-numbingly boring as her mother's. From her trips to foreign locations for modelling shoots, to attending celebrity parties and hanging around with the rich and famous at all the 'in' nights spots in London. It was the latter which started alarm bells ringing; Matt and the band were being tipped for stardom and here she was this pretty rich little parasite, poised and ready to make maximum exploitation from their newly found fame.

The lights dimmed outside the window and she heard the club's anthem *'Till the End of the Day'*, which indicated everything was around to get underway.

Able to see quite clearly now, she spotted Ella sitting at the bar with Issy and realised when Matt saw her, everything was going to blow up right in her face.

Jenny returned, breathless and smiling to join her two friends. 'Sorry, I got tied up chatting to Mick; he's on his own tonight. Nina's not well.'

'Nothing trivial I hope.' Issy said, turning away from her survey of the dance floor.

'Are you all right?' Jenny frowned at Ella. Issy pointed and Jenny raised her eyes to the scene in the room above the club.

'Don't worry, I'll get over it.' Ella hailed a waitress and they took another glass of champagne each. 'I suppose it was bound to happen.' she gave a casual shrug, 'Oh to hell with it, I'm not going to let it spoil my evening.' she raised her glass a little unsteadily. 'Not when there's all this free bubbly about.'

Mark Maddison pulled on his headphones and set the first disc of the evening on the turntable. *'Everlasting Love'* blasted from the speakers and soon the floor was full of people moving to the steady pulse of the music. The three girls joined them, Ella losing herself in the music, determined to enjoy the evening. As the record ended and they returned to their table she saw the door to Tad's office open and his party, still laughing and talking, descend to the dance floor in twos and threes. Matt, she noticed, still had the blonde in tow and they came onto the dance floor together.

'She's like a boa constrictor.' Jenny hissed to Issy, watching the way the girl locked her arms around Matt's neck.

'Even more interesting,' Issy eyed the door. 'The Abbotsbridge Mafia's just turned up.'

Ella turned to see Andy help himself to a drink and make his way through the crowds to join the Tates and the Knights. After a quick chat he turned, casually sipping his champagne, his gaze moving around the room. Spotting Ella, moments later he was standing at their table.

'Ella?' He looked puzzled. 'Didn't expect to find you here, thought you'd be with Matt this evening.'

'I am. He's…busy at the moment.' She tried to sound casual. The last thing she wanted was Andy gloating. 'People from the record company are here tonight.'

Andy looked across the dance floor and caught sight of Matt and his companion. 'Never mind.' He said, turning back to her with a smile. 'I'll look after you.'

Issy, about to deliver a suitably sarcastic response felt Jenny's foot nudge her ankle.

'Yes why not.' Ella was on her feet immediately. To hell with Matt, she wasn't going to waste the evening moping in a corner. If it was really over then tomorrow was the time to be miserable. Tonight she was going to enjoy herself. Andy, she decided, might have his faults, but he was OK really. It was obvious he knew what was going on but he'd been kind enough not to rub salt in the wound. In moments she was on the dance floor laughing and moving with the rhythm as if she didn't have a care in the world.

It was 10.00 and Mark was just about to bow out. He set up Cliff Richard's *'Congratulations'* to play as a prelude to Tad coming on stage to speak to those assembled in the club. After a short speech he introduced his guests to the crowd and then amid cheers and whistles, the band, came on one by one to be identified. Dressed in brown patterned shirts and orange velvet trousers, they greeted the audience before taking their place on stage. The Hammond organ under Paul's expert touch started up and they were off, straight into their warm up piece *'Gimme Some Lovin'*. Soon the floor was a moving mass dancing to the beat of the music.

Some time later, after saying goodbye to Sonny and the delegation from Centaur, who were eager to get back to London, Tad returned to his office with Matt. Pouring his son a glass of whisky he handed it to him, glad of a moment of solitude together away from the socialising and lip service they had all been paying that evening.

'Thank God for that.' Tad walked over to the window and looked down. 'Perhaps we can all get back to being normal human beings again.'

'It's only just beginning Dad.' Matt replied, joining him. 'Our lives will never be the same again, or at least mine won't. But it's all I've ever wanted to do. And I do know with the fickle nature of the business, I'm going to grab my moment while I can.'

'Very wise,' Tad agreed, seeing a lot of himself in his son. 'I enjoyed my time, although things were less cut throat in my day. The main thing is enjoy it but try to keep one foot in the real world.'

'Ella's been telling me that. She's been really supportive over these past few months.'

'What happened to her tonight?' Holding his glass to his chest, Tad turned his back on the window.

'I've no idea. If she'd been here I wouldn't have been lumbered with that dreadful Cassandra. I did ask Mum where she was, but she said she hadn't turned up.' Matt moved across the room to his father's desk, resting his glass on the leather inlaid top. 'I don't know what's wrong, but she seems to have been avoiding me completely since all this happened. She was OK when I spoke to her just over a week ago but I haven't heard from her since then. You know, she didn't even ring to congratulate us on getting to number one! I did think about going round to see her but everything's been so hectic; there's been no time and you know her mother doesn't give me a very warm reception unless I'm driving the BMW.'

Tad laughed. 'That woman's such an outrageous snob! Shame she wasn't invited, I think she would have hit it off quite well with the suits from Centaur.' He turned his attention back to the crowd below. 'They're really enjoying themselves down there, you know. It's been a great evening! Hang on a minute.' He paused, shading his eyes against the reflection of the glass. 'Ella *is* here, with Issy and Jenny.'

'What?' Matt walked over to the window and cast an eye over the movement below. 'Yes, you're right. What's going on?'

Issy and Jenny returned to the table, leaving Ella standing alone in the crowd applauding as the group finished and Jeff stepped forward to announce they were about to perform their number one hit. As he moved to the microphone and the music began she felt someone touch her shoulder. Matt stood there with a puzzled expression on his face.

'Ella where have you been?'

'I've been right here Matt.' There was a tightness in her voice as she took a step back from him. 'All night.' She held his gaze, her expression icy, 'I'm surprised you even missed me, you appear to have been having such a good time with your blonde friend.'

'That,' Matt reacted angrily, 'was not a good time Ella! I got landed with her because you didn't turn up!'

'To turn up, as you put it, you have to be invited. I wasn't.' She tossed her hair back off her face, eyes shining with anger, 'Probably because I'm not important to you any more.'

'Important? Of course you're important!' He reached out for her but she avoided his touch and turned away, moving carefully through the dancers, back towards the table where Issy and Jenny were waiting.

'Ella, stop!' Matt caught up with her, grabbing her arm and swinging her around to face him. 'Will you please listen to me for a moment! There's been a terrible mistake.' He reached out for her but she brushed him off.

'Leave me alone!' She pushed him away. 'I don't want to see you again. In fact I don't want anything more to do with you, is that clear?'

'You don't mean that.'

'Oh yes I do!'

'Ella, will you *please* listen to me.'

'Go away Matt!' She backed away, then turned and eased herself away into the darkness between the movement of bodies.

Matt stood there, watching her walk back to her table. The thought of her hostility upset him; he couldn't lose her now, not when everything else was coming together so well. She was the key to everything. He had to make her listen. He moved quickly to catch up with her, squeezing between the couples on the floor. He was within feet of her when he felt someone grab his arm.

'Just do as she says Benedict!'

He turned to find himself face to face with Andy.

'Keep out of this Macayne; it's none of your business!' Matt replied, irritated by the smug look on Andy's face.

'If someone upsets Ella, I make it my business. Leave her alone!'

Matt looked at Andy Macayne, standing there with that self-important tilt to

255

his head as if he had some divine right to interfere. 'I don't take orders from you!' He almost shouted. If the Macaynes thought they ran Abbotsbridge it did not extend to The Mill. This was his father's territory and he was not going to be spoken to or told what to do here by Bob Macayne's arrogant son.

'Can't you get it through your head, she doesn't want you anymore.' Andy looked at him contemptuously. 'She's had enough of you.'

'Just mind your own business!' Matt said irritably, pushing past him.

Everything after that came back as a blur. The band had just finished, everyone was standing clapping as he pushed between people. An unseen hand swung him around by the collar of his jacket and a fist connected with his face. He fell heavily to the floor. People around him screamed, the lights went on and he found himself lying there with the whole world going around. Someone propped him up and then Tad was there, kneeling in front of him, an anxious look on his face, shouting orders to Max to eject Andy.

The strangest irony crossed Matt's mind as he sat there trying to focus, nursing what would soon become a bruiser of a black eye. All the time he had been arguing with Ella, in the background they had been playing the love song he had written and dedicated to her, a song that was now sitting at number one in the charts. She had never known its significance, but even if she had, after the events which had taken place tonight, he doubted she would care much anyway.

Monday 6th May

'Well,' Issy looked at Ella across the refectory table where they sat having coffee after a late afternoon tutorial. 'You're the talk of the College today! Not many girls have two men fighting over them!'

'Oh do shut up Issy.' Jenny elbowed her angrily. 'You're being really insensitive!'

'Don't worry Jen; I'm used to what passes for Issy's sense of humour.' Ella said sourly, stirring her coffee. 'Anyway it wasn't a proper fight; Andy punched him that was all.' She grimaced as she brought her cup to her lips. 'It was all very embarrassing and of course my mother's in seventh heaven now.'

'Andy had no business interfering,' Jenny said angrily. 'It was between you and Matt. He shouldn't have got involved.'

'Well he did and now he has a six month ban from The Mill.' Issy was gleeful. 'It serves him right!'

'I agree, he deserves to be banned! He behaved like a thug!' Jenny agreed, 'Takes after his father!'

Ella set her half empty cup of coffee down in its saucer and looked at both of them. 'I'm sorry,' she said, getting to her feet and slipping on her jacket. 'I don't want to talk about this any more. I'm going.' She picked up her bag and slipped it over her shoulder. 'I'll see you both tomorrow.'

Arriving home twenty minutes later, she parked the Mini on the empty driveway and got out. Mondays was her mother's Ladies Circle afternoon which meant she would not be back until at least five. An hour's respite from the oratory on 'Poor Andy' which had been going on all weekend. She closed her eyes thankfully; at least that should give her enough time to relax with a coffee and the latest copy of '*Honey*'. As she bent into the car and pulled out her bag she noticed someone standing by the gate. She straightened up, frowning as he approached her.

'Peace offering.' He said, presenting her with the large bunch of red roses he was carrying.

'Thank you. 'She took them, running a finger over the perfect velvet of each bloom. 'They're beautiful.'

There was no response. He just stood there awkwardly, an uneasy expression on his face as if he didn't know what to do next. When the words eventually came, they spilled out in a torrent.

'Ella, I'm sorry, I'm so sorry!' His hands came together, fingers interlocking. 'And before you blacken my other eye, I know you're angry and you've every right to be. Can I just say it was all Mother's fault. If it's any consolation,' he gave a nervous laugh. 'She's had a good ticking off from both Dad and me.'

'It's O.K. Matt, when I thought about it afterwards I realised things didn't add up.'

'You did? So I'm not the bad guy any more?'

'No, ' She shook her head.

'And I'm forgiven?'

'Yes. Have you been waiting long?'

'Oh absolutely hours. Well, at least thirty minutes.'

'I didn't see you.'

'That's because I was hiding in the bushes next door.' They both laughed.

'Your eye looks painful.'

It's O.K. really. The boys think it makes me look tough.' He joked.

'I think it does too,' she smiled, 'Gives you a sense of danger. So, when are you leaving?'

'Tonight. That's another reason I had to see you.' His face became serious. 'because I won't be back in Abbotsbridge until at least Christmas.'

Locking the car, she said. 'Do you want to come in for a moment?'

'What about your mother?'

'Won't be back for ages.'

'Better not.' He shook his head. 'Ella, I came to see you because there's something I wanted to ask you. I wondered.....will you promise me something?'

'What?'

'That you won't give your heart to anyone else while I'm away.' He said nervously, colouring slightly. 'Because... because you mean everything to me.'

'I'm not going anywhere Matt.' She replied, reaching up and kissing his cheek. 'I'll be here waiting for you when you get back, I promise.'

After they had said their goodbyes Ella watched his car until it was out of sight before letting herself into the house. As she put the roses in water she felt euphoric. Although he hadn't said it in so many words she knew; he loved her, deep down he really loved her and that more than anything would keep her going in the months ahead.

Saturday 18th May

Andy Macayne sat on a wooden bench beside the river. He had just tried unsuccessfully to get into The Mill. After all the fuss surrounding the black eye he had given Matt a few weeks ago he thought he would lie low and wait until the whole thing blew over. By then he hoped Tad might either have forgotten about the incident or be so mellowed by his son's success that he would feel a little more charitable towards him.

It was not to be, however and was made worse by the fact he was not alone at the time. He had to suffer the embarrassment of being turned away by Max whilst Rich, Gareth, Bryony and Annabel were allowed into the club; his humiliation was now complete.

He could hear the music clearly as he sat watching the flow of the dark water and occasionally voices and laughter would drift towards him from the open windows of the building as the sky darkened and a cooling evening breeze blew up the river from the south. So what options were left open for him? It was clear that his four supposed friends had no intention of pleading for clemency on his behalf; they had simply waltzed through the open door, leaving him stranded in front of the large intimidating Max with his US Army crew cut and massive shoulders. Friendship he thought irritably, you couldn't rely on anyone these days.

He picked up a pebble and tossed it across the river, it skimmed the surface several times before disappearing into its dark depths. He was glad he had hit Matt Benedict. He was a louse who'd had it coming to him. Andy was sure he had been responsible for sending him off on a wild goose chase into the car park last January. How the car that was blocked in had got there he had no idea. It was a white Mini and one thing was certain; it was not there when he arrived. Someone had put it there deliberately. He had sorted the problem and returned only to find Ella circling the dance floor with the lacklustre Matt. Looking at the smile on DJ Mark Maddison's face, he sensed collusion.

Ah well, at least Ella was free from the clutches of Rock Star Benedict for good. The way was wide open for him again, and the time he had been waiting hadn't been wasted. She liked him, didn't believe the bad press he got. Now with Benedict gone it was time for him to move in for the kill. He couldn't wait to see all the envious faces once she was his. She was class this one, a real prize. But what then? Well the future was an interesting place. He knew he'd soon be bored once he'd got her to himself. Six months max and he'd be moving on, finding someone new. But that was the name of the game wasn't it, the constant cycle of attraction, pursuit and possession. Like many others he was merely a hunter of pretty women in an urban jungle.

All of a sudden he felt upbeat; there was a lot to look forward to really. Whatever was he doing sitting here letting the evening go to waste? The Red Lion, he decided. He would go to the Red Lion. Of course, it wouldn't be as enjoyable as Saturday night at The Mill, but Tony and the boys from the site would be there and he'd be able to have a drink and a laugh until closing time. It was better than nothing.

As he reached his car and unlocked it, he grinned to himself. Annabel's jacket lay on the back seat. They had been his passengers this evening, something he'd completely forgotten in all the turmoil which had taken place. Without him they faced an expensive taxi ride home. Ah well, perhaps there was some justice in the world after all.

On reaching the Red Lion he found the car park overflowing out into the road. Large notices announced there was a twenty first birthday for someone called Keith Green in the function room upstairs and a steady flow of guests had caused a log jam at the bar. It took him ten minutes to get a drink. As he waited he scanned the room, he saw faces he knew, but none of them belonging to the people he expected to be here. When at last he managed to get served he asked if Tony's crowd had been in. They had, and had gone on to The Plough. One of the carpenters was on his stag night and a pub crawl was in progress. Their eventual destination was The Mill. Maybe he could catch them there the barmaid said helpfully.

Andy sat in the corner staring into his double whisky, thinking about going home when he was aware of someone standing in front of him. He looked up and smiled.

'Hello,' He said. 'What are you doing here? I thought you'd be at the Club.'

'Not tonight,' she sat down opposite him, her grey eyes surveying him warmly. 'I'm a guest at the twenty first party going on upstairs. He's the brother of one of the girls on my course.'

'Really?' He raised interested eyebrows.

She smiled. 'You can come as my guest if you like.'

He was hesitant. 'But what if someone recognises me? I wouldn't want to get you into trouble.' he gave a weak smile.

'Don't be silly,' She laughed.

'It's no joke.' He made a miserable face. 'I'm beginning to feel like a social leper around here.'

'Oh come on it's not that bad. Look, I'm grateful for what you thought you were doing that night, but…...'

'*Thought what I was doing*, what does that mean?' He interrupted her. 'He publicly dumped you in front of a club full of people Ella! And then he came after you to rub your nose in it!'

'But that's the thing, he didn't. He was trying to explain. I found out the truth afterwards, it was his mother's fault.'

'And you are prepared to accept that excuse are you?' He raised his hands in exasperation.

'Well yes, why shouldn't I?'

'Because he's playing games with you.'

'Matt's not like that.'

'He'll hurt you one day believe me.'

'Andy,' She said with a weary sigh. 'Please, let's not fight. There's a party going on upstairs.' She stood up and reached for his hand. ' Come on, just let's agree to differ and go and enjoy ourselves. Please?'

'Oh....all right!' Reluctantly he drained his glass and hauled himself to his feet. 'Lead the way.........'

TWENTY FOUR

Friday 28th June

Ella let herself in through the back door of the house feeling a great sense of relief. The last examination, Commerce, was over. Tonight the three of them were going out to celebrate. All the Diploma examinations were set internally for the first year and the results were expected in a couple of weeks. After that the papers had to be forwarded to the Department of Education in London for their assessment and their final results, like those for shorthand and typing would arrive in mid-August.

Learning shorthand had not been easy for Issy and although both she and Jenny had given her some extra coaching, she still found it a struggle. She had scraped through the 50 words per minute in March and was hopeful of an 80 for the summer. The goal was 120 wpm by next summer. Ella was already writing at 110 and together with Zoë Ryan was being given extra dictation to push their speeds even higher.

The kitchen was empty. She was about to call out that she was home when she heard raised voices coming from the living room. Cautiously she walked down the hall, wondering, as Liam wasn't due home for another hour, who was with her mother? And why were they arguing?

The door was slightly open. Nick faced her, his back to the fireplace, while Jenny sat on the settee, hands folded in her lap looking up at Mel who stood between them both, her gaze directed towards her son.

'This is totally preposterous!'

'No it isn't! We love each other.' She heard Jenny say in a calm but determined voice.

'Jennifer!' Mel glared down at her. 'I do think my son is more than capable speaking for himself, thank you. He doesn't need you to do it for him.'

'Mrs Carpenter, I was only.....'

'Nick, for goodness sake say something!' Mel interrupted Jenny in mid-sentence. 'Is this how it's going to be? Her doing all the talking for you! What sort of man are you!?'

'What's going on?' Ella stared at the small group.

261

'Your brother has taken leave of his senses!' Mel's face was flushed with anger. 'He's engaged to be married.'

'What's the problem?'

'Jen,' Nick moved away from the fireplace. 'Seems she's not quite good enough for the grandson of landed gentry,' he said in a pompous voice, with a look of contempt for his mother.

'Oh Mother!'

'And you can be quiet!' Mel waved a warning finger at Ella. 'I know what I'm saying. Background is important. However,' she hesitated. 'There are other reasons as well. For a start Jenny's far too young! And how can Nick possibly settle down with someone he's spent more time writing to than being with? What sort of basis is that for marriage? It won't work!' She threw her arms up in despair. 'It will be a complete disaster!'

'But the main reason is my family.' Jenny looked up at Mel. 'Tell me, what exactly is it you object to Mrs Carpenter?'

'Jen don't......' Nick put a gentle hand on her shoulder.

'No, Nick.' She looked up at him with dark determination in her eyes. 'I want to know exactly what your mother's problem is.'

'Well I...' Mel hesitated, taken aback by Jenny's sudden assertiveness.

'Common are we?' Jenny began, 'Uneducated? Oh dear! Heaven forbid that my dad ever had to get his hands dirty for a living. But it was necessary, you know, because that's the way he built up his business. Honest, hard graft. So if you find him and my mum a little vulgar, a little inferior, that's your problem. The rest of Abbotsbridge don't. And let me tell you, I'd rather have them that way; better that than a stuck up, narrow minded prig like you!'

Ella watched in astonishment as Jenny having finished, got to her feet and walked from the room. She was always the quiet one at college, never outspoken, always polite. This had been completely out of character, but then her mother had dared to question the suitability of her family. It was the ultimate insult.

'Happy now?' Nick shot an angry look at his mother as he moved towards the door.

'You're my son!' Mel was unrepentant. 'I have a right to step in when I see you making a fool of yourself!'

'Wrong.' He stabbed a finger at her. 'You have no rights as far as I'm concerned. I've told you before you gave those up the day you walked out on us. I only came here because Jenny wanted me to. She was concerned about your feelings. Pity you weren't as concerned about hers!'

Mel rounded on Ella irritably, as Nick left the room. 'Well, now your brother's had his five penny worth, no doubt you'll have something to add!'

'I think everything's been covered quite adequately, don't you?' Ella said, pushing past her mother, eager to catch up with Nick.

She reached him as he was closing the front gate. Jenny, solemn faced, was sitting behind the wheel of her mother's green Cortina.

'Nick,' Ella called after him. 'Wait!'

'I have to go.' He said impatiently. 'The sooner we're away from this dreadful house the better.'

'Look.' She laid a comforting hand on his arm. 'I'm sorry she was so horrible to you both, but give her time, I'm sure she'll come round.'

'Ella I'm really not interested whether she does or doesn't.' He looked up at the creeper covered walls of the house then back at her. 'Do you know what her problem is? She's been treading all over Liam for so long, she imagines she has an automatic right to do it to everyone else!'

'She exasperates me too. She really is her own worst enemy.'

He shook his head. 'She *is* the enemy Ella. Manipulative and destructive.' he moved away from her towards the car. 'She tricked you into coming here and has been interfering in your life ever since. Niall, university and now Grandfather.'

'Grandfather?' Ella watched as Nick opened the car door. 'I don't understand.'

'He's phoned here and left messages. He wants to see you Ella, to say sorry.'

'I haven't had any messages.'

'Well he's definitely left them, on more than one occasion.'

Jenny looked up at him then at Ella and nodded.

'He spoke to Mother.' Nick continued. 'She promised to get you to call back. You've not phoned and he's very upset. He thinks you've turned your back on him.'

'Well I haven't.' Ella said angrily.

'Give him a call then.' Nick said tucking himself into the passenger seat. 'And from a phone box, not from in there.' He gestured towards the house.

After the car was out of sight Ella returned to the house to find her mother.

'Oh dear yes,' Mel had gone all breathless and fluttery, making her way to the hall, fishing a series of notes out from under the message pad by the phone and handing them to Ella. 'I quite forgot you know.'

Ella snatched the notes from her mother, giving her a glare she hoped would do more damage than words. After all, Mel had already been verbally battered by Nick so certain immunity to the spoken word had already set in. She found her handbag and left the house, making her way to the nearest phone box to make her call. Nick had been right. The last thing she wanted was to speak to her grandfather with her mother eavesdropping behind the kitchen door.

It was Mary who answered and called him to the phone.

'Grandfather,' Ella said, trying not to cry. 'I'm so sorry; I've only just got your messages. When can I come home?'

Friday 19th July

The red Mini, slowed, turned left and accelerated up the hill towards the farmhouse. Meridan Cross, rich in its summer colours, was now a place of change Ella reflected; a place without Niall. Her own life had seen changes too. Andy had become a regular fixture. He still moaned about having her company but not her heart. But how could she release that most precious part of her when Matt was still the focus of everything in her life. The Matt who had left her the bunch of red roses. The Matt who had promised to return at Christmas and who was now keeping in touch regularly with post cards.

Reminders of him were everywhere. In shop windows, newspapers and TV. There was no hiding from him. Their latest single *Window Dressing* was sitting at No 2 in the charts and Tad had the latest promotional posters of him and the group displayed in foyer of the Mill. Sandie Shaw's *'Always Something There to Remind Me.'* playing on the car radio just at that moment made his absence even more poignant.

The warm walls and newly painted windows of the farmhouse reflected brightly in the summer sun, the grey slate canopy of the front porch still leant slightly towards the sitting room window, clematis climbing untidily up its sides. The garden was a riot of colour, hollyhocks and delphiniums edge-to-edge with lupins and lilies. Mary shared Peggy Evas's passion for flowers and the roses in particular looked glorious. She parked the Mini in the open gravelled space in front of the farm and retrieving her suitcase from the back seat, locked the car and walked towards the front gate. As she opened it, Mary appeared at the front door, looking fresh in a pale green sundress, her strawberry blonde hair cut in a short bob.

'You made it then,' She said, smiling. 'I thought Mel might try and stop you at the last minute.'

'Liam's taken her off to Spain for two weeks - timed it rather well, didn't he?' Ella smiled, closing the gate behind her. 'Thankfully Mother has been totally distracted all week preparing her holiday wardrobe.'

'Hello Ella.' Richard appeared beside Mary at the front door, looking a little unsure.

'Oh Granddad,' Ella dropped her case and looked at him for a moment, then she was in his arms, hugging him. 'I've missed you so much!'

He held her close to him, his arms comforting.

'Dear, dear Ella, we've both been stubborn and foolish in our own way. But you're here now.' He broke his grip, holding her at arms length, shaking his head, smiling through his tears. 'Welcome home!'

In the warmth of early evening Ella reined in Merlin and stopped for a moment to look out across the valley towards Hundred Acre wood and the ripening swathe of the barley field below. It felt good to be back she thought as she watched the lengthening shadows across the fields, settling in to the familiarity of the village, surrounded by those who loved her. Of course she knew this was only a short respite and she would eventually have to return to Abbotsbridge and pick up her life with Liam and Mel once more. But it would be different now, she felt stronger and better able to deal with the challenge of living with someone as difficult as her mother. That strength had come from realising everything had come full circle and her life was happy and back on course again. She had a new career planned and had made peace with her grandfather. Everything was working out well; the one outstanding issue, Matt's return.

She smiled. Another of his postcards had arrived at Jenny's just before she left. There had been one every week since May with brief messages on what was happening with him and the band. This time it was wordier and showed a picture of Edinburgh Castle with a kilted bagpiper in the foreground.

'Here for two nights after a sell out concert in Aberdeen over the weekend.' He had written. *'It's been raining ever since we arrived. Despite that, everyone is upbeat about the tour - another sell out concert - everyone wants to see us. Edinburgh really is a beautiful city. Have had some time to myself so did some sightseeing and have even managed to complete a couple of songs for our next album. More news when we reach Liverpool - they want us to do a photo shoot at The Cavern. We'll be standing on the stage where the Beatles performed - how amazing is that? Matt xx. P.S. hope your exams went well.'*

As the sun disappeared below the tree line of Hundred Acre and the velvet blue of dusk crept into the valley Ella, still deep in thought, turned Merlin down the winding track and began her journey back to Willowbrook. Of course, the future was unpredictable; no one knew when tomorrow came what it would bring. But if there was one thing she could say with absolute certainty it was that Christmas this year was going to be special, very special.

LOVE, LIES AND PROMISES

Part two of the Behind Blue Eyes Trilogy

By

Joanna Lambert

1969

ONE

Tuesday 24th December

'I'm so sorry Ella. He rang this morning. It was a last minute decision by the record company.'

Tad Benedict looked into the face of the pretty dark haired girl at the bar and really felt for her. All around them, in his club, The Mill, people were in celebratory mood. It was Christmas Eve, laughter and music filled the place. Currently the dance floor was packed with revellers dancing to Creedence Clearwater Revival's *Bad Moon Rising.* Not the night at all to be delivering bad news like this. He could almost reach out and touch her disappointment.

'Switzerland?' Ella's grey eyes clouded and she shook her head as if she couldn't quite grasp what he was saying.

'Yes. One of their record company's other groups, the Spectators, were due to take part in a Christmas Eve live special out there. Aaron King the lead singer decided to get in some skiing when he arrived and is currently in hospital with concussion and a compound fracture of his left leg. So the Attitude were flown out last minute to take their place. Matt phoned from Zurich this afternoon, that was the first I knew of it.'

Ella felt Tad's hand on her shoulder as the news sank in and bitter disappointment washed over her. Switzerland. It might as well be the other side of the moon. And who wouldn't be disappointed on a night like this. She had been waiting since May to be reunited with him; had thought of nothing else. May - that had been a whirlwind time she remembered; Matt's band, the Attitude had been discovered, had a number one hit and been whisked away to London where their record company moguls had completely taken over their lives. First an album, then a UK tour. He kept in touch with post cards from each of their tour stops and had promised to return home for the festive season, to

3

meet her here in the club on Christmas Eve. The record company had no plans for them until Spring he said. Ironically, she decided, that was probably why he was now in Switzerland and not here.

'When will he be back?' She asked, hoping that at least they would have New Year together.

'He didn't say, but as soon as I hear anything I will let you know, I promise.' Tad squeezed her shoulder. 'Sorry I can't be more helpful, but that's as much as I know at the moment.'

Across the room he saw Ella's two friends Issy Llewellyn and Jenny Taylor coming off the dance floor. Time to leave, to let the sisterhood take over to provide the help and support needed to repair the damage he'd just inflicted.

Tad was a philosophical individual with an upbeat outlook on life. Although there had been this setback over Christmas, something which had also left his wife Faye frustrated and upset, he was sure it was just a temporary glitch. In a couple of days he guessed Matt would more than likely be returning to the UK and before they all knew it he would be back home to see the New Year in with friends and family in style. In no time at all everyone would have forgotten the disappointment they felt tonight. He wished he could given Ella these crumbs of comfort to buoy her up but was aware that only if he had been dealing in definites would his words have held any comfort for her this evening after receiving such disappointing news.

As he skirted the bar, he stopped and ordered a bottle of his best champagne. 'For the three young ladies in the corner.' he nodded to where the girls sat, Jenny with her arm around Ella's shoulder, all of them deep in conversation. As the person responsible for ruining not only her evening but possibly Christmas as well, it was the least he could do.

Author's note: When I approached Authors on Line with a view to publishing my novel, I was surprised to discover I had a very large manuscript on my hands. One which would translate into more than one book. 'When Tomorrow Comes' is therefore the first book of a trilogy. Now this has been published, I am working on finalising 'Love, Lies and Promises' and once this is complete, the third, 'The Ghost of You and Me' will follow.

Lightning Source UK Ltd.
Milton Keynes UK
01 December 2009

146912UK00001B/7/P

9 780755 204847